Such Good People

"Intricately plotted and deeply moving, *Such Good People* is a poignant examination of family, friendship, and the secrets we keep to protect those we love. Blumenfeld writes with nuance and compassion—this novel will linger in your heart and mind long after you finish the last page."

—**Alyson Richman,** *USA Today* **best-selling author of**
The Time Keepers

"*Such Good People* is a masterfully crafted, nuanced, and riveting story about the lengths we go to for the people we love. Blumenfeld's richly developed characters come to life and will stay with you long after the story ends. A thought-provoking, perfect book club pick. Don't miss this one!"

—**Elyssa Friedland,** *USA Today* **best-selling author of**
Last Summer at the Golden Hotel

"*Such Good People* is the moving story of lifelong friends managing the ripple effect of one fateful decision. Do the mistakes of our past define us? Is it enough to be a good person when the odds are stacked up against us? Blumenfeld writes a pitch-perfect, thoughtful tale of friendship and loyalty. A thrilling exploration of humanity and sacrifice with characters you can't help but fall in love with. This one truly shines."

—**Rochelle Weinstein,** *USA Today* **best-selling author of**
This Is Not How It Ends

"*Such Good People* is one of those multidimensional must-reads that wins both as a page-turning legal story about social injustice, prejudice, and redemption and an emotional, character-driven tale of love, family, and lifelong friendship. Fans of Tayari Jones's *An American Marriage*, Rebecca Searles's *In Five Years*, and Allison Larkin's *The People We Keep* will devour Amy Blumenfeld's latest triumph. *Such Good People* is Such a Good Book!"

—**Samantha Greene Woodruff, author of *The Trade Off***

"Blumenfeld's latest is as poignant as it is absorbing. An expertly crafted and wildly engaging exploration of the depth and resilience of human relationships. As main characters, April and Rudy each try to climb their way back from one tragic night in their youth, but their connection to each other is the focal point and crowning glory of this finely woven story. *Such Good People* makes for Such Good Reading. It's a *must*!"

—**Jacqueline Friedland, *USA Today* best-selling author of *Counting Backwards***

"An unputdownable story of lifelong friendship, family loyalties, personal ambition and the choices we make along the way. Blumenfeld's writing is engaging, nuanced, and sharp. Her complex characters and captivating story will stay with you long after you finish this book."

—**Rachel Levy Lesser, essayist and author of *Life's Accessories: A Memoir and Fashion Guide***

"Amy Blumenfeld's second novel is a thoughtful story about old friendships, the bonds of family, and long-buried secrets. *Such Good People* will leave readers wondering: Can you ever outrun your past? And even if you can, at what cost?"

—**Brenda Janowitz, author of *The Audrey Hepburn Estate***

"This beautifully rendered, heartfelt novel examines the bonds of family and lifelong friendships through a timely and insightful lens. *Such Good People* is such a good read!"

—**Jane L. Rosen, author of** *On Fire Island*

PRAISE FOR AMY BLUMENFELD'S

The Cast

"In *The Cast*, Blumenfeld deftly reminds us how friendship and love, when cultivated over decades, can transcend even the darkest moments. A heartfelt, moving page-turner."

—**Fiona Davis, best-selling author of** *The Address*

"This is my favorite novel of 2018. Your heart will grow after reading this story about the healing power of friendship."

—**Norah O'Donnell, Senior Correspondent, CBS News**

"A dazzling debut that challenges the boundaries of longstanding friendships. You'll laugh, you'll cry, you'll relate. But most of all, you'll wish it would never end."

—**Emily Liebert, *USA Today* best-selling author of** *Some Women*

"In her captivating and wholly engrossing debut, Blumenfeld pulls the reader in from the very beginning. She deftly handles the perspective of multiple characters, as well as writes about complicated issues with levity and grace. This well-told story is timely and relatable and leaves the reader wondering how she would handle similar situations."

—**Susie Orman Schnall, author of**
Anna Bright Is Hiding Something

SUCH
GOOD
PEOPLE

SUCH
GOOD
PEOPLE

A Novel

AMY BLUMENFELD

Published by SparkPress, a BookSparks imprint,
A division of SparkPoint Studio, LLC
Phoenix, Arizona, USA, 85007
www.gosparkpress.com

Published 2025
Printed in the United States of America
Print ISBN: 978-1-68463-322-7
E-ISBN: X 978-1-68463-323-4
Library of Congress Control Number: 2025900963

Interior design by Stacey Aaronson

For my parents.
The best good people I know.

1

April

NOW

From a thousand feet above ground, the city streets are a grid of magnificent milestones. As April leans her freshly highlighted caramel tresses against the lapel of Peter's blazer, she gazes across rooftops and scattered patches of green intrigued not by the beauty of Chicago's lakefront metropolis, but by the narrative before her. *How fitting*, she thinks, *to see life scrawled out like a signature from atop the John Hancock building.*

Down below stands the Drake Hotel, where they wed over a decade earlier. A few blocks away is Northwestern's Prentice Women's Hospital, where she delivered all three of their children. Out in the distance are the Garfield Park Conservatory and Notebaert Nature Museum—school field trip destinations where she'd been a parent chaperone. And there on the left, jutting into Lake Michigan along Navy Pier, is the iconic Ferris wheel—site of the sunset jaunt Peter had insisted upon the day they moved to Chicago. Newly engaged, madly in love, and utterly besotted by the romance of driving eight hundred miles in a U-Haul to plant roots in an un-familiar town, Peter believed riding a gigantic circle would be their perfect opening ceremony. "We'll have highs and we'll have lows," he'd said, pulling her close as they ascended into the sky, "but we'll sit side by side and take in the view together."

As they peer out the restaurant's floor-to-ceiling glass panes awaiting their table, Peter's familiar scent—Right Guard antiper-spirant mixed with a woodsy cologne she'd impulsively picked up at the Sephora checkout line—wafts through the linen fibers of his jacket. Somehow, the fragrance heightens her senses and enhances the romance of the moment like a well-curated movie soundtrack. "I can't believe it's really happening," she whispers. Peter kisses her head and wraps his arm around her back, just as he did that night on the Ferris wheel.

"Excuse me, Mr. and Mrs. Nelson?" comes a voice from behind. April and Peter pivot to find a young waiter with clasped hands and enviable posture pointing to a two-top in the corner of the room. "Your reservation is ready. Please, follow me."

April places her suede purse beside a small bud vase and the waiter chivalrously holds the back of an upholstered armchair as she descends into the seat. "Swanky!" she mouths to Peter from across the table and bounces her eyebrows up and down.

Peter grins. She knows he appreciates her steadfast unaffected-ness and how she remains the same grounded girl from Brooklyn's Avenue J despite their many years of midwestern comfort.

The waiter hands a leather-bound wine list to Peter, clears his throat, and deferentially offers a slight bow. "I'll be back in a moment with your dinner menus, but, um, I'd just like to say, it's truly an honor, sir."

Peter immediately stands and extends his right hand. "Aw, thanks. The pleasure is all mine . . ." he pauses, searching for a name tag on the waiter's lapel, "Justin."

"So, I, uh, I just wanted to let you know, sir, that it would be a thrill for me, really, if, say, you ever need a clerk or an intern or someone to get your coffee or file papers or pick up your dry cleaning . . ." He chuckles as his shoulders rise to his earlobes. "You're an inspiration, Mr. Nelson."

"Oh, come on now, that's very kind. Let's just take it a step at a time, shall we? The chickens haven't hatched quite yet, if you know what I mean," Peter says, knocking his knuckles against his forehead. "There *is* that minor issue of winning the election, so first things first. But I appreciate the support." He punctuates this with an elongated wink.

April knows being on the receiving end of sycophantic gestures is nothing new for Peter. He has garnered respect and admiration from others his entire life. In fact, the very first anecdote Peter's parents ever shared with April was how they recognized his leadership skills in second grade when he acquired sixty-five signatures from fellow students to petition the school board to sell cocoa with marshmallows in the cafeteria. He successfully argued that if faculty members at their Newton, Massachusetts elementary school could enjoy a cup of coffee in the teachers' lounge, then students were entitled to a warm beverage during the bitterly cold New England winters, too. The "Cocoa in the Caf" story had become family lore, and his parents got plenty of mileage from it at cocktail parties. But April is confident that for Peter, getting those signatures wasn't about being a leader or yearning to be seen and heard; it was purely about righting a perceived wrong and giving a marginalized group their due. It was all about empathy and action. No ego. That was his pixie dust at age seven, and it has remained to this day.

"Well, best of luck, sir. I'll be rooting for you." The waiter beams and then shifts his glance to April. "I'll go fetch those dinner menus now."

April takes a long sip of water until the waiter is out of earshot.

She knows Peter's a gem and deserving of the admiration as well as the promising recent polls, yet she can't resist the urge to gently rib him.

"Well, I'd say you've attained a solid C-list reality star status, Mr. Nelson." She smiles, raising her glass to toast. "I wouldn't put you on the B-list quite yet, but you're getting there."

Peter lets out a lengthy sigh. "This whole thing is completely surreal, you know? Good surreal, but still surreal." He fidgets with the utensils at his place setting and adjusts them into perfect alignment.

"Oh, honey, I'm so proud of you," April says, sliding her arm past the oil and vinegar bottles and reaching for his hand. "No one deserves this more than you." She interlaces her fingers with her husband's and rubs her thumb back and forth against his skin.

April can feel him staring at the burgundy polish on her nails and watches as his eyes drift over to the delicate diamond band encircling her finger. He smiles at her ring, his mind seemingly lost in his internal world, but she knows exactly what he's thinking.

"Man, was it pouring rain when I found this puppy." He chuckles, caressing the stones with the pad of his thumb.

April nods. She's heard the story about a million times. It was one of his favorites to tell—how the rain assaulted the sidewalk when he emerged from the subway station in New York's diamond district, how he sought refuge in a jewelry store near the corner of 47th Street and 6th Avenue to stay dry, how the chatty woman behind the counter pumped him for details about his bride, and how he acquiesced, despite his typically private nature. He didn't intend for the truth to sound so melodramatic. He certainly wasn't one for histrionics. But the facts were the facts. "I moved to New York to change the world," he told the clerk. "But it turns out, my world changed because I moved to New York." He pulled one of the clerk's business cards from a stack on the glass counter, flipped it over, and quickly jotted down those exact words. He knew they'd be perfect for the moment he got down on bended knee. This was the story he told April every year on the anniversary of their engagement. She could recite it verbatim.

"You know what, babe," Peter says, enfolding April's hands between his own, "tonight's about us. The next few months will be absolutely crazy with the election, so let's forget about work, the kids, your parents, everything. It's just you and me, kid. Old school."

April can practically feel her eyes sparkle. "*Old* school," she repeats with a laugh, and marvels at the fact that after all these years her husband still feels like a new addition to her life.

"Champagne?" she asks.

He shakes his head. "Nah. Too soon. It ain't over till it's over."

"Absolutely." She chides herself for overlooking how presumptive a flute of even Prosecco could be for someone as superstitious as Peter. "Why don't you pick?" she suggests, handing him the cocktail list.

While Peter scrutinizes the libations as if they were a front-page article in the *Chicago Tribune*, April gazes at him and lets out a little sigh. This is not an unusual occurrence. With his perfectly styled salt and pepper hair, cleft chin, and trendy tortoiseshell eyeglasses that skew both intellectual and middle-aged hipster, April never tires of her view. She even finds the mild scoliosis that rounds his shoulders and causes a small hump beneath his gingham button-down shirts to be sexy. And that night, like most other times, she gets lost in the scenery.

The waiter makes his way back to their table with two dinner menus tucked beneath his arm. As soon as he begins reciting the specials, April hears the cell phone buzz in her purse. It doesn't play any of the distinctive ring tones she's programmed for her parents' or kids' numbers, so she contemplates letting it go to voicemail. As she reaches into the bag to lower the volume, she notices a 718 area code. She tenses and picks up instantly.

"Hello?" She can feel her heartbeat quicken. As the only child of aging parents, an incoming call from any New York area code is a catalyst for full body perspiration.

"Yes, hi, I am looking for April Zagoda," says the voice at the other end of the line.

April jolts upright in her chair. She hasn't heard her maiden name used in over a decade. Her arms begin to tingle and her free hand forms a tight fist. She rises from her seat and motions to Peter—who is in the midst of asking the waiter to describe the artichoke appetizer—that she will take the call from an empty corner of the restaurant's dining room.

Oh no, this is it. This is the call. She's a nurse or an EMT or, oh Jesus, a coroner . . .

"Are they okay?" April blurts out, her voice cracking as she navigates a maze of tables toward a quiet corner of the restaurant. "Are they okay?"

"Excuse me?"

"Where are they? Are they hurt? Sick? What's wrong?"

"I'm sorry, I'm not sure what you are talking about."

"My parents!" she exclaims, finding a private spot beside the large picture windows.

"Your parents? Ms. Zagoda, I don't know anything about . . . I'm not calling regarding your parents. My name is J—"

"Oh, thank goodness," April sighs, cutting off the caller. She closes her eyes and attempts to recenter herself. "I'm so sorry, let's start over. How can I help you?"

"Ms. Zagoda, I'm calling from *The New York Times.*"

"*The Times?* Really!" April simultaneously feels a coil of tension release.

Growing up, *The New York Times* was the preeminent news source in April's household. Her father had the paper delivered to their home and would get his ink-stained hands all over her parents' white Formica kitchen tabletop. The fingerprints drove her mother crazy, but the routine of watching her dad come home from work, strip down to his sleeveless white ribbed undershirt, put a *Welcome Back Kotter* rerun on TV, and run his fingers along the newsprint was one of her fondest childhood memories. Her parents even kept a stack of Sunday magazines in a round wicker basket on the floor beside the toilet in their tiny, carpeted powder room.

"I'm assuming you're calling regarding my husband's election," April says. The thought of Peter being featured in *The Times* is almost as exciting as an election victory. "Before I put him on though, may I just ask, how did you know? I mean, I didn't realize people back home cared about local Chicago politics. Is this for the National News page? Did one of Peter's old colleagues in New York tip you off?"

April knows she's rambling, but she can't help it. Journalists make her uneasy.

"So your husband is running for office," the woman on the other end says matter-of-factly.

"Yes. State's attorney. Basically, what New York City would call the district attorney. He's been a litigator forever, as I suspect you already know. He just won the primary so now we're gearing up for the election."

"Fascinating."

"Yes." April closes her eyes to visualize the bulleted list of publicity talking points Peter's campaign manager had recently emailed her. "It was sort of unexpected, actually. When our kids were little, we volunteered a bunch. Wanted to meet other young families in our community, so we doled out food at a soup kitchen on Thanksgiving, delivered care packages to homebound elderly, organized a toy drive every December for children at the Ronald McDonald House in Chicago. We even helped clean up an old, abandoned lot and plant grass to create a greenspace and ball field."

"That's lovely . . ."

"You know what's funny? The more we volunteered as a family, the deeper our roots grew in the neighborhood, and the more invested Peter became in local politics. He was elected Alderman in our ward a couple of years ago and is now ready for the next step—state's attorney. I may be biased, but with his stellar record in New York and in Chicago, and his amazing heart, he really is made for this job."

"Mmmm," the reporter says. April can hear keyboard typing in the background.

"I'm sure you'd like to speak with my husband. He's right here, I'll put him on . . ." April starts walking back across the room to the table where she can see Peter studying the dinner menu.

"Actually, Ms. Zagoda," the reporter says. "I was calling to speak with you."

"Me?" she says, still baffled as to why this woman is not referring to her as Mrs. Nelson.

"Yes. I was wondering if you have a comment regarding Rudy DeFranco's release from prison?"

April stops mid-stride. Acid rises from her gut, as if the mere utterance of Rudy's name has eroded the lining of her esophagus. She does an about-face and returns to her spot in the corner of the room.

Several seconds of silence follow.

"Ms. Zagoda? Are you there?"

Shut your damn mouth, she cautions herself. *Just shut your mouth.*

"Ms. Zagoda, do you have anything to say regarding Rudy DeFranco?"

"Who are you? How did you get this number?" April snaps, her friendly demeanor vaporized.

"Ms. Zagoda, it has been many years since Rudy DeFranco was

imprisoned for the death of Bailey Jameson. There must be something you have to say now that he is being released."

How the hell do I gracefully get out of this?

"Ms. Zagoda? I know you are there."

Breathe in, two, three . . . April shuts her eyes.

"Any comment, Ms. Zagoda?"

Out, two, three . . . Images of Rudy's face, their childhood neighborhood, the handcuffs, the courtroom all flash across her mind like the grainy old slideshows her grandfather used to project onto his basement walls.

"Ms. Zagoda. How does it make you feel that Rudy DeFranco did time while you—"

April grits her teeth and interjects, "No. Comment."

"But look at your life and look at his. Ms. Zagoda, you must have something to say."

"My name is April *Nelson*," she pauses to let oxygen rise through her nostrils, "and I have no comment." She exhales and taps her iPhone to end the call.

April gazes out of the large windows overlooking her adopted city while she holds the silent phone against her ear to maintain the appearance that she's still conversing.

"Compartmentalize," she whispers aloud, and pledges to uphold a cheerful façade throughout the meal for the sake of her husband's sanity, as well as her own. Neither one of them can afford to crumble. She visualizes how the next hour will play out. She will order a glass of cabernet. She will listen as Peter speaks excitedly about the final weeks of the campaign. She will mention the beautiful book projects her first-grade students recently completed and acknowledge her good fortune to work at a school that feels more like a cocoon than a full-time job. She will remark how thoughtful it had been of her principal to reschedule the annual meet the teacher event so April's allegiances to her employer and husband won't conflict the evening before Election Day. And, most of all, she will ignore the blaring siren that has just gone off inside her body. She will disregard the uptick in her pulse, furtively glide her drenched palms along the edge of the tablecloth, and summon the strength to pretend that her marriage, children, career, friendships, and all she holds dear will not break at the same moment as the reporter's story. She can do this, and she will.

April stares out at the skyline—at all those landmarks dotting a map of the beautiful life she has created—and with all that she has, she straightens her posture, attempts another cleansing breath, and returns to her husband at the table.

Dinner is served.

2

Rudy

NOW

Rudy sits on the floor of his cell, organizing the lower shelves of a metal locker when the announcement comes over the PA.

He has just returned with his latest commissary haul—a bag of Cool Ranch Doritos, a travel-sized digital clock, and a pair of Reeboks. Each month his family wires cash via Western Union to his spending account, and every other Sunday he fills out a form with commissary requests. In the thirteen years he's been incarcerated, the bulk of Rudy's purchases have consisted of stamps, stationery, underwear, toothpaste, and toothbrushes. Occasionally he splurges on ice cream or chips, but generally, he is frugal. The fifteen cents an hour he earns cleaning stalls doesn't go very far. He's still got two years left on his sentence and wants to be prepared for the inevitable rainy days.

The Doritos this month are undoubtedly an indulgence. He considers it a birthday gift to himself. The clock and sneakers, on the other hand, are necessities. The commissary desk clock he bought when he was first locked up has recently bitten the dust and, in its absence, Rudy has found himself feeling increasingly unmoored. Tracking time is crucial when doing time. The ability to see hours and minutes tick away provides a sense of placement, and without it, Rudy finds he can easily grow confused and unsettled.

The Reeboks are a different story. They aren't a delicacy like the chips or a grounding force like the digital clock. Owning a pair of quality sneakers is an insurance policy. Good shoes are in high demand and low supply, but every once in a while, a shipment will arrive, and those days always feel like Christmas morning. This delivery is a particularly bountiful one. There are five styles of sneakers on the commissary list and each has a fan base. Certain inmates prefer the high-tops, some just care about the label, but all yield tremendous value in the prison's black market. Items are bartered all the time: clean socks for fresh produce, a good sweatshirt for a six-pack of room-temperature Pepsi. You never know when you might need to cash in on a favor, so having a pair of brand-new leather Reeboks secured in your locker is the equivalent of keeping a gold bar in your back pocket. Plus, sneakers are practical. They offer more physical stability and protection than the ubiquitous soft-toed slip-ons. In fact, some inmates even wear sneakers in the shower if they sense an impending brawl. One time, a prisoner wearing slip-ons reprimanded another inmate for talking too loudly in the phone bank. When the man didn't heed the request to lower his voice, the convict sauntered back to his cell, swapped his rubber shoes for sneakers, returned to the phone bank, and sucker punched the loud talker in the gut. That was one of the first lessons Rudy learned as a newbie inmate: Request sneakers, and when they arrive, keep them safe so you can either wear or trade them when needed.

Just as he's shifting some canned goods in his locker to make room for the new kicks, Rudy hears a garbled version of what he thinks sounds like his name echoing throughout the halls.

"Did you hear that?" Rudy asks, turning to cellmate Billy, who is lying on his thin unmade mattress, arms folded across his chest. His eyes are shut, but he isn't asleep.

"Hear what?" Billy mumbles.

"My name. I could have sworn it sounded like my name."

Billy grunts his disinterest and flips over to face the cell wall.

Rudy moves toward the door so he's closer to the hallway speakers. The garbled message is repeated, and this time, there is no doubt it is his name. "DeFranco report to the office."

Rudy's heart flutters as adrenaline courses through him. *What did I do? What did I do?* he agonizes while haphazardly shoving cans of tuna fish, mouthwash, and a spiral notebook back into his metal cabinet. As he fumbles with the lock, he tries to think of some indiscretion, a recent lapse or perhaps an offense he could have committed, but none come to mind.

As he waits for a guard to unlock his door, Rudy runs his fingers through his shaggy brown hair and stares through the barbed wire around the slit of his window to the electrical fence beyond.

Moments later, the guard appears. "You're up, DeFranco," he bellows, holding open the cell door.

Rudy nods and proceeds through the doorway, wiping the sweat on his palms against the sides of his starchy brown jumpsuit.

As he follows the guard down a hall and up a flight of stairs to the warden's office, he continues to rack his brain for any misstep on his part. Again, he fails to come up with anything he might have done wrong. Never, in over a decade behind bars, has he been punished. Quite the opposite, in fact. He's been a model inmate— promptly reporting for work, always following rules, respecting authority, keeping to himself.

When the guard knocks on the warden's door, Rudy instinctively straightens his posture and clears his throat as they await the signal to enter.

"DeFranco," the warden sighs from behind his desk. He seems burdened by simply uttering Rudy's surname. The room reeks of cheap air freshener, as if the warden cleared out a car wash's supply of rearview mirror deodorizers and hid them throughout his office. The man does not make eye contact. Instead, his gaze remains fixed on a stack of forms piled in front of him and licks his thumb and forefinger each time he flips a page to add his ball-pointed blue squiggle of an autograph.

Rudy stands in front of the desk, shoulders back, chin up, legs planted firmly on the floor a foot apart. "Yes, sir," he says steadily, trying to ignore the rapid thumping in his chest.

"Your number's up, DeFranco." The warden shakes his head in disappointment and glances up at Rudy somberly.

Rudy's mind flashes to a solitary confinement cell. He's heard horror stories of inmates being sent to the hole and can't imagine what he's done to deserve such punishment, but he's long past believing in appropriate outcomes. Prison is a world of its own and the fate of inmates is often subject to the whims of those in positions of authority. He knows he didn't deserve to go to jail to begin with, so the prospect of solitary confinement, while wholly unjust, would not be out of the realm of possibility given the outrageous trajectory of his life.

"Excuse me, sir?" Rudy's voice cracks. He immediately coughs to mask the squeak—just as he'd done as a pubescent teen—but the coverup is as ineffectual in his thirties as it was at thirteen.

The warden's eyebrow lifts and his mouth curls into a half-smile. "Gotcha." He chuckles louder than necessary and wipes his nose with the back of his hand.

Rudy recognizes this behavior. He has seen it many times before. It is the self-righteous air of someone drunk on power.

"You're outta here, DeFranco. Two weeks. Got your marching orders right here. Gotta say, you're one of the better ones. If it had been up to me, I woulda gotten rid of that Billy guy in your cell. Man, he's a lazy fuck. But you? You're a good worker. No complaints about you. Maybe that's why the bosses are cuttin' the strings with you coupla years early. Guess sometimes it works out for the nice guys."

The warden extends his arm toward Rudy and waves the signature pages in the air as if he's dangling a treat in front of a dog.

Rudy stands frozen in place. He opens his mouth to speak, but nothing comes out. He's unsure if this is a prank—if the people monitoring the prison security cameras are sitting back with a bucket of popcorn cackling at his gullibility.

"Well, you wanna go or what? Happy to keep you here if that's what ya really want, DeFranco." He snickers, pulling the papers back toward his chest and then extending them out again toward Rudy, teasing him with the prospect of freedom like it is all just a childish game.

Rudy steps forward and reaches for the documents. He wonders if his drenched hands will saturate the pages and render them void.

"Sign at the X on pages three, four, and six," the warden directs.

Rudy reads every word and signs his name in all the appropriate spots. His mind floods with questions about how this all came about, but he's too afraid to ask.

Lay low, he tells himself. *You'll get the details later. This is the first stroke of luck in thirteen years. Get out before it changes.*

"Thank you, sir," Rudy says as he hands the documents back to the warden. "Don't really know what to say other than thank you."

"Stay outta trouble, DeFranco," he says, his eyes glancing at something on his desk.

"Yes, sir. Thank you, sir."

The guard escorts Rudy back to his cell. After the cuffs are removed from his wrists and the cell door is closed, Rudy makes a beeline for his metal locker, retrieves a sheet of his best stationery from the top shelf, and begins composing the letter he has waited thirteen years to write to April.

3

April

NOW

"You okay?" Peter asks, looking over the restaurant's dessert menu. "You seem distracted."

Don't say a word about the reporter's phone call, she cautions herself. "Oh, I'm fine," April lies, flashing a reassuring grin. "Just thinking about the kids. I didn't hire a babysitter. I figured the girls are nearly eleven now, they're old enough to watch their brother for a bit, but I have a hunch the condo may not be standing when we get home."

"Maybe we should get the check, I've got a pile of work to do anyway," he says and raises his hand to grab the waiter's attention.

She can't get home soon enough.

As Peter scrolls through his phone in the back of the Uber, April stares out the window, gnawing on her bottom lip as they drive along Lake Shore Drive toward the South Loop. She doesn't notice the cityscape through the glass, or the whizz of passing cars, or even the heat blowing onto her face through the back seat vent.

All she can hear in her head is the tinny theme song of Mister Soft-ee's ice cream truck—the soundtrack of her early childhood.

She closes her eyes and is transported back to Brooklyn's Avenue L playground. She's running toward the tallest, most glittery silver mountain she's ever seen. She zooms past the swings, circumvents the seesaw queue, and delightedly waves to her mother who is read-ing on a nearby park bench. But as she extends her arm to grasp the metal slide's banister, April suddenly stops short. There's a boy, about her age, wrapping his palm around the handrail on the left just as her fingertips lay claim to the one on the right. He is clad in denim overalls, nearly identical to the pair she is wearing, except hers has a daisy stitched on the front pocket. Though they've reached the slide's ladder at the exact moment, no words are exchanged. There is no tantrum. No battle. No stepping over the other's feet to climb first. Just a silent stare-down during which April surmises that his eyes look like gigantic brown M&Ms.

"Rudy, honey, let the pretty girl go first," a woman's voice rings out.

The boy immediately releases his grip and moves aside to allow for April's ascension.

She climbs slowly, carefully, employing a one-rung-at-a-time approach before settling in at the summit.

"Hey," April calls, craning her neck to look down at the boy at the base of the ladder.

"Yeah?" he squints, hand at his forehead to block the sun blaz-ing behind her.

"Come. We'll go down together. I'll wait for you."

This is her most prominent childhood memory, the one accessed so frequently it's as if her subconscious has unlimited membership to a streaming service. It's also the one that triggers the most dichotomous emotions she's ever known—an amalgamation of tenderness, joy, devastation, and gut-wrenching guilt.

When the Uber stops, April's eyes jolt open and she returns to the present.

"Ape, you coming?" Peter asks. He's standing on the curb, holding the rear door open.

"Yep! Must have fallen asleep there," she says, shimmying out the back. "I think I'm going to zonk out the second my head hits the pillow."

April and Peter are greeted by the aroma of homemade chocolate chip cookies as they enter their condo. The enticing scent reminds her of a conversation she'd once had with a real estate broker who swore that baking prior to an open house would guarantee a sale. "Always stick a dessert in the oven right before a prospective buyer walks in," the agent insisted. "One whiff of apple pie or brownies from the kitchen, and they'll think, 'This is where I belong! Where do I sign?'"

Though olfactory manipulation is a questionable sales tactic, April knows there's truth to the power of warm confections, and this night is no exception. The fact that the entirety of her two-thousand-square-foot loft smells of cocoa and butterscotch is precisely what she needs. She doesn't care that cracked eggshells are strewn across her granite countertops, or that a glob of gravity-defying dough is protruding like a wart from her twelve-foot ceiling, or that she can hear the crunch of sugar granules every time she steps on her hardwood floors. Coming home to three children who just spent their Saturday night competing against one another in a bake-off is a dream. The scene is as heart-warming and adorably chaotic as a Nancy Meyers film. If she were a prospective buyer, she would undoubtedly close the deal right then and there.

After planting kisses on each of their children and petting their dog, Bocce, who is contentedly curled up atop an ottoman in the living room, Peter retreats to his "campaign headquarters" (a.k.a. the guest room) and April checks to make sure the kitchen appliances are turned off. The girls are conscientious tweens but have been left in charge without a babysitter just once before this evening. When all is clear, April makes a beeline for the master bedroom. In a singular fluid motion, she removes the silver hoops from her ears and punts her patent leather pumps into the closet as if they're little footballs. Still dressed in the ivory ribbed turtleneck, black miniskirt, and opaque tights she'd worn to dinner at the Signature Room, she crawls beneath the down comforter on her mattress and shuts her eyes.

She can't get the oddly familiar voice of the *Times* reporter out of her head.

Do you have a comment regarding Rudy DeFranco?

The question quickens her pulse and constricts her chest—physiological keepsakes returning like muscle memory after years of dormancy.

She curls into a tight fetal position beneath the duvet, hugging her knees against her breasts.

I have more to say than you could possibly print, she thinks. *Why didn't he tell me he was coming home? Why am I learning this from a fucking reporter? And how the hell did this woman get my number? I'm unlisted!*

April's eyes sting with tears.

Okay, what are you feeling right now? Name your emotions, she instructs herself as if she were talking one of her elementary school students down from a tantrum. *Is it fear? Confusion? Elation? Anger? Dread?* A tidal wave creeps up from the depths of her chest into her neck. She cups her hands over her mouth and presses her face into the mattress to muzzle the unstoppable wail.

"Mom?" Attie, one of her twins, hollers from the other end of the loft.

April quickly wipes her face with the edge of her white pillow-case, smearing black mascara and eyeliner everywhere. "Yes?" she bellows back through a crackling voice.

"Can we rent a movie on Amazon Prime?"

She clears her throat. "What movie?"

At that moment, Simon, her seven-year-old, pummels through the doorway of her bedroom and slides across the floor as if he's stealing a base in his little league game. She can hear the doorknob strike the wall behind it and already knows without looking that it has left a dent in need of repair.

"Tell Attie no! Say no, Mom! I'm begging. I don't want to see their dumb movie from like a hundred years ago."

"What do your sisters want to see?" she asks, extricating herself from beneath the comforter. She steps out of bed and heads to the en suite bathroom. She needs to wash her face. The kids can't see her cheeks tear streaked like this.

"Some stupid thing about cutting school. *The Avengers* is so much cooler." Simon clasps his hands in prayer beside the bathroom door. "Please!"

It's nine thirty and April isn't in the mood to play referee. She pats her face dry with a washcloth and shuffles down the hall to the family room sectional sofa where Attie and Rosie are snuggled, each with their own oversized cable knit blanket. *Ferris Bueller's Day Off* is on the screen.

"It's a classic," Rosie says, smiling sweetly at her mother. "My friend said it was filmed on her grandparents' street."

April runs her fingers through her tween's long ponytail—the silky texture and style an exact replica of her own from childhood. "That's certainly possible. I think it was shot in the northern suburbs."

"So who wins?" Simon asks, cutting to the chase.

"That's for you guys to decide," April responds as she swipes a cookie from the plate on Attie's lap. She can tell she's disappointed all three of her children with this response. "Figure it out. You're all very bright and know how to be fair. I've had a long day." April kisses each of their foreheads and retreats down the hallway past Peter, who is gesticulating wildly on a Zoom meeting in the guest room. She's relieved to see he's busy; she has no idea how to tell him about the call from the *Times*.

April quickly changes into pajamas, shuts the lights, and returns to bed, cocooning her entire body beneath the linens. The intimate space and absence of light reminds her of the forts she and Rudy constructed as children—how they'd throw sofa cushions and garbage bags onto the floor, grab flashlights and snacks, and play for hours in their own imaginary world. A smile spreads across her face as she recalls how those forts once inspired Rudy's grand idea of building a tunnel between their homes. They grabbed toy beach shovels and a plastic bucket in the shape of a crab and started construction by digging up April's backyard. It didn't matter that his apartment building and her house were separated by a major thoroughfare and a maze of Con Edison utility pipes; they were confident it was doable. When Barbara Zagoda gasped upon seeing her decimated property, Rudy sprang to his feet and motioned with his chin for her to meet him in the driveway for a private conversation. There was such an urgency and gravity to his demeanor, April didn't want to let on that she could hear every word from only a few feet away.

"Look, Mrs. Zagoda," he said, sliding his hands into the pockets of his shorts. "I just want to make sure you know, in case of emergency and what not, I can use this tunnel to get to April at any hour in case she needs me. Things come up all the time. Day and night. I want to be on call for her, you know?"

"Are you nine or forty-nine?" Barbara sighed.

April glanced over and could see her mother unfolding her arms which, a moment earlier, had been pretzeled tightly across her chest.

"We'll grow new plants, don't worry about that," Barbara said. "But y'know what you can't grow, Rudy?"

He shook his head.

"Kindness. And you've got that in spades. You remind me so much of your dad."

Even at that young age, April concurred with her mother's assessment. Rudy certainly resembled his father, Eddie DeFranco, an apartment superintendent who responded to handyman emergencies on a daily basis for the tenants of their building. Eddie was on call around the clock and made a point of telling residents he was at their service no matter how big or small the job, no matter the hour. In fact, April was at their apartment one Christmas when the landlord gifted Eddie a new uniform with the moniker "Super Super" stitched in red thread above the chest pocket.

Given his father's heroic status and epithet, Rudy's obsession with Superman was no surprise. In fact, when she and Rudy dressed up as superheroes, he'd knot a twin-sized bedsheet at the base of his neck and run zigzags up and down the sidewalk pretending to rescue people in need. April, on the other hand, would retrieve a green plastic "flying saucer" sled from her parents' garage, hug her knees to her chest, and cover herself with her "magic shell." She'd proudly claim to possess a trifecta of superpowers—invisibility, invincibility, and invulnerability—but often felt a tinge of guilt for choosing skills that prioritized self-preservation while Rudy consistently ranked the well-being of others above all else. Benevolence was in his nature, but it was also how he was nurtured.

With a cheek pressed against her mattress and a seven-hundred-thread-count sateen top sheet covering her body like a corpse, April silently mouths the questions that cross her mind. *Why's he getting out earlier than expected? Is he going back to Brooklyn? Who's picking him up? What's he gonna do when he gets home? Who's gonna hire him? Wait, is he even allowed to leave the house? How soon can I see him?*

April yearns to visualize the future. His future. Their future. If only she could flip ahead in the script. Act I of their lives started out great but tanked just before the interlude. *It's been a very long intermission*, she thinks. *What if the actors have changed?* In truth, she's different. And perhaps her greatest fear is that Rudy will be, too.

The air beneath the sheets has grown stuffy. April pokes her head and arms out and stares straight up at the ceiling fan. *Should I tell Peter about all of this?* she wonders. *Maybe, but not yet. I need more information first. He'll have questions and I won't have answers. It'll be too much of a distraction for him right now. I can wait to share the news.* She reaches for the cell phone on her nightstand and notices an incoming text:

> Georgia: Hey babe, just confirming yoga tomorrow morning? Still good?

She responds as if everything were normal.

> April: Yup! See you bright and early 🖤

"Shit," she groans. Typically, Sunday yoga with her girlfriends is a highlight of her week. Peter takes charge of breakfast and the kids' morning routines and she has a few hours to recharge on her own. But right now, she can't imagine having the wherewithal to leave the bedroom, let alone chat with friends or contort her body to resemble a triangle. She places the phone face down on her nightstand and attempts to fall asleep.

Though both her eyes and the bedroom door are shut, she can feel the reverberations of the base from the surround sound speakers playing the kids' movie down the hall. She can smell the aroma of freshly brewed coffee, which means Peter has just made a new pot and that this will be a late work night. Between the ambience in their home and the cacophony in her head, there's no way she's easing into a peaceful state.

"Forget it," she mutters aloud, surrendering to the impediments. Once again, she reaches for her phone, but this time, she types in a Google search:

> How to inform your husband you've secretly been in touch with your incarcerated best friend for the last thirteen years

She shakes her head, mocking her own entry, as if she were delusional to even tap the letters on the keyboard and think it would yield sage advice. She deletes the search history and types in Rudy's name instead but doesn't hit "enter."

Do I really want to go down this rabbit hole? she wonders. *Do I really want to be flooded with old trashy stories and undoubtedly a shit ton of misinformation? It's late. I already know I'm going to need every ounce of energy I can conserve. This is not a good idea. I'll hear from Rudy soon enough. Better to get legitimate information direct from the source than be fed lies off the internet. Shut off the phone, April. Go to sleep. Now.*

She acquiesces, shoves a set of foam noise plugs into her ears, hopes Peter will see the kids to bed, and eventually drifts off.

April arrives at the yoga studio the following morning as her friends are unrolling their cushioned mats parallel to one another on the hardwood floor.

"Hi, hi, hi!" April makes her way around giving each woman a quick peck on the cheek before settling into her usual spot beneath the window, the farthest location from the essential oil diffuser she abhors.

"Good morning, ladies," Corinne, the instructor, croons as she straightens her posture. "Please remember to turn off all electronics before we begin." She presses a button on a remote control that simultaneously dims the lights and cues up soothing spa music.

Though they enjoy stretching, posing, and breathing their way to a more centered existence, the best part of yoga is undoubtedly the "after party" in the studio's twinkly-lit reception area where they dish about their lives on a wooden bench beneath an oversized feathered dream catcher. The space is filled with whitewashed plaques of motivational sayings one might find on sale at Home-Goods—"Mindset is Everything" and "Let Your Soul Shine"—and though April deems the aphorisms to wax more tacky than poetic, the room's vibe is certainly inviting and warm. April and her friends typically linger until the students in the next class arrive, at which point they retrieve their jackets from an eggplant-colored wall cubby, fish their car keys from the depths of their tote bags, and relocate their gathering to the parking lot.

That Sunday is no different. Swigging from their stainless water bottles, key rings dangling from their polished fingers, they update one another on their personal headlines. Though there is only enough time for a highlight reel, they get the latest development with Dawn's ongoing custody battle, the plans for Ericka's son's Bar Mitzvah, and learn that Nina has yet to decide if she should accept the job promotion that would relocate her family to Hong Kong or stay put in Winnetka so her kids can play varsity lacrosse at New Trier. Children, aging parents, and, of course, opinions on what April should wear to Peter's Election Day victory party round out the conversation, but she doesn't allow Peter's career or her vacillation between a pantsuit and dress to dominate the discussion. She gracefully deflects, directing questions and attention to her friends.

Eventually, they boot up their cell phones, discover missed calls and texts, blow air-kiss farewells to one another, and fan out in the parking lot to their respective cars. As usual, Georgia and April steal a few minutes alone. This week's topic is a weighing of the merits and shortcomings of an Airbnb rental they found in Lake Geneva, Wisconsin, for their annual late December family vacation. After concluding that they will move ahead and book the house, April presses a button on her key fob to remotely unlock her car door. She can never remember where she parks and uses her Subaru's chirps as a compass. Turning her head toward the familiar sound, she notices Nina leaning against the hood of her car, hand on her heart, seemingly spellbound by her phone.

"Neen?" April calls out. "You okay?"

Nina doesn't respond. She's frozen in place.

April and Georgia shoot concerned looks at one another and jog over. The first thing April detects as she approaches is Nina's severely furrowed brow and slacked jaw. Typically, very little flusters Nina. She's a leader in crisis communications public relations, so to see the wind knocked out of her is jarring.

"What is it?" Georgia asks apprehensively.

April gently touches Nina's forearm. "Are you all right?"

Nina pulls away. "Oh, I'm okay," she says, the peak of her eyebrows nearly touching her scalp line. "Are *you*?" She turns her cell phone to April.

April looks down at the screen and just beneath a banner with the Associated Press (AP) logo are the words "Breaking News" and a headline: "State's Attorney Candidate Peter Nelson's Wife Linked to Homicide."

You're. Gonna. Pack. A. Bag.

Those are the first words April hears after seeing the headline. Though her chest rises and collapses with each breath, she is otherwise immobilized. Aside from a functioning respiratory system, the piercing chill of her friends' penetrating stares is her only proof of life. Time is frozen on a heavily loaded pause until she determines her critical next move. *What's the appropriate response?* she wonders. *Do I scream in horror? Laugh at the absurdity? Is there a path of least resistance here? Is it humor? Denial? Or do I go with a full-on mea culpa where I vomit out my past in the yoga parking lot and explain to these women—the ones whose children I've car-pooled, the ones with whom Peter and I have shared every New Year's Eve for a decade, the ones who have all moved to the northern suburbs yet I look forward to schlepping up to see on Sundays so we can laugh over our pathetic warrior poses and maintain our bond—that I have withheld critical information about my life? But do I really owe them anything? Aren't I entitled to privacy? And, after all, I have nothing to confess. I did nothing wrong.*

Before April can formulate a plan, she is interrupted by Nina.

"You're gonna pack a bag," she repeats her command. "One for you and another for your kids and you're gonna get the hell out of that condo before the press descends. Why you're living in a South Side converted loft with a buzzer security system instead of a doorman building in Lincoln Park is beyond me, but whatever, that's a conversation for another time. It's unbelievable how much crap the media makes up. Fucking whores. They'll do anything for a viral story. I mean," Nina chuckles, "it's not like I even have to confirm with you that this is absolute bullshit. But Ape, do you know how they could have even concocted something this ab-surd?"

Cars in the parking lot are beginning to blur together and April grabs onto Georgia's arm to steady herself.

"I got you." Georgia wraps her arm around April's waist and pulls her close.

April's knees weaken and a lump forms in her throat, physical manifestations of gratitude for the instantaneous support. It's mo-ments like these that she appreciates Midwestern manners and decorum. They may be biting their tongues and suppressing an urge to cross-examine her, but the unconditional support—or at least the appearance thereof—is precisely what she needs in this moment.

"Do you know anything about this?" Georgia whispers to Nina while rubbing circles on April's back. "What will this mean for Peter?"

April keeps her eyes closed and does not react to the conversation around her.

"Peter and his team are going to have to figure out Peter right now," Nina says while texting at a ferocious speed on her phone. April can hear her nails clack against the screen. "Maybe he stays put in the city to deal with this, maybe he disappears along with April and the kids. That's up to him and his PR crew. Oh, and April can't drive home alone right now. Georgia, can you take her car? Or give her a lift in yours? We can deal with moving the extra car out of this lot later."

"Of course, anything." Georgia says to April, "We'll pick up your stuff from the city and bring you guys to my house. You can stay with me."

Not one cell in April's body is fighting for autonomy. The comfort of having her hand held and guided like a child is invaluable. But then, the moment she thinks of herself as a child being ushered along, her own children's faces flash before her.

Attie.

Rosie.

Simon.

They're the ones whose hands must be held! This isn't just me, or Peter and me. It's all of us. The whole family is about to get hit.

Despite the adrenaline ricocheting through April's veins, her eyelids suddenly feel like bricks. She could fall asleep right there in the parking lot. Her face begins to tingle and the space around her seems off, as if the lighting has changed. She slowly lowers herself onto the pavement, sinking her head between her knees, like the crash position on an airplane.

"Here, drink this," Georgia insists, uncapping a bottle and bringing it to April's lips.

This sensation of feeling both numb and acutely aware of her surroundings is an experience April has known only twice before. The first was Rudy's arrest. The second was her expulsion from Rivington. Though the particulars varied—NYPD officers standing in her parents living room at 6 a.m. and university board members sitting around a mahogany conference table explaining their unanimous decision to flush her future down the toilet—the scenarios were a ripple effect of the same event. Now, as she swigs back water on the ground of a strip mall parking lot in Lake County, Illinois, all she can think is: *Here we go again. It's never going to fucking end.*

"Come on, we've got to get you home," Georgia says, gently helping April up from the pavement and guiding her into the car. "You need to see Peter and figure out a plan."

As they zip along Lake Shore Drive en route to the city, April gazes out of Georgia's passenger seat window searching for the landmarks that gauge her proximity to home. Lincoln Park Zoo, check. Sears Tower, check. Soldier Field, check. She yearns for the comfort of her children and the familiarity of their collective stuff. But as she envisions the toys, art projects, and framed photographs displayed on the fireplace mantle, her fingers instinctively curl around the seatbelt—one hand on the shoulder belt, the other on the lap—like a telepathic warning: *Strap in! Your world is as fragile as those snow globe tchotchkes you picked up on family trips.*

"You will get through this," Georgia says kindly, eyeing April's seatbelt situation. "*We* will get through this."

It's the *we* that does April in. The pronoun stings, the unconditional love igniting a torrent of guilt. *I owe her an explanation. But I can't. Not yet.* She rolls down the window and leans her head into the wind letting her hair whip haphazardly in every direction.

When April and Peter decided to leave New York and create a new life in Chicago, they made a deliberate choice to avoid any mention of her past. They saw no reason to voluntarily raise a red flag. When they began making friends in the community, April felt disingenuous. She grew quiet whenever everyone swapped stories about college or first jobs. She'd squelch any inquiries with: *Oh, I'm boring! College was what you'd expect! Nothing to report over here!* The more challenging social interactions, however, were the one-on-ones like coffee dates or walks with a girlfriend. Those were the times she'd find herself closer to the edge of spilling. *How will I have real friendships if I'm filtered and cagey?* she'd wonder whenever she was tempted to share. But then she'd remember the bottom line—her children—and how absolutely nothing was worth the risk of their well-being. After all, if there was one lesson she'd learned in life, it was how even the best, well-intentioned people remain human. Even the good ones are fallible. If she entrusted a friend with the entirety of the Rudy story, it could ultimately harm her kids. One slip, one leak, one missing word, one skewed detail, one questionable facial expression could alter the narrative.

Early in their marriage, before the twins were born, April and Peter agreed that she had to be the one to tell the kids. They needed to hear the truth from their mother who lived the experience—not through filtered, twisted gossip. Like first impressions, there would be only one shot to properly introduce them to the Rudy conversation, and the timing and messaging had to be on the nose. Attie, Rosie, and Simon needed to be mature enough to process nuance, perception, and facts, and they believed all three should be told together. It would be unfair to ask the girls to hold such a weighty secret until their younger brother matured.

Dread swirls inside April like poison as Georgia pulls into a parking spot across from the condo. *Does Peter know?* she wonders. *He must, the cell phone is practically an appendage. It's highly unlikely he hasn't received a text or email from someone. And if he hasn't, how the hell am I going to break this to him?*

All these years of deliberately muzzling herself, of putting up boundaries with friends, of waiting for the right moment to talk to her kids, it was all for nothing, she thinks. Her power usurped by a nine-word headline that is now forcing her hand; she's been robbed. All she has ever wanted is to do the right thing—especially by her children—and she knows at this very moment, her top priority is to be a united front with Peter and talk to the kids before they hear chatter from anyone else.

"Does the building have a service entrance in the back?" Georgia asks. "I know, I sound paranoid, but do you think the guy standing in front of your building is a member of the press?"

April squints to get a clearer look at the man outside the revolving door. "No. That's Bob in 5B. He's harmless."

"Guess I watch too many crime shows."

Now conscious of her surroundings, April surveys the area. Her eyes dart to the windshields of parked cars, to the sidewalks, to the darkened area on South Wabash beneath the EL platform—anywhere someone could be lurking. When she feels safe, they walk through the main entrance.

When they arrive upstairs, the condo is eerily calm. Simon is sitting cross-legged on the couch with a cereal bowl in his lap, hair disheveled, and staring like a zombie in footy pajamas at some animated show on TV. It's a typical Sunday morning.

April kisses her son on his head. "Hi, baby. Where's Daddy?"

Simon shrugs and shoves a spoonful of Rice Krispies into his mouth.

April walks down the hallway toward the bedrooms, Georgia

tagging behind like a loyal puppy. They peek into the girls' shared bedroom where Attie is rubbing the sleep out of her eyes and Rosie has her nose in a book, as usual.

"I've got the kids," Georgia whispers reassuringly. "I'll get them packed up. You go find Peter."

April continues down the corridor toward the guest bedroom. As she approaches, Peter steps out into the hall. She is about to ask if he's seen the headline, but one look at her husband's ashen pallor suffices as an answer.

"Peter," she whimpers, her hand rising to cover her mouth. More than anything she craves his reassuring embrace, the bear hug that always lets her know things will be alright.

Just inches away, he stands stone-faced and silent.

"Oh, babe . . ." She extends her arms, reaching for him. But as her fingertips graze his shoulders, he spins around, returns to his makeshift office, and shuts the door.

4

Jillian

NOW

T he Google Alert appears in Jillian's inbox just as she's un-
wrapping a sandwich at her desk.

As a veteran reporter, she is skilled at tuning out the
buzz of a newsroom. The multiple television screens, running stock
market ticker, ringing landlines, and constant din of journalists
crunching keyboards are soothing ambient sounds—not distractions.
She can think of no better meal companions than her ergonomic
chair and cell phone. Typically, she preps for interviews or sorts
through mail while eating in the office. But on this day, as she's
removing the wax paper and extracting a toothpick from her let-
tuce, tomato, and turkey on rye, an incoming message dings on
her computer, causing her eyes to shift from the overstuffed
sandwich to the monitor.

Years earlier, when Google Alerts came into existence, most of
her colleagues considered the technology manna from heaven.
What a gift to simply submit the name of an industry/company/

person and have any news delivered directly into your inbox. Naturally, when she signed up for this service, Jillian was interested in any information pertaining to her beat: Science. Climate Change. Environment. Public Health. Physics. Natural History. Neuroscience. Women in Science. But before she entered any of those terms into the search engine—before she even *thought* about the various scientific fields that would yield optimal results—she typed in the first three words that came to mind. They were the subject of her greatest curiosity and the surprising seminal source of her professional success: *Felon Rudy DeFranco.*

Not once in all the years since has there been a single story about Rudy. But now, just as she's about to take a bite of her lunch, the headline appears: "Coed Killer to Be Released After Years of Lockup".

Had she been chewing, she would've spit out her lunch. Instead, she leans in toward the monitor and clicks on the link.

There it is: Rudy's mug shot alongside a paparazzi-style photo taken outside the courthouse on the day of his sentencing. Jillian grabs the arms of her desk chair, her fingers curling, gripping its edges with the intensity of a passenger on a turbulent airplane. Even after all these years, there is something about Rudy's face that still manages to destabilize her. She wonders what he looks like now. Is he bald? Does he have crescent-shaped creases framing his mouth like parentheses? Or did he somehow manage to retain his boyish good looks?

She scans the story and quickly culls out the facts: He's getting released in two weeks; he'll be reporting to a parole officer in the New York City area; there is no comment from the deceased's family; and, most intriguing to Jillian, there is no mention at all of April Zagoda.

After reading the alert one more time, she takes a swig of Diet Coke, rewraps her sandwich, prints out a hardcopy of the story, and marches it down the newsroom corridor to her boss's office.

"Hey, you have a minute?" she asks, tapping a knuckle on the open door.

Todd, a bald, narrow-faced sixty-something with a mustard stain in the center of his necktie, looks up at her over the top of his reading glasses. There are three open newspapers sprawled across his desk and a salami omelet in a Styrofoam takeout container that has infused his office with the smoky aroma of over-fried bacon.

"Sure thing, come on in," he says, gesturing to the chair facing his desk. "Getting ready for the conference? I'm expecting another prize for you." He winks. "But no pressure kid, no pressure."

Jillian stares blankly for a second before her brain clicks into place. *Oh right*, she thinks, *the science conference*. It's the same event she covered a couple of years earlier that led to her multiple-award-winning five-part series.

"Yes, of course. Looking forward to it. But I'm actually here about something else." She smiles and hands Todd the printout. "So I, um, I'd like to cover this story."

Todd's furry eyebrows raise and form a unibrow as he scans the article. "Seriously?" he asks.

Jillian folds her arms across her chest. "Yes. Seriously."

"This is crime. And metro," he says, handing her back the sheet of paper. "This ain't your beat, kid."

As a seasoned, well-decorated reporter in her thirties she is hardly a kid, but doesn't mind his use of old newsman jargon. In fact, she likes it. It makes her feel as if she's surrounded by the likes of Woodward and Bernstein, like she's living a real-life version of *All the President's Men*.

"Oh, yeah, I know, it's not what I typically cover, but I thought . . ."

Todd has already lost interest.

"No one cares about this," he says, perusing one of the periodicals on his desk. "It happened over a decade ago. He's getting out. Big effin' deal."

I care! She wants to pound her fist on his desk but knows better than to lose her cool in front of a boss notorious for either making or breaking careers. Fortunately, she has always been on his good side. "I hear you, Todd, I really do, but, respectfully, I beg to differ."

Todd pulls the glasses off his nose and leans onto his elbows. "Gimme climate change, Jilly Bean. Gimme a new medical device that's gonna save the world. Do a profile on a prodigy doctor who's got a lead on a cure for cancer. I don't need you to tell me about a punk from the streets who killed a rich kid and did his time. If you care that much, let the folks over in metro know about it. They'll find someone to cover it. I need you here, writing what you know."

This is what I know, Jillian thinks. *And I know more than anyone else.*

"People will care about this, I promise you they will," she continues.

"She promises me!" he mumbles sarcastically. He now appears perturbed.

"Yes. I promise. This is the story that got my career going. I got my first stringer job after reporting it for my college newspaper." Jillian looks down at Rudy's mug shot. She's fixated on the fear in his eyes and recalls the first time those big brown irises had locked with her own. They disarmed her from moment one. There was a gentle sweetness in his gaze that made her feel safe, seen, and accepted. Unlike so many other boys she'd known, there was no entitlement in Rudy's glance, no airs. He was confident but not cocky. Charming yet completely grounded and real. His goodness was evident right there in his eyes.

"This guy is walking soon. You can't cover both him and the conference. I'm counting on you for another win this year."

"Okay," she sighs to Todd, defeatedly. "Message received."

⸙

Later that evening, while strolling in Central Park with her aging
poodle, Jillian stops to sit on a park bench. Farley instantly curls
up on the concrete beside her toes to soak up warm rays from the
setting sun. She pulls out her cell phone and types "Rudy DeFranco,
Brooklyn, NY" into the Whitepages.com website. Over one hundred DeFrancos are listed in the borough, but none named Rudy.
She racks her brain to recall the names of his parents. God knows
the press had had a field day with the story of the son of an
apartment handyman from Brooklyn murdering the son of an
investment banker from Westchester—she could probably dig up
their names with a modicum of effort but doesn't feel like going
down a rabbit hole while she's out walking the dog.

What about April? Jillian thinks, recalling that April and Rudy
had been childhood neighbors. Jillian searches for April Zagoda in
Brooklyn, and a second later, there's an address and phone number
right there on Jillian's cell phone.

Could April still be living with her parents? Jillian wonders. She
has no idea what became of AZ—April's nickname among the college newspaper staff back when they were in school together. April
had been a promising junior editor who signed her initials in big
block letters when approving galleys, and the moniker stuck.

Jillian's lips turn upward as she recalls the late nights and
weekends freshman year spent stressing over deadlines, guzzling
Diet Cokes, and smoking cigarettes beside the campus lampposts
at 1 a.m. as if it were midtown Manhattan and they were *Wall
Street Journal* reporters in need of a nicotine fix. Every story felt
like major news. Every headline would somehow change the
world. And with each byline, Jillian believed she was one step
closer to achieving her dream of winning a Pulitzer Prize. Their
world at the paper was insular, but she loved the bubble.

Jillian had heard a litany of rumors about April right after the scandal broke: April was taking time off. She was a hostess at a diner in Queens. She transferred to a community college near home and worked at a bagel store. She was temping as a secretary in Manhattan's garment district. No one knew the truth of what had become of April Zagoda following her expulsion from Rivington.

Jillian takes a screenshot of the Zagodas' address and phone number and saves it to a new file on her cell phone titled "AZ."

The following Saturday, Jillian drives to Brooklyn. If there is one thing she has learned about reporting, it's that you often get a better, more fleshed out story when doing research in person. Sure, she can get pretty far over the phone or with an internet search, but there is something about walking the streets and looking people in the eye that adds another dimension.

When she arrives in the late afternoon, there is a parking spot directly across from the Zagodas' home, but before exiting her sedan, she snaps a picture of the house and adds it to the AZ file. She then checks her appearance in the small rectangular visor mirror over the steering wheel, licks her fingertips, and flattens some flyaway hairs. *Game time,* she thinks as she walks up the stoop and rings the bell.

"Hello." Jillian smiles when the wooden door swings open. She is mindful to be friendly but not too eager. An elderly man is standing behind the rickety metal and glass storm door that spells out their house number in slightly corroded wrought iron letters.

"Can I help you?" he asks.

A woman's voice calls out from another part of the house, "Who is it, Steven?"

"Mr. Zagoda?" Jillian asks in her most gentle tone. She has shrewdly perfected what she refers to as "the chameleon"—a repertoire of various timbres and tricks to disarm sources and elicit information.

"I'm sorry, dear," he says placing a hand to his ear. "You're gonna have to speak up."

Jillian clears her throat and projects. "Oh, no problem. I was just asking, are you Mr. Zagoda?"

"Yes, I am, Steven Zagoda," he says kindly.

"Oh, hello, Mr. Zagoda. My name is Jillian. I went to college with your daughter, April."

He looks confused. "Rivington or Brooklyn College?"

"Oh, um," Jillian stammers. She wasn't aware April had ended up at Brooklyn College. "Rivington."

Mr. Zagoda shrugs nonchalantly. "Your name doesn't ring a bell. But any friend of April's is a friend of ours. Would you like to come inside? Have some tea? My wife just made some delicious blueberry muffins."

"Oh, yes, thank you, that would be lovely." Jillian feels a pang of guilt course through her as she steps onto their maroon living room carpet. *Focus*, she reprimands herself. *Stay in the moment.*

"Barb, we have company!" Mr. Zagoda bellows.

Barbara rolls her wheelchair into the dining room balancing a tray of muffins on her lap. She places it on the table and turns to greet Jillian.

"Hello. I'm Barb. Have we met?"

"I don't think we have. I'm Jillian," she says, extending her hand. "I was just saying to your husband, I know April from college. From Rivington."

"Mmm," Barbara nods, her lips pursing into a tight half smile.

Jillian can feel Barbara giving her a once-over.

"Sit, sit," Steven says, waving Jillian toward a ladderback dining room chair. "How 'bout some tea?"

"Sounds delightful. Thank you."

"There's an assortment of flavors right there on the sideboard table."

Jillian reaches for an individually wrapped bag of Orange Spice and notices a framed photograph of three children—two girls and a younger boy—beside the mahogany tea box. The kids are bundled in colorful winter gear and standing in front of a large reflective sculpture in the shape of a silver bean, which Jillian immediately recognizes as Chicago's Millennium Park.

"So what brings you to the neighborhood?" Steven asks, handing her the muffin tray.

"Oh, I was just visiting a friend and remembered April grew up in Midwood, so I looked her up online and saw she's still listed at this address. Figured I'd stop by . . . catch up." She casually wipes some crumbs off the tips of her fingers, hoping her nonchalance forestalls any suspicion about her visit.

"I'm sorry, dear. April doesn't live here anymore," Steven says. "It will always be her home, of course, but she lives—"

Barbara cuts him off mid-sentence. "Please forgive me, my memory isn't what it was, but you said you were at Rivington with April?"

"Yes, ma'am. We were in the same dorm freshman year, knew some of the same people, were on the newspaper together." Jillian takes a sip of tea. She's having difficulty reading Barbara. She can't tell if the woman is confused or suspicious. "We all missed April when she left . . ."

Silence.

Jillian blots the corner of her mouth with a paper napkin.

Steven clears his throat, breaking the lull. "I didn't catch your last name, dear. What did you say it was?"

"Jones. Jillian Jones."

Jillian doesn't feel the need to note that she went by Jill in college—never Jillian—and that her maiden name, Colburn, is the only surname April would recognize.

"Well, it's nice to meet you Jillian Jones," Steven says. "Do you live in New York? Married? Children? Job? Don't mean to pry . . ."

Jillian smiles and waves a hand in front of her face. "It's not prying. Let's call it curiosity, shall we?"

"Oh, I like her!" Steven laughs and glances at Barbara.

"Okay. So the answers to your questions are: Yes. Divorced. No." Jillian treads carefully. She knows he's posed four questions and she's offering only three responses.

"And where do you work?" Barbara asks, without skipping a beat.

"Oh, I, um, I teach . . . a writing class." She shifts uncomfortably in her seat.

It isn't a lie. She does have a side gig as an instructor for a writing workshop that offers courses from Screenplay 101 to Advanced Nonfiction Writing. The students in her Wednesday evening Introduction to Journalism class are all dreamers who yearn to be the next Jodi Kantor but are stuck in uninspiring day jobs. Teaching isn't Jillian's passion and she gains nothing professionally or financially from this commitment. She does it purely for the personal salve. The Wednesday night meetings are her version of going to church and she knows likely the closest she will come to a baptism for her soul.

"Good for you," Steven says kindly. "You know Barb's a former English teacher."

"Is that right?" Jillian takes another bite of her muffin.

Barbara nods. "High school. Twenty-eight years. Taught down the street at the Jewish school, Yeshiva of Flatbush. I retired a couple years ago. I was able to manage for a long time, but once my body started to collapse like a marionette without warning, I had to get out of the classroom. Couldn't have my students picking their teacher up off the floor. I was going to retire fairly soon anyhow, but I must say, this isn't how I planned to spend my time."

"How did you plan to spend it?"

"With my grandchildren."

"Oh, do they live nearby?" Jillian asks.

"They visit often," Barbara says cryptically and then winces.

Steven shoots up from his seat. "You okay, hun?" he asks lovingly.

"Just need to move."

He walks over to help his wife out of her wheelchair. "It's like ants in the pants," he explains to Jillian. "The feeling just strikes and she's got to get those muscles going."

"I bet the grandkids are a big help when they stop by. They visit on weekends?" Jillian is aware she's goading, especially given Barbara's physical discomfort, but gives it a shot anyhow.

"They're great kids," is all Barbara offers.

I can't push the envelope any further. "Well, I have to be going now," she glances at her watch, "May I use your restroom before I head out?"

"Of course," Steven says. "The powder room down here isn't working. Feel free to use the one upstairs."

Perfect. All I need is a minute or two to snoop around.

As she ascends to the second floor, Jillian notices how the Zagodas' stairwell resembles a museum gallery with framed family photographs spaced inches apart from one another along the wall. There is a picture of a little boy in a karate uniform, another of twin girls dressed in matching bathing suits, and one of Barbara and Steven with all three kids blowing out candles on a cake. Larger than the rest is a candid close-up of April and her husband laughing at their wedding. The flowing ponytail Jillian remembered as April's signature style in college is tied back in an elegant low chignon. Jillian thinks she looks pretty in the photograph. Content. Whole.

Upon reaching the landing she notices three bedrooms, a linen closet, and a bathroom. The first door on the left is slightly ajar and has a hand-painted "April's Room" plaque above the knob. She gently nudges the door open with her shoe and steps inside. A yellow heart-shaped pillow is resting against the head of a canopied bed and a stack of CDs—mostly billboard hits—is collecting dust atop a bookshelf. There are numerous spelling bee award ribbons tacked to a corkboard and just beneath it, on her desk, is a navy blue shoebox. There's an unopened letter addressed to this house, postmarked that week, laying atop the box with the return address:

Rudy DeFranco
Inmate # 07458952081
Wallkill Correctional Facility
P.O. Box G
Wallkill, NY 12589

Here we go, Jillian thinks as she snaps a photo of the letter. The lid of the box is askew revealing a stack of identical envelopes inside. *So they're in touch,* she thinks. *But why mail correspondence here and not to her home?* Jillian tilts her head to check if the letters have been opened, but can't tell from her angle and doesn't want to meddle. She takes a picture of the pile and promptly exits the room. Before descending the steps, however, she makes sure to stop across the hall to flush the toilet lest the Zagodas grow suspicious.

The upstairs bathroom is outfitted with pink and gray wall tiles and a pink porcelain sink. The space is authentically retro; no irony or kitch. Jillian can't help but compare it to the home in which she was raised where her mother had a contractor on speed-dial and their house was in a perpetual state of renovation to keep up with the latest trends. She never understood why her father cared to be the first of their friends to have a home gym, or why her parents rushed to carve holes into their kitchen ceiling the instant skylight windows became all the rage. They were constantly reaching, never satisfied, whereas the Zagodas' dated but perfectly functional bathroom lacks for nothing. And it is there, standing beside a shag carpet toilet seat cover and outdated periodicals, that Jillian finds herself envious of April, just as she was when they met freshman year.

Jillian returns downstairs to her hosts. "Thanks so much for having me, Mr. and Mrs. Zagoda. No need to get up. I can let myself out."

"Nonsense," Steven says and meets Jillian by the front door.

"It was a pleasure meeting you both. I'm sorry I didn't get to catch April. Would it be okay if I got her phone number? And an email?"

"Absolutely." He walks briskly into the kitchen, rips a rectangular sheet of paper from a "Proud Supporter of Public Television" notepad magnetized to their refrigerator, jots down the information, and hands it to Jillian. "I'm sure she'll be very happy to hear from you."

Given the suspicious vibes she is sensing from Barbara, Jillian isn't sure April's mother would have been as generous.

Later that evening, as she awaits the arrival of her sushi order, Jillian paces around her apartment in pajamas. She has her cell phone in one hand and the piece of paper from Steven in the other.

"It's just a conversation," she repeats aloud as if it were a mantra. "Just a couple of questions. It will be over before the doorman buzzes the delivery guy upstairs. You're an award-winning journalist. Make the damn call. You've interviewed thousands of people. You can do this. You *need* to do this."

She grabs a bottle of chianti from the fridge and fills a long-stemmed glass nearly to the brim. After a few hearty swigs, she heads to the desk in her home office, opens a spiral notebook, plugs her cell phone into the charger, and settles into the leather chair. She stares at the paper with April's name and number until the digits and letters blur. She closes her eyes, her mind transporting back to the night each of their lives changed forever.

She can feel herself at the party. The thump of the music. The stickiness in the air.

She can see herself trying to capture Rudy's attention.

She can see him repeatedly glance over at April.

Her insides twist and percolate with anger as raw and real as if she were her old self again. Jillian's eyes bolt open. She is back in her home office.

After one more swill of chianti, she picks up the phone and dials.

Ten minutes later, while chewing on a pod of edamame, Jillian marvels at what a difference a single telephone call can make. She has been in the business long enough to read people well, even over the phone, and it wasn't hard to deduce during her brief conversation with April that she's got a story to tell. With a husband in the midst of an election and her silence regarding Rudy, their brief chat felt like an unexpectedly delectable appetizer that left Jillian craving more.

Inspired and energized by her newfound knowledge, Jillian spends the next hour getting in touch with her Chicago-based press colleagues to see what they know about April and her husband.

She reaches out to her friend at the *Tribune*, but the call goes directly to voicemail.

She shoots off an email to an editor at *Bloomberg* and to a reporter at the Chicago bureau of the *New York Times*, but given that it is a Saturday night, no one picks up.

The last contact in her arsenal—her former intern—recently

started a gig at the Associated Press. As a newbie hire, Jillian hopes she might be working a weekend shift.

"Heather, hi!" Jillian says, perhaps a bit too enthusiastically.

"Jillian! So good to hear from you!"

After some pleasantries and catch-up, Jillian gets down to business.

"Tell me, what do you know about Peter Nelson?"

"The guy running for state's attorney?"

"Yeah."

"Not much. Pretty vanilla. Seems like he's got this in the bag. Why?"

Jillian can hear Heather typing.

"Oh, just curious."

Heather chuckles. "I worked with you long enough to know that you're never just curious. What's up?"

Jillian smiles. She misses speaking with Heather.

"You got anything interesting on his wife?" Jillian asks. "April Zagoda? Well, I guess now maybe she's April Nelson."

More typing.

"Nada. My sense is vanilla married vanilla. I think she teaches at a private school in the city. They've got a few kids. She volunteers for a bunch of community stuff. Again, may I ask why? Don't tell me 'just curious.' What's going on?"

Jillian lets out a long sigh. "Oh, just following up on a case that happened many years ago. I'm just sniffing around, seeing if there is any 'there there.' That's all."

"A case? What kind of case? Was it a medical malpractice story you covered? Were the Nelsons guinea pig volunteers for some scientific research gone wrong? Ooh! Does one of them have a rare condition? Man, that would likely seal the deal for his voters."

"Oh, you are dark! I'm proud of you! I taught you well!" Jillian laughs.

"Seriously! I could use a tip. I'm still breaking into this new job. I'd love to wow my editor."

"Don't worry, you were my top intern and they're gonna love you. Let's get drinks or coffee next time you're in New York. Gotta run! So good to hear your voice!"

She hangs up and immediately rummages through her desk drawer for a pen. Heather's comment sparked an idea and Jillian feels like a fool for not thinking of it sooner. She grabs a Post-it note and in bright red ink writes:

Monday 9 a.m.:

Call the medical examiner's office.

5

Rudy

THEN

t's 8 a.m. on the morning of Rudy's fourteenth birthday and though Eddie's already repairing a broken radiator in apartment 4R and Lorraine's on the bus heading to work as a cashier at Kings Plaza Shopping Center, they didn't forget to mark their son's milestone. When Rudy walks into the kitchen, he sees a stack of room-temperature Bisquick pancakes and a bottle of Yoohoo awaiting him, along with two envelopes. The first, a bright yellow square with red balloons along the perimeter, contains a birthday card in the shape of the number fourteen with $25 tucked inside. The second, a standard letter-sized rectangle, holds a piece of paper folded in thirds.

"Working papers," Rudy mutters as he unfurls the document beside his breakfast.

As he takes a swig of Yoohoo, Rudy recalls how his parents conferred the same gift upon his brother, Tommy, when he turned fourteen—the magical age when a minor in New York State can legally work after school and during vacations. As far as Rudy can tell, fourteen was a turning point in Tommy's life; it was when he became less carefree. Rudy wonders if the same will be true for him. Will he have time to ride his bike to Marine Park? Go for slices of pizza after school at DiFara's? Stroll around the mall smelling colognes with his friends? For years, he and April would giddily while away hours of winter break spinning inside the industrial-sized dryers in his building's laundry room. Would all that now end?

Later that evening, as the DeFrancos sit around the small kitchen table celebrating Rudy with Carvel ice cream cake, there's a knock at the front door. Rudy knows it's April.

"Hey, sorry I'm late," she says when he greets her. She's in pajama pants and an oversized sweatshirt, her hair pulled up into a loose bun. "Stupid math homework took longer than I expected."

"You're just on time!" Lorraine calls from the kitchen, already cutting April a slice.

Except for the year she had to have her tonsils removed, April and Rudy have never missed celebrating a birthday.

"Here you go," she says, handing him a crinkled ball of tissue paper. "I know. Not the best wrapping job. Hopefully the gift will make up for it. But open it now, before your parents see."

Rudy rips the paper and pulls out a key chain in the shape of a small blue ear. He inspects it at eye level, then looks at her quizzically.

"You said you wanted to get an earring, but your parents wouldn't let you. So, here, I got you an *ear-ring*? Get it?"

Rudy laughs. "Yeah, I get it. It's perfect. It's not a diamond stud, but it's the closest I'll get to one for a while."

"I got you." She smiles and tugs on her earlobe.

"Thanks, Ape." He pulls on his earlobe. "I got you, too."

"So, did you see the letter I left for you?" Eddie asks when Rudy and April enter the kitchen.

"You mean the working papers?" Rudy asks.

"Yes." Eddie places a hand on Rudy's shoulder. "Time for a part-time job."

"Actually, I was planning to apply for a job at the bagel store," April mentions. "We should do it together."

That's all Rudy needs to hear. Most of the employees are teenagers, and many of Rudy's friends frequent the popular spot, which means it could even be fun.

Days later, Rudy and April get hired on the spot.

The morning after middle school graduation, they set their alarms for 4:30 a.m. and meet on the corner of Avenue J to head over for their first day of work. April brings cups of chocolate milk so she and Rudy can sip and celebrate their inaugural walk as employees. Despite the bagel store's dispiriting décor—fluorescent lights illuminating brown countertops and yellowed wallpaper—its location adjacent to a subway station means the place is packed with hungry commuters. Customers queue up along the right side of the shop beside the beverage refrigerators and the line curves around to the left in front of the deli counter. The register is in the back, with a lift-up countertop where the personnel enter and exit. Girls are typically in charge of the cash register and boys stock the displays. Most teenage staffers flirt unabashedly and it is well-known local lore that by the end of the season, many workers will be connected by a Venn diagram of romantic liaisons.

Their summer is no exception.

During the early hours when foot traffic is heaviest, the team of ten teens moves fluidly behind the counter handing off cream cheese spreaders, blending iced coffees, and packaging whitefish into little plastic containers. But as soon as the breakfast crowd thins, cliques form. April befriends the quieter kids, the ones who can correctly calculate change without the subtraction function on the cash register, while Rudy gravitates toward guys like Marcus, the brash and beefy football player who pronounces his own name *Maw-kiss*, and Gabe, the chiseled shortstop on the Midwood High School baseball team. When these three aren't attempting to seduce female customers, they spend their time talking sports or plotting practical jokes on one another. The loudest girls on staff are drawn to Rudy's crew and dish out sexual innuendos as often as they dole out danish to patrons. They find reasons to brush up against the boys' biceps behind the deli counter and playfully swipe their backsides in the stock room. Rudy isn't particularly attracted to them, but they're a sufficient distraction from the purgatory of witnessing April's cheeks blush whenever she chats with Joe—an eighteen-year-old veteran staffer and the only one of the bunch who goes to Poly Prep, a private school.

Rudy manages to appear physically engaged with his own group while successfully listening in on April and Joe's conversations. It doesn't take long before he makes two important observations. First: Joe and April spend an inordinate amount of time talking about the merits of some guy he has never heard of named Atticus Finch, that Rudy would guess that both April and Joe have crushes on the guy. He's shocked this Finch guy has eluded him; he thought he knew every important player in April's life. Rudy wonders if Atticus lives in the neighborhood and makes a mental note to keep an eye out for him. Second: Watching April light up whenever she sees Joe makes his blood boil. He doesn't like the intention he sees behind Joe's eyes when he looks at her or the way he sounds so smooth and smart. And he certainly doesn't like her transformation . . . how she giggles at everything he says, becoming a more vulnerable and weaker version of herself. He knows all too well the motivations of teenage boys and has a burning urge to protect her—just as he had promised Barbara he would when they tried to dig a tunnel between their homes.

To Rudy's great delight, Joe stops working at the bagel shop in mid-August to prepare for college, but on his last day, he asks April for her phone number. Rudy watches the exchange like a spy through the glass deli counter; crouched low and peering over the tub of tuna salad as April retrieves a napkin from the dispenser and jots down her digits. *Jackass*, Rudy silently seethes as they hug goodbye.

Later that night, while lying on the top bunk of their shared bed, Rudy leans over the side rail and peers down at his big brother.

"Hey, Tommy, where's Dartmouth?"

"I think in New Hampshire. Or maybe it's Vermont? I'm not sure. But it's somewhere up there. Why?"

Relief washes over Rudy. Both states are far enough from Brooklyn that it really doesn't matter where Bagel Store Joe is headed. "I dunno," he replies coolly.

"There's always a reason." Tommy snickers.

Rudy lets out a resigned sigh and begins to throw a baseball above his head to see if it can skim the ceiling without leaving a mark. "So there's this doofus at the store who's got the hots for April and she told me that he left for Dartmouth today. I just didn't know where that was."

"Well, he's probably not a doofus if he's going to Dartmouth. I mean, idiots get into these fancy places all the time, maybe he's got connections, but chances are he probably isn't stupid. Does April like him?"

"How should I know?" Rudy snaps back and throws the baseball toward the ceiling again. This time it leaves a mark and a small chip of paint flies onto his bedspread. "Shit."

The room is quiet for a few moments until Tommy climbs out from his bottom bunk and stands to face his brother.

"What?" Rudy growls.

"You can hold your own. Don't be intimidated by the Einsteins."

"I'm not! I just didn't know where the guy is going to college. That's it."

Tommy shrugs. "Whatever. All I'm sayin' is don't sell yourself short with girls, with guys, with school, with a job, whatever. You're good. Got it?"

Rudy harrumphs and turns over on his pillow to face the wall. He can feel a lump form in his throat but coughs to make it go away. He knows he'll start to cry if he glances at his brother. Their father might be dubbed Superman, but to Rudy, his elder brother is equally heroic.

Two weeks later, as the Monday of Labor Day weekend rolls around, April and Rudy pick up their final paychecks and head to the DeFrancos' apartment to sit on the terrace and tally up their summer earnings.

As Rudy lays out his bills on the plastic stool between them, April laughs. "You're unbelievable! How did you make so much more than I did?"

Rudy dances his eyebrows up and down. "One word," he says, smiling broadly. "Bunny."

The significant gap between April and Rudy's profits is evidently due to a seventy-year-old regular named Bunny Fishbein. Whenever Bunny stopped by the store, Rudy would come around from behind the deli counter and place her order directly into her dark-spotted hands so she wouldn't have to reach over the glass casement and lose her balance. And each time, Bunny would bat her eyelashes and exclaim, "Oh, you give my husband a run for his money. See ya later, handsome." Though gratuity had never been his intent, their little repertoire proved to be quite lucrative.

As they chortle about Bunny becoming Rudy's sugar mama, the front door suddenly bursts open and then, just as quickly, slams shut, rattling the windows and startling them both. They shove their bills into the back pockets of their jeans and run inside from the terrace to find Tommy standing over the bathroom sink, trembling and panting as he douses his face with water.

"Are Mom and Dad home from work yet?" Tommy asks, trying to catch his breath.

"Not yet."

"Good."

"What happened, T?" Rudy asks, cautiously.

"Dammit," Tommy mutters, pressing a wad of toilet paper to his skin to stop the blood flowing from his chin.

Rudy and April watch, mouths agape, as Tommy inspects the rest of his face in the mirror. There is a two-inch horizontal gash running parallel to his bottom lip.

"I . . ." Tommy stops and grabs hold of the doorknob as a crutch for support. Slowly, he lowers his knees to the tile floor.

April darts to the kitchen and pours tap water into a plastic tumbler while Rudy tends to his brother.

Tommy leans his head against his knees. "I was mugged," he says, finally.

"Oh my God!" April and Rudy cry in unison. Rudy had heard about muggings in the area but didn't know anyone who had been victimized.

"Three guys. One held a steak knife to my face, another held my arms, and the third pulled my wallet out of my pocket. It was classic. Textbook. They were punks. I'm fine."

Rudy knows he's far from fine. Tommy's hands are still shaking.

"Here," April says, handing Tommy the water. She slides to the side of the room and begins biting her nails.

Rudy can sense she wants to go back to the safety of her parents' house where WQXR, New York City's classical radio station, is likely playing in the background with Barbara at the dining room table preparing lesson plans for the new school year. But he knows April doesn't have the heart to leave him to manage the crisis alone.

"You can go, I've got this," he says softly, giving her an out.

As expected, she shakes her head. "No way."

Tommy takes a few sips and closes his eyes. He's still wearing his cabana boy uniform.

"Were you mugged at the beach club?" Rudy asks.

"No. A guy who works at the club also lives in Brooklyn, just a few blocks away on the other side of The Cut. He offered to give me a ride back from Long Island. I told him I could walk home from his place. But I was too tired to take the long way so I . . ."

"No!" Rudy exclaims, his eyes bulging. "You didn't!"

Eddie and Lorraine always warn their boys not to walk through The Cut—an overgrown and imposing trenched area with railroad tracks that slices through their neighborhood. Though the rail lines are infrequently used, the tracks traverse a fourteen-mile swath from Brooklyn to Queens, and Lorraine heard that the grassy abandoned section was a magnet for muggers.

"Rud, you're not gonna tell Mom. Y'hear me? She'll kill me if she finds out."

Rudy nods obediently.

Tommy runs his fingers through his hair and continues, "I mean, it was broad freakin' daylight. I didn't think it would be a problem. But there were a bunch of idiot kids hanging out drinking beers. Can you believe it? Two o'clock in the afternoon! And they're acting like it's a goddamn tailgate at the Jets game. So I see them, look away to avoid eye contact, and pick up my pace 'cause I'm getting that sixth-sense creepy vibe. Next thing, they're up in my face." Tommy smacks the floor. "And all my summer tip money is gone. Gone!"

"Did you save your weekly paychecks?" Rudy asks.

"Of course I did! But the tips are the reason you take this kind of gig." Tommy groans loudly.

Rudy plucks several tissues from the box atop the toilet tank, turns on the faucet, and tests the water temperature with his index finger. When he's satisfied that it's mildly warm, he saturates the tissues and rubs them atop the bar of Ivory soap before dabbing Tommy's chin. "Stay still. Sorry if this stings." He then pulls out antibiotic cream and bandages from the medicine cabinet above the sink. April jumps in like a scrub nurse, unscrewing the ointment and tearing open the wrapper before offering them to Rudy.

As soon as the wounds are covered, Tommy announces, "Okay. Thanks guys. I gotta go."

Rudy's brow furrows. "Um, don't you think you should rest?"

"Yea, but I gotta take care of somethin' first," Tommy says, already across the hallway in their bedroom.

"Maybe I should go with you?" Rudy calls.

Tommy doesn't respond. He's too distracted yanking balls of tube socks from his dresser drawer and hurling them into the air behind him like snowballs. He reaches his arm to the depths of the drawer, removes a wad of cash secured with a rubber band, and throws it into his backpack. He then storms out of the bedroom, leaving articles of clothing littered across the floor. A moment later, he's out the front door.

Rudy and April glance at each other and without a word, trail Tommy who is already halfway down the building's stairwell.

They follow Tommy like silent shadows all the way to a drug store on the corner of Avenue M. Tommy struts with determination over to a display case with a small collection of red Swiss Army knives. He knows precisely where to go, as if he has rehearsed the moment in his mind's eye and is finally acting out the scene.

"Hey, how you doing?" he asks the store clerk with a head nod. "How much for the pocketknives?" Tommy bounces the pad of his index finger on the glass countertop above the display.

The clerk unlocks the display case, removes a model, and places it in Tommy's palm. He gently rubs his thumb over the white cross atop the candy apple red contraption. One at a time, Tommy methodically releases each of the various tools. He tests the scissors by cutting a piece of thread hanging from the hem of his T-shirt. Next the screwdriver, which he turns in circles as if uncorking an imaginary bottle of wine. He then removes the toothpick, inspects the nail file, and squeezes the tweezers as if he is trying to catch a fly with chopsticks. After tucking the tools back into their respective spots, he cautiously removes the blade.

Though small, the knife looks remarkably sharp, and Rudy wonders what his brother intends to do with it. He is confident that Tommy will not seek out vengeance on the thugs who mugged him, and yet, there is a look in his eyes that Rudy has never seen. It's a mix of unyielding determination and the unforgiving wrath of a toddler temper tantrum.

"Whaddya gonna do?" Rudy asks, shifting his gaze from the knife to his brother. He deliberately leaves the question open-ended, allowing Tommy to decide if Rudy's inquiry pertains to his intent to purchase or his intended purpose.

Tommy stares at the knife as he runs his fingers over the bandage on his chin. Then, with absolute certitude, he straightens his shoulders and announces, "I'll take it." He unzips his backpack and hands a wad of cash over to the clerk.

Like an enraptured student, Rudy soaks up Tommy's every move. As an ever-present silhouette since birth, he has experienced Tommy's life as intimately as his own—constantly watching, learning, embodying. On this day of metamorphosis, when his hero trespasses into victimhood, Rudy feels his own pulse race, his own throat choke with emotion, his own chest crush beneath what feels like the weight of a Mack truck, as if he were the one brutally assaulted.

And so, just as he has all his life, Rudy decides to mimic his big brother. He still isn't sure what Tommy plans to do with the knife, but if spending a portion of summer earnings in this fashion is suitable for his sibling, then it's certainly good enough for him. Rudy reaches into the back pocket of his jeans for Bunny's tip from that morning and places it atop the drug store counter. "Sir," he says politely, "make that two pocketknives."

6

Rudy

THEN

Peter Luger's Steak House is the Zagodas' preferred location to mark any special occasion. On the day April receives her letter of acceptance to Rivington University, Steven and Barbara take their family and the DeFrancos out for dinner to celebrate. But as much as April's matriculation is the culmination of her family's dream, it marks the commencement of a nightmare for Rudy. Sure, he's proud of her accomplishments and excited for the bevy of opportunities that await her, but he can't fathom life without April one block away.

When dessert and coffee are served, Steven rises to make a toast. He steps behind April's chair, places a hand on her shoulder, and looks across the table toward his parents.

"Do you know what today is?" he projects, seemingly for the benefit of his hearing-impaired mother and father.

"Tod . . ." Steven, voice cracking, raises a fist to his mouth to suppress a cry. "Today is the day *you*, April, fulfill *their* American dream."

Rudy glances over at April's Polish grandparents and sees they are enraptured by the whip cream atop their apple strudels. Her grandfather pokes at the white fluff with a fork while her grandmother mumbles something about how she'll never be able to finish a slice that large. They appear completely oblivious to the fact that their son is saluting them and their immigrant experience.

"Look at where we are." Steven nearly smacks a passing waiter as he gesticulates grandly at the dark wood paneling and ornate chandeliers. "A beautiful dinner at a beautiful restaurant with our beautiful extended family. So here's to a big, beautiful, bright future, April. Whatever path you take, I know you will always make us proud."

As Steven basks in the glory of his daughter's success with a raised beer stein, it occurs to Rudy that for the first time in his life, he fears the end of summer like a plague. *God help me,* he thinks..

When college move-in day comes, Rudy arrives early at the Zagodas' front door. As he steps inside, his eyes bulge. He has never seen their immaculate home in such disarray. April is on her knees shoving a hair dryer into an overstuffed storage bin and an obstacle course of luggage is strewn across the floor. Rudy tries to utter the words, "Good morning," but they stick in his throat. Instead, he curls his fingers, crunching the brown paper bag he's carrying.

"It's a mess. I know." April sighs. "No comments please."

"Hey, no judgment." Rudy stretches his arm over a stack of bath towels and hands her the crumpled bag.

"What's this?"

"Breakfast of champions," he says flatly and rubs an eye with his knuckle.

April peeks inside and finds a black and white cookie and a small iced coffee—her favorites. The napkin folded at the bottom is stamped with the logo of the bagel store that employed them every summer throughout high school.

"Aw, thanks, Rud." She takes a sip and smiles.

He nods and bends down to lift a duffel bag of clothing. "Big day. We got a lot to get done here. Better start."

"Yep. Your girl Bertha's waiting for you to work your magic."

Rudy has gone on enough car rides in the Zagodas' Buick—affectionately nicknamed "Big Bertha"—to know that April and her family are not nearly as spatially adept as anyone with De-Franco DNA. Whether it is a Sunday afternoon excursion to Costco on Long Island, or a family vacation like they all took to Virginia, Rudy is always the designated packer. Unlike April, who haphazardly throws items into the back seat, Rudy is methodical and patient. He has an innate ability to utilize every spare inch of interior car space without obstructing the rearview mirror.

Together they lug her belongings down the front stoop and over to the driveway. As they return inside for the second haul, Rudy spots Steven at the kitchen table studying the highlighted AAA Trip Tik. Beside his PBS coffee mug are several small circular plastic canisters that once held camera film. *Classic Steven*, Rudy smiles, realizing that in preparation for the trip, April's father has repurposed the black drums by filling them with the exact number of quarters they would need for tolls on the drive upstate. Beside the canisters are sandwiches wrapped in aluminum foil labeled "PBJ" or "Tuna" in Barbara's handwriting and a plastic bag with toothpicks which Rudy knows means she has sliced their lunch into bite-sized squares to minimize mess. Planning for this excursion is no different from any other family trip. The difference this time is where they are headed—both literally and figuratively—as April's departure marks a new chapter for everyone.

"So this is it," Rudy says after the last load is arranged in the Buick. He peers inside the windows to ensure there is adequate space for April beside the snack cooler in the back seat. "I think we got everything in."

Just as Bertha's trunk clicks shut, Steven marches over, map in hand. "Time check! Ten minutes to take off! Get ready and grab whatever you need for the ride. Unless there's an emergency, first gas stop isn't until the Catskills." He then pats Rudy on the back. "Thanks for your help, Rud. Don't know what we'd do without you."

"You'd have luggage falling out of your car," Rudy quips with a wry smile.

"Yes, that's certainly true. Listen, son, don't be a stranger now that what's-her-name over here won't be around as much anymore. You're still an honorary Zagoda."

"Thank you, sir. I appreciate it." Rudy can feel his eyes sting. He blinks away the moisture and gently taps his fist twice on the trunk as a distraction. "Well, safe travels! You got precious cargo there, Mr. Z." He points directly at April as he slowly walks backward out of the driveway. "Drive carefully."

"Will do!" Steven says with a wave.

"Aw shit, I forgot." Rudy spins back around to April who is still standing by the car. He digs into his back pocket and retrieves a keychain with a plastic tube attachment. "Here, this is for you."

She examines it. "No *ear-ring*?" she jokes.

"It's mace," he says seriously.

"Mace?"

"Look, I know upstate ain't the same as here, but just carry it to be safe, okay? You can take the girl out of Brooklyn, but you shouldn't take the street smarts out of the girl just 'cause she's in the middle of nowhere. You get me?"

She nods. "I get you."

"Hey, I'd build a tunnel to you if I could . . ." he says.

"I know you would."

"You call me if you need me, alright?" He tugs on his earlobe.

She smiles and does the same before opening her arms for a hug.

"Oh, before I forget, take this," she says, handing Rudy a slip of paper with her college phone number.

"Thanks," he says, forcing a smile. He places the paper in his pocket, pivoting on his heels, and begins a light jog toward the street, hoping she hasn't seen the tears that have spilled over his lashes.

"Speak to you soon!" she calls out.

"Knock 'em dead!" he hollers back, waving his hand in the air until he knows she can no longer see him.

As April drives away, Rudy heads directly to the bike room in the basement of his apartment building and grabs the blue ten-speed with the ram horn handlebars that he shares with Tommy. He bikes all the way down Ocean Parkway to Coney Island's Astroland and chains the tires, as well as the frame, to a lamppost on Surf Avenue just feet from the famed Cyclone rollercoaster. He purchases eight passes for the rollercoaster. Though he has enough cash for nine rides, he knows he'll want a Coke and Nathan's hot dog before biking home.

Rudy steps into the Cyclone's front car and buckles up. He squints as the sun shines brightly in the cloudless morning sky, bouncing off the Atlantic and illuminating the sidewalks. He loves when speckles of glass and rock embedded in concrete sparkle like glitter. It makes Brooklyn seem magical.

As the roller coaster jerks to a start he inhales deeply, filling his nostrils with warm, saltwater-tinged late-August air. His heart hammers in his chest as he ascends eighty-five feet to the peak. The slow click-click-click precariousness of the coaster's rickety wooden slats parallels everything he's felt inside recently—unmoored, unstable, flailing. When he finally reaches the top, Rudy grabs the handlebar in front of him and grips tightly with his palms. The car tips forward and a guttural roar emerges from his mouth as he plummets sixty miles an hour, the wind whistling in his ears. He can't recall ever emitting such a sound. It is deep and thunderous, as if he's emancipating a caged lion from his soul. When the ride culminates, he remains seated and hands another ticket to the attendant. He repeats this until he has completed eight consecutive rides. By the time he unchains his bike and satiates himself with a frankfurter and soda, he has expelled a good portion of the angst he has felt slowly building all summer. He is now ready—not necessarily ready for daily life without April, but at least he is prepared to face the day ahead.

The following weekend, while grabbing an extra toilet plunger to help his father deal with a rancid mess down in apartment 3A, Rudy sees a Post-it note next to the telephone in his parents' kitchen with "April called" written out in his mother's curly script. He smiles. He has been waiting to hear from her. He hasn't reached out, knowing April has a tendency to get homesick and fearing that a call from him might throw off her adjustment.

"Rud!" April exclaims upon hearing his voice. "Oh my goodness, how are you? I miss you so much."

A smile spreads so quickly across his face he can feel his cheek muscles contract. "I . . ." he starts but is interrupted.

"It's Rudy, my best friend, the guy I told you about," she says to someone in the background. "Hey, sorry, Rud. Some people from my hall were just hanging out in my room. They're about to leave, wait, hold on . . . Bye guys! I'll catch up with you later on the quad!"

Quad? Rudy thinks. She sounds different. Peppier.

"Sorry," she returns. "What's going on? What have I missed at home?"

"Absolutely nothing. How's college? How's the *quad*?" he asks mockingly.

"Do I sound like a John Hughes film already?"

"You sound happy."

"Thanks. I'm trying to keep busy. By the way, you should visit. There's a homecoming party next month if you want to come for that. Or any weekend, really. Think about it."

"Cool." Rudy has no idea how he would even get there. He wonders how much a Greyhound bus ticket costs.

"So they're setting up email accounts this week for us. Maybe you can borrow Tommy's computer and create one? Or do you get an email account through your new school?"

"Not sure." Rudy has enrolled at Kingsborough Community College, just four miles away from home, but classes have not yet started and he has no idea if registration comes with email.

"Listen, I gotta go," she says. "Say hi to your parents and Tommy for me. And think about visiting. Promise?"

"I will." Rudy hangs up and feels a sense of relief. *She sounds good. Really good. Settled. Happy.* Now he has to save up for a roundtrip bus ticket.

He goes into his parents' bathroom, grabs a bucket and plunger, and as he heads down to help his dad with the putrid disaster in 3A, he wonders what April will have for dinner in the cafeteria with her new friends.

At 5 a.m. on a Friday in November, Rudy fills a thermos of Coke, cuts a bologna sandwich into bite-sized squares (ala Barbara), and stores them in his backpack. He walks a few blocks to the subway station in Midwood and hops on a train to Manhattan where he catches the 6:30 a.m. Greyhound Bus.

The cloth window seat is more comfortable than he had anticipated, and the early departure hour yields a mostly empty bus. He sleeps the majority of the five-hour ride and arrives at April's majestic campus just as crimson, emerald, and golden brown leaves are cascading off the trees and forming piles on the ground. The school legitimately looks like the photos in the glossy brochure April had shown him.

Within seconds of exiting the bus, Rudy feels alien. He has never seen so many blondes, and everyone is wearing clothing with monikers he has never heard of: Choate, Andover, Bennington, Williams, William & Mary. Were they brands? Surnames? He wonders if the latter are the first names of the boy's parents. Rudy chuckles at how bizarre it would be for him to sport a T-shirt around Brooklyn with "Eddie & Lorraine" in big bold letters.

As arranged, Rudy finds the Dunkin' Donuts near campus and there, sitting at a table in the window, is April. Wearing denim overalls beneath a navy zip-up fleece, she springs up from her chair and bolts to the glass door to greet him.

"You made it!" she squeals, wrapping her arms around Rudy's neck.

He squeezes her tightly. It has been only two and a half months but feels infinitely longer. She looks exactly the same, but there is something discordant about seeing her in this environment.

"How was the ride? You hungry? Want to get something to eat or just drop your stuff and I can show you around?"

"I'm good. I ate on the bus. Show me your new turf! This place is amazing!"

April links her arm through his and together they walk down the street toward her dorm, backpacks slung over their shoulders, just as they had throughout childhood along Avenue J. As they cross the quad, April waves to several people and Rudy notices many of them wearing fleeces just like hers. She fits right in.

Later that night, following dinner with her hallmates in the cafeteria, they visit a boisterous off-campus sports bar where April, wine cooler in hand, shouts introductions over blaring music. He has never seen her drink alcohol. Once, at a high school graduation party, she sampled a beer by sticking her index finger into his red plastic cup of Budweiser. She recoiled the moment the pad of her finger touched her tongue and promptly cleansed her palate with three wads of Bubble Yum.

When April excuses herself to go to the restroom, Rudy leans his back against a faux-wood-paneled wall and scopes out the scene. The place is packed shoulder-to-shoulder with pearl-neck-laced girls in tight-fitting tops and boys wearing baseball hats with lacrosse sticks stitched over the brim. Two guys standing nearby clutch beverages against their chests and guffaw raucously. A third appears to be struggling to remove a cap from his glass beer bottle.

"You need some help there?" Rudy asks, pointing to the cap. He pulls out the little red Swiss Army knife from his pocket.

The guy's face lights up and he hands over the bottle. Rudy easily removes the metal top with the edge of his knife.

"Thanks, man! Cheers!" the guy says and turns back around to his friends.

Rudy is close enough to inspect the guy's fingernails. They are immaculate. He looks down at his own and regrets not having taken the time to rub away the black grease streaks before visiting that weekend. He begins to nibble away at the tip of his overgrown thumbnail when he feels a tap on his back.

"Hey," says a girl with shoulder-length brown hair. She is sylph-like and wears her purse strap diagonally across her torso.

"Hey." Rudy flashes a quick grin.

"You're in my economics class, aren't you?" she says, tilting her head coquettishly. "You sit in the back row?" She giggles.

"I'm sorry," he says politely, "I think you got me confused with someone else."

The decibel level of the music in the room suddenly shoots up, and the crowd cheers the song choice. Rudy can feel the soles of his high-top sneakers pulsating.

She smiles and cups her hand around her ear. "I can't hear you."

Rudy leans forward toward the side of her head. "We are not in the same class," he projects, enunciating each word.

"Really?" she yells into his ear, gently placing her hand on his upper arm. "Then where have I seen you?"

He shrugs. "I get mistaken for celebrities all the time."

She flips her hair and laughs. He didn't intend to sound flirtatious. The charm comes naturally, just as it had with Bunny Fishbein back in the bagel store.

"I'm Jill." She sticks out her hand as if it were a business meeting.

"Rudy." He nods. She has soft skin and a firm shake.

"Which house are you in?" she asks.

"I live in an apartment."

She looks at him confusedly. "Off campus?"

"I don't go here. I'm just visiting."

"Ah, you're from New York," she says, pointing to his New York Knicks sweatshirt.

"Very good, detective! Yeah, Brooklyn. Flatbush, Midwood, that area. You know it?"

She shakes her head. "I'm from Philadelphia. Suburbs."

At this moment April returns and slides her arm through Rudy's, just as she had during their afternoon stroll. "Hi!" April smiles warmly at Jill. "I'm April."

Jill pauses for a moment, her eyes darting back and forth between Rudy and April, as if her brain is trying to decipher their relationship.

"Oh, uh, hi," Jill says clunkily as she extends her hand for a shake. She's cordial but cooler than when she had first approached Rudy.

The three of them stand in the corner chatting for a while, Jill directing every question and statement toward Rudy, as if April is simply part of the décor like the neon Corona sign flashing on the wall above them. When did he arrive? How long was the bus ride? Is he being recruited to play on a team? What's his favorite sport, favorite drink? What does he do for fun? Rudy feels like it's an interrogation.

"It's getting late, no?" he says, turning toward April.

"It's only nine o'clock!" Jill chimes in before April can respond.

"Well, I've had a long day." He stretches and fakes a yawn.

"Where are you staying? The campus can get pretty dark at night. No city lights like where you're from. I'm happy to help you find your way if you're not sure where to go."

"Thanks. I think I've got it."

Rudy is determined not to be disrespectful to anyone in April's new world, but Jill is failing miserably at interpreting social cues. As soon as he catches April's eye, he furtively reaches for his earlobe. April grabs for her own and they smile widely at one another. The ear tug is a social rip cord, a secret signal they created back in middle school after she presented him with the earring keychain for his birthday. Somehow, the gift turned into a private joke which then morphed into a secret code for *have my back!* They've employed this tactic to extricate themselves from lame parties, awkward conversations, and to ensure April wasn't the last one selected for teams in gym class. Even if Rudy wasn't team captain, he'd convince whoever was to look past April's lackluster athleticism and call her name as a draft pick.

"I'm gonna get our coats, Rud, and then I think we should head out," April announces with a wink. "It was nice meeting you, Jill. Hope to see you around!"

"Oh, you too," Jill says robotically, her gaze remaining fixed on Rudy. "So how long will you be visiting?"

"Just the weekend."

"Well maybe we can meet up before you go? Can I get your number?"

"How 'bout I get yours?" he suggests.

Jill scribbles her digits on the back of a bar napkin and hands it to Rudy. "Call me!" She leans over to give him a delicate peck on the cheek.

Rudy smiles politely, waves goodbye, and exits the bar with April. As they walk back through town toward campus, he spots a trash can on a street corner. He crumples up the napkin and throws it in the bin.

7

Rudy

THEN

Six months later, while studying for his freshman year final exams on the bunk bed he still shares with Tommy, Rudy's telephone rings.

"Hello?" he answers flatly, cradling the receiver between his shoulder and ear. His attention is firmly focused on his work.

"So remember I told you I might have a meeting in Manhattan for this national college newspaper organization thing I'm involved with?" April jumps in, sans greeting.

"Yeah . . ." he loves that they can still start conversations this way.

"Turns out the university is paying for my trip. Free ride home!"

"Cool!"

"We have meetings during the day, but there's a schmoozy networking event this Thursday night on the Upper West Side. Want to come meet me at the end?"

"Do I want to see you? Yes. Do I want to hang out with a bunch of geeky wannabe reporters? Not so much."

"Fine, I'll make you a deal. Come, and if it's lame and snooty we can go somewhere else."

"Why don't we just hang in Brooklyn? You're gonna make me trek into the city on a non-rush hour subway schedule? Do you even care about me anymore?"

April laughs. "Come on! Please? I'll buy you Carvel next time I get home."

"Alright. Deal. I'll go."

"Yay!"

"So is there a dress code or something?"

"I don't care what you wear. Just show up."

As he hangs up, an image of a room full of Bagel Store Joes flashes in his head, which triggers a deep and lengthy groan.

At seven o'clock on Thursday evening, Rudy returns home from his final class of the week and walks directly into his parents' bedroom to retrieve an ironing board and steamer from their linen closet. He sets up the board beside his mother's bureau and fills the iron with water from the faucet he and his father recently installed in their bathroom sink. As the iron heats up, he pulls his nicest button-down shirt and only pair of khaki pants from his bedroom closet and returns to his parents' room, where he flattens the garments on the ironing board, smoothing out the creases exactly as his father taught him.

After a quick shower and a couple of Pop Tarts for dinner, he's ready. At nine o'clock, he exits the subway on the Upper West Side and walks six blocks to the address on Columbus Avenue. The smell of fried appetizers greets him at the door and it takes a moment after stepping inside for Rudy's eyes to adjust to the dim lighting. There's a large, crowded horseshoe-shaped bar and lounge in the back, narrowly spaced dinner tables with tiny votive candles in the front, and a spiral staircase near the entry leading to what appears to be a curtained second-floor loft for private functions.

Rudy stands patiently beside an empty hostess stand. He knows it is the proper thing to do given that the Zagodas always wait to be greeted and seated whenever they visit Peter Luger's restaurant. But after several minutes of feeling like a fool lingering next to an unattended podium, Rudy decides to take look around the venue for April's group.

About halfway up the spiral staircase en route to check out the private room, he hears someone calling out from down below.

"Um, sir? Hello? Excuse me, can I help you?" a woman snaps as she marches briskly toward the wooden lectern in her stilettos and black dress. Apparently the hostess has now returned to her perch.

"Oh, sorry, I'm just trying to find the newspaper group. Do you know where they are?"

She rolls her eyes and gives him a look as if she is shocked by his audacity to be alive. "There was an event up there behind the velvet curtains. You can check, but I believe it has ended. Next time, *sir*," she says as if she is being generous placing him in that category, "please be patient and wait your turn before entering." She punctuates her statement with a patronizing, saccharine smile that causes her nose to scrunch into a tiny orb.

What a bitch, he thinks. "My apologies," he says and proceeds up the remainder of the staircase. *This is the kind of shit I hate.*

When he reaches the velvet curtains at the top of the landing, Rudy paws at the heavy purple fabric to find an opening. After locating the break, he pulls the drapes aside and discovers an empty lounge with every indication that the party has ended. There are picked-over hors d'oeuvres platters, forgotten business cards on high-top tables, torn name tags littered across the floor, and waiters stacking dirty dishes into gray washing bins. Rudy shuts the curtain, but just when he is about to descend the stairs, he hears his name.

"Rudy? Is that you?"

Walking toward him from a restroom down the hallway is a girl who looks familiar, but he can't quite place her. His befuddlement must be evident.

"I'm Jill. Remember me? I met you last fall." She smiles. "At the bar? I gave you my number? On a napkin? You never called . . ."

Oh right . . . Jill . . . oh no.

"Hey, sorry 'bout that," he says with a shrug.

"Mmm," she nods skeptically, "that's okay. You're cute enough to get one strike. I'm forgiving." She playfully pokes at his chest. "Looks like we've got another chance. What are you doing here, anyway? Wait. Shh. Don't tell me." She raises her hand in the air as if she is in a classroom. "You're here to meet your little buddy, April."

Rudy nods. *My little buddy? This girl is really annoying.*

She folds her arms across her chest. "What's the deal with you two?"

"Deal?"

"Yeah. Are you going out with her?"

"Going out?" he asks with exasperation. "Me and April?! No, not at all. She's my friend. We grew up together. What are *you* doing here?"

"Same as April. Networking. Meeting alums and future bosses, I hope. Actually, I think I may have just landed a summer internship and possibly a stringer gig, fingers crossed."

Rudy doesn't know what a stringer is and doesn't care enough to inquire.

"Looks like your party's over," he motions with his thumb to the velvet curtains.

"Yeah. I think a bunch of them may be downstairs with the bar crowd. I'm not sure. I was in the bathroom and everyone just kind of left. Come, let's go check out the scene." She looks as if she might reach for his palm.

Rudy shoves his hands deep into his pockets before she can touch him. His quick reflexes have always been a gift.

As they make their way down the staircase, Jill stumbles and he instinctively wraps his arm around her waist to catch her fall.

She pauses and turns to face him. "Such a gentleman." She smiles and pecks him on the cheek.

He lets go of her waist and surreptitiously wipes his cheek as they step onto the main floor. They head to the backroom bar where Jill slides into a tufted banquette.

"Come sit," she says, patting the space beside her.

Rudy looks away to scan the room for April. The scene is a far cry from her college dive bar upstate. Instead of cheap beer and sports paraphernalia, this place has an air of sophistication and is chock-full of young professionals sipping expensive after-work cocktails.

"You want water or a soda?" he asks, rising on his tip toes to see over the crowd. He knows he will get carded if he requests anything alcoholic. In fact, he is surprised that a college networking event is being held at a restaurant with an active bar scene.

"No thanks," Jill says, cocking her head. "Come here. Talk to me. I don't bite."

This chick is the least subtle flirt I've ever met, he thinks. "Sorry, I need to find April."

Jill raises her eyebrows. "Interesting word choice. You *need* to find her? Or you *want* to? 'Cause I go to school with her and I've got to tell you, she is perfectly capable on her own. She doesn't seem to *need* you there."

Rudy winces. If Jill were a boy from the neighborhood, Rudy would tell him off and walk away. But she's a girl, and he was raised to always respect women, even the annoying ones.

"I'm gonna go get a Coke."

"Don't take long, I'll be waiting right here for you."

Rudy nods. *This girl is trouble,* he thinks as he heads toward the bar. *No effing way am I going back to her.*

The line to the bartender is a labyrinth of sheath dresses and button-down shirts, so Rudy walks to the opposite side of the horseshoe to find an opening. While rounding the curve he spots April alone in a secluded alcove of the room, her back against a wall, shoulders creeping upward. A tall twenty-something with fingers wrapped around a double old-fashioned glass is towering over her and leaning in close, mere inches from her face. He seems be to talking *at* April, not *with* her. A jolt of electricity ricochets throughout Rudy's body. He propels toward her.

"Rud! You made it!" she beams, tucking hair behind both of her ears.

Is that a sign—a double alarm? he wonders about their secret code. *Or is she just playing with her hair?*

"Bailey, this is Rudy. Rudy, this is Bailey," she says, her thumb now lingering at her lobe.

Yep. That's it, Rudy thinks, now certain this is a subtle version of their pact. He has his mission: *Be polite. Don't cause a scene. Get her out of here ASAP.*

"Hey." Rudy nods, offering his hand to Bailey for a shake. *Perhaps this is the path of least resistance.*

Bailey gives him a perturbed once-over and turns away. He can't be bothered.

What a loser!

"So, you're not gonna believe it, Ape, but I just saw that kid we used to play with all the time in middle school before he moved away. He's over on the other side of the bar. You gotta come with me to say hi." A lie, but it's the best Plan B he can concoct in the moment.

Before she even takes a step out of the corner, Bailey places his paw atop Rudy's shoulder. "Leave her alone," Bailey decrees, his baritone slow and slurred.

Who the hell does this guy think he is? Rudy wonders, shaking off Bailey's touch. He can now see the whites of this guy's droopy eyes are as ruddy as his cheeks. "Let's go, Ape."

She takes a step toward Rudy, but Bailey aggressively shimmies his loafered, sockless foot between them.

"She's not going anywhere with you, little boy."

"I'm sorry, Bailey," April says, straightening her posture. "But I am perfectly capable of making my own choice—"

"Oh, cut the shit . . ." he groans and coughs in Rudy's face. His breath reeks of alcohol.

"Back off," Rudy says, his tone firm. He feels like David against Goliath. If he had a slingshot, he'd aim directly at the jungle of chest hair sprouting from this guy's unbuttoned polo.

A quick image of Tommy crouched on the bathroom floor post-mugging suddenly flashes in Rudy's head. Instinctively, he slides his right hand into the pocket of his freshly ironed pants and glides his fingers over the smooth plastic surface of the Swiss Army knife he bought with his brother.

As April extracts herself from the corner of the room, her kitten heel accidentally catches in the buckle of Bailey's suede shoe. Unaware, she steps down hard.

Without a word, Bailey retaliates against Rudy, shoving his back against the wall.

"What the fuck, man? Don't touch me," Rudy says through gritted teeth. He is deliberately keeping his tone and actions in check. His priority is to safely get April out of there without making a scene.

"I can touch whatever and whoever the hell I want," Bailey declares, slugging back his gin and tonic and then spitting it in Rudy's face as if expelling mouthwash.

This idiot needs a little fear to sober up and come to his senses. Maybe this will work. Rudy pulls the Swiss Army knife out from his pants pocket and flicks open the two-inch switchblade as a deterrent. He keeps the knife low and discreet, pressed against his right thigh, but obvious enough for Bailey to see he is holding a weapon.

"Look at that little piece of shit!" Bailey guffaws before hunching down to grab the collar of Rudy's shirt. "Get *your* ass and your dressed-up *hussy trash* out of here."

Rudy can handle a personal attack on himself. He can handle being spit on and thrown against a wall. But a negative word about April is war.

"*Fuck* you, pretty boy," Rudy seethes.

Never, in all this time of carrying the Swiss Army knife, has he ever used it as a weapon. The blade has cut plenty of food and spread cream cheese, but never has it been used in a fight. He can feel the perspiration on his palms slickening the knife's plastic handle, but he tightens his grip and keeps it low against his hip.

Bailey lunges for the knife in Rudy's hand. They scuffle for no more than a few seconds before the knife clinks to the ground.

April immediately bends down, scoops up the knife, collapses the silver blade into its slot, and throws it into her purse.

"Come on," she says, grabbing Rudy's hand, hurriedly pulling him away while Bailey, seemingly unbalanced, takes a moment to steady himself.

As April drags Rudy toward the exit, he whips his head back and sees Bailey crouched on the floor of the alcove holding his arm. *Shit. Is that my fault?*

"Um, he looks hurt, Ape," Rudy says, his heart jackhammering against his rib cage.

"I'm sure he'll be fine. I want to get out of here."

The next thing Rudy knows, he and April are sliding across the vinyl back seat of a yellow taxi.

"Columbus Circle, please," she announces to the driver.

"What's going on? Where are we going?" Rudy asks. He has never felt more out of sorts.

"Home. We can get the B train at Columbus Circle."

"So why are we in a cab? Can't we walk it?"

"I want to get away from that bar and get home."

What the hell just happened? he wonders as they whiz past the elegant prewar doorman buildings along Central Park West. He has never gotten into a fight with anyone. Other than that time in elementary school when he wrestled another boy on the playground to determine who would captain a kickball game—he's been the peacemaker, not the aggressor. "You sure we shouldn't go back? Maybe make sure he's alright?"

She shakes her head definitively.

The car is silent until they stop at a red light at 72nd Street.

"Don't mean to pry," the driver says, staring at them through the rearview mirror. "But you kids okay? Looks like you've seen a ghost."

Rudy glances at April for guidance.

"Oh, we're fine, thanks," April says to the cab driver's reflection in the mirror.

"Just been a long day, that's all." She punctuates her statement with a polite, tight-lipped grin.

The driver nods satisfactorily and accelerates as the light turns green.

All Rudy can think of is the image of Bailey cradling his arm. *I hope he's alright. Did I do that to him? It happened so quickly . . .*

"So how do you know that guy at the bar?" Rudy asks.

April rolls her eyes. "I don't! Just met him! Maybe ten minutes before you walked over! His younger brother, Keith, works on the newspaper with me. I guess Keith invited him to hang out, sort of like how I invited you? I'm really not sure. He was clearly drunk and seemed like a jerk, but I didn't want to be rude to Keith's brother."

Rudy shakes his head disapprovingly.

"I mean, seriously, Ape. Next time, if you meet a loser like that, please, I beg you, just walk away. If for no other reason, the guy was a close talker."

"He *was* a close talker, wasn't he? His breath stank."

As they stand on the subway platform awaiting the B train to Brooklyn, a warm, humid breeze signaling an oncoming train causes a candy wrapper to go airborne and graze Rudy's cheek. As filthy as he feels, it is the first moment of happiness he has experienced all night. He can't wait to escape Manhattan and return home.

8

Jillian

THEN

T O DO:

1) Good impression
2) Network
3) Summer internship

Jillian tapes a sheet of lined notebook paper to the mirror on the back of her dorm room door and scribbles the to-do list in thick marker. While repeating the words aloud as a mantra, she opens her closet and pulls out the royal blue sleeveless sheath dress she picked up at Talbot's with her mother precisely for this sort of occasion.

"This is your ticket!" her mother had said an hour earlier when Jillian called to share the news that Rivington would be footing the bill for the college newspaper's editorial staff to attend a national conference in New York City. "I'm sure there will be lots of alumni journalists and publishers there. Opportunities like this don't come along every day, Jill. Go grab that brass ring!"

Jillian can think of no better way to wrap up the final weeks of her freshman year. Starting college this past fall was a milestone Jillian excitedly anticipated not because of the newfound independence or social opportunities it afforded, but because it was one step closer to starting her career. As soon as she arrived on campus for orientation, she made a beeline for the student newspaper. If she were to fulfill her goal of running the weekly by senior year, she knew she'd have to hit the pavement on day one.

Since September, she has reported on a trash can fire in the student center, written four movie reviews, covered two water polo tournaments, and is currently profiling a beloved biology professor on the eve of retirement. This story is her favorite. The aging doctor's passion for science is infectious and, at his suggestion, she's enrolling in Intro to Biology and Medical Ethics next semester.

Even as a young girl, she had an insatiable curiosity and uncanny ability to detect details that typically went unnoticed by others: the font on a restaurant menu, if someone's shoelaces were single or double knotted. Growing up, her father often joked that she could be a professional fly on a wall. Though it was said in jest, Jillian secretly wondered if such a job actually existed. One Halloween, she even fashioned a fly costume out of goggles and fuzzy pipe cleaner antennae.

The seminal moment came in sixth grade when she was assigned a make-your-own newspaper project. Jillian found each stage of crafting that paper to be more exciting than the next. Brainstorming article ideas was effortless. Interviews were a social life preserver—the structure and formality infused her with a confidence she often lacked with peers. And writing the copy, well, that was her sweet spot. There was a very specific buzz she'd get whenever she found precisely the right terminology to convey an idea or describe a scene. She couldn't explain the brain synapses that caused words foreign to her daily vernacular to rise from the depths of her consciousness and onto the page, but somehow they did, as if they'd been sitting on the edge of a desk in her head, arms raised, eagerly awaiting their turn.

Soon, it became clear that those seemingly insignificant details she'd always noticed actually had a purpose—they were secret weapons that could enrich a news story. Her eagle eye and talent for wordsmithing enabled her to be a conduit for truth. She entered every writing competition for which she qualified. By the time she headed to college, she knew that if she couldn't become an actual fly on a wall, she'd dedicate her life to being the next best thing: a journalist.

The following Thursday morning, Jillian boards a small van with her fellow staff writers and editors and heads to New York City. Five hours later, they check in to their midtown hotel, and by early evening she is showered, dressed, and heading to the conference's first event: a meet-and-greet in a private room of a bustling restaurant. It is a mild spring evening, and though her patent leather pumps are already causing her ankles to ache, she is distracted by the beautiful golden glow cast over Manhattan's storefronts and sidewalks.

As soon as she makes her way up the restaurant's spiral staircase and into the private reception space, she finds a corner of the room and busies herself by searching her purse. She unzips her handbag and rifles through the contents.

Pencil? Check.

Small spiral notebook? Check.

Touching the pencil's rubber eraser and the plastic coils of the pocket-sized notepad brings her comfort. She is armed.

Jillian works the room, stopping only to refuel with glasses of Diet Coke. She smiles. She asks questions—lots of questions as she knows people love to talk about themselves—and she listens attentively to the answers. When she's finished speaking with one professional, she quickly jots down their name and title on her notepad, then moves on to the next. She doesn't touch any of the hors d'oeuvres lest something get stuck in her teeth or sour her breath, and she certainly does not have any alcohol. By the end of the event, she has amassed a stack of business cards from alumni and local reporters, many of whom have encouraged her to apply for summer internships. One even proposed the possibility of a stringer position, which caused Jillian to smile so widely that a droplet of saliva spilled over the corner of her mouth.

By nine o'clock, the private event thins out and the multitude of Diet Cokes Jillian has consumed throughout the night have finally taken their toll on her bladder. Alone in the quiet of the restroom, she retrieves fifteen business cards from her black leather clutch and her heartbeat quickens as she runs her fingers over the names of the news outlets: *New York Post, Daily News, Wall Street Journal, The Brooklyn Eagle, The Queens Chronicle, NY1, Today Show, Dateline, Newsday, The Newark Star Ledger* . . . *Man,* she thinks, *could this night get any better?*

She carefully places the cards back inside her purse and then, as if it were a dream, she exits the bathroom and walks directly into the boy who has taken up residence in her mind for several months.

"Rudy?" she asks in disbelief. "Is that you?"

Though they'd only met once, his name rolls off her tongue as if she utters it multiple times an hour.

She can tell immediately by his befuddled demeanor that she has not made a similar impression upon him. Jillian remains unfazed and resolves not to squander this unexpected second chance.

As they descend the spiral staircase to the restaurant's first floor, she notices his bold striped socks. When she stumbles, he leans in to assist her down the steps, and the smell of his hair reminds her of the cologne-infused gels the boys back home in suburban Philadelphia started purchasing at the local drug store in eighth grade.

"Come sit with me," she says while sliding into a banquette in the bar's lounge.

"Thanks, but I need to find April."

Mmm. April, she thinks. *What's the deal with them?* Jillian and April do not socialize in the same circles but are acquainted well enough for Jillian to know April is a talented writer and likely her future competition for the top spot on the newspaper's masthead.

"Interesting word choice," Jillian remarks. "Technically, you don't *need* to find your *friend.* You *want* to find your friend. Just a grammar pet peeve of mine. People mix up *need* and *want* all the time, but really, they convey two very different desires. If you think about it, April doesn't *need* you here. I mean, I go to school with her and trust me, she is perfectly capable of managing on her own without you."

Rudy looks as if Jillian has thrown a dagger at him, and she wonders if she's been too harsh. Was her grammatical analysis off-putting? Too intense for this social situation? She didn't intend to sound mean, but perhaps he heard it that way? Though it seems his relationship with April is platonic, Jillian detects a distinct territoriality coming from Rudy. This triggers something deep inside Jillian. Not jealously, exactly. It's more of a need to win. Or at least a want.

When Rudy heads to the bar to order a soda, Jillian pulls out a small compact mirror from her purse and sets it out on the cocktail table. She reapplies her lipstick, eyeliner, and blush as she awaits his return. Several minutes pass. She looks over at the horseshoe bar from her velvet bench but is unable to spot him in the crowd. Several more minutes pass. She considers searching for him but would hate to lose the romantic banquette's prime real estate, so she stays put and begins ranking summer jobs in her head.

Just as she is staring into the distance, happily envisioning herself as a *New York Times* intern guzzling coffee while fact-checking a front-page story, Jillian's peripheral vision catches two people rushing past her toward the front of the restaurant. By the time she slides out from the center of the velvet bench, all she can see are their backs as they step out the door, hand in hand, one in a black dress and the other wearing khaki pants. Much of the crowd is dressed in a similar attire so she can't guarantee their identities, but based on her swinging ponytail and his striped socks, she can ascertain with near certainty who it is.

I knew it couldn't take that long to get a Coke! is her very first thought. *Liar!*

Jillian runs out onto the sidewalk to get a better look and confirm her suspicion, but she is too late. They're gone.

She heads back inside to see if she can find Rudy. *I'll give him the benefit of the doubt,* she tells herself.

Upon her return, Jillian hears a commotion coming from a small alcove in the back corner of the lounge. No one is screaming, but rumblings of "blood" and "fight" are clearly audible above the din. Some patrons take that as their cue to call it a night. Others, like Jillian, find their curiosity piqued and step closer. Within seconds, the background music falls silent, the dim lighting turns bright, and the hip vibe of the venue completely loses its mystique. A shroud has been lifted, as if everyone is now naked and exposed.

Seated on the floor of the intimate back nook is a tall blond man holding his bloody arm and venomously spitting out the words "fucking asshole" and "knife" over and over. Though not saturated, his polo shirt is dotted with blood and a bartender is using what looks like a dirty bar cloth to apply pressure to a wound. Two women in the crowd announce they are doctors and kneel down beside the man who looks to be in his mid-to-late twenties. One asks the bartender for an emergency kit.

Someone must have called 911 because the sound of sirens on Columbus Avenue is getting increasingly louder with each passing second until a throng of firefighters, police officers, and paramedics burst into the bar. As patrons make way for the crews and their gear, Jillian instinctively whips out the pen and tiny spiral notebook from her purse. She stands tall and follows the first responders, nudging herself into the epicenter as if she's a reporter at a crime scene.

"The guy was mental!" the man on the floor shouts as one of the doctors dabs hydrogen peroxide and applies a tourniquet around what Jillian thinks is a surprisingly small cut considering the amount of blood he is now shedding. "I was just talking to a girl and this thug comes over and puts his hand on her shoulder and tells her it's time to leave, like he owns her or something. So I take his hand off of her and I'm like 'don't manhandle her dude,' and the asshole takes out a fucking knife! A knife!"

Jillian scribbles down every word as if her life depends on it. She takes notes describing the bar's wood paneling. The blood dripping onto the floor tiles. The framed photograph on the wall above that is askew. The names on the back of the firefighters' jackets. The eerie silence in a room that moments earlier had been buzzing with conversation and music.

She knows the details are absolute gold, and despite being knee deep in the moment, she has enough presence of mind to realize this could be her big break. This is, without a doubt, an opportunity to seize and she is going to carpe diem the hell out of it. She'll run back to her hotel room, write up her account, and then dial the numbers on those business cards in her purse. *Those editors will be fighting each other for this story!* she thinks. *What better way to prove myself! It's just as well that I can't find Rudy. I'll be too busy writing this up tonight to see him anyhow.*

Jillian stands just feet away as a police officer questions the victim.

"Sir, what is your name?"

"Bailey."

"Bailey, can you describe the woman you were speaking with?"

"Smallish, her hair was up, I don't know . . ." he mutters, staring at his bloody arm. "Do you know how expensive this shirt is? And I just fucking bought it!"

"Bailey, do you recall her name?"

"I have no idea," he says exasperatingly, massaging his head. "I just met her. Something with an A? Or maybe an E? The hell do I know . . ."

"It's April," a voice in the crowd chimes. "The girl he was talking to—her name is April Zagoda."

"What is your name, sir?" the policeman asks.

"Keith Jameson. Bailey's my brother."

Keith! Jillian thinks. *Holy cow, that's Keith's brother!*

"Keith, how do you know April?"

"We go to college together. We're on the newspaper. That's why we're here this weekend. There's a conference. I introduced April and Bailey maybe a half hour ago, then I walked away to talk with someone else on the other side of the room. Last time I looked over, they were hanging out in that little space off the corner of the bar."

"Do you know the name of the man who was speaking with them?" the officer asks Keith.

"No idea," Keith responds. "I didn't see him."

"Did anyone see him?" the policeman asks, projecting his voice and rotating his head to scan the crowd. "Did anyone get a look at the man with April Zagoda?"

There are shrugs and blank stares all around.

"If anyone has information at any point, my name is Sergeant Costello, please let me know."

Suddenly, without warning, a gasp emerges from Jillian's mouth loud enough for the people standing in the vicinity to glance her way. She coughs to cover it up, lightly pounding on her chest as if something has lodged in her throat, and then fixes her eyes on her notebook, scribbling random words onto the paper as if she is oblivious to the eyes burning through her skin.

Oh my God, Rudy wasn't standing in line to order a Coke at the bar. He was with April. He was the guy Bailey described as being possessive of April. He was the one I saw running out the door.

Not wanting to miss a beat of the action, Jillian takes more notes: the thinning crowd, employees cleaning up, Keith piling into the ambulance behind Bailey, and the beefy paramedic squeezing Bailey's arm to stop the incessant bleeding. Eventually, when the scene quiets, Jillian slips into the private employee restroom near the bar.

"What do I do? What do I do? What do I do?" she whispers aloud, pacing back and forth between the toilet tank and the sink.

Should I tell the police Rudy did this? Oh my God. Do I even have a choice? Isn't it a crime to withhold information when a cop is asking for leads? Shit. I'm not sure.

Jillian can feel her armpits perspiring onto the fabric of her Talbots dress. It's humid and stuffy in the bathroom and she needs to sit down. She eyes the toilet seat cover. It is ancient, chipped, and loosely secured to the bowl with a single rusty screw, but she sits down because it a better option than the filthy floor tiles.

Wait a minute, I can't tell the police it was Rudy. If I'm involved in the story, no editor will publish my reporting. They'll claim there's a lack of objectivity.

Jillian shoots back up on her feet, walks to the sink, and wets some paper towels from the metal dispenser to dab beneath her arms.

But, breaking news doesn't just fall into your lap. This is a rare opportunity. I was in the right place at the right time.

She turns toward the bathroom door to exit, but just as she unlocks the handle, she hears a woman's voice.

"Oh, he was terribly rude, officer," the woman says, sounding as if she had been assaulted. "He just waltzed right into the restaurant and marched upstairs to a private party, like he owned this place. And then, when I politely asked him where he was going, he rolled his eyes! Most civilized people know that the proper thing to do is wait to be greeted by the hostess before entering. I mean, would *you* just dash upstairs if you were a guest in someone's home? I was hired as a hostess to greet people at the entrance for a reason."

"I understand," Sergeant Costello says sympathetically.

"And then . . ." the woman continues, lowering her voice as if she's gifting the officer invaluable gossip, "shortly after he arrived, he left with a girl. They were holding hands. Seemed in a hurry."

"Did you catch his name?"

"No, but he had these socks. I only noticed because his pants were a bit short, like he was walking into a flood."

Jillian leans the back of her head on the bathroom's thin wooden door, shuts her eyes, and releases a long breath. She's confident it's Rudy.

Do I corroborate and get involved? Or shut my mouth and write the story? she wonders.

Jillian takes a breath, straightens her back, and unlocks the bathroom door. Chin up, she walks over to the policeman and hostess.

"Hello officer," she says, infusing her voice with as much confidence as she can muster. "May I speak with you for a moment?"

"Absolutely, we were just finishing up here," he says and points to a nearby table.

As she takes a seat across from the officer, Jillian suddenly finds herself at a loss for words. Her eyes dart like pinballs between his badge, the gun on his belt, and the cap on his head. The sounds of the muffled voices on his walkie-talkie add to the weightiness of the moment. This feels very surreal. She has never been this close to a gun.

The lengthy silence between them and the cop's piercing stare as he waits for her to speak are torture. She knows she has to open her mouth at some point.

"How can I help you?" he asks.

"I, um . . ." She feels like Atlas—the world resting squarely on her shoulders.

"It's okay. Take your time," he says kindly. "Don't worry."

"I might have an idea about the, uh, person who walked out with, um, April Zagoda."

The cop's eyebrows arch. "That would be very helpful information."

Jillian envisions Rudy's face and feels a pang of guilt. "Well, I'm not totally certain, it's more of a hunch, actually."

"It's a start. Nobody else has come forward with any leads. Whatcha got?"

Jillian looks at the austere man across the table in his navy uniform. He is a symbol of strength, security, and integrity, the type of guy anyone would want in their corner. She then recalls that good journalists establish relationships with sources. Trusting, mutually beneficial relationships. Maybe Sergeant Costello could be one of those for her. He would be her first contact at the NYPD. That would certainly come in handy when she's a real reporter. Perhaps one day they could reminisce about how their professional relationship started when she was just a student journalist—how they randomly met at a crime scene on the Upper West Side, talking at a table.

"Miss? Are you okay?" Costello asks, interrupting Jillian's daydream.

"Oh, yes. Sorry." Jillian pulls out the pen and tiny notepad from her purse. She's just going to go for it. She'll try to strike a deal. *You've got information he wants, use it as leverage.* "Do you have any comment regarding this investigation?"

"I'm sorry, who are you? Are you with the press?" He runs a hand over the scruff on his chin. "I'm not speaking to reporters."

"Sergeant, I have reason to believe the man who left with April is a friend of hers."

"And how would you know this? Who are you with?"

She decides to answer only his second question and bypass the first. "I'm freelance. I mainly work for the *Post*."

It isn't a lie. Her college newspaper is actually called *The Post*, but it wouldn't shock Jillian if Sergeant Costello assumes she's referring to the *New York Post*.

"This is a new and ongoing investigation. I can't comment."

"Okay. Fair enough. Perhaps you can offer a few words about something else? More general. Like, have you seen similar cases? Would you say there are more people using knives as weapons these days? An uptick in crime on the Upper West Side? A need for metal detectors at bars and restaurants in the city? Anything? As a young reporter, it would be helpful for me to get a quote from the police department." *I don't care what you tell me! I just want a clip with a quote from the NYPD for my résumé!*

He studies her, seemingly trying to figure out her game. "I don't have time for this," he says, sliding back his chair.

You're so close! Don't let him slip away! "How about off the record?"

"Total anonymity?"

"Yes. You're a totally anonymous source."

"And in return you'll tell me what you know about the guy who left with April Zagoda?"

Jillian nods. *Are we actually doing this? Is he caving?*

Costello squints, apparently still deliberating about whether to engage.

"You want an anonymous quote about anything? Fine," he finally says. "There's been an uptick in bar fights recently. I think it would be smart for these places to hire more off-duty cops to work security. Maybe even invest in metal detectors."

Jillian bites down on her bottom lip to suppress her glee. *Stay cool.*

"Okay. Now it's your turn. What you got for me?"

She caps her pen, tucks her notepad inside her purse, and looks directly into Sergeant Costello's eyes.

"The guy you want is Rudy DeFranco."

9

April

THEN

After a long hot shower, April rummages through her purse in search of a hair scrunchie and discovers Rudy's blood-streaked Swiss Army knife. Between the bar's dimly lit alcove and the heat of the moment, she hadn't noticed the stains earlier in the evening. *Is this Rudy's or Bailey's blood?* she wonders as she scrubs the knife clean with two pumps of Neutrogena Acne Wash at her bathroom sink. She pulls out the tiny metal blade and digs a Q-tip into the crevices to ensure even the most miniscule specks are scoured away. The last thing she wants is for Rudy's cherished keepsake to be tainted because of an invitation she extended to a disastrous event. She was there when Tommy was mugged and appreciates how the boys matching candy apple red gadgets are so much more than they appear. It's their bond as brothers, their pride in being Eddie's sons, and the core tenets of their family's value system: be prepared, support others, protect the ones you love.

April had suggested earlier on the walk home from the subway station that Rudy sleep over, just like the old days. She'd need to return to campus soon, so this would be a nice window of time together.

"Ape, where are the potato chips?" Rudy whispers loudly from the base of the staircase. "They're not in their usual spot. Did your parents rearrange the cabinets?"

"Be there in a sec," she whispers back. She runs the knife under the hot water spout, blots it with a washcloth, and leaves it open to air dry atop the vanity.

When she joins him downstairs, she throws the washcloth and her dirty clothes into the laundry machine and carefully inspects Rudy's shirt and pants for blood stains. She sees nothing and adds them to the load. *Must have been Bailey's blood on the blade,* she thinks. *I'm sure someone got him a Band-Aid. The bar's got to have a first aid kit. I can't imagine his scrapes are any worse than the ones Tommy got when he was mugged.*

She joins Rudy in the kitchen and together they search for late-night snacks. It is so good to be home with him again. Watching him poke his head in the refrigerator and snag a couple of miniature Hershey bars from Barbara's secret stash in the vegetable bin rights something inside of her.

After lugging armfuls of junk food upstairs, Rudy pulls the trundle out from beneath her twin bed. She grabs linens off a shelf in her closet and together they set up his mattress. It's a seamless, fluid routine they have done for years and returns like muscle memory.

"So that Jill girl is pretty psycho, eh?" Rudy remarks as he settles in.

April can feel her forehead crease. "Did you see her tonight?"

"Yeah. When I got there. I was looking for you and ran into her."

"Eek!" April cringes.

"Yeah! *Eek* is right!"

She plops onto her bed. "Did I ever tell you that after you visited last fall, Jill kept asking about you? It must have been two solid months of, '*Is Rudy coming back? Can you give me his number? What's his last name?*' I bet she doodled *Jill DeFranco* at least a hundred times."

"I have that effect on women." He winks.

April clicks on the TV remote and begins flipping through channels.

A wide grin spreads across his face. "Ooh, what's your Vector Victor?" he asks when the movie *Airplane!* appears on the screen.

"How's your Clearance Clarance?" she shoots back.

"Roger, Roger." He adjusts his pillows.

As the film's opening music begins to play, Rudy grabs the remote control and mutes the sound. "So, can I ask you something?"

"Of course."

"Do you think I hurt that guy?" Rudy asks, his voice barely above a whisper. "He was holding his arm."

"No, Rud," she twists around so her stomach is now flat against her bed spread, "you were trying to calm the situation. If anything," she thinks of the bloody blade, "he probably hurt himself."

"Mmm." Rudy is contemplative.

"You did nothing wrong," she reassures him.

"But I feel badly."

"Rud, you did nothing wrong. He was a drunk jerk."

"What's that expression about a sheep in wolf's clothing?" he asks.

"I think it's a wolf in sheep's clothing."

"Yeah, that one." He points at her with the remote.

"Why?"

"You're very trusting. I'm not saying that's a bad quality, it's very nice. But do me a favor and keep your eyes open. I don't want to see you get hurt."

"You're the best, Rud," she says, reaching over and squeezing his hand. "But I'm a big girl. I can handle it."

"Yeah, I know you can. Just . . . some guys dress real nice but, you know . . . just be careful."

She smiles and nods.

He throws a potato chip at her and then presses play on the remote. Twenty minutes later, they are both asleep.

At 6 a.m., April wakes to the sound of pounding on the first floor of her parents' house. She shoots out of bed like a cannon and leaps over Rudy, who is curled beneath a blanket on the trundle. She flings open her bedroom door and gallops down the staircase where she finds her bathrobe-clad father standing in the foyer as four New York City police officers file onto the maroon living room carpet, hands on their holsters.

"Dad, what's wrong?" April shrieks. "Where's Mom?"

April's first thought is Barbara. For several months, April has sensed something off with her mother and her parents haven't been forthcoming with information. Before leaving for college, April noticed her mother moving a tad more slowly than usual. The change was certainly more subtle than drastic, and April convinced herself that it was merely a sign of aging. But the sight of uniformed officers flanking the china cabinet at that early hour ignites a wave of panic throughout April's body. It doesn't matter that they are police and not EMTs—if her father called 911, maybe the cops were able to respond faster than an ambulance crew.

"Is Mommy okay?" She can't recall the last time she referred to her mother as anything other than *Mom* or *Ma*.

"I'm right here," Barbara says, patting down her bedhead hair as she enters the room in her nightgown. "Steven, what the heck is going on?"

The sight of her mother brings a confluence of emotions April has never before experienced. She is relieved to know she can now expunge the mental image of her mother in distress, and yet, simultaneously, deep dread has just electrified her sympathetic nervous system like jumper cables to a car battery. *This can't be about last night. Could it?!*

"Sir. Ma'am. We're sorry to bother you, but we are looking for an April Zagoda," one of the policemen states flatly.

Oh my God. It is.

Both Barbara and Steven's heads rotate toward the staircase where April is leaning on the banister.

"Why on Earth would you be looking for our daughter?" Barbara, flabbergasted, walks over and protectively wraps her arm around April's waist.

Steven widens his stance and places his hands on his hips. "I'm sure there is a very logical explanation for this," he says, scanning the officers' faces.

The police look at each other knowingly until one of them takes a step forward. It's as if they're acting out a well-rehearsed scene in a play and this is his cue to speak.

"Mr. and Mrs. Zagoda, my name is Sergeant Costello, and these are my colleagues, Detective Ramos, Officer James, and Officer Strauss. We're with Manhattan's twentieth precinct. We'd like to speak with your daughter regarding an incident that occurred several hours ago on the Upper West Side."

April's entire body feels like pins and needles.

"Miss Zagoda," Costello starts, peering at April, "what do you know about a fight that took place last night?"

"Not much, really," she says, hoping the panic coursing through her isn't evident. She can actually hear the *whoosh, whoosh* of her blood pressure pulsing in her ears.

Costello pulls a notepad from his pocket. "Well, I understand you were present at the time. Is there anything you can share, perhaps about the argument or the men involved or anything related to the altercation?"

April has a sudden urge to run upstairs and bury herself beneath a heap of blankets with Rudy, the way they did as children when playing hide-and-seek with friends.

"April, dear? Is this true? Did you witness a crime?" her father asks.

A crime? she thinks. *Rudy and Bailey had a* scuffle. *I've seen guys fight like that at fraternity parties, but no one considers it a crime! The police aren't called to the frat houses. Why are the cops in my living room?*

All eyes are on April as she stands in her threadbare Midwood High T-shirt and the beloved navy Champion sweatpants she received as a gift on her fifteenth birthday. She can feel all of them—her father, mother, Sergeant Costello, and the three other cops lined up behind him like backup singers—awaiting her response.

She opens her mouth to speak but nothing emerges.

"It's okay, honey," Barbara says tenderly, squeezing April tightly. "Just tell them what you saw. It'll be fine. Don't worry."

"He . . . he was . . ." The words stick in her throat.

"It's alright, sweetie, go ahead," Steven says reassuringly.

"He was protecting me," she finally says.

"Who?" her parents gasp in unison.

"Did someone try to hurt you?" Barbara asks.

April shakes her head.

"Then who was protecting you? And why? From what? Or from whom?" Her mother's pitch rises with each word.

The cops simply stand there silently.

"It was just a stupid fight," April finally replies. "The guy was drunk and gross. We just left."

"Who is *we?*" Barbara asks. "The kids from your newspaper group?"

April shakes her head. She won't utter Rudy's name. She refuses to bring him into this mess any more than she already has by inviting him out. She could have easily just seen him over the weekend at home in Brooklyn. *Why did I guilt trip him into meeting me in the city?!*

"Who is *we*, April?" Steven asks, repeating his wife's question.

The silence in the living room is heavy. She feels cornered but will hold out as long as needed.

Costello steps closer to April. "Miss Zagoda," he says, breaking the stillness. "Would you happen to know where we could find a man named Rudy DeFranco?"

I won't do it, April thinks. *Nope. No way. I am not going to be the one to hand him over. I'm the reason he got dragged into this. If they want to take me in for questioning, fine. But no freaking way will I tell them where he is. Over my dead . . .*

"I'm right here," Rudy chirps from atop the staircase, rubbing sleep from his eyes. "I'm Rudy DeFranco."

Costello and his crew eye one another as their hands defensively slide down to the gun holsters on their hips. Costello juts his chin toward the staircase and all four of them carefully inch closer.

"Rud! Hey bud!" Steven instinctively brightens upon seeing him.

"Rudy, sweetheart." Barbara waves him over, and then yanks his forearm so she can pull him against her body. She now has one arm protectively draped around April's waist and the other around Rudy's. "Can someone please explain what is going on here? I am very confused."

"Mr. DeFranco," Costello says, hand still on his holster, "we understand there was an altercation last night at an establishment in Manhattan. A man was injured and is now hospitalized. We have reason to suspect you were involved. Would you like to tell us about it?"

Before Rudy can even part his lips to respond, Steven raises his hand.

"Rudy, you have rights," Steven says, stepping between Rudy and Sergeant Costello as if he is a human shield. "You don't have to answer any questions, son. You should have a lawyer before you say anything."

The cops make eye contact with one another, again, as if they are communicating telepathically.

"That is true, Rudy," Costello says, slowly removing the pair of handcuffs on his hip. "But you should know that you will need to give a statement. There is probable cause for your arrest."

"Arrest!" Barbara shrieks. "No, no, no, no, no! There must be some massive misunderstanding."

Tears begin to pool and cloud April's vision. "He was protecting me!" she whimpers. *This is not happening. This is not happening.* "Rudy was helping me! The other guy was a jerk! Go talk to the other guy!" For the life of her she can't recall Bailey's name.

"Mr. DeFranco, please turn around and place your hands behind your back," Officer Costello says.

"Oh, dear God . . ." Barbara cries, wobbling in place. "No! You can't do this! Oh my God! Oh my God! Not in my house! He's practically my son! You hear me? He wouldn't hurt a damn fly!"

Costello secures the first metal cuff around Rudy's left wrist.

"Mr. DeFranco, you have the right to remain silent . . ." he recites robotically.

"This isn't fair!" April weeps. "This is wrong! You've got this all wrong."

"Anything you say can and will be used against you in a court of law . . ." Costello continues.

"I need to sit down," Barbara gasps, reaching for the upholstered chair they inherited from Steven's grandmother.

"You have the right to an attorney. If you cannot afford an attorney, one will be provided for you," Costello states impassively.

April looks over and scans Rudy's face. His jaw is clenched and he is stoically staring at the framed family photos lining the wall along the stairwell.

"Mr. DeFranco," Costello asks, "do you understand the rights I have just read to you?"

"Yes, sir."

Costello fastens the second cuff on Rudy's other wrist. The click of the metal feels like a punch in the gut and April grows lightheaded. She sinks down to the lowest step on the staircase where she sandwiches her head between her knees: crash position.

"Where are you taking him?" Steven asks somberly.

"Twentieth precinct. Upper West Side."

"Rud, I know a lawyer," Steven offers. "I'll call him. We'll get this squared away. I promise. You'll be outta there in no time."

"For God's sake, Steven, your lawyer does trusts and estates!" Barbara shrieks. "What does he know about goddamn criminal law? Oh, Mother Mary, did you hear me? I'm so sorry Rud. You are *not* a criminal. I didn't mean to say *criminal* law. It's just what they call this kind of thing."

Steven runs his hands through his hair. He appears a bit less cool than earlier. "Well, I'm sure lawyers have lawyer friends in other fields, Barb. It can't hurt to ask."

Sergeant Costello shifts his attention to April.

"Miss Zagoda, we would like to ask you some questions as well. Just a witness account. Nothing more. We could do it here, but it might be easier down at the station. You're welcome to go in one of our cars now if you are feeling up to it, or feel free to stop by your own later this morning."

"We'll go now," Barbara interjects before April has a chance to respond. "Rudy's not going to sit in that precinct all by himself. I won't have it."

April doesn't want Rudy there alone either. "I'll go now," she manages to say. She desperately wants a glass of water and an aspirin.

"Mr. DeFranco, we'll need you to change into street clothing," Costello says. "Slip-on shoes only. No laces."

"Oh, dear God!" Barbara moans and rolls her eyes.

"And we'll need your wallet and passport."

"I don't have a passport, sir," Rudy says softly. "I've never been out of the country. And my wallet's upstairs in April's room. May I use the restroom before we leave?"

Costello nods and then looks at Barbara for direction.

"Top of the staircase," Barbara says in disgust.

Costello reaches for Rudy's elbow and escorts him upstairs.

"I'll be right here in the hallway," Costello explains. But as he's about to shut the bathroom door, he notices the Swiss Army knife sitting atop the vanity.

"Mr. DeFranco, is this yours?" he asks.

Shit. I left the knife out to dry on the sink! April realizes as she watches this unfold from her seat at the bottom of the staircase.

"Yes, sir. That's mine."

"Did you have it on you last night?"

No! Don't answer! You need a lawyer! April thinks. But it's too late.

"Yeah, I don't go anywhere without it. I carry it on me at all times. Ever since my brother was mugged, I keep it in my pocket."

April bolts up the stairs to interrupt before the conversation can go any further.

"Rud, I'm so sorry, I washed our clothes last night, but we fell asleep and I didn't put them in the dryer. Everything's damp. You'll have to borrow something to wear from my dad."

As April rummages through her father's dresser, Costello calls down to his colleagues.

Minutes later, three cops are sardined inside her pink childhood bathroom that still has a Hello Kitty shower curtain. April hands over a pair of Steven's jeans and a Yankees hoodie for Rudy and returns to the bedroom to fetch a pair of shoes. She tries to eavesdrop on the cops' conversation, but their voices are too low and muddled. As she reaches for her dad's loafers from a rack beneath the bedroom window, she notices two NYPD cars parked in front of their house. She presses her nose against the window screen, the exact same way she did years earlier when Rudy came over for their first playdate, and sees Detective Ramos retrieving a bag stamped with the word EVIDENCE in bold red letters from the trunk of one of the cars.

A prickly heat cascades over her body. *Oh God. The knife. I cleaned the knife. I washed away the blood. What's that called when you mess with evidence? Tampering? Shit. Did I tamper? Is it tampering if you don't realize you're tampering? Can't it just be cleaning? Wait. Will they arrest me too?!*

April exits her parents' room and sees Detective Ramos's gloved hand drop Rudy's pocketknife into the bag, transforming her friend's prized possession into a piece of evidence.

"Here's the address of the precinct," Costello says, handing Steven a business card when they return downstairs.

Rudy is beside them dressed in the clothing and brown penny loafers April had selected. He looks uncomfortable in the shoes, but she hopes the shiny copper pennies her father had squeezed into the slit on top will bring good luck.

"We're going to follow you," Steven says, snatching his car keys from a wall hook beside the front door. "We can go in tandem."

Standing at the edge of the driveway—the spot that had always been square number one of their hopscotch games and home plate for wiffleball tournaments—April watches as Rudy is escorted, hands behind his back, into the rear of Officer James's patrol car. She takes note of every move as the officer places his hand atop Rudy's hair, pushes his head down into the back seat, and buckles him in. She notices Rudy's face scrunch up as his cuffed wrists press against the vinyl. *He must be so uncomfortable*, she thinks. *I hope his skin isn't pinching.*

Though it is the logical next step after securing a seatbelt, the slam of the car door elicits a massive wave of separation anxiety on par with the homesickness she experienced as a child on the first day of school. She contemplates shouting *I'm so sorry! It's all my fault, I should never have told you about the party!* but refrains. Several bathrobed neighbors are already gathering on stoops. There's no need to add fuel to their speculation about why two cop cars are parked in front of her mother's geraniums.

"We need to get in touch with the DeFrancos," Steven remarks as the three of them pile into Big Bertha. "I can't imagine they won't allow him to call his parents, but who knows how much time he gets to talk. We should reach out."

No one speaks for the next thirty minutes, 1010 WINS news radio playing low in the background. The only other sound is of April unearthing tiny crumbs of food buried between the crevices of Bertha's cloth seats and flicking them onto the floor mats. By the time they arrive on the Upper West Side, Bertha is in need of a good vacuuming.

"Yes, hi, we're looking for Sergeant Costello," Steven says, walking up to the precinct's front desk.

"Take a seat," a uniformed receptionist says pointing to a wooden bench along the wall.

"Thanks. May we use the phone while we wait? We'd like to make a call."

As Barbara and Steven are led down a hall to contact the De-Francos, April takes in her surroundings. The precinct has a distinct musty-sweet odor—a combination of stale coffee and ink cartridges—and the walls are brown brick mixed with the same glazed rectangular tiles that lined the corridors of her high school. She knows she'll remember this day for the rest of her life.

"Hello, April," Sergeant Costello says as he approaches. "Sorry for the wait. Please follow me." He's all business.

She follows him to a small room with a square table and three metal folding chairs.

"Where's Rudy?" she blurts out.

"Room one with Detective Ramos. He's fine. Don't worry."

"You know, it was just a stupid fight," she says, the words flying from her mouth. "It happens all the time at frat parties. Why are we here? I don't understand," her voice cracks. Twenty seconds in and already tears are flowing down her cheeks.

Costello slides a tissue box across the table. "I just need to know what you saw and heard. That's all."

"That guy was drunk. Rudy was trying to help me. He didn't touch that guy . . ."

"Are you referring to the victim?"

The victim? She thinks, incensed. *I'm a victim! Rudy's a victim! That guy harassed us! Why is he the victim? Because he bled from a little cut?*

"Yes, I'm referring to him." She won't utter the word *victim*.

"Bailey Jameson," Costello clarifies.

"Yes. Rudy didn't start it. That guy laughed at Rudy and shoved him. He spilled his drink on him. Rudy said he didn't want a problem and tried to help me. Please believe me, Rudy's the best. I mean it. He's just the best. He's never hurt anyone. I swear."

"Why did he laugh at Rudy?"

Because he saw Rudy's measly knife, she thinks but doesn't say. She recalls her father's advice to Rudy back in their living room and realizes she should probably have a lawyer. "I think I should, um . . ." she starts, but feels impolite, audacious even, interrupting the flow of conversation. After all, she's not a suspect, just a witness.

"It's okay. We're just talking here," Costello assures April, clearly sensing hesitation on her end. He leans forward on his elbows. "You're doing great. This will all be helpful for Mr. DeFranco's case if we get the facts and have a full visual of the scene."

She takes a deep, ragged breath. "Okay. Well, um, the guy . . ."

"Mr. Jameson?"

"Yeah, he laughed at Rudy, and then he called me 'hussy trash' and came at Rudy."

"I see." Costello clears his throat. "Ms. Zagoda, as you know, a knife was recovered at your parents' home. Did you see that knife used at any time during the altercation between Rudy DeFranco and Bailey Jameson? Was it in Mr. DeFranco's hand? Did he strike Mr. Jameson?"

The sound of their full names sounds very official and scary. Tears sting April's eyes and she suddenly wants her parents but is determined to plow through.

"Yes, Rudy had a little knife, but all he did was take it out of his pocket. I can tell you for sure that that guy started the fight. He lunged at Rudy and then Rudy and I left. That was it."

"So you never saw Rudy stab Bailey Jameson."

"Oh my God! No! Never!"

"But there was a scuffle."

"Yes."

"And the knife was in Rudy DeFranco's hand at the time of the scuffle."

Don't say it . . . "I'm not sure. Like I said, the whole thing didn't last very long. That guy came at Rudy and the next thing I know, I'm looking down at the floor and I see the knife is there, so I pick it up and put it in my purse."

"*You* picked it up or Rudy picked it up?"

"I did. I didn't want anyone to step on it and get hurt. Plus, I didn't want Rudy to lose it. I know how much that knife means to him. I just grabbed it and threw it in my bag."

Costello nods. "I see," he says contemplatively and starts to scribble some notes on a pad.

"Is that how the knife ended up back at your home in Brooklyn . . . you put it in your purse?"

"Yes, sir."

"And when you came home, what did you do with the knife?"

"I rinsed it off."

"Where?"

"In the upstairs bathroom sink."

"What did you use to clean the knife?"

"Acne wash."

"And why did you rinse it off?"

She can feel acid swirl in her upper abdomen.

"It was on the floor of a bar. It was dirty. I figured I'd just clean it for Rudy."

"Did Rudy DeFranco ask you to do that?"

"No, sir. He was downstairs showering. Cleaning the knife was my idea."

"Was there blood on the blade?"

Fuck. "I . . . I'm not sure. I mean, I picked it up off the floor of the bar. It was dirty and sticky."

"Mmm." Costello scribbles some more notes. The pause in conversation ignites another surge of panic. *Did I just help or hurt Rudy? Am I in trouble now, too?*

"Could I, um, get some water?" she asks.

"Absolutely," Costello says. As he opens the door to exit the interview room, he nearly collides with Officer James, who is about to enter.

"Hey, got a minute?" James asks Costello. His face is more dour than April remembers from when he was standing in her living room.

As the men exit and linger in the hall outside, James lowers his voice, but the door is thin and she easily hear.

"That kid from Brooklyn is done," James says. "Call just came in. Victim coded early this morning. This ain't assault no more. DeFranco just got upgraded to homicide."

"Oh shit," Costello grumbles.

"The guy's family is loaded. Gated estate in the suburbs. Country club. The whole nine. Press is foaming at the mouth. We already got two photographers outside the precinct. They're asking for a statement."

This cannot be real. This is not happening. Suddenly, April can't breathe. Saliva pools along her gums. The sensations converge simultaneously, like an unforgiving tornado ravaging a small town. The room tilts and she bends forward, retching onto the tile floor. As she wipes the corner of her mouth with the back of her hand, she yearns, once again, for her mother. She needs to be held. Comforted. She knows the last place she should be in this moment is alone on a metal folding chair in a cold, bare room with nothing but a box of Kleenex and vomit at her feet. And yet, it is there that she remains, too fearful to abandon the space assigned to her by an officer of the law. She will obey. She will answer questions. She will not cause more problems for Rudy. She will do her best to clean up the mess—both the malodorous pool beside her and the deracination of their lives.

As she reaches for a tissue, she catches a sound coming from down the hall that is incomparable to anything she has ever heard before. At first it is piercing, then guttural. Both iterations are frightening.

Too scared to stay a minute longer in the interrogation room, she opens the door and finds an empty hallway. She looks to the left, then the right, and bolts toward the reception area to find her parents, but on her way she stops short.

"Rudy!" she cries upon seeing him in the corridor, still cuffed, and flanked by men in blue. "I'm so sorry, I'm so so sorry," she weeps.

"Ape, it's okay. I'll be okay. This will all get sorted out. I'm sure it's some big misunderstanding. We'll figure it out. Don't worry."

"Where are they taking you?"

"Central booking downtown," Costello answers. "He needs to be fingerprinted, put in the system, and arraigned."

Rudy lifts his chin high and inhales so deeply his chest puffs.

Costello tugs on Rudy's elbow and they begin to walk away toward a back door. She guesses they're trying to avoid press on the street out front. Eight hours earlier, she and her best friend were eating Pringles in her bedroom and watching Kareem Abdul Jabar copilot a turbulent flight in *Airplane!* Never could she have anticipated that in a matter of hours, her life would be just as stormy and surreal as a movie.

"I love you," April weeps as the officers pull him away. "I'm so sorry."

"I love you too," he calls out, his back to her.

April turns around to continue searching for her parents and that is when she hears another wail. This one is nearly identical to the first except it is followed by a loud thump. She picks up her pace and as she rounds the corner toward the reception desk, she finds Lorraine DeFranco passed out on the precinct floor.

10

April

THEN

To April's great surprise, sitting on a wooden pew during arraignments in Manhattan's Criminal Courthouse is not dissimilar to watching episodes of *Law & Order* on television. There are prosecutors with large accordion folders tucked beneath their arms, defense attorneys speaking in hushed tones to their clients, and everything from the leather penal code binder to the stenographer's wrinkled suit seem to possess a depressing brown patina. As far as April can tell, the only difference between the primetime drama and her reality is viewer perspective. Curling up beneath a blanket on your living room couch feels quite different than spending the day under fluorescent lights on a hard oak bench as you await the fate of your best friend.

Nearly twelve hours have passed since the cops entered the Zagodas' home and eight have elapsed since Rudy was finger-printed, photographed, and processed in the system. As the sun shines brightly in a cloudless sky over lower Manhattan, Barbara,

Steven, and April are now camped in a windowless courtroom alternating restroom and snack breaks between them to ensure someone is always present in the event Rudy's case is called. The DeFrancos had hoped to join, but when Lorraine collapsed at the police precinct that morning, the officers insisted she get checked out in the emergency room. So, while Rudy's parents are uptown monitoring Lorraine's blood pressure at Mount Sinai, the Zagodas are downtown awaiting his arraignment at 100 Centre Street.

At around 5 p.m, just before the shift change to night court, a door on the side of the courtroom that links to the holding pens opens and Rudy emerges, handcuffed, still clad in Steven's clothing.

"Court is now in session part AR1," a balding middle-aged clerk with glasses at the tip of his nose announces. "Honorable Michael Howard presiding."

"Appearances please," Judge Howard says, looking down from the bench as he leans back against the headrest of a tall leather chair.

"Richard Cossofski for the defense," says an older man in a slightly baggy blue suit standing beside Rudy. He's the lawyer Steven Zagoda's trusts and estates buddy recommended who kindly took Steven's phone call at 8 a.m. and rearranged his schedule to meet Rudy in the holding pens.

"Assistant District Attorney Donald Sketcher for the people," the prosecutor declares. He is bespectacled, scrawny, wears a pocket square in his light gray suit, and projects supreme confidence, which surprises April because he looks young enough to still be in college. She can't imagine he has been at the job very long.

The clerk clears his throat and recites a lengthy docket number. "People versus Rudy Dee Franco . . ."

It's DeFranco, you idiot! April silently seethes at the clerk's mangling of Rudy's name. It irritates her more than she knows it should. *Yet another injustice,* she thinks.

". . . Mr. Dee Franco is charged with murder in the second degree, possession of a concealed weapon in the first, assault in the first, tampering with physical evidence in the first."

"Counsel," the clerk says, "do you waive the reading but not the rights there under?

"I do, Your Honor," says Rudy's lawyer.

"People?" the judge asks, looking directly at the prosecutor.

"Your Honor," Sketcher says, "the People are serving felony grand jury notice and are inquiring as to cross."

"Written, oral cross is in effect, Your Honor," Cossofski says.

"The People are serving a Wiggins letter indicating their intent to present this case to the grand jury on the ninth floor of One Hogan Place at 10 a.m. on May 9," Sketcher says.

"Acknowledge receipt," Cossofski notes as he shuffles some papers.

This is like watching a play in a foreign language, April thinks.

"What are they saying?" Barbara whispers to Steven.

"Not sure. Maybe about whether Rudy wants to testify at the grand jury?"

The judge leans forward and writes something down before asking, "Mr. DeFranco, how do you plea?"

Rudy glances at his attorney for guidance. He looks lost, like a child seeking guidance from a parent.

Cossofski gently places an open palm on Rudy's back as a gesture of support. "Not guilty, Your Honor," Cossofski says on Rudy's behalf.

Sketcher takes a breath, stands tall, and shoves one hand in his pants pocket. It's as if he is readying himself to deliver a soliloquy he has dreamed about and rehearsed in front of a mirror.

"Your Honor, this defendant is charged with repeatedly stabbing a man with a knife at a party in New York County . . ."

April whips her head to Steven.

What? she mouths in exasperation.

Steven reaches for his daughter's hand and squeezes reassuringly.

That's not true! she mouths again.

He places his finger to his lips reminding April to stay quiet.

"After viciously attacking the victim, the defendant immediately fled the scene with the weapon. An anonymous tip led police to a private residence in Kings County where he was taken into custody. This is a very strong case in that there were multiple eyewitnesses and even confirmation from the defendant that he was, in fact, present at the establishment when the crime occurred. The defendant is facing a possible fifteen years if convicted of the top counts."

Barbara gasps loudly and a security guard standing against the wall of the courtroom inches closer, eyeing Barbara as if she's a live wire.

"I'll hear the People on bail," Judge Howard says.

Sketcher continues, "The defendant has every incentive to flee and not return to court, Your Honor. I respectfully request that bail be denied."

April's jaw drops. "Why would they do that? Can we object?"

"Shh." Steven places his index finger to his lips.

It's now Cossofski's turn.

"Your Honor," he begins. "We are dealing with a young man with no criminal history and strong ties to his local community. He has never even left the country. Mr. DeFranco was invited to attend a gathering where a young man tragically died . . ."

Oh my God. It's all my fault. Why the hell did I invite him?

"The victim allegedly attacked my client and although a scuffle ensued, there is no proof of how the victim died as my client left the party while the victim was alive. The victim was coherent and speaking with police who arrived at the scene approximately ten minutes after a 911 call was placed. There is only an allegation by an unnamed witness that my client, among the dozens of men at this party, is, in fact, the one responsible for the death of the victim . . ."

Who the hell is that unnamed witness? April wonders.

"Everything the People are alleging is just that—allegations," Cossofski continues. "Mr. DeFranco stands before Your Honor a good man accused of a heinous crime he desperately wants to clear his name of. He has every incentive to return to court for that reason. He is a lifelong New York resident and is currently enrolled as a part-time student at Kingsborough Community College where he is studying for an associate's degree in engineering. In addition, he works the weekend morning shifts at a bagel shop near his home and assists his father as a handyman at his apartment building in Kings County where his father is the superintendent. He is not on the payroll at the apartment building but does accept gratuity when assisting his father with repairs and maintenance. This is a good man, Your Honor. A really good young man. Hardworking. He is a devoted son, brother, neighbor, and friend with a longstanding record of contributing to his community. He has immense family support, and I have a good phone number for him and his family. Denial of bail is wholly inappropriate. I respectfully request that Your Honor set bail in an amount that his devoted family can afford to pay. We would ask that in the alternative, Your Honor consider releasing the defendant to the care of his parents. He will, of course, abide by any additional restrictions Your Honor would impose, such as a curfew."

Sketcher clears his throat and straightens his necktie. "Respectfully, Your Honor," he says with gotcha cockiness. "The only devoted family that *is* present in this courtroom today belongs to the victim. Despite the rawness of their loss, they have come en mass to this arraignment to see that justice is served. The death of Bailey Jameson, a recent college graduate with a bright future ahead of him, is a travesty. An absolute travesty. No family should have to experience what this family is going through. Again, Your Honor, the People request the defendant be held without bail."

April pivots and notices a somber family taking up a good portion of the back row. They must have quietly slipped in since her last bathroom break. They appear to be cut from the pages of an L.L.Bean catalogue—not unlike the kids she has met in college who wear sweatshirts with the names of boarding schools—except despite their bronzed skin and polished attire, they look absolutely drained. One of the women—the one clutching a leather tote against her chest like a security blanket—bears a striking resemblance to Keith Jameson.

"Your Honor," Cossofski volleys back, "let the record reflect that Mr. DeFranco's mother is currently under medical supervision at Mount Sinai Medical Center and his father is helping to care for her. They have a tight-knit family and upon learning of her son's arrest, Mrs. DeFranco fell ill. However, the defendant is supported in this courtroom today by close family friends."

Rudy begins to turn his head toward the Zagodas but is stopped and instructed by Cossofski to face the judge.

"We love you Rudy," Barbara mutters under her breath. The security guard shoots her a wide-eyed warning to shut up.

The courtroom grows still as the judge takes a few moments to peruse some documents on the bench. With nothing to record, the stenographer begins examining her nails. Something about the way she scrutinizes her cuticles and checks for chips in the polish deeply irks April. She is annoyed by how unaffected the rest of the world is by this moment in time. How can a cataclysm for one human being be just another day in the life of someone else?

April squirms uncomfortably in her seat, crossing and uncrossing her legs. She can only imagine what the day has been like for Rudy. She wonders if he's eaten. If he's been roughed up in the holding pens. Are his arms sore from being behind his back for so long? Has he noticed the golden inscription on the courtroom wall? *In God We Trust.* Does it bring him comfort? Or does he feel abandoned?

While everyone awaits the ruling, April sees that somehow, despite the handcuffs, Rudy has managed to intertwine all ten of his fingers so that he is holding his own hand. It is the saddest sight she has ever seen. If only she could stand beside him, place her palm in his, and absorb this entire debacle like a sponge so she can take the fall and he can walk away. She knows neither of them deserve this fate, but of the two, she should bear the guilt. Without her invitation, he would have stayed home. He would have studied for his final, probably eaten an Ellio's frozen pizza, watched TV, and gone to bed. Instead, he's now an accused criminal holding his own cuffed hands and standing before a judge who, at best, will set a bail the DeFrancos cannot afford.

"Having reviewed the standards," Judge Howard states while stamping and signing documents, "I find that monetary bail is the least restrictive means to ensure this defendant's return to court. I'm setting bail in the amount of $200,000 cash or $300,000 bond at 10 percent."

"Can you add a credit card option, Your Honor?" Cossofski immediately asks.

"Yes, I'll add a credit card option at $200,000 cash. This case is adjourned for grand jury action in part F on May 8."

"Thank you, Your Honor," both attorneys say, nearly in unison.

A court officer then laces his hands around Rudy's elbow to escort him to the holding pens. As he does, Rudy quickly turns back to the audience, and for a brief moment, his eyes lock with April's.

"Look ahead," the officer commands as they walk toward the exit.

There was no wink between Rudy and April. No nod. But

there was a connection. *At least he knows we're here*, she tells herself. Cossofski packs a bunch of papers into his attaché case and then unlatches a short red velvet rope separating the well from the audience section. After securing the cord's metal clasp behind him, he looks over toward the Zagodas and motions for them to meet him outside in the hallway.

"Okay," Cossofski says as they gather in the corridor. He places his briefcase on the ground between his feet then rests his hands on his hips. "Mr. and Mrs. Zagoda, do you know if there is anyone who can post bail?"

"Lorraine and Eddie can't afford it," Barbara states definitively. "And I won't sleep a wink for the rest of my life if I don't do everything in my power right now to keep him out of Rikers for even one night. So yeah, it's us. We're gonna do it."

Steven nods in confirmation. "I'm sure you understand, I don't have $200,000 just lying around though." He then reaches for the small leather wallet in the back pocket of his pants, removes a credit card from one of the slots, and skims the miniscule font on the back as if Visa must have an 800 number printed somewhere for how to post bail that exceeds your credit line.

"What happens if my parents and Rudy's parents can't get enough money to post bail?" April can feel the quiver in her voice.

"Unless bail is paid, he will stay behind bars until he sees the judge again."

Barbara looks over at Cossofski. "You say we get the money back if he shows up for all his court dates?"

"Yes."

"Well, Rudy's a responsible kid. I'll bet on him any day. Take us to an ATM. We'll withdraw whatever we can in cash and split the rest between our Visa and American Express cards."

"We don't have all of that liquid in our checking account, Barb," Steven says.

"Then take it from our retirement accounts," she says unequiv-ocally. "Rudy's good for it. We won't be out of the money. We can just replenish it later, right?"

"Yes. As long as he shows up," Cossofski reiterates.

"Okay," Steven sighs. "Let's go to an ATM. Then I'll call Amex and Visa to give them a heads up."

April is stewing, yearning to cry, punch, kick, scream, and curl up on the tile floor all at the same time. Instead, she stands beside her parents, digging her fingernails into her palms, and wishing she could go back in time to revoke the invitation she'd extended to Rudy to come out on Thursday night.

As the Zagodas and Cossofski exit the courthouse onto Centre Street, they pass a small huddle of reporters gripping microphones and tiny tape recorders. Several television cameras are anchored on tripods along the sidewalk. In the center of it all is Donald Sketcher and beside him are the people who were seated in the back row of the courtroom.

"The murder of a loved one is an injustice no one should ever have to know," Sketcher says, repeating nearly verbatim what he said during the arraignment. "A beloved son. A devoted brother. A friend. An athlete. A college graduate with a promising future."

The victim's family is silent. They let Sketcher and his slow, somber words be their mouthpiece. When they hand him some photographs of Bailey—posing with a lacrosse stick, in a tuxedo at prom, a few of their family on a boat at sunset—Sketcher holds the images above his head as if they are trophies. "It's an absolute trav-esty," he says as photographers' flashes explode like fireworks. "And believe me, there's going to be hell to pay."

Two hours later, April and Rudy are buckled in the back seat of Big Bertha, just like when they were kids. Steven is behind the wheel and Barbara is yakking away in a seemingly breathless run-on sentence.

"You hungry, Rud?" Barbara asks, not waiting for a response. "I can heat up a meatloaf or I got a Tupperware of your favorite sweet and sour meatballs in the freezer. I think I made them about a month ago. You know, you should only keep food frozen, especially meat, for like six months. Not sure where I heard that. My grandmother? Who knows. Doesn't matter. I've also got frozen chicken nuggets. Or we could pick up a slice? Actually, some eggs might be good. Easy and protein. Or would you prefer a bagel and butter?"

Steven reaches for his wife's knee. "It's okay, hun. I think he's got the idea."

"Thanks, Mrs. Z," Rudy says softly, his eyes closed. "I just want to go home."

The car is silent but for the sounds of passing traffic on the Brooklyn Bridge. Steven turns on the radio and a symphony on WQXR begins to fill the space.

Should I say something? April wonders, looking over at Rudy. His body is sunken into the cloth seats. There are no words. Small talk seems silly and awkward. She doesn't have the energy or presence of mind for a deep conversation about emotions or game plan and suspects Rudy doesn't either.

As she takes him in—still outfitted in the clothing she selected from her father's wardrobe early that morning—she notices irritation on Rudy's wrists.

"That hurt?" she asks, gently rubbing her finger over the red marks on his skin.

He opens his eyes briefly, shrugs, and shuts them again.

It is as close as they get to an acknowledgment of the day—the one she will always remember as the time she destroyed her best friend's life.

11

Jillian

THEN

illian doesn't move an inch as she watches April exit the courthouse.

She is standing in front of 100 Centre Street, shoulder-to-shoulder with seasoned reporters at her first press conference and, thanks to her disarming smile and quiet confidence, she has managed to snag a prime position at the front of the pack. No one bothers to check for press credentials. No one cares to ask who this young woman is or why she is here. With a fresh spiral notepad and sharpened pencil in hand, she blends right in as she furiously scribbles down nearly every word uttered by Assistant District Attorney Donald Sketcher.

"That party was a bloodbath," he bellows, as if there isn't a bouquet of microphones shoved directly in front of his face. "It was a senseless murder and I will personally see to it that this knife-wielding thug is prosecuted to the fullest extent of the law."

The Jameson family stands silently behind him, an ensemble

cast supporting Sketcher's leading man. With their linked arms and crinkled tissues dabbing away tears, they need not say a word. Their message is loud and clear: They are united. They are loving. They are victims. They are the good guys.

When Sketcher holds out a picture of Bailey in a varsity lacrosse uniform for all the cameras to see, Jillian's eye shifts past the framed photograph and notices April scurrying down the courthouse steps. For a moment, she considers bolting from the conference and following, but thinks better of the idea. *Do not squander this opportunity*, she thinks as the journalists beside her aggressively grill Sketcher. She's too shy to jump in and shout her questions above theirs, but fortunately, the queries she would pose are all asked and, by the end of the conference, she's got what she needs for a solid freelance article. Plus, by granting herself permission to be more of an observer than a participant, she is relaxed enough to pick up on details she might have otherwise overlooked: the initials *DS* stitched onto the cuffs of his shirt; the way his perfectly combed hair shines from newly applied hair gel; and, quite ironically, he is speaking to the media at the base of a wooden wheelchair ramp to the courthouse. Jillian is fairly confident this was unintentional, but for someone who seems to place a premium on appearances, this is a pretty befuddling gaff. *What kind of lawyer holds a press conference about the importance of fighting injustice while blocking an access ramp for wheelchair users?* she wonders.

After the Q&A ends and the media departs, Jillian remains on the courthouse steps watching Sketcher wave goodbye to the Jamesons as they are whisked away in black town cars. She studies the way he loosens his tie and then cracks his neck from left to right before walking down the street. Though it's now dinnertime on a Friday and she suspects he's heading home for the night, she decides to follow. Unsure of her objective or what she will say if they actually speak, Jillian is feeling emboldened and wily after nudging herself

into the press pool. She twists her long brown hair into a tight balle-
rina bun and pulls out a few strands to hang by her cheeks. She
knows the loose pieces soften her face and accentuate her youth.
She trails behind Sketcher like a shadow on concrete and then, as
soon as the crosswalk light changes and he steps into the street, she
strikes.

"Excuse me, sir?" Her voice jumps half an octave above its natural timbre.

He turns in her direction. "Yes?"

"I was just passing by over there," she says, pointing toward the
courthouse. "I noticed you were speaking to a crowd. Do you mind
if I ask what that was about?"

He studies her for a second and then takes the bait. "Oh, well,
I'm an attorney. The media is interested in a case I'm prosecuting."

"Gosh. What's it about? If you don't mind me asking, sir." She
is careful not to address him by name.

"A young man was murdered. Stabbed with a knife."

Play dumb, she reminds herself. "Oh, that's awful. Have you
done a lot of cases like this?"

"Mmm, pretty standard criminal law, unfortunately," he says,
checking the time on his wristwatch and picking up the pace of his
stride.

There is a momentary lull. Jillian knows she must think quickly
before she loses his attention but finds herself tongue-tied and
slightly starstruck given he was just standing in front of television
cameras.

"So, did you always know you wanted to be a lawyer?" she asks.
It's the only question that crosses her mind.

He seems puzzled. "What did you say your name was?"

"I'm Jill. It's nice to meet you." She extends her hand, but the
logistics of shaking while keeping in step with a brisk walker on her
left proves quite awkward.

"Well, yes, Jill. I've always known I wanted to be an attorney. Criminal law, especially."

"Some people are really lucky that way," she chirps. "Always know what they want and where they're headed. It's like they can feel it in their insides or something. I get it."

Lull. He checks the time on his watch, again.

Don't drop this ball, she thinks, trying to keep pace. *This is your chance to get a source at the DA's office, just like you did with the cop.*

"I'm planning on law school," she lies. "Would it be okay if I got your card? Would love to sort of pick your brain about your experience. Being a prosecutor sounds like a dream job."

"I really don't have time for this, but here's the main number for the DA's office." He stops, pulls a scrap piece of paper out of his pocket, and scribbles down a phone number before sprinting toward a subway station.

When Sketcher disappears underground, Jillian inspects the letterhead on the memo paper. It has his name printed at the top, but the employer is not the DA's office. Instead, it's a private firm located in Hoboken and the number has a 201 New Jersey area code.

Confused, she walks to a pay phone across the street, drops in some change, and dials.

A woman picks up on the first ring. "Law Group. Martha speaking, how may I help you?"

"Oh, hi there," Jillian says, surprised and grateful to catch someone still at work so late on a Friday. "I'm trying to find the best way to reach Donald Sketcher. Is this it?" Although she's got the Manhattan DA's office number, she figures this is an innocuous way to dig for more information.

"Mr. Sketcher left the firm about a month ago. May I help you?"

Interesting. "Any chance you know where I can find him? Perhaps a number or email?" *This might be a good way to get a direct line to him and not have to deal with the DA's press office and the potential headache of being asked for press credentials.*

"Hold please . . ."

Though Jillian can tell Martha has muzzled the telephone receiver, her voice remains clear.

"Hey Fran?" Martha calls out to a colleague in the background. "Are we supposed to give out Sketcher's new number? I've got someone on the line asking for him. No, I don't know who she is. What? You want me to tell her what?! I'm pretty sure if I say 'jackass moron' I'll get fired. You're a hoot, Fran." Martha clears her throat and returns to Jillian.

"I'm sorry ma'am, I'm not at liberty to disclose Mr. Sketcher's contact information. May I assist you with something else?"

"Oh, that's okay, thanks. Have a good weekend."

Jillian hangs up and scribbles down: "jackass moron" on her notepad. She then hails a taxi back to her hotel.

As she makes her way up the FDR Drive, she sits in the back of the cab flipping through the pages of her notebook. *There is* so *much here*, she tells herself. Plenty of material for a solid article and then some. Her mind sputters with story ideas, but she knows time is of the essence. Editors are impatient. News gets stale fast. If she wants to pitch a piece, she's got to move quickly.

An hour later, Jillian settles into a van with her faculty advisor and fellow club members. When news broke of Bailey Jameson's death, Rivington insisted the group leave the conference and return to campus. Everyone is on the van except April Zagoda and Keith Jameson, who are spending time with their families. Unlike Thursday's break-of-dawn trip to Manhattan when the students were abuzz with excitement, the Friday night drive back to campus is somber and silent. There is a profound heaviness in the air that has either induced sleep among the passengers or spawned distant stares. The only interior light on the darkened ride is the one directly above Jillian's seat, which shines brightly over her head as she finesses her pitch. By the time they pull into the school parking lot at midnight, the draft is complete. She disembarks the bus, races to her dorm room, and arranges the cocktail party business cards she collected in order of importance. The top card belongs to the editor she will call first, and if the editor does not respond promptly, she will move on to the next.

The following morning, the first call she makes is to a business reporter at *The New York Times*. She gets his answering machine and leaves a message.

The next call is to the Associated Press. The reporter picks up but tells Jillian the AP is already on the story.

The third call is to an editor at Gannett—a network of national and local newspapers. The editor is intrigued and asks Jillian to email it over so she can take a look.

Jillian hangs up, grabs her notebook, and spends the next twenty minutes typing up the story written in her notebook. She reads it over twice to check for spelling and grammatical errors and then, after five quick jumping jacks and a shake of her legs as if she were about to run a marathon, she leans over the keyboard and clicks "send."

Given the colossal adrenaline rush of a dream coming true, Jillian is unable to sit still. She unpacks her duffel bag from the trip, does a load of laundry, showers, slips on some sweats, and with a towel turban wrapped around her wet hair, transcribes every note from her spiral pad onto her computer for safekeeping.

That afternoon, Jillian walks across campus through a dreary drizzle to pick up hot chocolate and a French cruller from her favorite coffee shop. She's mentally preparing for rejection by the editor at Gannett and decides to treat herself to soften the potential blow. The café in town is two doors down from the sports bar where she met Rudy, and suddenly, she thinks of him tenderly. In this moment, he is neither a story idea nor an opportunity to leverage her career; he's Rudy, the boy with the deep brown eyes and crooked smile to whom she was drawn by a force so overwhelming it felt as if they were destined to meet. For months, she had replayed that night over and over in her mind's eye. She could hear every word of their conversation. She could smell his citrusy cologne. She could see his high-top sneakers planted solidly on the bar's sticky floor and envision the way his shoulders raised when he dug his hands into the front pockets of his jeans. Never could she have imagined that this would be the fate of the guy she hoped to one day call her boyfriend.

When she returns to her dorm room, Jillian kicks off her wet sneakers and notices a flashing light on the answering machine. She places the half-eaten cruller on her desk and presses play.

"Hello, Jillian, this is Beth, from Gannett. Wanted to let you know your story looks great. We'd like to run it in the tristate area local papers, and there's a good chance it will go national in *USA Today*, but I'll have an answer on that later after the editor's meeting. Anyway, I've got a couple of questions, minor nits, nothing major. Please give me a call back so I can get this in the hopper. Also, would love to hear what other story ideas you've got. Alright. That's all for now. Speak soon."

"Oh my God," she whispers aloud and replays the message to make sure she has heard correctly.

After the second listen, she begins pacing around her dorm room. *Okay, okay, I need at least three more pitches before returning Beth's call. I can't blow this opportunity.* She grabs her notebook and flips through the pages. As she looks over the content, story ideas from various angles come on like a flood. *How 'bout a profile of Bailey Jameson? A profile of Rudy DeFranco? A personal essay about coming into town for a conference and ending up at a crime scene? Oh, and I'd love to do a long form magazine-style piece related to Sketcher. Not sure what, but there's definitely something there, I can feel it.*

Armed with her pitch list, Jillian sits cross-legged on her extra-long twin bed mattress and dials Gannett.

"Jill, hi!" Beth greets her warmly. "I've got to say, I'm very impressed by your work. Really well done for someone your age. You've got a bright future ahead of you."

Jillian's cheeks flush. She wishes she could record this conversation.

"So listen, I'm going to email you my notes. There are a few minor holes—nothing you can't handle. If you can get it back to me by four o'clock, we'll run it nationally."

If I can get it to you by then? Jillian thinks. *I will move mountains . . .*

"And, if you're interested, I'd love to try you out as a stringer on a regular basis. Your eyes and ears are very strong."

At 4:01 p.m., with the achy euphoria of a marathoner at the finish line, Jillian collapses onto the throw pillows she and her mother purchased at Bed, Bath, and Beyond. *I guess we were destined to meet after all,* she thinks as she closes her eyes and envisions Rudy. *Fate, indeed, brought us together, just not for the reason I expected.*

12

April

THEN

U ntil this moment, April has never pondered the difference between "murder" and "manslaughter." But as she sits in the DeFrancos' living room, staring at the newspapers fanned on their coffee table featuring Rudy's mug shot, the distinction has never been so important.

Across from her on a Queen Anne chair is Rudy's defense attorney, Richard Cossofski, whose liver-spotted knuckles and silver combover remind April of her late grandfather. The De-Francos, Zagodas, and Cossofski are crammed into the apartment to discuss Rudy's options: go to trial or accept a plea bargain that Cossofski anticipates will be made by the Manhattan DA's office at any moment.

"That Sketcher guy is a real cowboy, and the reporters are the cattle he's corralled," Cossofski opines. "He's shouting murder from the rooftops, and even convinced the grand jury to indict Rudy on murder and manslaughter in the second degree, but Sketcher knows

damn well this isn't a murder case. Man 2, maybe. But not murder."
Cossofski reaches a hand into the breast pocket of his ivory button-
down shirt and pulls out a cough drop.

"What's the difference?" April asks. So many unfamiliar legal
terms are being thrown around it's dizzying.

"Murder is premeditated—there is an intent to kill. Manslaughter two is different; it lacks the malice. As we all know,
Rudy didn't plan this crime. He had no scheme, no intent. That
prosecutor? Sketcher? Believe me, he knows that. It's all part of
gaming the system. They overcharge the defendant, grandstand
to the press, and then negotiate with us for a sentence that's less
severe than the original charges, but more than the defendant
probably deserves." Cossofski untwists the lozenge's paper wrapping and pops it into his mouth.

"Why are they publishing these lies about my baby?" Lorraine
asks, weeping as she reclines on the couch in her white terrycloth
robe. Rudy, seated beside her, plucks a tissue from a nearby box and
dabs his mother's cheeks.

"Come on, Ma, you know the answer," Tommy says, eyeing the
stack of tabloids he picked up at the corner bodega earlier that
morning. "They're gossip rags. Sensationalized junk to get people to
fork over cash. It's a business. When you get a prosecutor standing
in front of a courthouse spewing this crap, they think there's no
need to fact-check him. They're hearing it from the horse's mouth."

"Did you see that quote in the *Brooklyn Eagle* from Mrs. Brown
in 2A?" Lorraine cries. "She says, 'He was always a good kid.' Can
you believe it? She said *was*! He *is* a great kid! And then she tells
them we're a nice, hardworking family and how you just never know
what people are really like behind closed doors." Lorraine sits up
and crunches her fingers around the piping of a throw pillow.
"There are no goddamn closed doors around here! This is who we
are! We ain't hiding nothing! There ain't no cover! We're good

people! We take care of people! My husband is the goddamn Super Super! And Rudy is his best helper! You know how many times my son has plunged her toilet and unclogged her goddamn bathtub drain, pulling out nasty fistfuls of her gray hair? Has he ever complained, even once? No! God as my witness, this boy, this beautiful, beautiful boy, is not a murderer . . ." Her voice breaks. "There is no one better! You find me a better child, a better friend, a better brother."

If she didn't know better, April would swear she'd scored front-row seats to a play or one of those experiential performances where actors mingle with audience members. Never has her life felt this surreal.

"Shhh . . . It's okay, Ma, it's okay," Rudy says, wrapping his arms around Lorraine. "I'm gonna be okay. Don't you worry."

Rudy's stoicism is shattering. Barbara dabs the corners of her eyes with a crumpled tissue and the staccato of men clearing their throats sounds across the room. As April shifts in her seat to distract herself from what she knows will be an ugly cry, she suddenly feels sore from head to toe. Her muscles ache like never before, yet she's done no heavy lifting.

"It's my fault!" Tommy suddenly cries out, hands shooting above his head. "It's all my fault. I never shoulda let you buy that friggin' knife. I wasn't thinking. If I hadn't been so fired up that day, we wouldn't be here. I fucked it all up. You were just a kid following your big brother who was supposed to do the right thing and set the example. I should be the one paying the price, not you." Tommy's lower lip begins to quiver.

You're wrong, April thinks. *You may have inspired the knife, Tommy, but I'm the one who pushed Rudy to go to the party.*

"Listen," Cossofski interjects, glancing at his wristwatch and then squinting at the wall clock to double-check the time. "Sometimes shit happens and there's no one to blame. Whatcha gonna do . . ."

April is surprised by both his cussing and his casual tell-me-something-I-don't-know manner. *Is that unprofessional or is he simply too old to care what comes out of his mouth?*

Just then, Cossofski's cell phone rings. "Okay gang, it's Sketcher. I'm going to take this outside in the hall. Be back shortly." His knees crack loudly as he rises from the couch.

The room grows quiet and somber as Cossofski steps into the corridor by the elevator bank to negotiate Rudy's fate. With its harsh fluorescent lighting, brown metal doors, and chipped taupe walls that could pass for a relief map thanks to eons of layered paint, the cold antechamber feels like the antithesis of what it is— an artery to a warm family home.

"I think you should eat something, Lorraine," Barbara says softly, breaking the silence.

Lorraine sniffles. "You think I can eat at a time like this?"

"Well, at least drink something. Stay hydrated."

"I'll get you some water, Lorraine," April offers. The tension in the room is unsettling; it's impossible to sit still, she needs to move, especially given the stiffness in her muscles.

As she fills a glass for Lorraine in the kitchen, April notices the space is a complete mess. Dishes are piled high in the sink, countertops are covered in crumbs, and when she pokes her head inside the fridge, it smells of spoiled produce. After a quick sniff around she discovers the culprits—moldy lemons and an old onion—which she discards immediately. She then tidies up, fills a garbage bag to the brim, and lugs it out a special service entrance door in the kitchen that leads to a trash chute. While stuffing the bag down the compactor, April hears Cossofski's and Sketcher's voices echoing out in the hallway. Cossofski must have put the call on speaker. She gently closes the trash door so it doesn't creak and crouches down to sit on a nearby stairwell step.

"You've got no case! The grand jury was a slam dunk," Sketcher crows. "The autopsy may be pending but we don't need a medical examiner's report to know the facts. There was a fight. Your guy pulled a knife. There was blood. My guy was taken to the hospital and your guy fled the crime scene with the weapon he admits was his. How much more evidence do you need? DeFranco should be away for murder. And if you don't think there is a chance at a murder conviction, certainly you must acknowledge this was Man 2."

"As you say, the medical report is still pending."

"Listen Pops, I've got a former pediatric—pediatric!—heart transplant patient here. A freaking society family from Westchester. And a charitable one, no less. It was the fastest grand jury indictment I've ever seen. You know as well as I do you didn't put DeFranco or Zagoda in front of the grand jury for a reason. It's because you know that even if you had a medical report, you wouldn't have a chance in hell of winning."

Hearing her own name quickens April's pulse.

"And speaking of April Zagoda," Sketcher's nasal voice is loud and clear, "as you know, the cops interviewed her as an eyewitness. I've got the notes right here. She picked up the knife from the floor, put it in her purse, fled the scene of the crime, and cleaned it. I mean, come on. If that's not tampering, you tell me what is!"

Oh my God! I'm screwed too! April's torso instinctively lurches forward; her arms protectively wrap themselves around her legs and her mouth presses against her kneecaps. She has formed an upright fetal position.

"You kidding me?" Cossofski sounds irate.

"Hey, people swallow joints all the time and they get charged with tampering . . ."

"First of all, Zagoda picked it up because the knife could have hurt someone if it remained on the floor *and* she knew it belonged to DeFranco. That's why she took it from the scene. And by the way, she handed the knife over to the cops without incident when they found it at her home. She didn't conceal anything and was fully cooperative. Where are you going with this?"

Sketcher is quiet. "I'll tell you what," he finally says as if he's about to propose the deal of a century and do Cossofski a favor. "If we tack on a count of tampering with physical evidence to DeFranco, I'll look the other way with Zagoda."

He wants Rudy to take the fall for me? Oh my God, how did we get here?!

"'Look the other way?' What on Earth are you talking about? She did nothing wrong!"

"I'm offering your client a plea. I'll drop the murder count, if he pleads to Man 2 *plus* tampering."

"Ah, I see." Cossofski laughs. "If you can't get *her* on tampering, you're gonna go after *him* even though he had absolutely nothing to do with picking that knife up off the floor? Where did you go to law school? I'll make sure my granddaughter takes it off her application list."

"Hey, listen, I'm happy to go to trial for murder," Sketcher ignores Cossofski's dig. "As I said, I don't need the pending autopsy and neither do you. I got a blade, a wound, a bunch of blood, a death, and a defendant who fled the scene. How are things looking on your end, Pops?"

What an asshole! April thinks, utterly aghast.

Cossofski clears his throat. "Listen, kid," he says calmly. "I know you're new on the job. What is it, about a month now under your belt at the DA's office? I've got a few decades on you. You're over your skis on this. I'm going to give you the rookie benefit of the doubt here and offer you a chance to start this conversation over."

Sketcher doesn't skip a beat. "I'm happy to go to trial."

Cossofski lets out a long, frustrated sigh. "I've got a guy with no priors here. A good kid with lots of references who will vouch for him. He did not *flee* the scene, as you say. DeFranco and Zagoda both claim in their *individual, separate* interviews with police that Jameson was an aggressive drunk who started the altercation. Whatever action taken on DeFranco's part was self-defense, and when there was an opening to leave and go home, Zagoda and DeFranco took it. In my view, that was self-preservation, not fleeing a crime scene."

"You got any witnesses who can support this?" Sketcher sneers.

"You know as well as I do there are no other eyewitnesses. They were in a secluded area of the venue."

"I rest my case."

The long pause in conversation is worrisome. April buries her face in her hands. *What is happening? Say something, Cossofski! Do something!*

Finally, Cossofski clears his throat. "Make me your best offer, Mr. Sketcher," he says flatly.

"I knew you'd come to your senses," Sketcher gloats.

April can hear the flipping of pages. It must be Sketcher because she knows Cossofski walked into the hallway with nothing but his cell phone.

"Alright. Forget the tampering. Forget Zagoda. I'll drop the murder count," Sketcher says definitively. "But DeFranco's going to have to plead to Man 2 or we go to trial. Final offer. Pick your poison. I'll give you two weeks to decide and then I rescind the offer."

"I'll speak with my client. We'll get back to you."

The sense of relief regarding her own acquittal lasts but a moment. April is immediately engulfed by guilt for the brief respite of joy. *I don't understand . . . Of the two of us, didn't I make the bigger mistake? I washed blood off the knife. I put our clothing in the laundry—maybe that could have somehow helped Rudy's defense? All Rudy did was hold a stupid little blade as a scare tactic to protect me! He didn't stab anyone! Yeah, Bailey died and that's awful, but it's not Rudy's fault. They should forget about both of us, but if anyone is in trouble here, shouldn't it be me for tampering?*

The distinct high-pitched creak of the DeFrancos' front door sounds, which she knows means Cossofski is returning to the apartment. April scoots back into the kitchen where she notices the water glass she'd intended to bring to Lorraine ten minutes earlier. *Shit!* She grabs it off the counter, takes a few sips, and fills a fresh tumbler with ice for Lorraine. When she returns to her seat in the living room, Barbara shoots a look at her daughter as if to say, *Where have you been?*

"Okay. So as it stands now," Cossofski begins, returning to his spot on the sofa. "Option one is we go to trial and hope the jury hasn't seen these headlines or bought into the DA's bullshit caricature of the Brooklyn thug versus the suburban prince. I'm sorry if that's crude or offensive to anyone, but I'm just telling it like it is. If we go to trial, Rudy will be charged with murder . . ."

Lorraine whimpers softly at the mention of the word.

Cossofski glances up at her but carries on. "Option two, we take the plea the DA is offering. Rudy'll still be charged with murder, they can't change the charge, but they can drop the top count which is murder if he pleads guilty to manslaughter in the second degree."

"Why wouldn't we go to trial?" Tommy asks. "He's not guilty. I mean, this was self-defense! The guy came at Rudy! Rudy said it, April saw it. I get that a trial is risky, but I kind of feel he deserves his day in court. You know, that whole 'the truth will set you free' thing. Jury of your peers and whatnot. I didn't think justice was a negotiation."

"Absolutely. He's undoubtedly entitled to his day in court. Self-defense is what we got in our corner. And listen, if we go to trial, I'll argue the heck out of it, but the fact that the grand jury wasn't having it doesn't bode well for how it would play out in a courtroom. I know this isn't easy, but we need to take into consideration what could happen if we pass on the plea bargain. I'm just trying to be real here. This isn't a case where a defendant is saying, 'It's not me.' Rudy admits he was there. The knife that cut the victim belonged to Rudy. He says he opened the blade. Whether or not he *intended* to use it as a weapon . . ." Cossofski shrugs, "it's still a weapon. These are indisputable, established facts that don't work in our favor. I have colleagues that would simply tell you what to do and walk away if you didn't follow their advice. I'm not going to do that, but I'm going to give it to you straight."

April swallows hard. Her head is still woozy.

"Here we go: If Rudy takes the plea and admits he's guilty of manslaughter in the second degree, he'll be looking at up to fifteen years. Hopefully less given he's a first-time offender and will probably have good behavior, but I can't promise it will be less than fifteen. If he gambles with a trial and is convicted of murder, he's looking at significantly more time."

"How much more?" Tommy asks.

April lowers her eyelids, bracing for the answer.

"Could be life," Cossofski says matter-of-factly.

"What?" Lorraine screams. "You're his lawyer! Fix this! Is this a joke?"

April pinches the bridge of her nose. *I need a pound of Advil.*

"I'm doing my best, Mrs. DeFranco," Cossofski says. "But I need to be honest with you. If Rudy chooses to go to trial, yes, in theory the jury could believe his version of what happened and find him not guilty, but there is a good chance, a very good chance, they won't and he could face decades in prison. In a trial, a carefully worded question during cross examination or a passionately delivered summation by the DA can be like kryptonite with a jury. Even if the DA says grandiose things that get overruled or stricken from the record by the judge, once the words are uttered they can be like little droplets of poison that seep into the minds of the twelve people in that jury box."

"What about the medical examiner's report? Why don't we wait for that?" Tommy asks.

"I can subpoena it, but it will take some time. And while I can't promise, I don't think it will win us any points in the end. The victim was a heart transplant patient. The sympathy card can't be ignored here. I've been around the block a few times and I can tell you, based on decades of experience, this isn't a pretty picture for us. I'm here if you want to throw it all against the wall, but . . ." he shakes his head, "even if we wait for the autopsy and go to trial for the chance of a win, this can take years—years of feeling like you're riding a raft in class-five rapids with no guarantee you won't drown in the end. And, there is a ticking clock on the DA's plea offer. You've got two weeks to decide and if you don't take it, we go to trial."

"So what are you saying?" Tommy huffs.

"What I'm saying," Cossofski looks thoughtfully at the ceiling fan for a few beats before shifting his gaze to Rudy, "is I need to know if you're a gambling man. I need to know how patient you are. I need to know if you're willing to wait months or even years living in limbo before going up against a cowboy in a courtroom that will be packed with a family that looks as pure as if they just walked off the Mayflower. Or, if you'd prefer to swallow your medicine now and get this all behind you sooner rather than later."

Except for the intermittent shouts of "Tag, you're it!" coming through the screen window from children playing outside on the sidewalk, the room is still. April's eyes moisten remembering when she and Rudy were those kids.

"I think maybe we fight this . . ." Barbara says softly, wringing her hands.

Tommy nods his head, but then Eddie abruptly rises from his seat.

"I would like to speak with my son," he announces softly but assuredly. His chin is high, shoulders thrown back.

Rudy promptly releases his arms from around his mother and follows his father out the front door of the apartment.

The following week, while checking her campus mailbox in the student center, April notices a thin envelope with *Office of President, Rivington University* on the return address. She rips it open immediately.

> *Dear Ms. Zagoda,*
>
> *I hope this message finds you well. I am aware of the unfortunate experience that recently occurred and would like to invite you to meet in my office this Friday at noon. Please call to confirm the appointment with my assistant. I look forward to seeing you.*
>
> *Sincerely,*
> *Daniel Cole, PhD*

He's just covering his ass, she thinks. She can't imagine the president of a university truly cares how she's feeling. *It's optics*, she tells herself. *He needs to make an effort, at least on the record, to express sympathy.*

Two days later, April is seated on a tufted cabernet-colored leather couch in the reception area outside Cole's office. Her arms involuntarily wrap themselves around her stomach as she waits.

"Ms. Zagoda," Dr. Cole says flatly when he finally opens a heavy wooden door. His navy pinstriped suit, royal blue tie and polished lace-ups fit perfectly with the decor. "Please, come in."

He turns to enter the room, and she follows. The mahogany paneling, marble busts, and brocade drapes make her feel small and scared.

"Ms. Zagoda, I'd like you to meet Mrs. Bass, our legal counsel, and Mr. Greystone, head of the board of trustees," he says as they approach a glistening rectangular wooden table. Each person has a folder, legal pad, and fountain pen symmetrically arranged in front of them as if it were a place setting at Buckingham Palace. April doesn't register either of their names; she is too shaken by the nearly identical way each one flashes a quick toothless grin and then averts their eyes. It's as if they are clones and there's a mastermind standing behind one of the hideous window treatments pressing a button that turns their faces on and off.

"Here, please take a seat." Cole points to a nail-head trim armchair at the head of the table. He then saunters over to a bar cart along the wall, reaches for an intricately cut crystal water pitcher, and fills a drinking glass designed with the same diamond-shaped pattern. "Well, Ms. Zagoda, let me start by saying we are deeply saddened to learn of what occurred last week in New York City. So very unfortunate on so many levels." He places the glass in front of her, walks the length of the table, and sits down to face her at the opposite end. "How are you feeling in the wake of all of this?" he asks, tilting his head sympathetically.

April takes a sip. She has no idea how to answer that question. "I'd say it has been a pretty surreal week."

"I have no doubt. No doubt at all."

The room is eerily still. *This is creepy.* April glances at the nearby grandfather clock. *I hope this doesn't take long.*

"Ms. Zagoda, we want you to know that given the circumstances, it would be fully understandable if you need to take some time off from your studies. An extended period to regroup and reflect would not be unreasonable."

April looks around the table. The man and woman are staring blankly at their notepads. "Oh, no, that's okay. I think staying at school and focusing on my work is probably what I need most right now. Normalcy. Staying on track. Keeping busy."

"Mmm." Cole nods. "Ms. Zagoda," he says slowly. He seems to be choosing his words judiciously. "What you experienced is a *trowww-ma*. I'm sure you are aware."

The way he slowly draws out the word trauma sounds deliberately pretentious. She's never heard anyone pronounce it any way other than rhyming with *drama*.

"And with trowww-ma, sometimes it's best, if gifted the opportunity, to take time to heal."

"I appreciate that, sir. Thank you. I'm open to speaking with the counseling office on campus. If you have the name of someone specific there you could recommend . . ."

"Yes, we do have a very strong counseling center. But have you considered devoting your time, perhaps at home, to processing and reflecting? As I said, we would be fully supportive."

April squints her eyes. *Reflecting? What does that mean? And why isn't he hearing me?*

"Thank you. I really do appreciate that. But again, I think staying on campus is the best choice for me right now. Emotionally."

"If I may," interjects the lawyer. "I think what Dr. Cole is trying to express, Ms. Zagoda, is that it may behoove you to take some time off." She has a sweet kindergarten teacher voice and enunciates clearly as if April is dense.

"Yes, I understand. Thank you. But I'd prefer to stay," April says, forcing a smile.

Bass straightens her posture beneath her white silk blouse. "April, dear, how do I say this . . ." She glances over at Dr. Cole, who nods. "We are encouraging you to take a leave of absence. Full time." There is both pity and calculation in her eyes.

Leave of absence?! "Yes, I understand this is an extraordinary circumstance and I will likely be processing this *trauma* for years to come, but I want to be here. At school. Please. I will schedule regular therapy sessions with the counseling office. I promise I will do whatever it takes. I need the distraction. I can't be home right now."

Both Bass and Greystone raise their eyebrows at Cole, clearly signaling a cue.

"Ms. Zagoda," Cole says, pausing to let out a sigh, "we have come to the unanimous decision that it would be in the best interest of our school at this juncture if you were to take an indefinite leave."

It is almost as if April can hear the shoe drop from the ceiling's dentil molding and come crashing down on the Persian rug beneath her feet. "I'm sorry, are you kicking me out?" she asks, her voice cracking. She's unsure if her disbelief will erupt in the form of laughter or tears.

The room's silence is confirmation.

"You're kicking me out," April states definitively, as if she needs to hear herself say the words. A wave of heat spreads over the entirety of her body. Her breath feels like fire and her cheeks are hot to the touch.

"Suspension until further investigation seems to be the most appropriate response at this time," Cole says dryly.

April stares directly at him as she takes a few demure sips of water to cool down. "I don't understand," she says, surprised at the words that have just emerged from her mouth. Normally, she would simply accept a decree from an authority figure, but in this moment, she is feeling uncharacteristically emboldened. "I'm suspended? Are you saying I'm guilty until proven innocent even though I've done nothing wrong?"

Cole taps the head of his pen on the table. "It's quite complex, really. I'm sure you can appreciate that."

April looks up to the ceiling to prevent the tears pooling in her eyes from spilling onto her lashes. "What happened was tragic, but I'm not sure why I am being punished."

"Ms. Zagoda, our university has a firm policy of not condoning violence of any kind."

"Rudy was protecting *me* from potential violence." Her voice is now trembling. "He saw an inebriated man getting too close to me, so he stepped in. That's the extent of *my* involvement. I would think you'd be grateful someone tried to help one of your students."

There are glances around the table.

"With all due respect," Cole says, "that is not the extent of your involvement."

"I'm sorry. I don't follow." She can feel sweat dripping like a loose faucet beneath her arms.

"Our discretionary fund paid for the newspaper club to attend the conference in New York City, which means the entirety of the weekend fell under the rubric of a school event, not a personal vacation. You were not at liberty to invite any member of the public to the networking event."

"I did *not* invite Rudy to the networking event. In fact, I was very deliberate in telling him to arrive *after* the private event ended and to join me in the public space downstairs where everyone was hanging out . . ."

"At a bar," Mrs. Bass interjects with an expansive Cheshire cat grin.

"Well, it was a lounge section of the restaurant and there was a bar there. Regardless, it was a public space. Rudy arrived after the private newspaper event ended. And by the way, Keith Jameson did the same with his brother."

"Bailey Jameson is a graduate of this university," Cole snips. "Mr. DeFranco has no affiliation . . ."

"How old are you, dear?" Mrs. Bass cuts in before April can get a word in.

"Nineteen."

"Are you aware of the legal age to consume alcohol in the state of New York?"

"Yes, twenty-one."

"Were you consuming alcohol, Ms. Zagoda? Why were you at a bar?"

What the hell is going on? She may as well be on a witness stand in this kangaroo court. "I was drinking ginger ale. I swear."

April can hear Greystone snicker.

"It's true! I hadn't eaten at the networking event and needed something calm on my stomach." Her heartbeat quickens. "Also, this whole evening was organized by the newspaper club. I didn't choose the venue for the networking party. They did. And, as you mentioned earlier, this school paid for me to attend. I went where I was instructed to go."

"Yes, dear. We were delighted to cover the cost for you and the rest of the club and are very pleased you were able to enjoy it," she says. "But when that gathering ended, on your own volition, you relocated to a bar."

"We *all* did! Everyone just moved downstairs once the private party ended."

"Not *everyone* was there, dear. Your faculty advisor returned to the hotel when the event ended."

"I was never told I had to leave."

"You are a representative of our school and underage drinking is illegal."

"Again, I wasn't drinking. I'm getting the feeling that you think I did something wrong. Please tell me what I did. I'm really, honestly, at a loss here . . ."

There is a lengthy pause before Cole says, "Ms. Zagoda," his voice is deeper now, more commanding, "the board of trustees has convened, we have consulted with our legal team and come to a unanimous decision that your enrollment at Rivington is suspended until further notice. We encourage you to withdraw to tend to personal matters at this juncture. Reflect on your actions."

There it is again. Reflect on my actions?

"We are generously giving you an opportunity to save face, Ms. Zagoda . . ."

Save face?!

"But if you decline this offer, we will have no recourse other than to issue an official statement announcing your suspension."

This is completely illogical, she fumes internally, but is confident that screaming *bull shit!* or *I'll see you in court!* would be completely futile. They've made their decision, and she knows she lacks the emotional energy as well as the finances to sue a behemoth like Rivington.

"Final exams are almost here. Can I just take them and get credit for the year?" It's a Hail Mary pass, but she's got nothing to lose.

"This is effective immediately. Your transcript and credits will accurately reflect the work you have done up until this point in time. You have the weekend to collect your belongings."

April takes a long sip of water. *Here it is,* she thinks. *This is the proof. I was right. I am to blame and this is my sentence. Rudy will be caged, and I will be released.*

Suddenly, her lap is saturated. She checks the glass of water for a leak but is surprised to see no liquid has spilled. A warm trickle travels down her leg from thigh to ankle. It is at this moment she realizes she has wet herself.

With nothing left to say, April reaches into her backpack and removes the compact rain poncho she had bought earlier in the year at the campus bookstore. She stealthily ties it around the waist of her pants before anyone notices the mess. She thinks back to Rudy's father in the living room, and the dignified way he held his head high when they met to strategize Rudy's defense earlier in the week.

"I am not a gambling man, Mr. Cossofski," Eddie DeFranco had said softly but steadily when he returned from the hallway holding Rudy's hand. "I need my son. I'm not getting any younger. Better I should have him home in fifteen years than in fifty. He will take the plea. No trial. We can't risk it. But for the record, for whatever that's worth, this haggling between lawyers is a sham. This isn't the 'liberty and justice for all' that my family came to this country for. We'll play your game if it means he will come home sooner, but my son did not kill that man."

Channeling Eddie DeFranco, April lifts her chin. "Thank you, Dr. Cole," she states graciously, kowtowing to yet another injustice. She then rises to her feet, smooths out the poncho for maximum pant coverage, and walks out the large wooden doors to the quad where she makes a beeline for the nearest restroom.

13

April

THEN

Originally, April's plan for sophomore year had been to rush a sorority. Instead, she is spending her second year of college with ex-cons.

Had she not been kicked out at the end of her freshman year, she would have ultimately needed to take a leave of absence. Of this she is certain. Frat parties and semi-formals lose their luster once your best friend is arrested in front of your mother's china cabinet. There's no turning back after something like that.

Instead of writing her final freshman term paper at a cubicle in the packed college library, she sat alone in her childhood bedroom crafting a ten-page letter to the sentencing judge attesting to Rudy's stellar character and begging for leniency. On the day her classmates packed up their dorm rooms and moved out for summer break, she spent the afternoon in a Manhattan courtroom watching Rudy—clad in his father's best suit—stand before a judge and admit guilt as part of the plea bargain with the prosecutor. If that wasn't soul crushing enough, he then got a venomous verbal lashing from the Jameson family as they read a victim impact statement in court referring to Rudy as a "raging monster" and how his imprisonment would "never feel like justice, but will at least provide some solace knowing he will not be able to destroy another family." It took every bit of willpower April could muster not to kick and scream from her spot on a courtroom pew.

But what hurt the most—more than the Jamesons' statement and more than the pounding of the judge's gavel, which reverberated through her body like an electrical current—were the brief seconds at the conclusion of the plea. Shortly before Rudy was whisked away, he quickly turned toward the audience and locked eyes with her. She watched as his lips curled inward as if he were biting down on the flesh inside his mouth, and how his big brown irises had turned glossy. Not once in this entire debacle had he seemed this unmoored.

"I love you," she mouthed and blew a kiss with the tips of her fingers.

He furtively tugged on his earlobe, employing their secret "let's get outta here" signal. This time, however, there was no escape. The guard reached for Rudy's arms, cuffed his wrists, and in seconds he was gone. Their covert code had been transmitted and received, but his cry for help went unanswered.

I failed to save him, was all she could think as she sat in the pew, too numb to cry. As the reporters, prosecutors, and Jameson family filed out of the courtroom, her mind returned to the day she and Rudy met on the Avenue L playground. *We'll go down together, I'll wait for you* were the exact words she'd said from atop the metal slide. Her promise became the foundation of their friendship as well as the invisible, invincible cord connecting them—a cord that extended between his apartment and her house, then stretched to

Rivington University, and would now reach all the way to a prison in upstate New York.

And it was then, as she slowly rose from her seat and stepped forward into this new chapter, that April made another promise—this time to herself. *We may not be going down together right now, but I will wait for you.*

"I'll never abandon you, Rud," she whispered aloud as she headed toward the courtroom exit. "And I'll be the first in line to welcome you home."

Now, just months later, April's life seems wholly foreign to the one she once lived. Each day, instead of strolling up a grassy hill to calculus class or meeting friends for Taco Tuesday dinner in the cafeteria, she drives Big Bertha to a nondescript red brick building in an industrial section of Queens dotted with car repair shops and adult video stores. There is steel construction scaffolding outside the entrance and a small square placard with *The Prentice League* beside the glass front door. Finding a parking spot on the weekends is easy when the neighborhood is barren, but congested weekdays are a challenge and she often parks in a garage, justifying the fees by telling herself it's a fraction of the cost she paid to attend a private college, live on campus, and enroll in a meal plan.

April's schedule is set in stone. Monday through Friday mornings she takes courses at Brooklyn College and by the early afternoon she is tutoring math, reading, writing, or job interview skills in one of the whitewashed cinderblock classrooms at the League. Saturdays and Sundays she is there, without fail, by 10 a.m. *If Rudy's time is regimented*, she thinks, *then mine will be too.* Plus, she has no interest in socializing.

Volunteering at an organization that helps recently released prisoners integrate back into society had been April's idea. After

Rudy's sentencing, she spent much of her days and nights thinking about how he would while away his time. She would look at the clock and wonder, *Is he eating lunch? Taking a shower? Reading a book from the prison library?* She feared minutes would turn into months and eventually he would fall so far behind academically he'd lack any motivation to stay on track for a college degree. As an education major, April had long planned to devote her career to teaching children and setting them up for success. But what about Rudy's success? How could she help him visualize a promising future and work toward the day when he would be an employable, educated, free man?

Shortly after his sentencing, April came up with an idea. Each week she'd use the Xerox machine in her father's home office to photocopy her most intriguing school assignments. Any reading material she thought Rudy might enjoy she'd stick in an envelope and send to him. If he wrote back, perhaps he would ask questions and they could create a study group, albeit in a pen pal format. In fact, when she proposed the idea to Rudy in a letter, she put a smiley face next to the word *pen*. She hoped her pathetic pun might elicit a tiny grin.

The second part of her plan was to figure out what life would eventually look like for Rudy after release. If she could get a lay of the land now, if she could see for herself the challenges he might eventually face upon reintegration, she could find a way to get him ahead of the curve so he'd be prepared to hit the ground running. April called up Cossofski and asked if he knew of any programs where she could volunteer her time. And that's how she discovered The Prentice League.

Until now, April had never heard the terms "holistic services program" or "halfway house," let alone given an iota of thought to the struggles of life post-incarceration. But as soon as she arrived for her interview, she could literally feel her eyes widen. As she rode the elevator to the director's office wearing her favorite pink houndstooth skirt and a leather tote dangling from her shoulder, she wondered why the two men standing beside her had bulky devices protruding from the bottoms of their pants. When they exited together onto the third floor, she overheard a receptionist direct the men to a room for ankle bracelet monitoring. Then, as she proceeded down the linoleum hallway to her interview, she passed a room where a woman was organizing piles of clothing onto racks labeled "suits," "dresses," "tops," "pants," "jackets," and "shoes." When she poked her head inside, the "boutique manager" explained that these donated items help clients who can't afford appropriate work clothes. *Brilliant!* April thought as she continued down the corridor. She hadn't been there more than a few minutes and already her world had expanded. If they'd have her, she'd give them all the time she had to offer.

Over the last several months, April has become a fixture at the League and a beloved tutor in the education department. Some days she teaches basic literacy. Other days she prepares clients for their High School Equivalency diplomas or college entrance exams. And then there are times when she finds herself acting more of a quasi-therapist—helping to foster confidence and allay test-taking anxiety while working to improve standardized test scores.

On the Friday after Thanksgiving, as she sifts through her desk drawer in search of a paper clip, there is a knock on her office door.

"Good day, ma'am. Sorry to disturb you. Are you Ms. Zagoda?" asks a svelte, soft-spoken older gentleman, hands clasped in front of him.

April guesses he is in his late sixties, early seventies. He has high cheekbones, a receding hairline, and eyes the color of mocha.

"Hello," she smiles. "Please, come in."

"Thank you, ma'am. My name is Hollicott P. Bradley. Pleasure to meet you." He's wearing frayed slacks and his tweed overcoat has weathered brown suede elbow patches. Despite the sleeves being too short for his lanky arms, there is an elegance to this man.

April points to a nearby folding chair. "Please make yourself comfortable, Mr. Bradley. Are you new to the League?"

"I am." He nods. "Just released on Wednesday."

"Congratulations. Well that must have been quite a Thanksgiving gift."

"Indeed. Yes, indeed."

"How can I help you, sir? I haven't received your file just yet so I apologize, I'm not familiar with your case."

"Oh, there's not much to tell, really. Made some mistakes. I used. I sold. Did my time. What can I say? Now I'm here." His cadence is matter-of-fact, yet gentle. "I just asked a lady down the hall where I could find someone to explain this." He reaches into the inner pocket of his blazer, removes a folded piece of white paper, and hands it to April. "She told me to see you."

April unfurls the paper. It is a photocopy of Rudyard Kipling's poem, "If."

"Someone gave it to me while I was away and I kept it on the wall beside my cot all these years. I've stared at it every day. Memorized it. I can recite every word standing on one foot, but I don't get it. I need someone to translate it."

"I would love to," April says sweetly. She knows this poem well from Honors English class in twelfth grade. "In fact, I have some notes on it at home. I'll bring them in and show you."

His eyes crinkle into little half-moons.

"If you like, I can give you a preview now," she offers and repositions her chair next to Mr. Bradley's so they can read the lines together. "Basically, Kipling is talking a lot about stoicism and rising above adversity. Here," she points to the top of the page, "if you take a look at this first part, he writes about keeping a level head and trusting yourself in times of trouble."

"Mmm. Yes."

"Then, later on, he says you've got to be able to endure things like hearing your words get twisted and things getting broken, but you must find a way to pick yourself up and start again."

"Oh, mercy, don't I know it."

April waits a beat, hoping he might elaborate, but when it's clear he has nothing more to share, she says excitedly, "So here's a great section." She points to the verse:

If you can fill the unforgiving minute
With sixty seconds' worth of distance run,
Yours is the Earth and everything that's in it,
And—which is more—you'll be a Man, my son!

"Want to take a guess at the meaning?"

He stares at the page and shrugs. "Something to do with life being like a marathon."

"Yes, good! Maybe Kipling's saying if we can stay positive, be kind, bounce back, and never take a moment for granted—we will succeed? What do you think?"

Mr. Bradley places his hand over his heart as if he is about to recite the Pledge of Allegiance. "Thank you," he says tenderly. "I think that sounds about right."

"My pleasure." April folds the sheet along its creases. "If you don't mind me asking, who gave you this poem?"

"A librarian . . . he retired a few years ago and gave it to me the day he left . . . where I was."

April has come to appreciate the breadth of reactions to prison life among those recently released. Some openly acknowledge where they have been, almost wearing incarceration as a badge of street cred. Others are eager to distance themselves as soon as possible, struggling to even utter the word "prison," as if the blemish will cease to exist if they can erase the word from their vocabulary. It's too soon for April to determine where Mr. Bradley lies on that spectrum. With only forty-eight hours of freedom under his belt, she suspects he may still be trying to parse it out himself.

"Well, I must be going now," he says, carefully sliding the paper inside the pocket of his lapel.

"Please come by again soon. We can study anything you like. Or just chat." It's people like Mr. Bradley who enable April to see a silver lining in the sharp left turn of her life. When she gets a moment like this—to teach and connect—it means she has managed to find fulfilment, rather than fault, in the justice system. It's a kernel of glory in this complex and layered present.

"'Preciate it, ma'am," he says, lifting April's hand and lightly kissing her knuckles.

April isn't sure she's old enough to be referred to as *ma'am*, but she remains thoroughly charmed as he bows his head before leaving the room. Had he been wearing a fedora, she's confident he would have tipped it in her direction.

Over the following months, Mr. Bradley regularly stops by April's office and a routine is swiftly established. He raps lightly on her office door before entering, takes the same seat beside her desk, and they begin their sessions with a discussion of what she is learning in college. One by one, they run through her courses. He selects the subject order—history, English, psychology, Spanish, political science, etc.—and she fills him in. They talk about her professors and homework assignments, analyze literature, and dissect political theory. It's as if her classes are a delectable buffet and he is ravenous for the knowledge she's acquiring.

It doesn't take long for administrators at the League to notice their bond as well as the change they've made in each other's lives.

By the time the annual gala fundraiser rolls around, the dinner committee deliberately seats them together at a high-profile donor table so their connection is on full display.

On a warm spring evening before sunset, The Prentice League's formal gala is held in a massive loft space in Manhattan's Chelsea neighborhood. Floor-to-ceiling windows face westward over the Hudson River and the sounds of jazz hang in the air as investment bankers and corporate lawyers mingle with League staff. Photographers from all the society publications are in attendance—*Page Six, New York Magazine, The New York Times Sunday Styles Section*— snapping pictures of tuxedoed men and bejeweled women sipping champagne as city lights twinkle in the distance.

When the League's director takes to the podium and asks guests to find their seats, April zigzags through the crowd to locate her assigned table. As she nears, she notices Mr. Bradley has already arrived and is rearranging some items atop the white linen tablecloth.

"What'cha doin'?" she asks.

He winks mischievously at her. "Oh, nothin'," he says and excuses himself for the restroom.

April spots her name calligraphed on a small rectangle of folded cardstock near a salad plate and exchanges pleasantries with the woman on her right. Soon, the house lights dim, the room quiets, and as the director begins his opening remarks, a man in a suit and tie slips into the empty chair on April's left.

"Ooh! Just in time," he whispers to no one in particular.

"I'm sorry," April says quietly, "I believe that spot is taken." She would hate for Mr. Bradley to return from the restroom to find his seat occupied.

The man's thick but tidy eyebrows furrow and he reaches for his place card. "Looks like I'm right where I'm supposed to be," he says, handing it to April as proof. "But I'm happy to swap with someone else if you like."

April inspects the card, which reads: *Mr. Peter Nelson.*

Confused, she does a quick scan around the table and notices Mr. Bradley seated on the opposite side looking thoroughly tickled. A mischievous grin is sprawled across his face. Though he's too far to eavesdrop, he seems enraptured by her interaction with Peter as if he's watching an engrossing silent film. All that's missing is a bucket of popcorn in his lap. He tips his head forward toward April, just as he did that first day in her office. Back then though, it was a gesture of gratitude for her poetry lesson. This time, his message is indubitably: *You can thank me later.*

"No, no, that's okay," April says, returning her attention to the man beside her. "Looks like my friend has made other arrangements."

"I'm Peter," he whispers.

"I see." April smiles, glancing at his name in her hand. She then grabs her own place card and offers it to Peter. "I'm April." The words emerge from her mouth more flirtatiously than she intends.

He strokes the dark stubble on his cleft chin as he examines her card in his hand. "I see." He grins, a single dimple appearing on his cheek.

April can feel herself blush. She turns her head away and toward the stage where the director is teeing up a video about the history of The Prentice League. For the several minutes they sit quietly side-by-side, respectfully focusing their attention on the enormous projector screen above the stage. When the presentation ends and dinner is served, chatter around the ballroom swells and she can sense an awkward silence hanging in the air between them. Peter shifts in his chair to face April, but instead of sparking a conversation he is distracted by Mr. Bradley, who is walking toward them.

"Enjoying your evening?" Mr. Bradley asks ebulliently as his eyes dance back and forth between April and Peter. "I see you two have met."

"Yes, we have, my friend," Peter says.

"Wait, how do you two know each other?" April asks.

"Oh, we're old buddies," Peter says, winking at Mr. Bradley.

She detects sarcasm in his tone.

"This dashing gentleman and I met about a half hour ago in the coat-check line," Peter explains.

"Mmm . . . dashing," says Mr. Bradley proudly as he adjusts his bowtie. "I like the sound of that."

"And how are the two of you acquainted?" Peter asks.

Mr. Bradley clasps his hands together as if he is about to pray and positions them in front of his chest. "Ms. April here is the best teacher I have ever had."

"That's very kind," she says diffidently. "Well, Mr. Bradley is the best student I've ever had. He asks the most thoughtful questions." *Shift the conversation away from me. Focus on him. The last thing I want is to talk about why I'm here and involved with the organization.*

Mr. Bradley rests one hand on Peter's shoulder, the other on April's, and then raises his chin toward the crystal chandelier descending from the ceiling.

"'If you can fill the unforgiving minute with sixty seconds' worth of distance run, yours is the Earth and everything that's in it,'" he preaches as if he is standing at a pulpit in church. "Fill the minute, kids. Run the distance!" He pats their backs as if it is an exclamation mark at the conclusion of his sermon.

"Kipling." Peter smiles.

"Yes!" Mr. Bradley exclaims. "And this lovely lady can tell you all about it while I search for some mini hotdogs. Excuse me."

April and Peter watch in silence as Mr. Bradley strolls over to a young cocktail waitress halfway across the hall to make his request. She must either be confused or not comprehend what he is saying because he soon begins gesticulating to describe the appetizer. As he sticks his left index finger inside the loose fist he has formed with his right hand, it appears to April that he is making what could be construed as an obscene gesture to the young woman.

"Oh shit!" April gasps when the waitress hurriedly walks away from Mr. Bradley.

Peter and April spring up and head over to allay the situation, but before they reach Mr. Bradley, the waitress has already returned with a platter full of pigs-in-blankets.

Peter and April look at each other and break into laughter.

"You want to get some air?" Peter asks, pointing to an expansive outdoor patio.

"Sure," she grins.

"That Mr. Bradley seems like quite a guy," he remarks as they walk past an ice sculpture shaped like the Statue of Liberty.

"Yes, he certainly is," she marvels, now cognizant that Mr. Bradley's scheme to stealthily swap his own place card with Peter's had been the catalyst for this entire meet cute.

"So, you come here often?" Peter joshes, chivalrously holding the patio door open.

April emits a robust giggle and is instantly embarrassed as her response is heartier than Peter's inquiry warrants. "No, first time. How about you?" There is a chill in the evening air and she shivers, her bare arms suddenly sprouting goosebumps.

"You're cold, here, put this on." He removes his suit jacket and drapes it over her shoulders before she can decline.

Okay, she thinks, immediately warmed by both the fabric and its woodsy scent. *You have a choice to make. If you're not ready for new friends, you're certainly not ready to date. Even a guy as cute this one. You see where this is heading. Watch yourself.*

"So what's your connection to The Prentice League?" she asks. The words practically fly out of her mouth as if her subconscious has lost its patience with her self-imposed period of mourning and is decidedly taking charge.

"Oh, well, none so far," Peter says. "I'll be doing some pro bono work for them soon so my boss suggested I come here tonight, get to know the organization. He's on the board and had an extra ticket."

"Pro bono?" she asks. She has never heard the expression.

"Yeah, basically volunteering to do free legal work for them in my spare time."

"A lawyer with spare time. Huh."

He chuckles. "Minimal spare time. But I make room for the things that are important. I'd love to help out in person, but logistically it's a challenge. Reviewing documents is definitely not as fulfilling as face-to-face work, but it's something. What about you? How'd you get involved?"

Where to begin? There's no way, "Oh, you know, just trying to cleanse my soul and gain a little insight into what my incarcerated best friend is going through" will fly.

"Well," she pauses, choosing her words carefully. "It's not unlike your story, actually. I wanted to help, heard about the League, and now I tutor there."

"Cool. How often do you go in?" Peter asks.

"Every day. Some days I stay longer than others."

A waitress balancing a tray of egg rolls suddenly appears beside them. "Care for some?" she interrupts. April declines, but Peter spears one with a toothpick and dips it in duck sauce.

"How do you balance that with work?" he asks before taking a bite.

It suddenly occurs to April that Peter must think she is much older than her actual age.

"I'm still in school. I go after class."

"So it's an internship?"

April shakes her head. "Purely volunteer," she says, almost under her breath. She does not want to invite any more accolades.

"You're in school and you spend every day tutoring ex-cons?"

April isn't sure if Peter thinks she is the most bizarre woman he has ever met or if she is Mother Theresa, but either way, she is itching to change the subject. The small talk about her life and the ensuing praise are beginning to make her feel deeply vulnerable.

"So where are you from?" she asks, swiftly turning the tables.

"Boston. Newton, to be exact. It's a suburb just outside."

"How'd you end up in New York?"

"Oh, it's not very original or exciting. Pretty standard path. Went to college, then law school, decided I was destined to change the world," he puffs his chest facetiously, "took a summer internship at a firm in Manhattan, they offered me a job, I passed the bar exam, started working, blah, blah, blah. Anyway, you seem much more interesting. How'd you end up here?"

"Oh, it's not very original or exciting." She smiles coyly, mirroring his response. "Born and bred New Yorker." April notices Peter's sole dimple make an appearance again.

"You've never left?" he asks.

And here we go . . . Play it cool . . .

"Actually, I did leave for a little bit," she says cautiously, "but then I came back home."

He cocks his head. "So are you one of those people who personifies that *New Yorker* poster? You can't survive anywhere else because everything beyond the Hudson River is amorphous, unlivable, foreign terrain?"

"Guilty as charged!" she chirps, raising her hands as if she were being arrested. A sharp pain stings her chest. *Guilty as charged? Did I really just say that?*

Her sudden discomfort must be evident because a sobering look of concern washes away the flirtatious grin on Peter's face. "Is everything okay?" he asks. "Did I say something to upset you? I'm so sorry if I did."

"No, I'm sorry," she says somberly, her fingers delicately grazing the dark hairs on Peter's forearm. "It's just . . ." She scrambles for a viable excuse, anything other than the truth—that she feels like a horrid, selfish human being for enjoying her night on a gorgeous rooftop with twinkling little lights and lanterns while Rudy is alone behind bars. "It's just, uh, I've got a term paper to write," she lies. "It was really so nice to meet . . ."

"Stay," he insists. "It's only eight o'clock. How 'bout you stick around a little longer, but we make it productive? We can talk about your paper, discuss your thesis statement, organize your source list. I don't want to brag but I've got a talent for numbering footnotes. I could be very useful."

Gosh, he's adorable. She can feel herself softening. "Are you always this persuasive?"

"I was the moot court champion of Bigelow Middle School and Debate Club president at Newton High," he shrugs sheepishly. "I even dressed up as Atticus Finch for Halloween when I was ten."

"Really?" she smiles, imagining a younger version of Peter trick or treating as a defense attorney while his friends wore Smurf costumes. "*To Kill a Mockingbird* was my favorite book growing up."

"Same. It's the reason I applied to law school."

April is enchanted, just as she had been with that older boy who worked in the bagel shop when she and Rudy were kids. *Ugh, Rudy . . . What am I doing? This isn't fair.* "I'd better—"

"Stay," Peter cuts her off before she can say *go.* "You think you'd better stay. That's what you were about to say, right?" He grins. "So what's your paper about?"

"My paper? Oh, yes, um . . ." Staring up at Peter's chiseled face, she can't erase the image of Rudy in a prison cell. "I'm sorry," she finally says, defeatedly. Guilt has eroded her ability to remain present and keep up witty banter. "I really have to go."

Peter sighs disappointedly. "It's okay. I get it. I can't imagine you have much time for homework given how often you tutor. Can I at least walk you out?"

"Oh, you don't need to do that. There are some really amazing people at the League, you should meet them."

Peter gazes at her for a beat and then says, "I think I already have."

A cool breeze whips across the patio. She tightens Peter's jacket around her torso and catches another whiff of his musky scent from the lapel. The fragrance and fibers are cozy and inviting, beckoning her toward him, and yet, she remains frozen and mute, unable to reconcile the civil war between her head and her heart.

"If you reach into the left pocket there," he instructs, pointing to the blazer. "I think there might be a pen."

She sticks her hand inside and pulls out a black ballpoint.

"Good," Peter says and digs into the back pocket of his pants to retrieve April's place card—the one she handed him at the table earlier that evening.

"You kept it?" she asks, pleasantly surprised.

"I had a feeling I might want to remember this night." Peter says, offering her the place card. "Would you mind writing your number on here? Maybe we can go out sometime, you know, when you don't have a term paper?"

"I'd like that." She scribbles her information on the inside fold.

Never before has April known magic like this. Nor has she ever been so conflicted. But as she stands beside Peter, warmed by his blazer and optimism, she feels—for the first time in a very long time—hopeful.

14

Peter

THEN AND NOW

Peter is abuzz as he climbs the stairs and unlocks the front door of his third-floor walk-up.

"Hey man." He nods to his roommate nestled on the couch. There's an empty pizza box and two cans of beer beside his bare feet on the coffee table.

The unsanitary condition of their apartment is on par with a post-party frat house. Dishes are perpetually piled in the kitchen sink and an exterminator's business card shares a magnet on the refrigerator door with a Chinese restaurant delivery menu. It's a tossup which vendor they dial more frequently. His bedroom is tidy, but the air is musty due to the hundred-gallon fish tank he inherited from his grandfather that sits atop a corroded wooden stand wedged between his mattress and a wall. As a junior associate in a white-collar law firm, scouring scum from plexiglass on a regular basis is low on his to-do list, but he also doesn't have the heart to toss the tank, and so it remains in his room, perpetually coated in green slime.

Peter heads directly into his bedroom, shuts the door, and retrieves the place card with April's phone number.

Do I call tonight? he wonders, flipping the paper between his fingers like a tiny baton. *Or is that too eager? Tomorrow? Next week? Three days? Five? What the hell are the rules?*

He strips down to a T-shirt and boxers, grabs a yellow legal pad, and begins drafting a script of what to say whenever he does decide to call April.

The following evening, just after he finishes a chicken salad sandwich at his desk, Peter tapes the yellow paper to his computer screen. He hasn't been this nervous to call a girl since seventh grade when he asked Suzanne Congro to the winter dance.

A man answers on the first ring. "Prentice League, how may I help you?"

Confused, Peter checks the number on the place card. He thought she had given her home number. "Um hi, is April Zagoda there?"

"I'll transfer you. . ."

He takes a long swig of water during the silence.

"Hello, this is April."

"Oh, hey April. This is Peter. Peter Nelson? The guy from The Prentice League thingamabob . . ." *Thingamabob?!*

"Hey Peter. How are you?" She sounds more professional than flirty. *Ooh, did I misread the cues? Maybe she's not interested . . .*

"Good. And you? Didn't realize I was dialing the League. You're still at work?"

Obviously she's still at work, you schmuck, he thinks and rolls his eyes at his daftness.

"Yes. I'm here more than I'm home so I figured I'd give you this number. I'm actually heading out in a minute. They close and shut off the phones at seven."

Peter checks the clock on his desk. It's 6:58 p.m. "Guess I'd better make this quick, then." He glances at his script and reads it verbatim:

So, I had a really great time with you last night and I was wondering if you'd like to grab dinner sometime.

There is a pause on the other end of the line. His pulse quickens. He had not considered she might decline his invitation. But before he his mind can go down a rabbit hole, she responds.

"I'd love to."

He clenches a fist and pumps it in victory. "Great. How 'bout this Saturday?"

"I'll be working at the League until five. You want to meet me here?"

"Perfect. Maybe you can show me around the place before we head out."

"Great. Thanks. See you then."

"Yeah, see you Satur—"

The phone system cuts off, abruptly ending the call.

Peter hangs up the receiver and immediately grabs the Zagat restaurant guide off his bookshelf. He flips through the narrow burgundy manual until he finds the section for Queens and dogears the pages with the most intriguing eateries near the League.

On Saturday afternoon, after a run around the reservoir in Central Park, Peter puts on his finest jeans and a blue and white checkered button-down shirt, rolls up the cuffs, runs a drop of gel through his hair, and takes an unfamiliar subway line to a section of Queens he has passed through only once while attending a firm outing to see a Mets game. As he exits the station and ascends the subway stairs to the sidewalk, he is greeted by dozens of shiny hubcaps shimmering like Christmas ornaments on a chain-link fence. He surveys the adjacent abandoned lot and grows uneasy. Having lived in the city for several years, he prides himself on being a streetwise New Yorker, but feeling this out of sorts reminds him how vast and diverse a metropolis this is—after all, his adopted Manhattan is just one of five boroughs. Unlike his bustling Midtown East neighborhood, this pocket of the city is eerily still at 5 p.m. on a Saturday. He quickens his stride and when he arrives at the League, a sense of relief washes over him.

"Hi, I'm Peter Nelson. Here to see April Zagoda," he tells the security guard at the front desk.

The heavyset woman in a stone gray uniform eyes him up and down. "ID," she says coolly.

He hands over his Massachusetts driver's license and she exhales loudly while recording his information in a ledger.

"You'll get it back when you leave, take a seat," she mutters and punches some buttons on a telephone.

A minute later, a stairwell door opens and April appears. Peter instinctively rises in her presence. *She looks different*, he thinks as he takes in her delicate baby blue sundress and cardigan sweater. With her high ponytail and understated makeup, she is effortlessly beautiful—more so than he remembers from the gala.

"Hey," she says softly, walking over to greet him. She rises onto her tiptoes to give him a peck on the cheek. "Did you have trouble finding the place?"

"Nope. Not at all. Piece of cake. I even did some window shopping. There's a nice selection of hubcaps around the corner if you're ever in the market."

"Good to know." She laughs.

They head up the stairwell and April proceeds to give Peter a tour. He sees the clothing boutique, the job postings tacked onto bulletin boards, the coffee lounge, and finally, her office classroom.

"So, this is it," he says, looking around her room. "This is where you change lives."

"Oh, please," April rolls her eyes. "I help people study for tests. We chat. That's all."

"Don't be so humble." He walks over to her desk and notices a small, framed photograph of two young children dressed in superhero costumes. The colors are muted and remind him of the countless photos his parents took of him and his siblings. Peter picks up the frame and admires it. "Is this you?" he asks.

"It is," she says matter-of-factly.

"And your brother, I assume?"

She shakes her head but offers nothing more.

"So where are we going?" she asks, grabbing her purse from a coat closet and swinging it over her shoulder.

"Corona. It's a neighborhood in Queens. You ever been?"

"Ahh," she responds without skipping a beat. "So it's going to be you, me, and Julio down by the schoolyard?"

Peter gasps, impressed by her quick wit and musical reference. "Paul Simon! You know the song!"

"Know it? Are you kidding? I grew up on Paul Simon! He and my mother both went to Forest Hills High School. She plays his music all the time. I know every lyric."

This girl is very cool.

Despite arriving on time for their reservation, Corona's Park Side Restaurant is fully booked and the patrons lingering at their assigned table have yet to pay their bill. The bar area is packed so Peter and April stand in the narrow entryway taking in the bevy of framed celebrity photos hanging within centimeters of one another along the walls, including autographed headshots of local news anchors, restaurant managers with their arms around movie stars, politicians with upward pointing thumbs, and a sampling of voluptuous women in animal-print stoles beneath the awning of the famed Italian eatery.

"Nelson! Nelson party of two!" a tuxedoed host eventually calls out.

Peter raises his hand and they follow the man as he zigzags between tables. The restaurant has multiple rooms, at least two dining floors, and every inch is humming. They pass multigenerational families sharing platters of baked ziti, a post-christening celebration with a sleeping baby in a nearby stroller, a bridal shower with diamond ring–shaped mylar balloons, and numerous couples out for dinner on a Saturday night. Some are dressed to the nines, others are in jeans and sneakers. The crowd is as ethnically diverse as the attire. As they head to a back room with large greenhouse windows overlooking a garden of porcelain fountains and ceramic busts, Peter is delighted to see they have honored his request for a relatively quiet corner table.

"So," Peter starts, after they put in their dinner order. "How's my friend Mr. Bradley doing? I kind of feel like I owe him one."

April grins and picks a chunk of fresh Parmigiano-Reggiano off the little dish beside the bread basket. "He's doing well. He's going to be taking the test for his high school equivalency diploma soon. We've been studying. I think he's got it."

"I hope this doesn't make you uncomfortable, but I'm sort of in awe. I don't know many people who have a job where they can see an immediate impact on people's lives the way you do. And you aren't even compensated! I admire it tremendously, but I don't get it. Why is a college girl like you hanging out with Mr. Bradley—as charming as he is—and not partying it up with your girlfriends? Not that I'm judging, I'm not. Believe me, I was certainly not a wild guy in school. I'm just curious."

"I'm compensated in other ways," she says cryptically, nibbling on a corner of cheese.

Peter looks her directly in the eyes, waiting for her to elaborate. When she offers no more, he can feel his smile collapse a bit. "I'm sorry, I just don't follow."

She sighs. "It's complicated."

Peter nods sympathetically but remains mute, hoping she might expound to fill the void.

"It's a long story . . ."

He can feel her beginning to cave and suddenly he feels guilty. "I don't mean to pry. We don't need to talk about it if you don't want to."

"No, it's okay. It's just, I, uh, it's still kind of fresh."

Change the topic. Don't be an ass. She's clearly uncomfortable. "Forget I asked. Tell me more about my buddy Mr. Bradley. The guy seems like a genuine stud."

April chuckles. "Oh, he is! Everyone loves him."

"What's his story?"

"You know, it's such a shame. Bright, good guy. Had he been born into other circumstances his life would have been completely different. Lost his parents young, got into drugs, ended up selling, went away for a while, cleaned up his act, got a job as a truck driver, married, started selling again for extra cash because they wanted to start a family, got caught, went away again for a longer time, his wife divorced him. It's just really sad all around. But he's a good, sweet, intellectually curious man."

"Wow."

"I know. If I told you the number of stories I've heard like his, you wouldn't believe it. It's like variations on the same theme. I feel like the world is broken. Somehow, I don't know, it sounds incredibly cheesy, but I kind of feel like I need to fix it."

An electric charge runs through Peter like a thunderbolt. He has never known anyone—other than himself—with such an innate drive to improve the world. Most people in his orbit are singularly focused on chasing six-figure bonuses and 401Ks.

Over the next two hours, as they share an artichoke appetizer, Caesar salad, and Eggplant Parmigiana, April and Peter get acquainted with the basics: family, favorite television shows, impressionable books, a mutual love of both rap and Rat Pack, and an idolization of a single character in literature: Atticus Finch.

"I intend to name my first child Atticus," he declares as he signs his name on the check at the end of the meal.

"Atticus Nelson?" she laughs.

"What? I'm serious! I've heard worse!" Peter smiles as he neatly stacks the bills for a cash tip and secures it on the table beneath the pepper shaker. He looks up at April. "Ready to go?"

She nods. "Thank you. This was delicious."

"Yeah, Zagat came through. This place is awesome. You feel like dessert?"

"Always," she says excitedly. "Lemon Ice King of Corona? It's across the street."

"You read my mind." He reaches out his hand. She slides her delicate, smooth fingers into his. They fit perfectly and remain entwined until their orders of flavored ice—pineapple for her, pistachio for him—are passed through the storefront window. He doesn't want to let go but needs to pay the man at the counter.

"Should we sit over there?" Peter suggests, pointing to a nearby park bench beside a bocce court. As they settle and watch old men play ball beneath string lights, April decides to open up. Peter isn't sure why she has chosen this particular moment to share, but he listens attentively and doesn't question her timing.

She tells him everything. Every detail. Between spoonfuls of tangy crushed ice, the events of her life erupt from her mouth like volcanic ash. Though they've only just met, he trusts when she says she has never told anyone. The sincerity in her voice, the way her eyes pool just before Rudy's name emerges from her mouth, the vivid depictions of his arrest, the arraignment, the sentencing, the aggressive prosecution, the lies and decimation of Rudy's character in the media, her expulsion from Rivington, her decision to volunteer at the League, her need to see his face in that photograph on her desk—with every word there is a distant look in her eyes, like a veteran sharing tales from the battlefield. It's as if she's reliving the experiences in real time right there on the park bench beside Peter.

"Thank you," he says when she's done. He can sense a dam has broken and all he wants to do is lift her up so she won't get swallowed by the flood.

She dabs a tear from the corner of her eye with a napkin.

"You didn't have to share all that, but I'm grateful you did."

"Well, there you have it. This is me. All of me."

"No." He shakes his head. "That's not all."

She looks at him quizzically. "No, it is! I promise, I left nothing out."

This girl has no idea how special she is. Peter leans forward and reaches for her hand. "Sorry, that's not what I meant. What I should have said is, that's not *all* of you. These events—they don't define you. Not even close. Did they happen? Yeah. But that's not the entirety of your story. Something tells me your story is just beginning and what you shared with me . . ." a smile broadens across his face, "well, I'm pretty confident that was just the prologue."

April blots another droplet by her lash line. "You're sweet. You must think I'm a total nut job. Major baggage here. I should probably have that yellow caution tape wrapped around me. Anyway, I'll completely understand if you want to go home and call it a night. I can drive you back to Manhattan if you want, or drop you at a subway station . . ."

Peter gradually lifts his hands and gently places them on her face, one palm on each of her cheeks. Slowly, he leans in and kisses her mouth. Her lips are plump, soft, and taste like a piña colada. When they pull apart, April remains fixed, her eyes still shut, as if she is holding on to the moment.

"There's nowhere I'd rather be," Peter says tenderly. April is unlike anyone Peter has ever met. At twenty, she is eight years his junior, but more mature, wise, and grounded than any of his peers. He could tell there was something unique about her when they met at the gala, but now, after this evening, he is smitten.

Her lids lift and expand to a wide-eyed gaze directly into his pupils. He feels raw, already tethered to and protective of her.

"You deserve happiness, April. You can be a friend to Rudy, but also build a life for yourself. The two are not mutually exclusive."

She says nothing, but he can tell she is processing the message.

He leans in and kisses her again. This time they linger, embracing on the park bench for several minutes until the sounds of bickering bocce players intensifies and kills the mood. Peter tries to ignore the distraction, but when one elderly man shouts, "Stop grabbin' my balls!" at his friend, it's impossible to focus. April and Peter untwine themselves and burst out laughing.

"Want to take a walk?" he proposes. "Maybe we should leave these guys to sort out their business."

"Good idea."

They stroll over to Flushing Meadows Corona Park where children are playing on fields illuminated by streetlamps and parents are gathering in clusters of beach chairs enjoying post-picnic dinner conversation. They walk past the New York Hall of Science and the towering Terrace on the Park party space, and note how striking the giant globe structure from the 1969 World's Fair is despite its dire need of a paint job.

As they exit the park and make their way toward Big Bertha,

they pass a woman on the sidewalk selling flowers out of a painter's bucket.

"For your lady?" the woman beckons, waving a long-stemmed pink rose in Peter's direction.

"Absolutely!" he says and notices her nameplate necklace as he hands over payment. "Thanks, Julia! Keep the change."

Peter pivots toward April to present her with the flower and when he does, he leans into her ear and sings softly, "A ros-ee for the Queen of Corona. From me and Julia, probably not too far from a schoolyard."

It takes a second to register, but when it does April's face lights up. "Paul Simon's song!" she laughs. "It's as if you planned it!"

Peter drapes his arm around her shoulder. "Well, if I had, I would have asked Paul to serenade you instead of me. I got the height, but he's got the pipes."

April looks up at Peter and smiles. "It worked out perfectly. It was meant to be."

He couldn't agree more.

Peter decides to wait until the end of April's senior year to propose. It will be her graduation gift, but he'll deliberately ask the day *after* commencement so as not to detract from the significance of either milestone. The culmination of college marks the end point of an experience that began with unimaginable heartache for April and will forever be linked to her friend, Rudy. The day after graduation, however, will mark a new beginning that is tied solely to Peter. The first day of the rest of their lives together.

"I moved to New York to change the world, but it turns out my world changed because I moved to New York," he proclaims on bended knee atop the roof where they first met the night of The Prentice League gala. He had contacted the event coordinator at the venue in advance, explained his intention to propose, and arranged to get access to the space. Charmed by his plan, the manager provides complimentary champagne and surreptitiously snaps pictures from behind the sizable bouquet of pink roses Peter ordered. When they exit the roof as giddy, teary-eyed fiancés, they hail a cab to Brooklyn to share the good news in person with Barbara and Steven and call Peter's parents in Boston.

"I knew it! I knew it!" Barbara exclaims when they walk in the door, April's shiny solitaire leading the way. "Steven! Come!"

On command, April's father bounds into the living room and beams. "Aww, geez, look at that sparkler! And the ring ain't bad either." He winks and pulls them both in for a hug. "I'm so happy for you guys."

Over the last eighteen months, Peter has gotten to know the Zagodas quite well. Because April lives at home and he visits often, the four of them have shared innumerable meals, played plenty of Uno, and taken enough walks around Midwood that Peter could be a tour guide. He needs no more proof that with the Zagodas he has won the in-law jackpot.

"And I'm happy for us, too," Barbara says, swallowing hard. "We're getting another son."

Another? Peter wonders. *April doesn't have a brother. I must have misheard...*

It takes the sudden sobering of their faces and a feeling of air being sucked out of the room for him to catch on, and when he does, Peter is unsure how Barbara's comment should make him feel. Flattered that she is fond enough to call him a *son*? Jealous that someone else could also be worthy of the title? Heartened to be welcomed so warmly into the family? Irritated because this once-in-a-lifetime moment now feels tainted?

This is the first time April's parents have ever referenced Rudy in Peter's presence. Neither his name nor that chapter in their lives has ever been discussed. In fact, the topic of Rudy has rarely come up since their first date by the bocce courts in Corona. The few passing remarks she has made have always sounded more like tender reminiscences of a deceased relative: *Oh, Rudy could have fixed that broken faucet—he used to fix everything* or *Oh, Rudy loved this restaurant . . . their blueberry pie was always his favorite.* The only difference as far as Peter can tell is that people don't mail greeting cards to the dead; April sends a letter to Rudy every year on his birthday and Christmas.

"Ape, what do you think? You want to call the DeFrancos? Tell them the news?" Barbara bites her lip, seemingly unsure.

We haven't even called my folks yet, Peter thinks but doesn't say. Strangely, this gearshift reminds him of two things. First is the *In Memorium* montage at the Academy Awards when the entertainment industry pauses to honor colleagues who have passed. Second is a wedding he recently attended for a Jewish friend who, at the conclusion of the ceremony, stomped on a glass to symbolize that even in happiness, it's important not to forget moments of sorrow and feeling shattered.

"No Ma, not yet." April shakes her head assuredly. "I want to call the Nelsons first."

Peter plants a kiss on her forehead. Her insistence on prioritizing his family feels like a victory. *Maybe our marriage will be the antidote to all the fragmentation this family has experienced.*

Excitement returns when they speak with Peter's family. But unlike the Zagodas, his mother presses for details: *Are they willing to get married in Boston? What color scheme does April have in mind? Do they have a season preference? Have they considered Cape Cod?*

They dodge her questions, claiming the details have yet to be discussed, but in truth, April has no desire for hoopla and Peter doesn't care enough to advocate for it. Were she interested, he could easily get on board with an eight-piece band and a limo filled with groomsmen, but she yearns for little more than a marriage license and a slice of carrot cake.

It can take time to peel guilt from joy, he reminds himself, envisioning the emotions like two stubbornly adherent swatches of Velcro. *If Rudy's absence from a wedding reception will be too heart-breaking for her to bear, so be it. I've got the girl. I don't need the "Electric Slide."*

The following week, Peter's boss summons him to his office. Peter assumes it is a congratulatory meeting as word has spread around the firm of his betrothal, but he is taken aback when the first words out of Stan Abrams's mouth are not "congratulations" but rather, "What do you think of Chicago?"

"Chicago?" Peter asks, surprised.

"Yes."

"I've never been."

"Really?"

"Yes, sir."

"Hmm. Well, I suppose you should check it out because I have a proposition. Our firm is expanding. We're opening a branch in Chicago's West Loop. What do you think of heading up that office?"

"Me?"

"Yes, Peter. You."

I guess this isn't the right time to tell him I was contemplating a transition to the public sector.

"I'm flattered, sir. Thank you!"

"We'll cover all costs, help you find a home," Abrams says. "I'll have a team supporting you every step of the way."

Despite his deep affinity for Atticus Finch's defense attorney character, Peter's singular focus throughout law school had been to become a prosecutor. His summer internships were always at a DA's office—first in Boston, then in New York. Then during his third year, he met a young partner at Abrams's firm who convinced him to apply for an associate position. "You've seen what it's like working for the government. Going to the firm will be good for you—different clientele, different cases, different lens on the criminal justice system. Plus, you'll pay off your student loans faster. Go get a taste of white collar and then in a few years become a public servant. It's a good plan."

It was sound advice and Peter has no regrets about his path. He has paid off his loans. He has gotten great experience with a variety of cases he might not otherwise have encountered. Recently, however, he has been feeling the itch to return to the public sector. The more he thinks about it, the timing could be ideal as it could enable him to plant roots and feel settled in the job before starting a family. On the other hand, though, the opportunity to manage the firm's satellite office and build it from scratch is quite enticing.

"Thank you, sir," Peter says, shaking Abrams's hand over his desk. "I will discuss with my fiancée and get back to you."

"I believe this could be a very good fit. Let me know soon."

Peter heads back to his desk and immediately pulls out a notepad to make a pros-cons list before calling April.

PROS CHICAGO

1. Great résumé builder
2. Founding an office is a unique opportunity
3. Romantic to start a marriage by planting roots in a new city

4. *Wholesome Midwest could be a good place to raise a family*

5. *April can apply to grad school in Chicago instead of NY*

6. *Can always come back if it doesn't work out*

7. *Fresh start for April. New city with no memories or reminders of what happened with Rudy. Might help her move on.*

He puts a star next to number 7.

<u>*CONS CHICAGO*</u>

1. *Leaving New York—hard for April?*

2. *Delays plan to exit the firm and transition to public sector work*

3. *Taking the bar again!!*

Seeing it written out on paper helps, but he could be swayed either way. There are certainly fewer cons, but they're weighty ones. In the end, April's happiness reigns supreme. If she isn't on board, he'll turn it down.

"Oh my God, that's incredible!" she squeals later that evening, wrapping her arms around Peter's neck. "I'm so proud of you!"

"So? What do you think?"

"Oh, gosh, Peter. How can you turn this down?"

"Really? You're on board?"

"I mean, for me, it's just my parents. That's the hardest part—

leaving them. But as long as you're okay if I come back to Brooklyn whenever I want to see them . . ."

"Are you kidding? As often as you like. Car, train, plane, whatever. We'll make it work."

As soon as they break the news to Barbara and Steven, they're pummeled with aphorisms.

"Spread those wings and fly! Carpe diem!" Barbara claps in excitement. "Give it a go! You can always come back home if it doesn't feel right."

"I agree with your mother," Steven says. "Do it. But I'm warning you now, if you turn into one of those people who think deep dish pizza is better than a normal slice, I change the locks."

"Well," April says, "there's zero chance of that happening, so I guess we're moving to Chicago."

Six months later, Peter and April are standing in a small, carpeted conference room at Chicago's famed Drake Hotel. The venue has the cachet and sophistication to satisfy his mother, but the intimacy to accommodate April's desire for a small family-only celebration. With her hair in a low, loose chignon and a slinky white satin spaghetti-strap gown purchased off the rack at Marshall Field's department store, she makes a stunning, elegant bride. The moment is captured by one of Chicago's top wedding photographers, hired by Peter's parents as a surprise gift. "Well, if my friends and relatives can't be here in person," his mother whispers in his ear the morning of the wedding, "at least I can send out one hell of a holiday card."

In another surprise move, his mother submits her favorite photo of the wedding day to the Celebrations section of the *Chicago Tribune* and it runs the following week with the caption: April and Peter Nelson, Drake Hotel. The bride is a graduate student in education at DePaul University; The groom is a partner at Abrams Law Firm, LLP.

"I guess we've officially arrived," Peter says when they open the newspaper and see the candid taken of them walking outside the hotel near Lake Shore Drive.

April cringes. "Ugh."

"I'm sorry. I had no idea my mom was planning this . . ."

"Well, you know what's the best part?" she says, softening. "Look at that . . . we're April and Peter Nelson. I'm April Nelson."

Peter knows this is a new beginning for both of them, but for April, her new moniker is a rebranding—a clean, fresh slate.

"That's my favorite part too, Mrs. Nelson," he says.

Within the year, Peter's satellite office is up and running smoothly, but the itch for government work does not abate. Always true to his word, he will not renege on his commitment to Abrams, but he begins networking at dinners and conferences with members of Chicago's criminal justice community. He meets social workers, public defenders, prosecutors, and judges in both Cook and Lake counties and continually returns home from each event inspired to someday make the transition.

Soon, they are pregnant with the twins: Attie and Rosie.

A few years later, Simon comes along.

They outgrow their rental apartment, buy a condo in the South Loop, and before long, their home is filled with soccer cleats, piles of laundry, and a black lab named Bocce. A dry-erase calendar nailed to the kitchen wall governs their lives. Annual family pictures taken in nearby Grant Park replace older photographs from their earlier years in New York, and the small, framed snapshot that had once been a treasured fixture atop April's desk at the League is no longer displayed. Peter suspects it is buried somewhere in an old shoebox in the bowels of April's walk-in closet. That's not to say Rudy has been discarded like outgrown clothing; it's more a matter of demotion. The all-consuming attention he once garnered has shifted to a focus on career and parenthood. But twice a year—on Rudy's birthday and at Christmas—April writes a lovely card and Peter deposits it into the mailbox on the sidewalk outside their loft. Peter always checks the addresses on envelopes he mails before inserting them one-at-a-time into the mail slot—a habit he inherited from his mother—and whenever he sees the prison address on the front, pride swells in his chest.

She has done right by Rudy, and by us, Peter thinks every time he mails those cards.

Seeing the words "correctional facility" diagonally beneath their return address in the upper left corner reminds him of April's resilience and strength. He's always believed in her power to persevere and create a fulfilling life post-Rudy, but the way she has managed to compartmentalize—to ensure he is not forgotten while simultaneously tending to her own happiness—gives Peter a sense of peace.

But one Sunday morning many years later, as Peter exits their marble lobby to deposit Rudy's birthday card in the mailbox, someone shouts his name.

"Mr. Nelson!"

Peter whips his head around.

"How's the campaign goin'?" the man asks as he raises a camera to his eye and quickly snaps a picture.

Ahh, the press, Peter thinks. *Guess someone is doing a story on the upcoming election.*

"Hey, good morning!" Peter waves, holding the letter he is about to deposit in the mailbox.

A flash goes off.

The bright light is harsh and Peter can feel himself wince. He wishes he'd put a baseball cap on before leaving the condo. His bedhead is out of control and the baggy sweatpants are doing him no favors.

Click. Click. Click. The camera shutter's staccato beats pepper the air as he inspects the envelope for Rudy before inserting it into the slot.

"You're out early today," he says jovially to the photographer.

The man doesn't respond. He's all business.

"Well, have a good day," Peter says after he has deposited the letter. He walks briskly down the street to a café and checks the time on his watch. He's got a conference call soon and has to be home in time for the kids so that April can drive up north to her weekly yoga class.

Before entering the coffee shop, Peter looks over his shoulder to see if the man is still standing up the block. He is, and he's now yielding a larger, more telescopic lens. Peter ducks into the coffee shop like a movie star dodging paparazzi and places his order. By the time he heads home, the man is gone.

Two hours later, while making blueberry pancakes for his kids, there's a call on their landline.

"Peter!" his campaign manager is breathless. "Have you seen it?"

Peter flips the pancakes on the griddle and licks a bit of batter from his finger. "Seen what?"

"Oh, shit. Really? You haven't seen it?" he says.

He lowers the flame on the gas stove's burner and walks down the hall to his office where he left his cell phone to charge.

"I have no idea what you're talking about, Dale, but whatever it is can't be as bad as you sound."

"Check your email," Dale says frantically. "Right now."

"Okay. I'll call you right back."

Peter boots up his phone and sees there are seventy-nine new texts and over two hundred email messages. Nearly all contain a link to an AP story: "State's Attorney Candidate Peter Nelson's Wife Linked to Murder."

Four photographs accompany the article.

The first is of a disheveled-looking Peter squinting at the camera while stepping into the coffee shop.

The second is of him wincing as he holds a letter beside a mailbox.

The third is a zoomed-in shot of the front of that envelope where Rudy DeFranco's name and Wallkill Correctional Facility are spelled out in April's perfect penmanship. On the upper left-hand corner is the Nelson's home address.

The fourth is the wedding photo his mother submitted years earlier to the *Tribune*.

"Oh my God," Peter mutters aloud and collapses into his desk chair. *I'm ruined!* He does a quick Google search and sees that internet rags have already piggybacked off the AP report and are blasting baseless, sensationalized headlines at lightning speed:

State's Attorney Front-runner Is Penpals with
Wife's Incarcerated Ex-lover

Nelson's Wife's Dark Past:
What Else Will Come Out Before Election Day?

Wanna-be State's Attorney Nelson Has Felon Brother-in-law

What the hell?! How is this possible?! He immediately picks up the phone and dials Dale.

"I'm on it," Dale says upon picking up. "But I'm already getting calls from reporters. Do you want me to respond? You want to have a press conference? Ignore it and let it hopefully die out?"

Peter runs his fingers through his still unwashed hair. He hears one of the kids turning the TV on in the family room down the hall and knows without looking that it's Simon watching his beloved morning cartoons.

"Give me a minute to process this. I'll call you back." Peter hangs up and can feel his lip begin to quiver the way it did when he was a little boy about to cry. But instead of reaching for the tissue box at the edge of his desk, he kicks the wall beside his office door with the force and precision of David Beckham. The paint chips and cracks instantly unfurl like spider veins up to the ceiling.

"Fuck!" he exclaims. "Fucking Rudy! How many fucking lives is he going to fuck up!" Peter knows he needs to shower. It will calm him and he does his best thinking while standing in the steam. Not to mention, he is feeling absolutely filthy. As he steps out of his office to head to the bathroom, he hears the lock click on the front door. April is home from yoga. He is fuming and can't face her right now. Though he knows she doesn't deserve to be the focus of his fury, he can't dismiss the overwhelming urge to scream at her. Why couldn't she have just left this guy in the dust? He's not a relative. He's not an ex-husband. He's her fucking overprotective neighbor who got her kicked out of college and put her through hell. He nearly ruined her life and now, by association, he may do the same to her husband.

"Oh, babe . . ." April extends her arms, reaching for Peter as she comes down the hall. But as her fingers brush against his shoulders, he instinctively recoils as if she is diseased. He turns, walks back into his office, and slams the door.

15

Jillian

NOW

"I cannot believe she would pull a stunt like this!" Jillian hisses while staring at photos of Peter Nelson on her laptop. She is sitting cross-legged on her living room couch scrolling through the AP's report, utterly aghast at how deftly Heather, her once sycophantic intern, has scooped her.

Jillian grabs her phone and dials Heather's number.

"Hey Jillian!"

Bitch! is the first word to cross Jillian's mind, but she knows better than to let it slip. "Well hello, Nancy Drew," she chooses instead. "Just saw your piece on Peter Nelson. That was some speedy reporting you did there."

"Oh, it's nothing." Heather giggles. "You piqued my interest in the Nelsons when you called the other day."

"Mmm..."

"I figured with the election coming up it wouldn't hurt to get some candid shots of Peter, so I sent a photographer to hang out outside their home. Peter seems like an early riser—the kind of guy who goes out for a jog at six and negotiates world peace by eight. So while my guy was standing by the Nelsons' front door, I did some investigating back at the office. As you know, my time management skills are pretty on fleek!"

"Yes, quite." Jillian rolls her eyes.

"Turns out Peter's as plain vanilla as I had suspected, but oh my gosh, his wife! That schoolteacher was involved in a murder! I couldn't believe it! And it gets better! As I'm reading these stories online about April and the homicide case, the photographer comes back to the office. We start loading up the pictures and guess what? When he zooms in on the one of Peter standing by the mailbox, we notice the address on the envelope he's holding. It's the prison in New York! They're sending a freakin' letter to the killer! I mean, you can't make this shit up! It's gold!"

Hearing Rudy's name interspersed with the words *murder* and *killer* stings deeply.

Jillian had never been reckless in her youth. She had never experimented with drugs, alcohol, or sex. Instead, her rebellion came in the form of conscious carelessness: a self-issued hall pass permitting jealousy, ambition, and ego to take the wheel. The glee in Heather's voice reminds Jillian of her younger self and she vows to prevent the same mistake from happening twice.

"Well, just a little piece of advice, if I may," Jillian offers with a tinge of condescension. "Mind your reporting. Slow and steady wins the race."

"Not anymore!" Heather fires back with a chuckle. "It's more like you snooze, you lose."

"Trust me. It's better to run a solid story than Swiss cheese, even if it takes a little more research and time to fill the holes."

There is a brief silence. "I'm sorry, Jillian, I'm not sure I follow."

"I know you're excited to move beyond the assistant position and the fact checking may be left to your underlings now, but just a friendly reminder to triple check everything, including the minutia. Don't rush or embellish your story to rack up the likes. Get it right. I'd hate to see you slip and fall so early in your promising career." *Not to mention the harmful ripple effect inaccurate reporting can have on innocent lives*, she wants to add but refrains.

"Well, I appreciate that. Thanks," Heather says curtly. "I'm getting a call on my other line so gotta run. Let's talk soon! Bye!" Click.

Jillian narrows her eyes as she stares at the phone in her hand. "Okay, Heather," she says aloud. "Game on."

For Jillian, competition has always been stronger fuel than caffeine. Unfortunately, having spent the last two decades as a science and medical journalist, her crime reporting skills are stale. She hasn't flexed that muscle in years, and asking colleagues for help is a risk given how Todd, her boss, has made it abundantly clear there is no straying from her beat.

Though Heather's attempt to commandeer this story is irritating, Jillian doesn't regret reaching out. The best thing to emerge from their initial conversation was Heather's assumption that Jillian was trolling for a tip about some sort of disease or malady plaguing the Nelson family. Though that had not at all been Jillian's intent, Heather's hypothesis sparks an idea and ignites something inside her. It's the same magical intuition and adrenaline surge she gets whenever a story feels right . . . when it clicks into place, and she knows she's onto an idea that can go the distance.

On Monday morning, after brewing a fresh pot of coffee and emailing Todd that she is taking a sick day, Jillian arranges a notepad, mini tape recorder, and a handful of mechanical pencils on the glass table in her living room. She twists her hair into a claw clip and sinks into a sofa cushion, her fully charged laptop at the ready.

"Here we go," she exhales. It feels like the dawn of a new school year. She's alert, excited, and ready to make her mark.

The only way to set her conscience free is to do the research. There is no other way to tell the true story or absolve any guilt for allowing her young ego to overshadow accuracy. She'll need every document to form a full picture—the court file, interviews, police records, autopsy report, and the arraignment and sentencing transcripts.

She opens her computer to the NY Courts website and within seconds of typing Rudy's name into the electronic records search page, she's in and scrolling. Without question, the most heart-wrenching parts are the character references addressed to the judge. Prior to sentencing, friends, family, bosses, coaches, and neighbors wrote letters in the hopes of humanizing Rudy. The goal was for the judge to view him as a person, not simply "the defendant." There was a handwritten note on pink stationery from a neighbor named Bunny Fishbein who lovingly referred to him as a "mensch." There was a baseball coach who made a top twenty list of anecdotes exemplifying Rudy's kindness, selflessness, and team spirit. Numerous teachers elaborated on his peaceful nature and innate curiosity, and Mr. Marino, his boss from the bagel store, described how he wept for hours upon learning of the arrest. "I gave him his first job the summer he was fourteen, and he's been working for me ever since," Marino wrote. "He's my boy. I trust him implicitly. Hard-working, disciplined, responsible, punctual, he's the last kid I would have ever thought this would happen to."

The most powerful letter, however, was from April.

Your Honor,

As you might suspect, I have never composed a letter quite like this before. I know many people are writing to you in support of Rudy DeFranco, and I am confident every single one of them will tell you what a truly wonderful person he is as well as how absolutely shocking this unfortunate situation is for him, his family, and our community. In that regard, this letter is no different. Rudy and I met as young children on a Brooklyn playground when he stepped aside to let me have the first turn on a slide. In all the years I have known him, that kindness, consideration, and reflexive desire to put others before himself has never waned. His character is consistent. He is loyal, thoughtful, selfless, and big-hearted. He's the guy who instinctively lends a hand to anyone in need and somehow knows just what to say to lift spirits and make days brighter. I love him dearly and couldn't be more proud to call Rudy DeFranco my best friend.

I suspect the difference between this letter and the others you will receive is the fact that I was with Rudy on the night of the incident. I invited him to the event and will undoubtedly live the rest of my life knowing that my invitation paved the path to this nightmare.

I have seen the distorted media coverage and I feel the need— not just as Rudy's friend, but as someone who values transparency and accuracy—to share my truth and what I witnessed that evening.

When Rudy arrived at the restaurant/bar, I was speaking with Bailey Jameson. Bailey and I were introduced by his brother, Keith, a new friend I had made while working on my college newspaper. Bailey was quite drunk. He was slurring his words, spitting saliva as he spoke, and as he stood over me—my back against a wall in a corner of the room—I could smell the alcohol on his breath. Rudy approached and was a gentleman. He was protective and gracefully tried to lead me out of what was an uncomfortable situation. He did not touch Bailey. He did not initiate a fight. It wasn't until Bailey became belligerent that Rudy pulled the little Swiss Army knife from his pants pocket, but even then, he kept it low and by his side to avoid confrontation. It was purely a deterrent. He did not raise his hand or thrust it at Bailey as has been reported in the press—that is wholly untrue. What actually happened was that Bailey shoved Rudy first. Rudy tried to avoid an altercation—he is not one to fight—but Bailey was aggressive. A scuffle initiated by Bailey ensued and when it ended, Bailey was still yelling, and Rudy and I left to return home to Brooklyn. That was all. Though I had never witnessed one before, it seemed to me this was no more than a standard bar fight.

I don't know if this information will influence your sentence, but I needed to share my version of the story. Your Honor, you must know that Rudy was protecting me. He wasn't looking for trouble, and he certainly wasn't looking to hurt anyone. He has been touted as a belligerent thug by the prosecutor and that description has carried over into the headlines. This characterization could not be further from the truth. We—his family and friends—have deliberately bitten our tongues. We have stayed out of the media and opted not to refute the despicable descriptions made by Mr. Sketcher, the assistant District Attorney, as we don't want to add fuel to the fire. I'm sure you can imagine how frustrating and infuriating it is to see a person you love be raked over the coals, have their character decimated, and realize that you can do nothing but stand by and watch from the sidelines lest it make the situation worse.

Please know, it is not lost on me that there is another tragedy here as well. I am fully cognizant that the Jamesons are suffering too. I am deeply saddened for their loss and wish them much strength and comfort. I suspect Rudy's incarceration will offer

them a sense of closure, but closure does not equate to justice.
Given what I witnessed that night, as well as all that I know
about Rudy DeFranco as a human being, I am confident that
something is amiss. Rudy is not responsible for ending Bailey
Jameson's life. Please have leniency.

> *Respectfully,*
> *April Zagoda*

Jillian stares at April's letter and wonders what went through
the sentencing judge's mind after reading it. She knows Rudy was
given up to fifteen years for manslaughter, but did anything change
as a result of April's words? Did anyone investigate this case further? As far as Jillian can tell, the answer is no.

She returns to the court files online and lands on Bailey's hospital-issued death certificate. But all that is written is: "Pending further studies."

There must be an amended certificate somewhere or an autopsy
report or something from the medical examiner, she thinks.

She flips through the files and discovers a handwritten note on
a yellow legal pad. There is no date on the page and no indication
of whose messy cursive jotted down:

Cardiomyopathy
A-fib
1.5-inch arm laceration + suture
ETOH (alcohol) ↑
~~Heart Trans~~

Ahh, Jillian thinks upon seeing the familiar scientific terms, *now this is my wheelhouse.* A-fib (atrial fibrillation) she knows is a rhythm disturbance and cardiomyopathy is a weakening of the heart muscle. Though it is unclear why these conditions are mentioned and included in the file, she can only surmise that they refer to either the defendant or the victim. And, given that she knows Rudy had not been drinking on the night of the crime and Bailey was unquestionably blitzed, she concludes that the anonymous note is in reference to Bailey's health. She combs through the remainder of the court documents in search of an autopsy report but finds nothing.

Over the years, Jillian has penned numerous medical features for the newspaper. One of her most talked about special series—the first to land her a guest appearance on *The Today Show*—was about cardiovascular issues. She knows from years of reporting that alcohol can have a nearly instantaneous effect on heart rhythm; a single drink can double the odds of a bout of A-fib occurring within the next few hours. Excessive drinking is certainly cautioned for those with cardiomyopathy or A-fib. Additionally, if she is correct that this note is referring to Bailey's medical history, he most likely would have been prescribed anticoagulants to prevent blood clotting. That's standard protocol for someone with A-fib and cardiomyopathy.

Mouth agape, Jillian stares at the computer screen. *Well, getting cut by a knife isn't good for anyone, but if this guy was on blood thinners and had preexisting heart problems, maybe he bled excessively from the cut on his arm.* Suddenly, her mind is rabid. *I've gotta talk to Arielle.* She snatches her cell phone.

Jillian has a bevy of sources at the ready whose brains she can pick. She goes right to one of her favorites and texts Dr. Arielle Snyder, an expert in heart failure, to schedule a call. Seconds later, Jillian's phone rings.

"Hey, you caught me at a good time," Arielle says, the sound of her heels clicking loudly in the background. "I'm heading back to the office from a meeting. What's up?"

"Thanks. I'll get right to the point. I'm doing a story about a guy who died. Mid-twenties, was shit-faced drunk and in the middle of a bar fight when he got a shallow knife cut on his arm. History of A-fib, cardiomyopathy—"

"Cause of death?" she interrupts.

"My understanding is he bled out."

"From a shallow cut on his arm? That's seems a bit farfetched."

"Yeah. I'm having a hard time buying it. I feel like there's something else going on. It's not adding up."

"Yeah, it's not adding up because it's probably a load of crap."

This is why Jillian loves Arielle. She wears pearl earrings and red-bottomed stilettos but curses like a truck driver and always tells it like it is.

"If this guy were my patient, you betcha he'd be scared shitless of standing within ten feet of a bottle of booze and I'd have him on an anticoagulant with regular checkups to make sure the dosing is consistently right. Was he taking a blood thinner? Did he have the right dose? Was he med-compliant?"

"I have no idea. Not a clue."

"Well, chances are if the guy was as drunk as you say, he probably was not a model patient. And if his doctors prescribed a blood thinner—and I can't imagine any responsible cardiologist not insisting on one—he probably didn't follow their advice. I mean, yes, in theory he could bleed out from a small cut, but I think it's unlikely. Another option is he could have thrown a clot. If he was irresponsible and didn't dose his anticoagulants properly, he could have stroked out. Or . . ." her voice ticks up excitedly, as if she's enjoying playing the detective game, "he could've had internal bleeding related or unrelated to the fight. May not have been the knife at all. A normal, healthy man in his twenties doesn't die from this sort of scenario unless there is something unreported. This guy could have been a ticking time bomb having nothing to do with the cut on his arm and no one knew. You need to talk to his doctor. Get a medical report if the autopsy isn't available yet. Who's his doctor?"

"I don't know."

"Hmm. All right. Bear with me, I'm walking back to my desk. I have an idea . . ."

Jillian hears a door creak open.

"Good morning, everyone!" Arielle says cheerfully. "Eliana, can you please hold my calls for the next few minutes? Is Mrs. Liat set up in exam room three? Yes? Great. Please let her know I'll be in to see her shortly."

Another door clicks followed by the tapping sounds of a keyboard.

"Okay," Arielle says. "I'm at my computer. What's the guy's name? I'll see if he was a patient at one of the hospitals in our network."

"Can you do that?"

"Why not? I won't access his chart, but I might be able to at least find out who his doctor was."

"That would be very helpful. His name is Bailey Jameson."

"J-a-m-e-s-o-n?" Arielle asks, spelling out each letter.

"Correct."

"Hmm. I don't see a Bailey listed anywhere, but there's a bunch of Jamesons in our network . . . Catherine, Elliot, Garrett, Keith. . ."

"Keith! I know Keith! He's Bailey's brother. I mean, assuming it's the same Keith Jameson."

"Well, looks like this Keith sees one of my colleagues in the Westchester satellite office."

"Interesting," Jillian says.

"Look, I gotta go. I've got a patient waiting."

"Thank you, Arielle. This is helpful."

"Yep. Keep me posted."

Jillian hangs up and wraps her hands around an oversized mug of lukewarm coffee. Hearing Keith's name triggers an image she'd long ago committed to a storage room in her brain. It's as if the memory were waiting patiently all these years on a bakery line, and finally its number has been called. At the time it occurred, she'd convinced herself it was just another one of her inconsequential fly-on-the-wall observations. But now, years later, she realizes how perceptive and astute it had been, like a sixth sense.

She closes her eyes and her mind travels back to that fateful night at the college newspaper networking event. She was standing in a buffet line and saw Keith—a senior and the sports editor of their paper—chatting with an alumnus. The man extended an invitation to grab a drink at a bar later that evening. Keith graciously declined, explaining that he had plans to meet up with his brother.

"Is your brother Bailey Jameson?" the man asked.

Keith nodded and folded his arms across his chest.

"Wow, now that's a name from the past. How's he doing? We were in the same fraternity. He was a year ahead of me. Geesh, that guy knew how to have fun. Is he still traveling abroad? Or working abroad? Something abroad . . . Europe? South America?"

Keith widened his stance and shifted his weight from leg to leg as he mentioned something about Bailey being back in New York.

"Bring your brother!" the man insisted. "I know a place where they brew their own beer. From what I remember of Bailey, it'll be right up his alley!"

Keith asked for a rain check, shook the man's hand, and walked away toward a table with neatly arranged water bottles. Jillian followed.

"You know, you just passed up a great opportunity." She nudged

Keith's elbow like an annoying younger sister. "Why didn't you accept that guy's offer?"

"I don't drink." He shrugged indifferently.

"You're a senior. Aren't you twenty-one?"

"I don't want to. Not my thing."

"Well, *sports* is your thing, isn't it? You could just sit and hang out. Networking is very important for your career, you know."

"I don't need to sit in a smoky bar with a bunch of drunks. I'll follow up with that guy, I'll get his contact number, it'll be fine."

Jillian opens her eyes and they land on the spiral notepad on her apartment coffee table. She stares at it for a moment and then another memory appears. This time, it's the after-party.

She was standing within feet of the cops, a reporter's notebook in hand, when she first saw Bailey Jameson, a slobbering, foul-mouthed, lanky-legged inebriated mess on the barroom floor. His back was against the lower portion of a wood-paneled wall and from her vantage point, Jillian could see him rubbing his chest in concentric circles, as if to relieve heartburn. Keith was kneeling beside him, dread and concern written all over his face. As Bailey was loaded onto a stretcher and rolled outside to the waiting ambulance, Keith stood on the sidewalk speaking with two paramedics who were taking notes on a clipboard about whatever Keith was sharing.

The scene flashes before her and then ends as quickly as it appeared.

"I wonder if Keith was giving the EMTs Bailey's medical history," Jillian says aloud inside her empty apartment. She walks barefoot into her kitchen and grabs a box of crackers from her pantry.

Back on the sofa, snacking on Wheat Thins, she opens her laptop and goes directly to Facebook. Sure enough, Keith has a page. Jillian scrolls through his list of over two hundred friends and notices a handful of familiar names from Rivington. She clicks on each of their profiles long enough to see many college romances didn't last past graduation. She learns her freshman year resident advisor is now a CPA who recently went on an Alaskan cruise, and Devon, a former fraternity president, is now a herpetological vet and head of the southeast region of the Association of Reptilian Veterinarians. *Who knew?* Jillian is thoroughly intrigued but stops short of plunging further down a rabbit hole. *Focus!* She redirects herself and returns to Keith's profile. His page has a photograph of his wife and four children at Disney World. It says he lives in Larchmont, New York. The only other identifying information is a hyperlink to a website for a private medical group. She clicks and sees he's an orthopedic surgeon and founding partner at the practice. *God bless the internet.*

Jillian leaves a message with Keith's receptionist as well as a breezy email asking if he'd be willing to act as a source for a medical story she's reporting. She doubts he'll be inclined to talk if he knows she's seeking information about his deceased brother, so she banks on the publicity angle. A shout out in the *Times* is hard to turn down. Sure enough, two hours later, Keith's number appears on her caller ID.

"This is Jillian," she answers.

"Well this is a pleasant surprise," he says, his baritone as deep as she remembers.

"Keith! Thanks for calling back. Great to hear your voice."

"Likewise. I'd ask what you've been up to all these years but frankly, I read your stories all the time in the paper, so I'd feel like a big fat phony if I pretended not to know. Gotta say, you did a great job on that elder care series last year. I thought the piece on the visiting nurse service was particularly interesting."

"That's kind of you. Thanks. You know," she chuckles, "I could ask what's keeping you busy these days, but I, too, would feel like a big fat phony because, full disclosure, I completely stalked you."

He laughs. "How can I help?"

She begins pacing around her apartment, as if she needs the momentum to propel the lie she is about to serve up.

"So, I'm working on an article profiling top doctors in various specialties in the New York area. My team and I are putting together a special insert. After some online sleuthing I came across your name. I'm wondering if you could speak to the sort of conditions you treat, memorable cases, rewarding aspects of your job, why you chose this field. It's lighter than my usual fare, but important nonetheless." Jillian hopes he doesn't grow suspicious. This is the type of article she could have written half-asleep as a rookie journalist back in college.

There is silence on the other end of the line. Jillian wonders if he has driven into a dead zone without cellular service. "Keith? Did I lose you? Can you hear me?"

"Yeah," he sighs, "I'm here."

"Oh, good."

More silence. She supposes he is mulling it over, which is surprising given that it's a total puff piece with free advertising.

"Would you like to meet for breakfast tomorrow?" he asks. "I've got rounds early in the morning but have a window from about seven to eight."

"Just tell me where and when."

"I'll be at Lenox Hill. Meet me on the corner of 77th and Lex and we'll find a spot. That work?"

"Absolutely. See you tomorrow."

The following morning, Jillian and Keith are facing one another in a booth at a small coffee shop on Manhattan's Upper East Side. After a bit of pleasantries, it's all business. He seems tense as she pulls a mini tape recorder out of her leather tote but doesn't object to her using it. She is mindful to smile as she lobs softball questions his way: What kinds of surgeries does he perform? Does he have a specialty within orthopedics? What are the greatest rewards and challenges of the job? As he answers, she is convinced he has bought into the ruse.

A waitress comes by with Keith's pancakes and Jillian's fruit cup. They watch silently as she lowers the white porcelain dishes onto the table. When she walks away, Jillian poses what she calls "the gateway" query—the one she hopes will lead to the most revealing and intriguing response.

"So," she says, stabbing a piece of cantaloupe with her fork, "what inspired you to get into orthopedics? There are so many specialties out there. Why this one? What spoke to you?"

Keith slices the stack of pancakes in half with surgical precision. He then rotates his plate and cuts each of the halves in half to create four perfect quarters. As he rests the knife on the edge of the plate, he leans forward onto his elbows and looks Jillian directly in the eyes.

"Listen Jill," his tone now soft and intimate. "I didn't sleep last night. I couldn't stop thinking about our breakfast this morning." He turns and glances furtively out the window beside them onto Third Avenue. "I've spent years wondering how I'd handle this," he whispers, "how it would unfold, when it would happen, *if* it would ever happen, whether I'd have the guts to say everything I've kept inside all these years."

Jillian can feel her eyes widen and pulse quicken, unsure where he is going. Her hands grip the curve of the vinyl bench seat, bracing herself for the ride.

"Hearing from you yesterday, Jill . . . well, I'd say it was the green light I needed."

"Green light?" Her head cocks slightly to the left.

"Heaven knows I haven't had the guts to make the first move."

What? "Keith, I . . . I . . . I'm afraid I'm not following . . ."

He pushes his glasses up the bridge of his nose. "So, you asked what inspired my interest in orthopedics . . ."

"Yes."

"Well, I'm going to give you my stock answer and that's the one you can run in your story."

"Okay . . ."

"I've always loved sports. I wasn't much of an athlete so I became a doctor for athletes—fixing bones, helping them heal so they could improve their game. Basically, I picked this specialty so I could hang around the sports world."

She smiles politely, curious what awaits.

"Now if you put that away," he says, pointing at her tape recorder, "I'll tell you the back story, but it's just between us."

Though he doesn't ask for their conversation to be off the record, she acquiesces without hesitation, promptly sliding the palm-sized device into an outer pocket of her tote bag.

Keith is quiet for a moment and then says, "I had a really hard time with what went down when my brother . . ."

"It was awful. I can't even imagine . . ."

He turns his head around to ensure there are no patrons or waitstaff within earshot. "My family was a wreck. I knew the truth, but I shut my mouth. Told myself I was being a loyal brother and son, and that the right thing to do was to just stay quiet."

She nods sympathetically, not wanting to interrupt or derail his train of thought with a question.

"I don't know if you remember, but I wanted to be a sports reporter and work for ESPN."

"I do. What changed?"

"Oh, life. You know. Decided to go to med school. Save some lives, change some lives for the better. I picked sports medicine and orthopedics, 'cause, like I said, I could still keep a toe dipped in that world."

She waits a beat. "So, are you saying you found your calling after Bailey was killed?"

Keith takes a large bite of pancake and chews slowly. "I wouldn't describe it like that."

"Pardon?" she asks, unsure if he is responding to the word "calling" or "killed."

"It was more of a pact."

Ah . . . calling. "A pact? With whom? God?"

He shakes his head. "No. Me."

She stays quiet, allowing the silence to build.

"Some seriously messed up shit went down, Jill. I was muzzled. Wasn't allowed to speak about what I saw and heard. I needed to find another way to . . . I don't know . . . feel lighter? I figured putting out good and righting some wrongs in the world was the antidote, and what better way than to be a doctor, right? Wasn't my top choice, but it was a good choice. I guess you could say I was trying to reverse the karma."

"Karma?"

He takes a swig of ice water, places the plastic tumbler back on the table, and lowers his voice to a whisper. "April should have never been kicked out of Rivington. And that kid with the knife . . . Rudy." Keith pulls a paper napkin from a dispenser on the table and wipes the corners of his mouth. "That kid got screwed."

Jillian casts a quick surreptitious glance downward to check the outer pocket of the tote bag beside her. The recorder's tiny red light is still on. The tape is still rolling. She raises her eyes back up to meet Keith's. "I'm listening," she says, striking the perfect balance of sympathy and curiosity. "Tell me everything."

16

April

NOW

t's only 7 a.m., the dawn of a new day, and already April can tell it won't be any better than the last twenty-four hours.

First, she's running on no sleep. Peter slamming the office door in her face when she returned from yoga Sunday morning stung, but she figured they'd talk after he cooled down. That never happened. He spent the majority of the day at his desk trying to quell the firestorm, and when he did briefly emerge from his hole for food, he avoided April's eye as well as any conversation with her unless it pertained to the kids. Despite their vow never to go to bed angry, they did, for the first time in their entire relationship. She lay awake all night waiting for him to join her, but he never did. And now, the light is poking through their bedroom window and it's Monday morning. Too late to talk. She needs to get ready for work.

En route to school, she drives over a pothole. This causes the large coffee sitting in the cupholder to spill and saturate her black pants. And if that isn't enough, when she lifts a stack of student book reports from the back seat of her car, the rubber band encasing the papers snaps and sets aloft a flurry of cockeyed penmanship all over the school parking lot. She stomps on some, grabs at others, and while she manages to retrieve all the documents, most of her first graders' projects are crinkled or torn. "Fuck me!" she mutters repeatedly as she gathers them into a pile.

Now, with the papers secured in her work bag and her clothing stained but dry, she locks the car, takes a breath, and marches into school.

"April! Hi! Hi! Hey there!" Jenna, the school secretary, sputters as she plows through the waist-high wooden swing gate to greet her. "Dr. Herman would like to speak with you in the teachers' lounge. I'll go with you." Jenna places her palm on the small of April's back, hurriedly ushering her into the main hallway.

"Can this wait?" April asks. "I came in early to set up bulletin boards." *And avoid the tension at home with my husband,* she thinks but doesn't dare reveal.

"No, Dr. Herman was pretty clear. As soon as you arrived I was to let you know about the meeting."

Dr. Herman, a Brooklyn native, worked with Barbara Zagoda for many years in the English department at Yeshiva of Flatbush in Brooklyn until he relocated to Chicago for a plum position as the head of one of the city's most prestigious private schools. When Peter and April moved, Barbara connected them with Dr. Herman so they'd know someone nearby in case of emergency. Once April received her master's degree in education, Herman scooped her up as a first-grade teacher. Other than her volunteer work at The Prentice League, this is the only full-time job she's ever had.

Upstairs in the lounge, April does laps around the faculty kitchenette as she awaits his arrival. The room is long, narrow, and smells like microwaved enchiladas.

"April, dear," Dr. Herman greets her. The pity in his eyes is a giveaway; she knows he's seen the headlines. "May I?" he asks, his arms extending for a hug.

She swallows hard. His thick New York accent cuts right through her and she is instantly homesick. Her face begins to contort and she knows it's just a matter of seconds before it morphs into an ugly cry.

"Oh, come now, it's all going to be okay," he says, pulling her into his chest.

Dr. Herman's blue and gray plaid blazer smells like her father's aftershave and she is pretty certain her dad owns the same knit tie. This is as close to her father's embrace as she could possibly get.

"It's okay. Let it out. Let's sit, shall we?" he says, directing her to a worn leather couch beneath the lounge's sole window.

She sinks into the soft cushions as he slaps a "Meeting in Progress" placard on the door.

"You're going to get through this," he says sweetly. He reaches for a Kleenex box on the table and sits down beside April.

"Thank you." She sniffles.

"We are here for you. I am here for you. My family is here for you. And your school family is here, too."

"I appreciate that. I really do."

"But," he inhales, "there are some matters we need to discuss."

Her stomach drops.

Dr. Herman stands and walks over to the kitchenette sink where he fills a plastic cup with water. The creak as he turns the knob shut feels ominous, a fateful prelude to calamity. He returns and hands her the cup with a polite yet taciturn smile.

She takes a sip and waits for him to initiate the conversation.

"So, April . . ."

Here it is.

"Like I said, I'm here for you 100 percent. You tell me your needs, I've got your back."

But...

"But there was a meeting of the board of trustees late last night."

Ah, here we go. It's college all over again. Those fucking board....

"And, well, hmm, how shall I say this . . . they feel . . ." he rubs his hand over his tightly trimmed beard, "they feel this is a bit of a distraction for the school."

She nods. "I'm sorry," she whispers, tears pooling again in her eyes.

"Oh, no, dear, it's not *you. You're* not the distraction. Everyone loves *you.* It's the publicity. The attention. We've gotten a few calls from the media and last night the president of the board got a call at his home."

"At home? About what?"

"Oh, just, silliness. Don't worry, we've said 'no comment' to every inquiry."

"But what did they want to know?"

"About your history at the school, about Peter's involvement in that crime years ago, about whether our school does criminal background checks before hiring staff to work with children, if we knew about your 'record' before signing a contract years ago. I'm telling you, absolute insanity. You have no criminal record! They don't know you! They don't know the story. They're baiting us. They're on a fishing expedition. They're looking for headlines."

Oh my God, I'm never going to escape this! Never!

"Sweetheart, it's noise. That's all it is. Noise. I've known you nearly all your life. I've watched you grow up. I know your family. I know you. I know how our students follow you around like the Pied Piper. I've gotten pulled aside by more parents gushing compliments about you than I have for any other member of my faculty. You're the gold standard."

He sandwiches her hands between his and continues, "Listen, I knew about everything when I hired you, but I didn't care because it was *mishigas*. Craziness. Noise. You, your family, you're all such good people. Such good people. And sometimes, good people get hit. This situation is a prime example of that. Stuff happens to everyone, but the measure of a person, in my opinion, is how they rise above. You, April, you rose. You overcame."

"Thanks."

"Don't thank me. It's the truth. But it's also true that the board was not aware. So until they get up to speed on the details, they want you to lay low."

"Lay low? Am I fired?" Visions of the Rivington boardroom flash across her mind.

"No! Absolutely not. It's just until the press calms down and they can sort all of this out."

"Sort what out?"

"How to handle it. You know, how to respond to parents, reporters, that kind of stuff. And while they're busy doing that, they feel it would be best for you to take some time. Be with your family, circle the wagons so to speak. Then when things aren't so hot and they realize this is much ado about nothing, you'll come back. Think of it as a little vacation." He shrugs.

"Are they upset you hired me?"

"Not that I am aware. But even if they are, I don't regret it for a second. You've been a gift to our school."

"Some gift." She rolls her eyes, horrified by the thought that Dr. Herman's career could be affected. "What about my class? What will you tell my students? I'm sick? On vacation? They shouldn't hear lies..."

"The kids'll be fine," Dr. Herman reassures. "We'll figure it out. Listen, you're going to get a call from the president of the board of trustees today. He's going to give you the bottom line I just gave you, but I wanted to get to you first so you're prepared. From their perspective, they've got a school to run. Private school parents to please. If there are photographers outside and reporters calling, it's bad PR and a headache."

"I get it. The easiest solution is to cut out the problem. I've been down this road before. I know the drill."

The school bell rings loudly in the hallway. Though the yellow buses won't pull in for another half hour, April and Dr. Herman look knowingly at one another; the teachers will file in momentarily.

"You might want to get going," he suggests. "I'll check in with you later."

After a quick embrace, April races downstairs. Instead of pinning crayon drawings to a bulletin board as planned, she clears her classroom of all personal belongings before the students arrive. She claws up her lip balms and hand lotion tubes from a desk drawer and drops them inside a plastic grocery bag. Her chunky knit cardigan, the one reserved for chilly winter days, falls to the floor of the coat closet as she yanks it off a hanger. Anything of value—the framed photo of her own children, a cherished birthday card, a personalized mug brimming with sharpened pencils—is thrown haphazardly into an egg crate.

When she's done, April briskly trots out a back door and heaves everything into the trunk of her SUV. All she wants is to hear Peter's voice. He's the only person who can convince her that everything will be all right—that her job status is a temporary hiatus and not a repeat of college, that her involvement in a crime over a decade earlier will not tarnish the reputation of a sweet elementary school principal, that a single photo of Peter mailing a letter will not derail his career, and, most importantly, that their marriage will not combust.

April picks up her cell phone and calls Peter. She knows he must be made aware of her job situation in case the news is leaked to the press, but suddenly she stops and ends the call. The thought of presenting what will undoubtedly be another source of frustration and disappointment for him is too much to bear, especially since they haven't spoken since the headlines broke. She was gutted when he pulled away from her touch; she cannot come home to a greeting like that ever again.

April glances at the digital clock on the dashboard. Buses teaming with kids will arrive any minute. She buckles her seatbelt and steps on the gas, bolting off school property and onto a residential street around the corner. She parks, shuts the engine, and reclines the seat to a nearly flattened position. Hidden beneath the car windows, she stares up through the sunroof at the bright morning sky—a promising robin's-egg blue with scattered cotton ball clouds.

"What the hell is going on?" she whimpers aloud, utterly depleted.

Everything feels off—the smell in the air, the way the daylight shines through tree branches. It is as if she's viewing Earth through a psychedelic filter. She has never done drugs, not even marijuana, but briefly entertains the thought that something she ingested—oatmeal? coffee? chewing gum?—was spiked. Her equilibrium is undeniably askew and the need to escape is urgent. Not the car, but her life. All she wants now is to be enveloped in the warmth of her parents' home—the maroon carpet, the dated upholstered chairs, the oxidized newspaper clipping from Dear Abby and the photocopy of the Scarsdale Diet that have been magnetized to the refrigerator door for decades. Perhaps it was the comfort of Dr. Herman's familiar accent, or the way he smelled like her dad, but never, in all her years of living in Chicago has she felt this homesick for New York.

Just then, a text comes in.

Georgia: Hey, just checking in. You going
to the girls' soccer game after school?

Ignoring her friend's query, April types back:

April: You home now?

Georgia: Yup.

April: Can I come over??

Georgia: Aren't you teaching small
humans today?

April: No. Can I come over?

Georgia: Of course. You okay?!

April: Can I borrow a pair of
pants?

Georgia: Ape, what's going on?

April: Be there soon.

Twenty minutes later, April pulls into Georgia's circular driveway in Highland Park. She is standing at the front door of her center hall colonial holding a pair of bubble gum pink sweatpants in one hand and crisply ironed black slacks in the other.

"Wasn't sure which look you were going for so you've got both ends of the spectrum—Brittany Spears or corporate mom. I have jeans as a middle ground if you prefer."

April kisses Georgia's cheek and reaches for the sweats. "These are perfect, thanks," she says.

"Coffee? Tea? A shot of vodka?" Georgia asks as April ducks into the bathroom.

"Peppermint tea would be great, thanks," she calls back through the closed door, holding onto the porcelain pedestal sink for balance as she peels off her clothes.

When she walks into the kitchen, Georgia is filling two mugs by the stove. April slides into the upholstered bench seat beside the dining table and gazes out the bay window into the backyard. "Gosh I love those trees," she says adoringly. Every time she visits, April is taken by the magnificence of Georgia's two large weeping willows. Their gorgeous pendulant branches flirt with the grass as solid trunks, wide and wise with age, sit steadfastly anchored into the dirt. It's a wonder how they appear so sad yet beautifully strong and resilient at the same time.

Georgia brings over the mugs and settles into a seat across the table. "Ape, your eyes are bloodshot. What's going on?"

April lifts the steaming cup to her mouth, but it burns her lower lip upon contact. She winces and fills Georgia in on her morning as it cools.

"Oh craaap," Georgia moans softly.

"I know."

"How'd Peter take it?"

"Haven't told him yet."

"Don't you think you should?" Her eyebrows arch high.

"Yeah, I just have to time it correctly." April blows on her tea. "He's gonna flip. He's in survival mode, holed up in his office or on a conference call. Honestly, I've never experienced this version of him. He's prickly. It's like he's . . ." she pauses, her mind searching for the most apropos adjective, "possessed."

Georgia nods. "I suppose it's understandable. The negative press was a major curveball, but Peter's the most levelheaded guy I know and," she smiles, "he adores you. So, okay, he's temperamental right now. We've all had our moments."

April doesn't share that their typically effortless banter and comfortable lulls have morphed into an icy, gut-wrenching silence at home.

"Thanks again for taking my kids when the shit hit the fan."

"Oh, please. Don't even mention it! Having them here is always a treat for my kids. I'll take them anytime." Georgia licks her lips. "So Ape, you know I love you, right?"

Shit. April instinctively holds her breath and braces for another hit.

"Here's the thing." Georgia interlaces her fingers around her mug. "People are talking. They're making comments to me because they know how close we are. They assume I knew. I've been blowing them off, not returning texts, changing the topic, but that will only last so long. I'm trying to figure out if there is something I can say to shut them up or put out the fire. I'm not armed with the facts so I feel sort of vulnerable, you know? Like I'm not well-equipped to shoo them away."

Though Georgia's tone is kind, April detects a hint of victimhood.

"What are they saying?"

"It doesn't matter . . ."

"Of course it does! You can't tell me people are talking about me and then not share what they're saying."

"I'd prefer not to," she says, her lips forming a tight O as if she's sipping through a straw.

"Then why did you raise it?" April is incensed.

"I'm just trying to be helpful."

"How is *that* helpful?"

Georgia's eyes are now glossy. "I didn't mean to upset you. I'm just trying to do the right thing. Say the right thing, whatever it is you want me to say. I'm just a good girl from the Midwest. I don't know from these things."

"And I'm a good girl from Midwood! You think I landed in Chicago fresh off a real-life *Law & Order* set? You think any of this feels natural to me? That it has ever felt deserved?" April retorts.

She turns and glances out the window into Georgia's backyard. April feels as forlorn as those willow trees look.

"I'm really sorry, Ape. I didn't mean for it to come out that way." Georgia sniffles and grabs a napkin from the holder on the table. "I just feel ill prepared. I guess what I'm trying to say and clearly failing miserably at communicating is, how can I help?"

"What are people saying?" April asks again. She doesn't typically care about others' opinions, but she is itching to know what is being uttered behind her back. As long as she's already lost control of the wheel, she may as well brace for the crash. "Who's still my friend?"

"Honestly?" Georgia asks.

"Honestly."

"There are more people genuinely concerned about your well-being than those pumping me for gossip. Most want to know if you're okay. If Peter and the kids are okay. If they can do anything like deliver meals, run errands, that kind of stuff."

"Geez, it's like Peter's a widower." April shakes her head. The only thing she abhors more than the spotlight is pity. And the one thing she loathes more than pity is being a burden. "I'm sorry people are bothering you. You shouldn't have to deal with it. You should know it's not like I intentionally hid this from you or Nina, or anyone. It's history. I mean, I don't know *everything* that happened to you in high school or the escapades Nina had in college."

Georgia reaches across the table for April's hand. "You don't need to explain yourself to me. You shouldn't have to deal with this either. Just know I'm here in whatever capacity you need."

"Thanks," she says, genuinely relieved that the swell of tension has seemed to abate.

"So you want to role-play out what to say to Peter about the job?" Georgia asks.

April groans. "Maybe I tell him I've decided to quit and just stay home for a while?"

"There's no way he'll buy that."

"Why not?"

"Listen, I don't judge anyone's life choices, but you're not cut out to be a lady who eats omelets at Country Kitchen on the daily. Don't lose yourself in this."

"I know, but I—"

April's cell phone rings, interrupting her train of thought. She looks at the screen. It's the nurse at her kids' school.

"Hello?" she picks up, trying to hide the rattle in her voice. Her hand instinctively covers her heart; she's not sure how much more it can take today.

"Mrs. Nelson, this is Nurse Allison. Everything is fine. We just have a bit of a bellyache," she says slowly, her voice high-pitched and singsong. Her use of *we* leads April to believe at least one of her children is within earshot of the nurse. If not, this woman has an awfully puerile way of speaking. "I'm calling because I'm here with *both* of your daughters. I've taken their temperatures and am happy to report neither one has a fever, but they do look quite pale."

"Thank you. May I speak with them please?"

"Absolutely!"

A moment later, April hears a barely audible, "Mommy?" on the other end of the line.

"Attie?"

"Hi Mommy," she says softly. "My stomach really hurts. Rosie's does too. Can you come get us? Or maybe Daddy can come? We need to go home right now." The girls suddenly sound as if their voices have regressed to their six-year-old selves.

They never ask for Peter before me, she thinks. *They know. Someone must have said something.*

The nurse returns to the line. "Hello again." April can hear both girls sobbing in the background. "They're welcome to relax on cots in my office for the remainder of the day, but I think they might be more comfortable at home."

"Understood. I'll leave right now."

It isn't until they are in the subterranean garage of their building, walking from their designated parking spot to the basement elevator bank, that the girls finally start talking.

"Tell her!" Attie whispers to her sister.

"No, *you!*" Rosie hisses back.

"Tell me what?" April asks, carrying their schoolbags.

The girls glance sideways at each other but divulge nothing.

"Tell Mom *what?*" April repeats, more sternly as they approach the elevator.

Attie is chewing on a beaded bracelet, her wrist pressed against her mouth, and Rosie is pretzeling her arms across the buttons of her pea coat. "Well . . ." April says expectantly as the elevator dings its arrival. She presses the button for their floor. "I'm waiting . . ."

"I can't," Attie says, now clutching her stomach.

"Fine, I'll do it," Rosie harrumphs. "Hannah told Ilana a secret. Then Ilana told Erin. Then Erin told me. Then Jessie came over to me at the water fountain and said the same thing and she's not friends with Hannah, Ilana, or Erin. So she heard it from someone else."

"What secret?" April asks.

"And then . . ." Attie pipes in, ignoring April, "I went to the bathroom and saw Rosie crying and she told me what they said and then I started crying."

"Oh, guys, I'm sure it's just a big misunderstanding. It can't be that bad." As an elementary school teacher, April is a seasoned pro at dealing with social issues and telephone games gone wild. "What did they say?"

Rosie inches closer to Attie and reaches for her hand before beginning to speak. "They said you helped kill someone in New

York. They said your boyfriend went to jail and that Daddy's trying to make our family look good, but even though we seem nice we're actually not and all their parents talked and no one is allowed to come over to our house anymore."

"That's preposterous!" April says as the elevator doors open. She steps onto the carpeted corridor and widens her arms for a hug. "Come my loves. Mommy's here, it's going to be alright."

Attie steps toward April but before they make contact, Rosie grabs her sister's arm and pulls her away. "Daddy!" Rosie screams, dragging Attie down the hall to their condo. "Daddy where are you?"

April can't look. She can't watch her daughters flee as if she were some sort of monster. "Girls!" She calls out. "Girls, please. Come back." But when the front door creaks open, she knows they've disappeared inside and that once again, she is alone, this time on her knees, with two hot pink backpacks beside her on the vestibule floor.

17

April

NOW

April cracks open the door of Peter's home office and pokes her head inside.

He's on a call. No surprise.

"You got a minute?" she whispers.

He spins around in his swivel chair, gives her pink sweatpants a once-over, then spreads his index and middle fingers into the shape of a V. For a brief moment, she's hopeful this is a sign of peace, a white flag to end the chill that has sprouted between them. She glances at the rumpled bed sheets atop the sofa across from his desk and wonders if the peaceful hand gesture means he'll return to sleeping in their bedroom. But when Peter mouths "two minutes" to the wall above her head instead of her face, she swiftly returns to reality, closes his door, and heads to the kitchen.

Peter finds her a few minutes later. "What's going on? Are the girls sick? I heard them come in but couldn't get off my call." He looks down at April's legs. "And what's the deal with this situation?"

"It's been a morning. I'll get to the pink sweats later. Right now we need to triage."

"Triage?"

"Yes, triage." She knows the kids' immediate well-being trumps any discussion of her employment. "Listen, the twins know about the headlines."

"Fuck!" he exclaims, clinching his thick hair with both hands.

"I know," she grumbles as she arranges Saltines on a plate for the girls. "Needless to say, it was upsetting and confusing, hence the stomach issues and the call I got from the school nurse to pick them up."

Peter begins pacing around the kitchen island. "Fuck! Fuck! Fuck!"

She has never heard her proper Bostonian husband curse so much. *Stay calm*, she implores herself. *He's lost control, I need to pilot this plane.*

"We've got to talk with them," April says evenly. "They need facts and reassurance. And then we'll have to speak with their school to devise a plan if an issue arises again in the classroom."

"*We?*" he bristles. "I'm not the one who created this shitstorm."

She whips her head around. "What's *that* supposed to mean?"

"Oh come on, April. It's not like my controversial petition for hot chocolate in second grade is the skeleton in the closet here. I'm not the one with the past."

"Are you kidding me? You knowingly married into that past. You took it on. I hid nothing from you. Not one thing!" *What an ass! This isn't my husband . . .*

Peter opens his mouth but places a finger against his lips as a blockade.

"What?" She glares.

He shakes his head, refusing to utter whatever is on his mind.

"Just say it!"

"I've been on the phone with my publicity people all morning . . ."

"And?"

"And we need to address this head on. We should issue a statement or, better yet, hold a press conference."

"About what?" April turns toward the sink and runs her hands under the faucet even though they are perfectly clean. Both the warm water and not having to look at Peter are surprisingly soothing.

"Oh please. Come on, April. You know exactly *what*. Stella thinks we need to lay it all out there."

"Who's Stella?"

"The PR people just brought her on board to help deal with this crisis. The headlines are too damaging. So either I stay quiet, take the hits and allow the negative press to poison my name, or I give some context to this crap and hopefully reverse it. I'm leaning toward the latter. Stella says we need to come out and tell people exactly what happened so we distance you from the crime. You should explain how Rudy was simply some guy you knew from the old neighborhood and you were just trying to help a familiar face out of a bind. And then we brush it off and say something like 'no good deed goes unpunished' or whatever."

April can feel her jaw slack. "Some guy from the old neighborhood? You're kidding, right? Tell me this is a joke." She reaches for a dish towel on the marble counter and wrings it with her hands as if she's trying to asphyxiate its cotton loops.

Peter shakes his head. "We need to squash this story. Today. It's just going to continue to get worse. We need to tell the people the truth, and tell it together. You and me as a unit."

"The *truth*? You think the truth is that Rudy is just some kid from the old neighborhood? Are you insane? He was my best friend! And I was the one in 'a bind' as you say. He was protecting *me*. I am not disowning him. I will not diminish him. And I will never, ever brush him away like a speck of dirt."

Peter's face flushes a shade of crimson she has never seen. "So you'll dirty up my life and abandon me instead? You won't support your husband, the father of your children, but you'll stand by a man who's doing fifteen years for homicide?"

"He didn't kill anyone!" April screams. She glances down the hallway to check that the kids' bedroom doors are closed. *Thank goodness they are*, she thinks.

"He pled guilty to manslaughter!"

"That was bullshit."

"He had a knife, April! You need to accept the facts. He might be a decent guy and this was a one-off mistake, but honestly, who does that? Who whips out a knife at a networking event?"

April glowers at Peter in disgust. "I cannot believe we are having this conversation right now," she hisses and walks over to check the digital thermostat on the wall. The condo suddenly feels like a sauna even though it reads sixty-eight degrees.

"*You* can't believe it?" Peter balls his fists. "*I* can't believe it! I can't believe that I have to practically beg for my wife's support in a moment of need—a need, by the way, that only arose because of *her* life, not mine—and she won't give an inch. Not a single inch. All I'm asking is that you make a statement to explain it all away. Answer a few questions, smile, and tell the press that Rudy and that whole debacle was simply a blip from your childhood and that's all this . . ." his arms stretch to take in the expanse of their family home, "this, is your *real* life—not the shitty place you came from."

She shakes her head incredulously. "*'The shitty place I came from.'* Wow. So now it comes out. So that's what you really think of my family, my home, everything I love in New York."

"That's not what I meant," Peter fumbles, attempting to backtrack. "You know that's not what I meant."

"Fuck you," she spits at him.

"April," he steps closer, reaching out for an embrace, but she recoils.

"I'm sorry I'm such a burden, Peter."

"My God, April. Why is this so hard to understand? *You* are not the burden. *Rudy* is the burden. This *mess* is the burden. As my wife, please, help me erase the mess."

"I can't do this right now." Her voice cracks. "We have two kids down the hall who could use a snack. I can't have this fight . . . And why is it so goddamn hot in here? Is the air not working?"

Peter walks over to the thermostat and presses a button. "It'll cool off soon."

Unfortunately, she knows he's referring only to the temperature, not the tension in the room.

"Listen," he turns to face her, "this doesn't have to be a fight."

"Peter, you can't ask me to stand in front of the world and resurrect the past—a past you and I deliberately tried to leave behind when we moved here. And you certainly can't ask me to publicly disavow a person I love. A person who lost years of his life because he was protecting me. I'm not turning my back on him. He's family. Never. I'm sorry, I won't do it." She thinks back to their childhood, the slide, the ear tug, how they were always there for each other, the promise she made to herself to be there when he got home. "It's a hard no."

"A hard no, eh?" Peter straightens his spine. "A person who is *like* family, not actual family—that's the guy you'll fall on your sword for? That's the one you won't turn your back on? I have news for you. He's not the only guy who changed his life to protect you. Look where we're fucking living April. I started my career from scratch in Chicago because of your baggage out East. I changed my life to protect you too and this is how I'm treated?"

"Illinois isn't a prison cell! Don't twist my words. I'm not saying I won't support you."

"I don't need to twist your words, April. You said it yourself. He's the person you love."

"Stop. You're acting like you're in middle school. I know how important this election is for you. And it's important to me too because I love you. If you need me, I'll be there. I will smile and be the dutiful wife standing by my man . . ."

"Oh, no, no, April. No. You've made it very clear. You're standing by your man."

His words sock her in the gut. "Cut the crap, Peter. He's not my man. You are."

Peter's thick eyebrows wriggle like caterpillars. "Are you sure?"

April closes her eyes and collects herself before stepping into the girls' bedroom. "Room service!" she says as she enters. April can see Peter has already staked out his spot in the corner. His legs straddle Rosie's desk chair while his arms hang limply by his sides like a defeated chimpanzee. Muscle, skin, and bones scream what he refuses to say: *The onus is yours, bitch. Clean up this mess.*

April settles in at the foot of Attie's bed. "Wanna come join us, Ro Ro?" she asks, patting the space beside her.

Rosie nods but chooses the opposite end. The girls rest their heads side-by-side on a single pillow by the headboard, their loose hairs intertwined and indistinguishable. A lump forms in April's throat and she swallows hard, unsure if the beauty of their sisterly bond or her fear of a united front against their mother is the trigger.

The magnitude of the moment is not lost on her. As she takes in their innocent, expectant faces, she is keenly aware that the choices she is about to make—her words, her tone, her attitude and outlook—will imprint deeply and likely remain for the rest of her daughters' lives.

April glances over at Peter for support, but after a split second of eye contact he shifts his gaze to the floor. All he offers is the wave of an open palm, like a gentleman insisting she walk ahead and lead the way.

Though the specifics are not the same, April is reminded of her time at The Prentice League. While she never spoke with the children of incarcerated parents during her years as a volunteer, she had occasionally spotted them around the office and it always broke her heart to see pure young lives tainted by such grown-up issues. To witness an arrest, to watch a mother suddenly disappear from home, to attend family gatherings without a father, to contend with gossip and rumors, and to digest the reality that you have been passed an inescapable legacy through no fault of your own, is simply tragic. On occasion, April has wondered how Rudy will handle the topic should he become a father one day. What will he tell his kids? When will he tell them? Will he be defensive? Stoic? An open book? His conversation will undoubtedly look very different than April's, and yet, there will be common tropes.

April and Peter had always known the day would come when they would share April's past with their children, but never did they expect a public outing to force their hands. Perhaps they were naïve to think a run for office wouldn't dig it all up. As far as they knew, it had never been on anyone's radar—neither personally nor professionally—in all the years they had resided in Chicago. They had moved on. They had proven themselves to be cherished and valuable assets in their communities, effectively rubbing out the past. But here they are, or, more accurately, here she is about to saddle her daughters with the news that they have been infected by some deleterious matrilineal gene. It's one thing to inherit an elevated risk for a certain disease—like a BRCA mutation linked to breast and ovarian cancer—but it is quite another to contaminate your own child through human error, even one in which you were only peripherally involved.

April takes a breath, focuses on the girls' faces, and begins, her voice aquiver. "Guys, let's, uh, let's talk about what happened today in school. Is there anything you'd like to ask or discuss?" Given her background in early childhood education, April is privy to the cardinal rule when dispensing delicate information to kids: Make them your guide. Share the basics but create space for them to pose questions. Then tailor responses to fit their inquiry. Offer no more, and no less, than what is asked.

Rosie cups her hand around her sister's ear and whispers something that elicits a shrug from Attie. April's heart pounds at the sight. She can feel the girls' respect fading with each passing second and it's clear Peter has no intention of jumping in for the save.

"Well." April smiles reassuringly, channeling her commanding teacher persona. "I'd like to share some things with you if that's okay. First of all, you need to know that Dad and I love you so much. You can tell us anything. We don't care if it's good or bad. Whatever is on your mind, you can always, *always* come to us. Got it?"

Flat miens, but at least they're locked in and making eye contact. She knows they're listening.

"Second. What you mentioned a few minutes ago in the elevator—about the things kids said at school today—that must have been really hard to hear. And pretty confusing."

She assures herself as she awaits a response. *That's good. Reflect back what they told you. Be patient, you're doing great. You've got this.*

After a few seconds, Rosie sits up. "Did you kill someone?" she asks, point blank.

"No," April shakes her head definitively, "absolutely not." *Don't cry*, April commands herself. *Keep it factual and clear and for God's sake, do not cry.*

"Did you *help* kill someone?" Rosie follows up, threading her pink polished fingers through the holes in a crocheted blanket. She stares into her lap and frowns, something she does whenever she's upset.

"Never, ever. No." April is careful to keep her voice even and strong.

"Do you have a boyfriend?" Attie asks.

"The only boyfriend I have is sitting right over there." She points her thumb toward Peter, who is now rubbing his temples. "I don't have any other boyfriends."

"*Did* you have a boyfriend who killed someone?"

"No."

Rosie leans her back against the bed's wooden headboard. "Do you have a friend in jail?"

Okay. Here we go.

"Yes, I do," April says confidently, her voice lilting upward ever so slightly. "My friend Rudy. He's been in prison for a while. Since before you were born. Since before Dad and I even got married."

"Why?" Rosie pushes. "Why is he in jail? What did he do?"

"Well, he got into a fight one night many years ago. He didn't start it. And he didn't mean to hurt anyone. But the man he fought died the next day and Rudy got blamed for that man's death."

Attie clutches her stuffed giraffe so tightly it appears she may decapitate it. "He died the next day because of the fight, or from something else?" she asks.

Out of the mouth of freakin' babes. If only Attie could have been Rudy's lawyer.

"Well, sweetie, that's a really great question. I'm not sure."

"So if you didn't do anything bad and Rudy's not your boyfriend, why would people say those things about our family?" Rosie asks. "Why would they lie?"

"And why would our friends say they won't come to our house

anymore?" Attie whimpers, burying her face in the giraffe's neck.

Peter huffs. "Oh my God! Who said that?!"

"A bunch. Ellia even pretended not to know me, like I was invisible," Attie sobs. "She just walked past me like we never had sleepovers or anything,"

"How dare they!" Peter fumes. "That's just horrible." He squints accusatorially at April.

"We'll get to the bottom of this, I promise," April assures the girls, shoving the tension with Peter inside an internal waiting room to be dealt with later. "Your friends will be fine. Don't worry. What matters right now is that you know the truth. And the truth is that yes, a friend of mine went to prison many years ago and he is getting out soon. That's it. That's all. That's the whole to-do."

"Ellia says he was 100 percent for sure your boyfriend," Attie states, arms now folded.

"Ellia has no idea what she's talking about." April wants to tack on that that spoiled penthouse-residing brat whose sixteen-year-old sister drives a custom designed Range Rover is full of shit, but she refrains.

"Did you love him more than Dad?" Rosie asks.

"Guys." April raises her hand to shut this down. "Rudy was *never* my boyfriend. Just a friend." Through her peripheral vision April can see Peter anxiously stroke the stubble on his chin. "I love your dad very much. I love Rudy, too, but differently. I love Rudy as my friend."

"Does Dad know your friend?" Rosie inquires.

April looks over at Peter then back to the girls. "No, they've never met." She wonders if this is the end of the interrogation. *Please ask for Fritos and the Disney Channel . . .*

"Why did Ellia say that Daddy is trying to make our bad family look good?" Attie asks, barely above a whisper.

That mother fucking Ellia.

Peter shifts uncomfortably in his chair and grumbles something unintelligible.

"Honey, I can't tell you why people say what they do," April shrugs. "The reality is, you can't control other people. Not their actions or their words. The best thing Dad and I can do as parents is to arm you with the truth and the confidence to know who you are and where you come from. And you guys should hold your heads high because you come from a family that loves you deeply, that is kind, hardworking, honest, and generous."

"It's not fair," Rosie says with a pout.

"You're right." April sighs. "It's not."

She desperately wants to go on a rant about how the justice system is flawed, how the press can be careless, and how those at the helm in our courtrooms and newsrooms must be judicious and cautious with their powers or else the entire system will break. Instead, April crawls from the foot to the head of the bed and kisses both of their noses.

"I love you guys, it will be okay," she says as she nuzzles them in a three-way embrace. April wishes Peter would get up from that desk chair and join them. At a minimum he could offer a supportive wink or gesture of unity in lieu of his muted stone face.

Rosie and Attie reward her with gentle pecks in return, proof her message has not only been delivered but heard. *If only I were as easy a sell*, she thinks.

An hour later, Peter is back in his office and April is pacing around her master bathroom talking with Nina.

"I can't, Nin, I just can't!" she insists. "There is no way I'm issuing a statement or standing in front of a microphone talking about this."

"Agreed. There will be no statement from you." Nina's voice

booms through the receiver. "Listen, I've met Peter's PR guru, Stella. It's a small industry. We've crossed paths enough times for me to know the woman's not an idiot, but there are two schools of thought on how to tackle these sorts of situations. One camp says you face negative press head on. Deny, deploy, describe in detail, do whatever it takes. The other camp is passive: Keep your head down, mouth shut, and eventually you'll suffocate the headlines."

"Well, it looks like Peter and I are in different camps. What should I do?"

April can hear voices between Nina's panting breaths. She's either on a treadmill in front of a loud television or briskly walking along a crowded street.

"What should you do, April? What should you do? You should take care of you is what you should do. Listen to your gut."

"I have to go home." April swallows hard.

"You are home."

"No, New York home. Honestly, I'm homesick. I've missed my parents and New York before, but not like this. I guess all the Rudy stuff resurfacing brings me back and makes me realize no one here gets it. Not Peter, not you, not Georgia, not my kids. I need a little fix. This is a need, not a want."

Nina is quiet for a beat. "Well, if your gut's telling you to get out of Dodge, do it. Get a reset."

"I know, but Peter will go ballistic."

"Will your friend be out of jail yet?"

"I don't know. I'm not sure what day he'll be released. But regardless, I'm craving a visit with my parents."

April can hear the whirr of Nina's treadmill along with a breakfast cereal jingle playing through the phone. She's definitely exercising beside a television.

"Okay, here's what I'm thinking," Nina says. "Peter can take care of Peter. If he issues a statement, that's his statement. If he decides to have a press conference, it's up to you if you want to smile and stand next to him, but I would strongly advise you not to say a word."

"Yes, but Stella's point is we are a unit, and voters need not only to see but *hear* us as a united front."

"Well, I disagree. I think you can be part of a marriage but maintain individuality. No offense, Ape, but this is your stuff, not his. Was Peter involved in that crime? No. Did he even know you at the time it occurred? No. Just because you two are legally wed, does that mean he inherits your stuff even if he had nothing to do with it? I don't think so! And by the way, same goes for Rudy and you. He pulled a knife, not you. It's unclear to me why you've taken such a hit."

April sits atop the toilet seat cover and rests her forehead in her hands. She's in no mood to dissect the drama. Right now, all she needs is a plan.

"What about the kids?" April asks. "You think I should take them with me to New York for a few days? Gosh, it would be great to just pluck them out of here. Getting spoiled by grandparents would be a fun distraction for them."

"Perhaps," Nina says evenly, "but the reality is that it will be harder for the kids to get back into a routine when you return to Chicago. Plus, the comments from their friends will just be on pause. I suspect they'll have to deal with questions eventually. It might be wise to just maintain normalcy. Keep the routine going. You know what I mean?"

"Yes, but how am I going to leave them? Peter's swamped. There's no way he will make three lunches, successfully navigate the bus schedule, get them on time to after-school activities, work his day job, manage the campaign, and gracefully figure out the media. There's simply no way that's happening."

"*You* do it all the time."

"True, but I'm not dealing with a campaign on top of everything. In all fairness, it's a lot right now. He's got a ton on his plate."

"How about asking Georgia? Not my place to volunteer others, but your kids are in the same school. It's only for a couple of days. I'm sure she wouldn't mind taking them."

"That's not a bad idea."

"Yeah, I have those every so often," Nina jokes. "Alright. Go to New York and recharge, just keep your eyes open. I can't imagine there will be reporters camped out in your parents' driveway, but if I'm wrong and someone rings the doorbell or approaches you at a store, just shut your mouth. And for Pete's sake . . ."

"For *Pete's* sake?" April smiles.

"Ha, yes, for *Pete's* sake, and your own sake, pack a hat and sunglasses. You don't need a story blowing up about you running off to New York and leaving Peter behind."

"Got it. Thanks, Nin."

April hangs up and immediately texts Georgia.

> Hey, need a favor.

Georgia: Of course. What's up?

> April: Can you take my kids for a
> few days while I go to New York?
> And . . . Would you be able to
> book round-trip flights for me? I
> will absolutely reimburse you.

April does not want to pay for the flights on her joint credit card with Peter. The last thing his campaign needs is for anyone to assume he paid for his wife to disappear during a PR crisis.

Georgia: Send me dates and I'll take care of it. In terms of tickets, just clarifying, am I getting one ticket for you and one for Peter? Or are you flying solo?

What a loaded question, April thinks.

April: Yes. I'm flying solo.

18

Rudy

NOW

"DeFranco!" a guard bellows from the prison corridor.

Rudy is sitting at the edge of his mattress, dressed in a fresh jumpsuit, when he hears his name. He rises and stands at attention, unsure what to expect.

The soles of the guard's shoes squeak against the concrete floors and the clang of his key ring grows louder as he nears Rudy's cell. This moment is over a decade in the making and Rudy's prepared. He has cleared his locker, bartered two pairs of unused cotton socks for two empty cardboard produce cartons, and packaged up a significant fraction of his life. Fortunately, the only items he cares to keep are lightweight: handwritten letters, photos, and a couple of paperbacks. The one thing missing is certainty. Today's the day he has been promised, but if there's a single lesson he has learned, it's that nothing in life is guaranteed.

"DeFranco," the guard calls again, now unlocking the steel cell door.

Rudy's stomach falls. *They've changed their minds. That's it. I'm stuck here.*

"Get your shit," he commands, eyeing the boxes in the corner of the room. "Time's up."

With the two repurposed fruit boxes cradled in his arms, Rudy follows the guard down the main hallway, through several security clearances, and then to a chamber with small nooks that reminds him of the dressing rooms at Loehmann's department store. Lorraine used to take the boys shopping with her when they were still young enough that no one seemed bothered by their playing with Matchbox cars on the fitting room floor. Somehow, a synapse in his brain has connected this sterile jail to girdled women squeezing cellulite-dimpled flesh into discounted dresses.

"Strip," the guard says curtly, pointing to one of the cubicles.

Rudy gently places his boxes on the ground and removes his clothing. He can feel the man watching his every move.

"Hold your balls and bend over."

Rudy knows the drill. He lifts himself and leans forward at a ninety-degree angle. Unlike his first strip search years earlier, this guard doesn't touch him. *Perhaps they care more when you enter the system than when you exit,* he thinks.

"Get dressed." He watches as Rudy steps back into his jumpsuit, slips on his shoes, and signs his name on a sheet of paper.

"Parking lot's through those doors. Good luck." The guard turns and walks away without a formal send-off, as if Rudy's freedom is simply a check off his to-do list.

Alone in the hallway, Rudy stares out of the floor-to-ceiling glass walls. The morning sun shines brightly, beckoning him outside and making this auspicious day feel even more promising. He has imagined this very instant since the day he was incarcerated. He'd suspected he would make a mad dash, like an Olympian out of the starting blocks, and yet, here he is, immobile.

What if reality doesn't live up to the fantasy of life back home? he wonders, looking down at the boxes beside his feet. A stack of envelopes sits on top. Thirteen years of correspondence from those he loves most secured by a thin brown rubber band. The sight of their handwriting, his parents' Brooklyn return address, the browned edges of the older letters—all of it replaces his reticence with reminders of a loving, happy home that he has not seen in far too long. Then, as if a gun has fired in that Olympic race, he propels forward out of the starting blocks.

Pushing the door handle is surreal. The simple act of placing his own palm on the metal bar and walking outside unescorted, unencumbered by cuffs on his wrists, feels foreign. He follows a concrete walkway as it curves around the corner of the building. There is grass on either side of the path and a wooden placard with an arrow beneath the words: Visitor Parking. As soon as the lot's blacktop comes into view, Rudy hears his brother's voice.

"Rudy! Rooooodaaaaay! Over here!" Tommy is sprinting toward him, arms waving high above his head like a possessed cartoon character.

Rudy accelerates to a jog but stops short when one of the boxes he is carrying topples to the ground. Postcards and books scatter over the asphalt. He crouches to clean up the mess and when he gazes upward into the sun, his brother is there, standing over him.

"God, it's good to have you back." Tommy's voice breaks. He extends a hand and pulls his brother up into a hug so constricting that Rudy lets out a cough. "Let's get out of here, klutz. I got a change of clothes for you in the trunk." Tommy grabs both cartons and leads the way to his red sedan.

Rudy is beaming. The good-natured ribbing along with his brother's familiar scent of Irish Spring soap envelops him like a warm blanket. "Thanks," Rudy says, furtively glancing inside the car windows to check for his parents. He isn't surprised by their absence. Lorraine so abhorred seeing Rudy in prison she broke out in hives before each drive upstate. Eddie tolerated the visits a bit better but had grown increasingly quiet over time. With each passing year, he said less and less to the point where their time together became more painful than joyful for Rudy. The memory of his father as a jovial man was of greater comfort to Rudy than witnessing the aged, muted version. But he didn't have the heart to tell Eddie to stay home. Uttering those words would have wrecked him, and he hated to think about the emotional or physical impact that rejection could have on his father.

"Yeah, Ma's been in the kitchen for days," Tommy says, clearly sensing Rudy's curiosity about their parents' whereabouts. "She's cooking, freezing, baking, freezing. It's endless. She got a whole new set of Tupperware and already went through two of those aluminum foil rolls. I don't think there's any room left in the fridge. We're gonna eat like freakin' kings. You should go away to prison more often."

Rudy laughs. Oh, how he has missed his brother! "So what's Dad up to?"

"He's doing some work in the apartment. Don't tell him I told you. I think it might be a surprise. So act like you had no idea, okay?"

"What kind of work?" he asks as they deposit the boxes in the trunk.

"Our bedroom, I mean, uh, your bedroom. I told you I moved out a while ago, right?"

"Yeah, of course," Rudy replies, though it was actually Lorraine, not Tommy, who informed Rudy in a letter.

"Needed my own space given how I work with Dad and all." Tommy's voice dips a bit more somber. "Twenty-four-seven got to be too much, you know?"

Two minutes in and already the elephants have begun their parade. There's the issue of family time—Tommy's abundance versus Rudy's years of forced separation. There's the topic of compromise—Tommy sacrificing his budding accounting career because Rudy was unable to do his share to help their aging father manage the building. And then, of course, there's the matter of Tommy's privilege to live independently while Rudy spent over a decade in a cell block. But now is not the time to dig in. This is his moment to celebrate. In fact, the rest of his life is going to be a celebration. *Lookin' forward, not backward*, he's decided is his new mantra.

"Man, I'm excited to see your new place!" Rudy smiles, hoping to put Tommy at ease and assuage any guilt his big brother might feel for forging ahead with his life. "So, what's dad doing in our bedroom?"

"I don't know, but it's been like a time capsule from when we were kids. The bunk beds, the dresser, the *Sports Illustrated* covers we taped to the wall . . . He wants to surprise you with the new paint and whatnot. Like I said, don't tell him I told you."

"Got it," Rudy promises. He ducks into the car to swap his prison uniform for the brand-new hooded sweatshirt and track pants Tommy brought. Rudy peeks inside a shoebox and finds a fresh pair of Nike sneakers.

"These yours?" he asks, pointing to the high-tops.

"No, yours."

"You serious? T! Are you crazy?" he exclaims, running his fingers over the smooth white leather and navy swoosh.

"It's the least I could do."

Rudy can't remember the last time he was dressed in new clothes from head to toe. "Hey, I still got it goin on or what?" he asks while shimmying into a shoe.

Tommy takes in the entirety of Rudy's appearance. "Of course you've got it goin' on!"

Rudy waits for the follow up—a gentle punch on the shoulder or a sarcastic retort about how Rudy gets his good looks from

Tommy—but there is nothing. It's like Tommy's on his best behavior.

"Can you cut these off?" Rudy asks, pointing to the tags.

"I don't have a scissors," Tommy says.

"Yeah, you do. Just unfold it. It's next to the blade on the pocketknife."

Tommy pauses before responding. "I, uh, I don't have that anymore."

"You don't have what anymore?"

"My Swiss Army knife. I got rid of mine a long time ago."

"Oh." Rudy nods as if this makes perfect sense, even though the thought of Tommy parting with his once prized possession is shocking.

No brotherly ribbing? No more knife? Okay, so it's a little different, he thinks as he rips the tags off with his hand. *But holy cow, I'm in a car! In real clothes! Sitting next to Tommy!*

As they pull out of the lot and descend a winding wooded path to the main county road, Rudy adjusts the radio dial to find a music station without static. Deejay voices cut out on every frequency and they decide the endeavor is futile until they emerge from the sticks and enter civilization. About an hour into the trip down the New York State Thruway, Tommy pulls up to a fast-food drive-through for Cokes, burgers, and fries. Rudy's mouth waters as the clerk passes their order through the window. *Oh my God!* He moans as a whiff of grilled onions wafts out of the bag and into the car.

"Pace yourself." Tommy laughs. "This is just the appetizer. Wait 'till you get home and see what Ma's got for you." He reaches for the stereo knobs on the dashboard and pumps up the volume now that they have a clear signal of New York City's Z100 radio station.

As they accelerate onto the highway, Rudy rolls down the window. With a sixty-five-mile-an-hour breeze in his face and Beyoncé blasting through the Toyota's speaker system, he begins to feel his shoulders loosen and can sense the same in Tommy. He grabs a couple of fries from the bag and dips them into a small container of ketchup, relishing the taste of freedom. *I can handle this*, he thinks, leaning back against the headrest.

"Thanks for everything, Tommy," he says, staring ahead at the open highway. "You're the best."

Tommy smacks him playfully upside the head. "Gimme a burger."

Ahh, there it is. Now I'm home. Rudy smiles.

The aroma of fresh tomato sauce, garlic sautéed in oil, and oven-baked chocolate greet Rudy as soon as he walks off the elevator onto the fluorescent-bulbed hallway. If he shut his eyes, he'd swear he'd just entered a five-star restaurant.

"You're early!" Lorraine exclaims upon opening the door and seeing Tommy. "Was there no traffic? Did you speed?" She interrogates her eldest son, her face contorted in confusion and concern as she unties the apron strings around her neck. "Wait a minute . . ." Panic sets into her voice. "Where is he?! Don't tell me. Oh, no, did they keep him?"

Rudy is crouched down on his knees behind his brother; it's a game they've played as long as they can remember. "Hi Ma!" He smiles, poking his head over Tommy's shoulder.

"Ahhh!" Lorraine shrieks. She shoves Tommy aside with such force that he loses his balance.

"Oh God, oh God," she begins to sob, pulling him into her bosom. "My baby! My baby!"

Lorraine's mother hen is poised and ready for her close-up. The suffocation that would have been abhorred when he was a teen is the exact nourishment he needs right now.

Eddie, on the other hand, is more reserved. "Hey, hey, look what we have here." He smiles broadly, patiently waiting for his wife to release their son. When she does, Eddie kisses Rudy's cheeks and each of his hands. He is undoubtedly overjoyed by his boy's return, but he's soft spoken and possesses an air of depletion, as if he's long overdue for retirement.

Witnessing the change in his father incites a wave a sadness in Rudy. He is doubly grateful now for the early release.

As they walk inside and drop Rudy's boxes in the hall closet, he notices the dining table is set for seven, not four. "What's this about?" he asks Tommy, pointing to the three extra place settings.

His brother shrugs. "Ask Mom. I don't know."

Just then, the intercom buzzer sounds in the kitchen, alerting them to guests in the lobby. Lorraine presses a button on the wall and leans into the speaker. "Come on up," she chirps excitedly, then purses her lips and shoots Rudy a mischievous look. Her eyes twinkle as they widen.

Minutes later there's a knock on the door. "Rudy, baby, can you get that for me?" Lorraine asks, sounding just as she did when he was young and she'd ask him to run an errand at the corner bodega.

Rudy heads to the entryway where he is greeted by Steven Zagoda's outstretched arms.

"Our boy is home!" Steven exclaims.

A hard lump instantly forms in Rudy's throat. Steven's warm exuberance, as well as the possessive "our boy" feels like a hero's welcome. For the first time all day, he teeters on crying. The emotion hadn't hit him when he saw his parents, perhaps because he was prepared. But Steven Zagoda? That man was there at the start of it all and was still standing strong, cheering at the finish line. There's something quite moving about the steadfastness of those who see you through from arrest to reentry.

As they hold an embrace in the DeFrancos' foyer, Rudy's peripheral vision detects movement in the corridor. When he turns his head toward the motion, he sees Barbara seated in a wheelchair and

April holding the handlebars, steering her mother down the hall toward the apartment.

An electric shock shoots through his body, involuntarily straightening his spine.

While it's surprising to see Barbara in this condition, Rudy's gaze is fixed on April. Everything and everyone else blurs. She looks just as beautiful as he remembers, except her hair has changed. The color is lighter, and the length is a bit shorter but still substantial enough for the ends of her signature ponytail to brush against the shoulder of her denim jacket. Though she's wearing flats, her diminutive frame is a towering presence that notches up the energy in the atmosphere. He wants to wrap his arms around her and never let go. And yet, just as he was overcome by a reticence leaving the prison, his muscles feel weighty and fixed. *I can't believe it has been thirteen years. Thirteen years!*

Though she had offered numerous times when he initially went away, Rudy discouraged April from visiting him upstate. At first, it was because he didn't want the image to imprint in her mind. He was ashamed and knew a prison-issued jumpsuit was a far fall from the framed photo they had of one another in superhero costumes as kids. *Superman is supposed to transform into Clark Kent*, he thought, *not a felon.* But as time passed, he discovered an additional reason to dissuade her: the fickleness of prisons. He couldn't bear the thought of April having to endure what his family had experienced.

One time, while Eddie and Lorraine were on the highway en route upstate, the warden announced he was stopping all visits that day. No reason was provided and Rudy was unable to contact his parents. It broke his heart to know they were schlepping four hours north only to be turned away and then ride four hours back home without ever laying eyes on their son. Another time, Tommy did the drive and it started snowing halfway into his trip. By the time he arrived, the prison ended visiting hours "due to inclement weather," which meant he was shooed away as soon as he pulled into the visitor parking lot. And then there was the Saturday when all three members of his family made the trip together for his birthday. Rudy was so excited, he pressed his clean jumpsuit by putting it under the mattress the night before. Perhaps seeing a crisply creased uniform might make Lorraine worry a bit less, he'd thought. But twenty minutes into their three-hour allotted visitation, an officer came over and said there was a "situation" at the prison but gave no additional explanation. Lorraine cried and Tommy cursed under his breath, but no one dared challenge authority. The DeFrancos knew that if they made a stink with a corrections officer, Rudy would pay a price. So they remained mute and instead of ending the visit feeling uplifted, Rudy watched his family walk away degraded and powerless. This boiled his blood. He realized then that while it was one thing for *him* to be dehumanized and disrespected, it was significantly more painful to watch that treatment inflicted on loved ones and know that there was nothing he could do to stop it. *April's never coming to visit*, he decided after his family left that day. The thought of her getting turned away after making a long drive or being subjected to the whims of an officer in a foul mood was simply not an option. *I'd rather not see her than worry about her well-being.*

"What are you standing here like a statue for? Go!" Steven pats him on the back. "Go say hello. They can't wait another second to see you."

When Rudy and April lock eyes, they both break into smiles that form pockets of jubilation in their skin, crevices of delight that one day will become crow's feet. With the wheelchair a blockade between them, he first kneels down to greet Barbara at eye level.

"Hit the brakes, sweetheart," Barbara instructs April. "This boy deserves a proper greeting."

As April adjusts some levers on the wheelchair, Barbara kicks out the foot pedals and pushes herself up to a standing position. "Come here, Rud, let me look at you." She puts both hands on Rudy's face and kisses his forehead.

Rudy can see Barbara's body is thinner; her cheeks are sunken and the skin on her arms more crepe-like, less taut.

"Okay, you two, that's enough. Now it's my turn!" April squeals, carefully lowering Barbara back into the chair. She wheels her mother over the floor saddle into the DeFrancos' apartment, secures the brake, and immediately wraps her arms around Rudy's neck. "I can't believe this is real. I just can't believe it. I've missed you so much," she whispers, then pulls away to take him in. "Oh, thank God you're home," she says and goes back for another squeeze.

Like Barbara, April's body has changed. Not drastically, she has always been slim, but she's harder—more fit and toned. The youthful plumpness that once filled her cheeks has faded; even her jawline is more angular and defined. *She smells different,* Rudy thinks as he breathes her in. Her scent is sophisticated and musky, no longer the flowery lotion/spray combo he remembers her stocking up on whenever there was a sale at the Kings Plaza Shopping Center. "I've missed you, too. It's so good to see you." *I'm not letting go until she does.*

"Ahh, Lorraine made lasagna, I can smell it from here," Barbara remarks.

"You know her well!" Rudy laughs, and he and April naturally break apart.

"I do," Barbara states. "Her lasagna is my weekly Wednesday dinner. Did you know your mother prepares meals for me?"

Rudy is not at all surprised by Lorraine's generosity.

"Ever since I started using this thing," Barbara says, tapping the wheelchair's armrests, "it has been a lot harder to do stuff. Your mom comes over and paints my nails, other times we go for a stroll and run errands, and she always makes extras of whatever she's cooking. Steven's gained ten pounds!"

Steven rubs his protruding gut as proof.

As if on cue, Lorraine bounces out of the kitchen, a gingham apron tied at her waist. "Can you believe it, Barb?" she says, pointing at Rudy. "We survived. Thank God that's over."

Not completely, Rudy thinks. Yes, he's home and the early release is an undeniable blessing, but a long road remains, including an ankle monitor, a curfew, and weekly check-ins with a parole officer for the duration of his sentence.

"Come, everyone, food's gonna get cold." Lorraine waves the two families over to the dining table.

April begins to maneuver Barbara's chair but Rudy intervenes.

"Here, let me . . . I haven't driven in years!" He chuckles, and as he reaches for the handles, his fingers brush up against April's left hand. The prongs of her diamond-encrusted wedding band scrape against his knuckle and his mind instantly reverts to their first summer at the bagel store when April had a crush on an older boy. He doesn't remember the guy's name or what he looked like, but Rudy vividly recalls lying in his bunk bed, throwing a baseball in frustration at the ceiling, and asking Tommy if he'd ever heard of a place called Dartmouth. "Don't be intimidated by the Einsteins," Tommy had said. "And don't sell yourself short."

As the two families gather around the rectangular table— Eddie and Lorraine at the heads, Steven and Barbara on one long side, the "kids" together on the other—Rudy can think of no better homecoming.

"A toast," Tommy says, lifting a can of Coke before they dig into the large serving platters dotting the table. "To the greatest brother a guy could ever have. Welcome home, buddy."

"To Rudy!" they cheer.

Less than twenty-four hours earlier, he was eating off a plastic tray in a mess hall, unsure if administrators would come through on their word to release him. He tried not get his hopes up when fellow inmates began placing bets. If anyone asked what he was most looking forward to, he'd feign indifference. But in truth, all he wanted was a stroll through Midwood—to see the mom-and-pop shops, the schoolyard playgrounds . . . the fractured sidewalks, aged trees, and fire hydrants that sprayed water on scorching summer afternoons—and to be with those dearest to him. Now, with April to his left and Tommy on his right, Rudy's equilibrium has returned; fantasy has become reality right here on the plastic-covered dining chairs.

As Lorraine begins to serve the meal, April's phone rings and she quickly pulls it from her jacket pocket to check the Caller ID. Rudy sees "Peter—ICE Husband" flash across the phone screen. *Ice husband? What does that mean?* He contemplates asking April to clarify the pairing of these incongruous terms but lets it go.

April stares for a second at Peter's name, seemingly weighing whether or not to answer the call, and then slides the phone back into her pocket.

Rudy can feel her tense. Her cheeks flush and the corners of her mouth—which had been upturned since their reunion at the front door—have fallen.

"Can you please pass the salad?" April asks politely.

When Lorraine brings a bowl over to scoop a helping onto her plate, April's phone rings again.

"Ugh," she harrumphs. "What now?" Once again, April retrieves the phone from her jacket pocket. This time, Rudy can see the screen says "Georgia—Cell." April reflexively skids her chair away from the table and picks up the call. "Hey," she says softly, concern in her voice as she walks over to the hall. "Everything okay? The kids okay?"

Rudy watches as she sticks a finger in one ear and presses the phone to the other.

"Oh, okay. Yeah, Simon's blue sneakers are in the duffle bag. If you don't see them inside, check the outer pocket. I can almost guarantee there's a plastic storage bag of tank tops in the girls' luggage, but in the rush of the moment I may have forgotten to actually put it in the suitcase. It might still be sitting on Attie's dresser at home. Honestly, it's a good thing I even remembered their underwear. Sorry you have to deal with this. I appreciate everything you're doing. It's royally sucky . . . No, we haven't spoken. He just called, but I didn't pick up. I can't deal right now . . . I'll call to check in later. Thanks again."

When April returns to the table with what Rudy can easily tell is a forced smile, he knows something is amiss.

"You alright?" he asks.

"Of course!" she says, leaning her head on his shoulder. "How can I not be? I'm here with you, aren't I?"

We need time alone to talk, to catch up, he thinks.

"How long you in town?" he asks.

"Couple of days."

"You want to come with me tomorrow? I've got to meet with my parole officer. Sign some forms."

"Absolutely. Whatever you need, I'm yours." She smiles.

Rudy couldn't have asked for a better homecoming.

The following morning, April pulls up to the corner of Avenue J in front of Rudy's building.

"What happened to Big Bertha?" he asks as he steps off the curb, shocked to see April behind the wheel of a Honda instead of her parents' faux wood–paneled 1980s wagon.

"That girl retired years ago."

Rudy shakes his head. "End of an era."

"It happens." She shrugs. "So how you feeling?"

He lets out a long sigh. "Like a million bucks. I mean, I know the whole ordeal isn't totally done, but it's soooo good to be home. I feel like I can finally see the light at the end of this screwed-up tunnel."

She reaches over to the passenger seat and squeezes his hand. "We've got a new start now and it's going to be great. I just know it."

Rudy wonders what she means by "we." Their families' collective trauma? Or are she and Rudy embarking on a new chapter?

"So how's everything in the Windy City? Husband, kids, job? Everyone good?"

"Yeah, yeah, status quo . . ."

"Status quo?"

"Okay." She exhales, releasing air like a deflating balloon. "You really want to know?"

"More than anything."

"So I'll paint a picture of my daily routine . . ."

For the next thirty minutes, April regales Rudy with the logistics of working a full-time job and raising three children with a myriad of after-school activities and commitments. He learns about the shockingly slutty costumes for Attie's dance competitions, the social drama surrounding Rosie's tennis team, and how Simon became the goalie for his peewee ice hockey league because the coach felt he spent too much time waving to the audience whenever he skated across the rink playing other positions. There is no mention of Peter—ICE Husband.

"Hey, you think I can fit into that parking spot?" April points to a narrow space between two cars on a side street.

"It's tight. Want me to do it?"

"Can you?"

"Are you doubting my skills?" His mouth is agape in mock disbelief.

"No, Rud. I mean, are you *allowed* to drive a car?"

"Shit. You're right. I forgot. No I can't, not yet." Rudy opens the door and stands on the sidewalk waving her through as she parallel parks.

With its rubber plants, relic coffee maker, and hallway corkboards, the New York State Department of Corrections & Community Supervision is as generic an office space as they come. After checking in, they are introduced to Gene, Rudy's parole officer, who swiftly ticks off the rules of his early release.

"No alcohol, no drugs, no weapons, no leaving New York State without permission. You are allowed to leave the house between 7 a.m. and 9 p.m. but must be home by curfew or it will be considered a violation of your parole. If you want to go anywhere outside of the state of New York, you must submit a formal request for approval well in advance. I want you back here to check in once a week for the next month. If that goes well, we'll space out the visits. Got it?"

"Yes, sir."

He slides a stack of signature pages in front of Rudy, hands him a ballpoint pen, straps on an ankle monitor, and they're done.

Rudy smiles as they exit the building. "This is way better than what I had. Honestly, I don't care if they chain me to the living room couch. I'll take it."

As they make their way down the sidewalk, though, Rudy stops and rotates his right foot.

"What's wrong?" she asks.

"It feels weird. I think the strap's cutting into my skin."

"Maybe it's too tight? Let me check. I don't want you to get a blister . . ." April bends down and rolls up the cuffs of Rudy's pants, exposing the monitor. She gently rotates the device so a piece of plastic doesn't rub against his shin. "Is that better? Or do you want to go back inside and have them adjust it?"

Before he can answer, a rapid-fire noise startles them. It's in close proximity and incessant. April and Rudy turn toward the sound, and several flashes go off. Then, just as quickly as it began, the clamor ends and they spot a photographer running away.

"What was that about?" Rudy asks innocently, looking down at April, who still has her fingers wedged in the strap. "You think someone famous walked by? Aw, that would suck if we missed it!"

April quickly rolls down the cuffs of his pants. When she stands, Rudy notices she has lost all color in her face.

"You look green, Ape."

"How's your ankle?" she asks, brushing him off.

"Better. You sure you're alright? You don't look so good."

"Uh, yeah. Let's go home."

Worried she might be lightheaded, he reaches for her hand and together they walk around the corner to the parking spot.

Another flash goes off.

Suddenly, April retracts her hand from his. "Get in the car," she seethes through gritted teeth. "We need to leave. Now."

19

Peter

NOW

"I cannot believe this!" Peter shouts, slapping the *Chicago Tribune* with the back of his hand. "There are so many levels of wrong with this I don't even know where to begin."

April is back in Chicago curled into a fetal position on the couch in Peter's home office. Multiple newspapers with photos of April and Rudy are strewn across Peter's desk. There is one of them exiting the Department of Corrections, one of her bending down to fix his ankle monitor on the sidewalk, another of them walking hand in hand, and one sitting side-by-side in her parents' car.

"First of all, you didn't even mention you'd be seeing him," Peter fumes. "When I agreed to your whole New York trip, it was because you said you needed to visit your parents and that your mom wasn't well. I didn't give you shit about booking it without consulting me first. I didn't harangue you about the fact that it's the height of my campaign and my wife should be by my side. I agreed to it because you said you needed to be there and I promised you when we moved to Chicago that you could see them any time. Did I expect it to be when I needed you most? No. But when I give my word, I give my word. I just made one, *one*, very clear, explicit request that if Rudy happened to get released while you were in New York that you were *not* to see him because I knew reporters would be on the prowl. But did you listen or care about what your husband had to say? Hell no!"

April pulls the hood of her sweatshirt over her head like a remorseful teenager on the cusp of punishment.

"And while we're on the subject of Rudy, let's just get it out there, shall we? What's the deal with you two? Did you sleep with him? Are you in love with him? Like, just tell me the truth. Put it on the table, April. Was he the one you loved but couldn't get 'cause he was locked up, and I was the consolation prize because I wasn't doing time for murder?"

"It wasn't murder . . ." she mumbles.

"Oh my God! *That* is what you have to say for yourself? Are you kidding me? You're quibbling over the formal charge from the Manhattan DA's office after everything else I just said?" He thrusts the newspaper onto the floor in fury. "Well, now I have my answer."

"Stop!" April sits upright. "Do I love Rudy? Yes, I do. But I love him like an old friend. A cousin. A best friend. Whatever you want to call it."

"So you never . . ."

"Never what? Hooked up with him?"

"Yeah."

"No!"

Peter shakes his head. "Well, even if it never happened, I find it hard to believe that a guy who killed another dude simply because he was talking with you doesn't harbor some feelings. I'm telling you, I'm a guy. There's no way he spent thirteen years behind bars and the thought of winning you over never crossed his mind."

"It's not like that." April rolls her eyes.

"Whatever. You owe me," he states definitively, pointing at her face. "My election is around the corner, and you're going to clarify all this crap before the polls open."

"Clarify what *crap*?" April raises her fingers to form air quotes.

"Whatever it is they want to know."

"Who's they?"

"The press, the voters, anyone asking."

"We've been through this already. I don't want to speak about this publicly, Peter."

"Well, I'm not going to lose this election, April." He can feel his nostrils flaring. *There's no way I'm letting this opportunity slip away without a fight. I've come too far.* "We tried playing this game your way when you disappeared to New York, and that made matters worse. Now we're going to play by my rules."

"I don't know about that . . ."

"Oh, I do," he says assuredly and takes a swig from a water bottle before pounding it onto the desk with a thud. "Heck, if there's one thing I *do* know, it's that if I lose this election, it'll be because of you. So let's try to avoid that, for both our sakes."

April shoots a look of disgust toward him that he has never witnessed in all their years together. The room is silent as they stare at one another, both seemingly frozen and unsure how to navigate this unfamiliar terrain. If he weren't so incensed, her revulsion would reduce him to tears and spur groveling on bended knee for her forgiveness, followed by an extravagant flower delivery. He has certainly spoken in tones and words that have never before emerged from his mouth, but, in fairness, he has also never felt betrayal this profound.

April's lower lip begins to quiver. "Peter, I'm not talking about this with the media. Rudy has a chance to start over, and the more we discuss his case, the more likely the story stays alive and the harder it will be for him to move on. Reentry isn't easy, you know that."

"Jesus effin' Christ, April! The more we *don't* discuss this case, the more likely my campaign will die!" Peter punches the air in frustration like a bruised and bloodied Rocky Balboa in a final round with Apollo Creed. "And need I remind you that I had nothing to do with this case? Nothing! I inherited it from *you*. Just get out there, answer the reporters' questions about your involvement, and minimize your relationship with Rudy. The story will spike for a hot minute and then cool off. It's the only way to divorce me from this mess."

"Nice. Really nice. Are you trying to do the same with me?" she says sharply.

"No, no, no," Peter stammers. He pinches the bridge of his nose. *I've got to cool this down. We're going too far off the rails.* He looks around at the photos and plaques in his office—his diplomas, pictures of their family, academic and professional trophies, certificates of appreciation from local charities—this moment is the culmination of a lifelong dream. But it is a dream he has only ever envisioned with a wife standing beside him—a Jackie to his Jack.

"It's quite the opposite, actually," he says more calmly, pulling out his desk chair to sit down. "I want the world to see my beautiful, lovely better half who, out of the kindness of her heart, got roped into a mess when she was just a kid. If you explain it all away, I guarantee you'll win their sympathy. You're the only one who can salvage the election. It's not me, Ape. You've got to be the one to talk. We're so close I can feel it. Please. This is me begging you."

When a tear trickles out of the corner of her eye, he knows he's gotten through. *Don't berate the witness, counselor. You've got her right there in the palm of your hand.*

"Okay," she says, wiping her cheek. "I have an idea."

Peter straightens his spine, each vertebra lining up and standing tall like readied soldiers.

"What if . . ."

He tilts forward on the desk chair, preparing to accept her olive branch.

"What if, instead of me doing the talking, *you* get out there and clear Rudy's name."

I thought we were making some headway here. His posture collapses as swiftly as it had sprouted.

"Just hear me out. You don't even have to mention Rudy by name. You can be totally honest and say, 'I'm aware of the situation in the news and although I personally was not involved in what occurred many years ago, I wholeheartedly believe this was a travesty. Like many of you, our family can relate to unfortunate situations—times when we think, there but for the grace of God go I. This was one of those situations and our hearts go out to all involved.' And this is where you shift. You bring it back to your message about why you are running for State's Attorney."

He ponders her idea. "So spin the story and use it as leverage."

"I suppose, if you want to be crass about it . . ."

"I'm just stating the obvious." He shrugs. "So let me get this straight. We say . . ."

"*You* say," she corrects, "that you have a track record of being a compassionate attorney, a history of community service, and in the context of all this stuff, we as a couple understand better than anyone the importance of having responsible people in power . . . people dedicated to the pursuit of justice."

Peter paces around the room wringing his hands. "But it still doesn't address the photos of you in New York. You know they're going to ask."

"Just because they ask doesn't mean you have to answer. You can say it's a private matter or, better yet, didn't you learn in law school to answer a question with a question? Throw it back at them."

"But I'm a public servant . . ." He's feeling very fidgety and grabs a small wooden gavel from his bookshelf—the one he received as a gift from his parents upon graduating law school—and begins twirling the handle. Never in his life has he had to cover anything up. Never has he felt dirty, impure, or the need to be slick. Authenticity and honesty are as much a part of him as his DNA, and he can't believe that April of all people is the one trying to change him.

"A public servant who has a right to privacy as much as everyone else," she snaps. "Take control of the message. Pivot."

Peter considers this and picks up his cell phone. "Let me see what my PR people say."

Seconds later, Stella is on the line. Peter puts her on speaker and gets her up to speed.

"Hmm. Will your wife at least stand next to you when you talk?" Stella asks. "It's important for people to see family support."

Peter raises his eyebrows expectantly at April as he lets Stella's question dangle in the air.

April points at the cell phone, then presses a finger to her lips, signaling that she wants Peter to mute his conversation with Stella.

He presses a button and holds up the phone as proof. "It's muted. She can't hear you."

"I'm not saying a word at the press conference," April clarifies.

"So, is that a yes?" he asks.

She nods. "Yes."

Peter feels a slight swell of optimism.

On the Sunday before the election, Peter stands behind a bouquet of microphones in a crystal chandeliered conference room on the third floor of Chicago's Hilton Hotel. He is dressed in a crisp navy suit with a periwinkle silk tie, his hands commandingly gripping the sides of the lectern.

Stella is planted in the front row, directly in his line of sight, and April, adorned in an ivory dress and gold bangle bracelets that clang every time she moves her hands, is just a few feet to his left. There are about ten rows of cushioned brocade chairs on either side of the center aisle and while it's not a packed house, there is a sizable buzzy crowd with a handful of television cameras set up on tripods along the perimeter.

"Hey, everyone, thanks for coming this morning. Don't want to take up too much of your time, I know everyone's busy . . ." He can feel himself stalling and glances over at Stella, who offers a wink of reassurance. "So, as you may know, there has been some attention brought to a matter completely unrelated to my campaign."

A reporter's hand shoots up and he feels his pulse quicken. *Stay calm. Stay on message.*

"Yeah, so . . ." Distracted, he scans his note cards resting on the podium.

"I'm here to set the record straight and take this opportunity to speak to you all as I would my friends."

There's a bit of feedback from the microphone, which causes a high-pitched sound to reverberate in the room. As a hotel employee walks over to adjust the mic wires, Peter reviews the talking points in his head. *Keep it simple. Don't be defensive. Don't focus on Rudy. Talk about criminal justice reform. Importance of having good people in office.*

When the mic is fixed, Peter continues. "As I was saying," he flashes a nervous grin, "long before I met my wife, she attended a gathering in New York City. A crime took place that night and it involved someone she knew. This individual pled guilty, was incarcerated for several years, and has recently been granted an early release from prison. I have never met or spoken with this individual. I have never been involved in any aspect of this case. It has no bearing on me, my professional record, my lifelong commitment to the pursuit of justice, my decades as a lawyer in good standing, my many years of volunteer work, or my ability to, hopefully, serve as Chicago's next State's Attorney." His palms are saturated and he surreptitiously wipes the sweat against his pants. "And with that, I'll take some questions."

Nearly every hand in the room rises.

Peter reaches for a glass of water from the shelf beneath the microphones. As he takes a sip, he glances over at Stella and notices a strained look on her face. The confidence she projected minutes ago has faded and morphed into a pencil-chewing, furrowed-brow concern. *Shit. Did I not hit all the marks?*

"Yes, in the back of the room." Peter points to a petite woman with a sleek blonde bob.

"Mr. Nelson. I'm Heather Jenkings with the Associated Press. My question pertains to the relationship between your wife and Mr. DeFranco, the young man who was incarcerated for homicide. Were you aware of the degree of intimacy between them?"

Peter smiles. This question is not unexpected. "I can assure you, Ms. Jenkings, they were no more than neighbors. Next . . ." Peter points to a man in the second row.

Heather raises her voice. "I have a follow up, Mr. Nelson. In your experience as an attorney, would you say it is typical for someone to willingly post nearly a quarter of a million dollars in bail for a person who's merely a neighbor? Is that common?"

What the hell is she talking about? "Excuse me?" Peter places a hand beside his ear as if he hasn't heard her.

"Surely, you're aware, Mr. Nelson, that your wife's parents shelled out $200,000 bail for Rudy DeFranco, essentially paying for an accused murderer to be released following his arrest prior to sentencing. I was curious how you felt about this matter and if, as State's Attorney, you have a position on bail reform laws. Do you share your wife's inclination to return criminals to the street and will that impact your policies going forward should you become State's Attorney?"

Stay positive. You are in control. You drive the message. You determine the headline.

"I was not aware that my in-laws had posted bail, but I am hardly surprised." He turns briefly toward April and though she is ashen, he smiles broadly as if he couldn't be more thrilled by this news. "They are compassionate, generous human beings. As I mentioned earlier, I had absolutely no involvement in this case. I've never met Rudy DeFranco, I don't know his family. This was a blip in my wife's life prior to meeting me. What I *can* tell you is that I have every confidence in my wife's judgment, her values, her morals, and the same can be said for her parents. They're humble people who don't need recognition for performing acts of kindness. Knowing my in-laws as I do, I have no doubt they were thoughtful and considerate in their actions. And as for your question about bail reform, though I did spend several years practicing law in New York, I cannot speak to current policies in that state. In terms of Illinois, as you are probably aware, bail reform is a very important issue. I will certainly explore policies relating to cash bail, pre-trial release, and work with colleagues to determine when a citation is called for versus an arrest. I believe strongly in the relevance of drug treatment as well as mental health courts, and I welcome the opportunity to discuss this further. Now, for the gentleman in the second row . . . I'm ready for your question . . ."

"Yes, hi, Mr. Nelson, I'm Matt Julius with NBC 5 News. I was just curious if Mrs. Nelson might offer a comment about her role in the criminal case. I appreciate that this was her experience, not yours, and so in light of that, I was hoping she might be able to provide some insight about it all, specifically the nature of her current relationship with Rudy DeFranco and why she was recently with him in New York shortly after his release."

Smile. Smile. Smile. Exude confidence.

"Mr. Julius, this isn't a press conference for my wife. She's a citizen with a right to privacy."

Don't look back at her. Do not turn toward April. Peter is certain that if he does, he will buckle. Anger and betrayal will hijack the façade he's desperately trying to maintain.

"Let me ask you a question, Mr. Julius. If you knew of someone going through a hard time, would you show up or would you conveniently disengage and leave that person to fend for themselves? Out of sight, out of mind."

"Sir, this is not about me."

"And this is not about my wife. But you asked a question and I'm going to answer it. If you were that person, Mr. Julius, the kind who minds their own business, you wouldn't be alone. Many people choose not to make waves in their own lives. It takes a special kind of human, one with an expansive, open heart, to be there in the good times and in the bad times for the people they . . ." Peter catches himself. *Don't say love.* ". . . look out for, like family, friends, or neighbors. And frankly, it's no surprise to me, or anyone who knows my wife or in-laws, that they would step up. That's the way they're all wired. That's the way my wife was raised, and the values she and I try to instill in our children—to be there for others in times of need. My wife is a beauty inside and out. I'm one lucky guy. Okay. That's it for today. Thank you."

Peter reaches for April's palm, and with sweaty interlaced fingers they walk off the stage. *I handled that as best I could. Man, she owes me.*

"You finished strong. You deflected very well," Stella says as the three of them ride the elevator down to the lobby. "There's a black

SUV waiting on South Michigan Avenue. Get in fast and I'll call you in a bit."

When they exit onto the sidewalk in front of the hotel, cameras ricochet as Peter helps April into the car. As soon as the driver shuts the door, they both sink into the buttery back seats.

"Thanks for what you said, it was really nice." April tilts her head to rest on Peter's shoulder, but he reflexively jerks away, suddenly needing to retrieve the cell phone from his jacket pocket.

He ignores the compliment and begins scrolling through emails. *I can't believe I had to do that. I can't believe you put me in this position. This was supposed to be a smooth sail but you've got us treading in place, and now, if I'm lucky, I won't sink.*

"Peter? Did you hear me? What you said was really sweet. Thank you."

He cocks his head and looks disdainfully at her.

"What? What is it?" April asks.

"Why have we never discussed that your parents posted his bail? I had no idea."

"I don't know." She shrugs. "It's not like it was a deliberate omission. It just never came up in conversation. Why does it matter?"

Peter slams his thumb into the red seatbelt button to release the straps so he can turn his whole torso to face her head-on. "Don't you think that's a detail I should have been aware of—that you should have told me at some point over the years? I had no inkling your parents were so involved. Why didn't his parents step up? How did they convince your parents to foot the bill?"

"Peter," she says calmly, shaking her head, "it wasn't like that. There was no convincing."

"It was nearly a quarter of a million bucks, April! Your parents aren't loaded. Why would they post money they don't have to bail out a kid who isn't theirs? They don't have that kind of dough just lying around. They probably needed a loan or credit line or second mortgage. That's a lot of effort for someone who isn't your flesh and blood. Unless, of course, they were buying their way, or *your* way, out of something."

"What the hell is that supposed to mean?" she spits back.

"Look at it from an outsider's perspective," he says, pounding a fist onto the middle seat between them. "Why would your family ante up and not Rudy's? It doesn't make sense."

"Do you have any clue how strapped his parents were? Lorraine was a cashier at Alexander's department store and Eddie was a building super. We weren't rich either, but at least my parents were professionals with regular paychecks, a pension, and a 401K . . . a totally different ballpark than the DeFrancos."

"Yeah, I appreciate that, but still, from the perspective of someone naturally skeptical like, say, a reporter, it seems overly generous. In my mind, it's now fifty-fifty on whether we start seeing headlines that there was some sort of coverup for your involvement."

April looks as if she has just caught a whiff of something foul. "Oh my God. You've lost your mind. There was absolutely no coverup . . ."

"I know that, but will the press buy into the purity of it all? That's my point. We'll have to see . . ." Peter leans back and rebuckles his seatbelt.

The car slows as they approach a bit of traffic. The space between them grows quiet. All Peter can hear as he stares out the window is the hiss of air filtering through the car's air vents.

"I'm not sure you appreciate how awful this was on so many levels," April says, barely above a whisper as she opens her purse to retrieve a packet of tissues. "Especially for Eddie, Lorraine, and Tommy. You have no idea how they were treated throughout this whole ordeal. After Rudy's arrest, their bank dumped them. Completely out of nowhere. No warning. One day Eddie and Lorraine are depositing their paychecks and the next they're getting a letter in the mail saying the bank has terminated their account. When they called up to ask if it was a mistake, they were told that the bank was under no obligation to disclose the reason to the client. Legally the bank had the right to do whatever they wanted. Can you believe that?"

"That's terrible."

"Yeah, it was a shit show. Turned out that Rudy's name popped up on some list of criminals and the bank didn't care about guilt or innocence. They asked no questions and made no effort to learn the facts. All they wanted was to wash their hands of him. And then, because his account was still linked with his parents' accounts and with Tommy's, the bank kicked the whole family out. Guilt by association. Eddie and Lorraine were forced to drain their checking and savings and put the cash in a fireproof safe in my parents' basement. Do you know how demoralizing it is to have to ring your friend's doorbell to make a withdrawal? It was like my parents' basement became their ATM. Eventually, one of the smaller local banks agreed to take them on, but that was only after my dad pulled strings with some friends of friends."

Peter shakes his head. "Yeah, that's awful." He has heard of this happening to clients but has never had a personal connection—not even a few degrees removed.

"And by the way," she continues, her voice still soft, as if she doesn't want the driver to hear. "It was the same with their credit cards. They were dropped without warning despite perfect credit. Never missed a payment and all of a sudden Lorraine was buying a birthday gift for Tommy when her Mastercard got denied. She was mortified, especially because it happened at her department store and her friend was ringing up the purchase."

Peter releases a long sigh. "This is horribly sad and I'm sorry to hear it. But why didn't you ever tell me? It's a significant part of your life, April. I shouldn't have learned about it from a reporter at a press conference. I was totally thrown off."

"I'm sorry. It's not like I was deliberately hiding it from you. The bail thing just never came up."

"It's the type of thing that should have. At least in preparation for the election."

Peter closes his eyes. He can feel a bizarre tug-of-war inside him, as if his heart and mind are holding opposite ends of a long, corded rope. It seems as if every cell in his body is being forced to choose a team—either the one filled with compassion and empathy, or the other whose rally cry is, *she screwed you.*

Peter's phone rings. It's Stella. *Saved by the bell*, he thinks. *Now here's someone who I know has my back.*

"Is she with you? You still in the car?" Stella's tone is curt and crisp.

Peter assumes she is referring to April. "Yes."

"Fine. Call me when you're alone."

Peter can't decipher her tone, but it feels urgent and triggers a surge of adrenaline. "Yep. Will do."

20

Jillian

NOW

t's 7 a.m., thirty minutes before her flight is scheduled to depart from JFK, and Jillian is sitting at home in fleece pajamas, crafting an email to her boss. Though it has been her intention all along to beg off with a last-minute ailment, she feels no guilt about scrapping professional responsibilities for full immersion in the Rudy-April saga. Peter's recent press conference is making headlines in Chicago, and Keith Jameson texted earlier in the week to see if she is free to meet today on the Upper East Side. "I'm definitely making the right choice," she says aloud to herself. *No doubt at all.*

> Dear Todd and Crew,
> I'm sorry to be writing this in the eleventh hour, I know it's poor timing on my part, but I'm not feeling well and will not be joining you in Sweden for the conference, at least not

today. There's no way I can board a plane right now. Will
keep you posted. I'm here for any questions, brainstorming,
sound boarding, etc. Call or email with anything at all. Safe
travels!

Best, J

"Ahh," she exhales after sending. *Plate cleared.* She shuts the
laptop, throws a winter coat over her night clothes, and heads
across the street to her local Starbucks. As she waits in a lengthy
line to pick up her drink order, she notices her phone light up with
text messages wishing her a speedy recovery.

Thank you! she types back to each one. *Send updates!*

With a vanilla iced latte in hand, Jillian returns to her building's lobby where she sees her neighbor, Jordana, waiting by the
elevator bank.

"Hey there, coming back from a run?" Jillian asks, taking note
of Jordana's teensy jogging shorts on the chilly November morning.
Her bony, lanky legs look about a mile long.

"Yeah, just did a loop around the reservoir," she says, still
catching her breath.

"Good for you. That's impressive."

"Stress reliever. I find it helps before going to work."

"Makes sense. You still practicing law?"

"Yep." She wipes sweat from her brow with the back of her
hand. "Same job since law school."

"Wow. That's rare these days." The elevator opens and the
women step inside. Jillian presses the button for their floor. "Remind
me . . . DA's office?"

"No. Legal Aid. I do defense."

"Right . . ." Jillian's mind begins calisthenics. "So, this is kind of
a random question, but would you happen to know people in the
DA's office?"

"Yes. Absolutely."

"It's probably a long shot, but did you know an assistant district attorney from years ago named Sketcher? Or a defense attorney by the name of Cossofski? I don't think he was with Legal Aid though."

"Are you friends with Sketcher?" Jordana asks.

"No." Jillian takes a sip of her drink.

Jordana sighs with relief. "Okay, good. Sketcher was . . ." She shakes her head censoriously. "I hate to bad-mouth anyone, but he was kind of a slimeball. Rumor was his application got rejected like three times from the DA's office before a bunch of strings were pulled, and then after he worked there for a bit they quickly regretted it and let him go. Last I heard, he had billboards on the Jersey Turnpike advertising his private practice. Like one of those 1-800 type of things with a big close-up of his face."

"Interesting," she says, knowing she will research the heck out of this later. "And how about Cossofski? Do you know him?"

"I met him once or twice a long time ago. Seemed like a nice guy. He had worked in the DA's office for a while before going to defense. He was an 18B lawyer—that's a private lawyer who represents indigent clients. Cossofski definitely had friends on both sides of the aisle. I remember him being pretty savvy and political about that kind of stuff. Never wanted to ruffle any feathers with people in the DA's office or on the defense side."

"That's got to be a challenge in the courtroom, no?"

"Yeah, he wasn't a street fighter. Certainly not a go-for-the-jugular type, but perfectly capable for bread-and-butter misdemeanors like drug possession or trespassing violations. I'd probably want someone else representing me if I were facing a more serious charge. He retired a while ago."

The elevator dings and the doors open onto their floor.

"Have a great day!" they say simultaneously and walk in opposite directions down the corridor.

Back at her desk, Jillian scrolls through the research file she's created on Rudy's case. She's still flummoxed by the anonymous missive scrawled onto a stray piece of yellow legal pad.

Cardiomyopathy

A-fib

1.5 inch arm laceration + suture

ETOH (alcohol) ↑

Heart Trans

How on Earth did this random note make its way into the court's electronic records? she wonders. As she sifts through documents, Jillian notices that the cursive on the memo matches Sketcher's distinct slanted penmanship at the bottom of several signature pages. *He must have written that note. But when? And where would he have gotten this information?*

As soon as the clock strikes nine, Jillian dials the office of Phinneas Kennedy, the Chief Medical Examiner. They had spoken on several occasions over the years when she needed clarification on a medical story, and he had always been an insightful source who didn't mind taking Jillian's calls.

"Hello, Dr. Kennedy, this is Jillian Jones," she says, leaving a message on his voicemail. "Hope you're doing well. I'm calling because I'm working on a story and I'm trying to get some clarity on an issue. When you have a moment, please give a call on my cell. Thanks."

Three hours later, the ME returns Jillian's call just as she is about to meet Keith Jameson on East 86th Street at the entrance to Carl Schurz Park. Given Keith is tight on time, he takes priority and the ME goes to voicemail.

"Hey, good to see you again." Jillian smiles as she and Keith settle in on a bench overlooking the East River. Though pale, he is dressed impeccably—brown suede lace-ups, a crisp white button-down shirt, and navy slacks with a sharp ironed crease down the center of the leg.

"Thanks for meeting me, Jill. I'm sorry, I must seem so needy . . ." He's already rubbing his palms together.

Needy? No. Anxious? Yes, she thinks but doesn't dare say. "Not at all! How can I help?"

"So, I really enjoyed speaking with you at the diner and I think getting some of that stuff off my chest . . ." he clears his throat, "well, it felt good to let it go."

This guy needs a therapist, Jillian thinks.

"There's a lot more I need to tell you, Jill. Just gonna jump in, okay?"

"I'm here. I'm listening." She nods sympathetically, wishing she hadn't forgotten her microcassette recorder. She glances at her cell phone and contemplates using the voice recorder app but her battery is too low and it would cut off mid-conversation. *Just focus and take in every word,* she implores herself.

Keith has progressed from palm-rubbing to hand-wringing. "My family really screwed April and that kid who went away."

"Rudy?"

"Yes, Rudy."

"What do you mean by 'screwed,' Keith?"

"Fucked over."

She laughs. "I know what 'screwed' means. I'll rephrase the question. *How* did they screw April and Rudy?"

"Jill, my brother was very drunk that night. For multiple rea-sons he should have been laying off the booze. Aside from being an alcoholic, he was taking a slew of medicine—for years, mind you—that specifically states on the packaging that patients should refrain from alcohol consumption. He had a heart transplant in middle school and was literally a poster child. He and my mom spoke at conferences, did an ad campaign and fundraiser for organ donation awareness, and as long as he was under her roof, he was med compliant with the immunosuppressants, anticoagulants, what have you. The second he went off to college, it was like wings sprouted and he couldn't fly away fast enough. He drank, partied, got in trouble, and I'm sure you can guess how adherent he was to his pill schedule and doctors' appointments. You'd think someone who faced death would be vigilant about healthcare, but it was the opposite. It was like he was finally living for the first time."

"That must have been so frustrating for your family. To come that far and then watch him self-destruct."

"It was. Especially for my mom. She was on the board of two pediatric cardiology charities and a leader in the organ donation community. It wasn't a good look. She was mortified by his behavior and did whatever she could to prevent the dirty laundry from getting out, which only made it worse."

"Like what?"

He shakes his head. "Oh, I could give you years of examples of my parents coddling and enabling . . . but with this, she sank to a whole new level. I thought it was bad when she finagled the 'study abroad at rehab' situation, but what she did after Bailey died was beyond the pale. My mom is the reason April got expelled. She told the school she'd cut off all funding unless they got rid of the 'young lady who invited that monster to the gathering and ruined her life.'"

No way! Jillian can feel all tension release in her jaw. *They seriously kept this pressure campaign under wraps!* More shocking than the news is the fact that she never heard any rumors pertaining to it on campus.

"I love my parents. I do," Keith continues. "They're such good people. But they were in over their heads for years with my brother. After he died they had a need to point as many fingers as they could, and April was low-hanging fruit. She was a freshman with a generous financial aid package who had not yet made any great contribution to the school. She was hardly a loss to the university."

"And the school just went along with it?"

"Think about it. It could have been a colossal nightmare for Rivington if they didn't honor the wishes of major donors who just lost their son—an alumnus and former poster child for organ donation who survived a heart transplant, went on to attend a top university founded by his ancestors, and then gets assaulted at an event that was peripherally organized by the school and dies? Come on, Jill. From the administration's perspective, this wasn't rocket science. April was expendable. Kicking her out was the path of least resistance. So they made up some bullshit excuse and got rid of her."

"And you knew about all of this as it was happening?"

"I'm not proud of it, but yes. I heard my mother screaming into the phone when she was threatening Daniel Cole." Keith stops walking and closes his eyes. For a minute he doesn't say a word, and Jillian doesn't push.

When he lifts his lids, Jillian can see the whites of his eyes have turned pink and glossy. "I didn't know what to do." His voice cracks ever so slightly and he swallows. "I stood by my parents. They're my parents . . . they were in pain. I didn't have the heart to point a finger and call them out. We were in mourning. I mean, my brother wasn't a saint, but he was still my brother. You do what you need to do for family."

"Right . . ." Jillian nods sympathetically.

"But what happened to April, ahh . . ." He shakes his head and stares off into the distance over the East River. "That's haunted me. There were several times when I wanted to reach out to see how she was doing, but I thought better of it. Didn't want to unearth all that stuff again. Better to leave it alone, you know? So I did. And then time just went by. Speaking of time . . ." He checks his watch. "I'm gonna have to go in a few. Back-to-back patients all afternoon."

They near the end of the promenade and turn down a winding walking path leading back to East End Avenue.

Don't let him leave just yet. There's a loose thread. Push a little more, she plots in her head. *He mentioned something about Rudy, follow up before he walks away.* "You'd said your mom did something to Rudy? What was that about?"

"Actually, with Rudy, it was what she *didn't* do. It was not like what happened with April where my mom was on the attack. With Rudy, she was mute. She didn't care that this kid's life was ruined simply because she refused to talk publicly about Bailey's medical issues. She should have been more forthcoming."

"And you knew about this, too?"

"Yes, but unlike April's expulsion where the crap excuse was obvious to me, I couldn't be sure about this one. I had a hunch but wasn't positive."

"A hunch about what?"

"About a good guy getting screwed so my mom could keep our family name clean. About what actually led to Bailey's death."

"Didn't you ride with Bailey in the ambulance? Weren't you at the hospital?"

"Yes, but when doctors asked me about his medical history, all I shared was his heart transplant in middle school. I didn't give more. I didn't know his daily pill regimen off the top of my head! It's not like I kept a list of his meds on a piece of paper tucked inside my wallet in case of emergency. We weren't like that—we were never close. He was older, spent time away in rehab. Sports was really our only common ground. Honestly, if I could turn back time, I would never have told Bailey I was in town. It just seemed like the brotherly thing to do given he was living in Manhattan and I'd be visiting. I guess hindsight's twenty-twenty . . ."

She bites down on her tongue as a reminder not to interrupt his flow.

"Heck, you want to know what's really bugged me all these years?" He kicks a pebble with the toe of his shoe. "How I didn't call my mom from the emergency room. She would have known exactly what he was taking, or *supposed* to be taking. It was like her full-time job. She would have been able to rattle off prescriptions and doses. Even if he wasn't compliant, it could have at least provided some information to the ER docs."

"Go easy on yourself, Keith," she says kindly as they pass Gracie Mansion, the mayor's residence. It's sprawling front porch and Victorian style remind Jillian of a southern plantation. She wonders if the Jamesons' house in Westchester is as large and intimidating as this home.

"Yeah, well, it is what it is. I saved my mom's face instead of my brother's life. It's that simple." He checks the time again and bends down to give Jillian a hug. "I'm sorry, I really do have to go. But I'll call you. To be continued."

As soon as he disappears down the block, Jillian hails a cab. She can't wait another minute to get home and record everything she's learned.

Between the transcription of their tape-recorded meeting at the diner and the notes she has just frantically typed up, Jillian's "Keith" file is thirty pages long. She saves the document on her desktop and prints a hard copy as well.

For the first time in her life, Jillian is indifferent to how this endeavor will impact her career. She is propelled forward not by the promise of professional reward, but by a mutation of personal gain.

Investigating this story is a personal salve, and while the motivation may be foreign, it feels perfectly right.

The next task on her list is to return the call from the ME.

"Phinn Kennedy," he says, picking up on the first ring. For a sixty-something-year-old man who works with dead people all day, he's remarkably sprightly.

Unlike many journalists for whom press officers are the gatekeepers, Jillian has direct access to much of New York City's medical world without the burden of red tape. She has covered the health beat for years and formed relationships with countless sources along the way. Several, like Dr. Kennedy, warmly welcome her calls. After a brief recap of his recent trip to the Bahamas, they get down to business.

"So, I'm working on an investigative piece," she begins. "The court file has a death certificate for the victim that says 'undetermined,' but I don't see any updated form and I can't find anything else official about how this man died."

"If there is an external cause of death, it would not appear on a hospital-issued death certificate. The hospital usually puts 'pending' or 'undetermined' if it's an external cause like a homicide. They hand it off to us and then we fill out the certificate once the autopsy is finished and we're done with our investigation. That can take a while though—weeks, months—because often, additional information like medical records, police reports, and lab tests are needed before a final determination on cause of death is made. What's the victim's name?"

"Bailey Jameson."

"B-a-i-l-e-y J-a-m-e-s-o-n," he announces each letter as he punches it into the system. "Okee-dokey. We've got a one-and-a-half-inch laceration to forearm, subcutaneous with no tendon involvement. His blood alcohol content was .15, which is significantly elevated. His INR level was through the roof, so that could be a sign of liver disease, which wouldn't be shocking if the guy drank this level of alcohol on a regular basis. Alcohol, as you may know, makes INR spike."

"INR?" Jillian asks.

"International Normalized Ratio. It tells you how long it takes for your blood to clot."

"So he was clotting all over the place?"

"No. The opposite. If the INR is that high, it means he had an increased risk of bleeding. In other words, it would be hard for him to stop bleeding."

"So even though he had a superficial one-and-a-half-inch cut on his arm that didn't hit any tendons, he could have a serious bleed given the high INR?"

"Yes. But hold on. There are more notes . . . bah, bah, bah, bah, bah," he tuts while perusing. "Okay. This guy's got a doozy of a history here. Atrial fibrillation. Cardiomyopathy. Heart transplant as a kid! Yikes! Ooh, wait, here it is . . . Bingo! He was on immunosuppressants which is standard care for transplant recipients, but if the guy was drinking and noncompliant with those immunosuppressants, he could have developed recurrent afib or cardiomyopathy and that would explain why he was on blood thinners."

"I don't need a medical degree to know that blood thinners and alcohol don't mix," Jillian remarks.

"Correct. An occasional beer or glass of wine here and there is probably fine. But looking at his liver, I'd say he wasn't a moderate consumer. Honestly, his INR is so off the charts I wouldn't rule out an overdose of blood thinner. He could have been inconsistent with his medical care. Maybe he took pills one day, skipped the next day, skipped weeks altogether? I've seen it all."

"Okay, so Bailey couldn't stop bleeding. But how do you die from a minor cut on your arm?"

"There's more to the file. Hold on . . ."

Kennedy mutters indecipherably into the telephone receiver until he returns to the conversation. "Your guy had a brain bleed," he announces. "That's what took him out. Musta hit his head at some point."

"He died of a brain bleed? Not the cut on his arm?"

"Correct. He had excessive bleeding, but the arm wasn't the cause of death. According to hospital records, he'd gotten a bunch of sutures on his forearm shortly after he arrived in the ER. I've got a photo right here of the stitches. The guy didn't die until hours later."

"Interesting. Did they do any scans?"

"Yeah. Only his heart. They must have seen the scar on his chest and shit their pants. But the heart and chest were clear."

"Why didn't anyone scan his brain when he came in?"

"Well, that can be complicated. I started my career as an ER doc. I saw drunks come in all the time. When a patient arrives in an altered mental state, it can often be attributed to alcohol instead of a head injury. A good ER doc will order a scan of the head on anyone altered, especially if they come in after a fight. But when a patient has a blood alcohol content as high as this guy, some docs may choose to let them sober up first, and then observe and reexamine later. That can take time. And if the patient is still altered when sober, then they'll order a scan of the head."

Okay. Let me get this straight, Jillian thinks. *So his heart and chest pass muster. He gets a handful of stitches from the knife wound on his arm, and it stops the bleeding pretty quickly. They give him IV fluids and at some point Bailey starts bleeding in his brain and dies. But they didn't scan his head when he arrived so no one caught it.*

"You know, he could have had a cranial bleed all along," Kennedy continues. "It could have happened at the scene or even before that night. The skull is pretty tough. It can take a hit and be okay. Sometimes you hit the head and it's game over, but it can take time. Either way, if you're dealing with a patient already on unmonitored levels of blood thinners, well, it ain't gonna help."

Jillian's whole body erupts in goosebumps, her flesh confirming what her mind already knows—she's got a winner of a story. "I wonder why there is no mention of this in the court file if it is in your records. Forgive me if I sound naïve, but do you typically speak with the attorneys on criminal cases?"

"Sometimes. Not always."

"Do you recall speaking with either the DA or defense on this particular case about these findings?"

"I keep a paper trail of everything. But those sorts of personal notes are in a different file away from the lab stuff. I like to separate church and state, if you will. Off the top of my head, no, I don't remember this case. But I'll double-check. Sit tight."

A minute later, he's back.

"Alrighty." He rustles some papers and lets out a long sigh. "Just one conversation for this case. It was a quickie. From 12:05 p.m. to 12:11. I spoke with a gentleman named Donald Sketcher from the Manhattan District Attorney's office."

"Yes, he was the prosecutor on the case."

"Says here we discussed the cardiomyopathy, the A-fib, the high alcohol levels, heart transplant, the INR, the 1.5-inch laceration on the forearm, the sutures, evidence of warfarin in the toxicology report, and that there was a major bleed."

"Did you tell him the cause of death?"

"Yes. I told him it was a bleed. Intracranial hemorrhage."

"You specifically told Sketcher the bleed was from the brain, not the cut on the arm."

"That's correct. Subdural hematoma. Classic hit your head, no one knows, then hours or days later you collapse."

"And when did you speak with Sketcher?"

"June 3."

That's after Rudy pled guilty to manslaughter, but before he was sentenced by the judge, Jillian realizes. *Did Sketcher know about the brain bleed and not tell Cossofski because Rudy already accepted the plea deal?*

Jillian grabs a pen from a drawer, writes *June 3!* on a stickie note, and posts it on her desk lamp.

"Dr. Kennedy, after you spoke with Donald Sketcher on June 3, did you two have any follow-up conversations?"

"No."

"And you never spoke with Richard Cossofski, the defense attorney?"

"No. Never."

"Were you aware that the defendant was charged with murder, pled guilty to manslaughter in the second degree, and was sentenced to up to fifteen years in prison? The party line in all the press was that the victim bled to death and the assumption was that it was due to the knife cut on his arm."

"Oh, I'm sorry to hear that. I didn't know. I don't usually follow the cases once we've signed off. My own view is the victim's wound was too shallow to cause his death."

"Why wasn't the real cause of death publicized?"

"That's beyond my paygrade."

"Got it. I have one last question. Let's assume for just a second that the victim's INR had been normal so he had the ability to clot. And let's say he was completely sober and there was no injury to his head. Do you think he would have bled to death if all he had was that cut on his arm?"

"If it were just that exact 1.5-inch cut on his arm and everything else in his body was quote-unquote normal? No. I can't imagine he would have succumbed to a superficial laceration that didn't even nick an artery or vein. If you hit an artery, blood will spurt everywhere. But this wasn't that kind of slash. Not even close. My nephew's a chef and has gotten much worse on the job. It wasn't the knife cut that did Bailey Jameson in. The kid who got locked up for this didn't know it, but he was dealing with a live grenade. Bailey Jameson was a ticking time bomb."

Cha-ching! Jillian thinks. "Well, this has been extremely enlightening. Thanks for your time, Dr. Kennedy."

Jillian hangs up the call and goes directly to her kitchen where she uncorks a bottle of pinot noir. As she leans her back against the edge of the countertop, swirling wine higher and higher like little tidal waves up to the rim of the glass, she processes the conversation.

Why didn't someone on Rudy's defense team talk with Dr. Kennedy before taking the plea deal? Why would Cossofski advise accepting the plea deal without knowing the cause of death? And if Cossofski knew it was a brain bleed as well as the extent of Bailey's medical issues, why didn't he fight harder for Rudy? I need to talk to Cossofski...

She returns to her desk and types in a Google search for Richard Cossofski. The first hit to appear on the page is his obituary.

So much for that approach . . . She takes another swig of wine. *Who do I know in criminal defense?*

Ten seconds later Jillian grabs her keys, a pencil, and a notepad, and walks down the corridor in her slippers to Jordana's front door.

"Hey, sorry to bother you," Jillian says when Jordana greets her wearing an elegant silk blouse and flannel pajama pants. "I would have called or texted but I didn't have your number. Is this a bad time?"

"No, your timing is perfect." Jordana smiles. "I just got home from work. Make yourself comfortable."

Jillian glances around the apartment. There are scooters and helmets lining the foyer, a large black duffel with a protruding baseball bat at the end of the hall, and half-consumed bottles of blue Gatorade adorning the ledge of the pass-through window to the kitchen. *This place is so alive,* she marvels as she settles in on the living room's plush gray sofa. *Our layouts are identical, but the vibes are so different.*

"So what's up?" Jordana smiles, twisting her long blonde strands into a messy bun as she plops down on a leather club chair across from Jillian.

"I'll get right to the point," Jillian says. She reveals everything she's learned about Rudy, April, Peter, the lawyers, and her conversation with Dr. Kennedy. As swiftly as Jillian divulged Rudy's identity in exchange for a quote from the cop on the night of the crime, she's as eager now to clear his name. "The thing that baffles me is why Cossofski didn't wait for the autopsy report to come in before having Rudy enter a guilty plea."

Jordana cocks her head for a moment before answering. "I mean, obviously I wasn't there and I haven't reviewed the file, so I can't be so bold as to say this was ineffective assistance of counsel, but yeah, this was a puzzling approach. It is possible the DA put an expiration date on the plea offer. That happens. Maybe Sketcher said he'd rescind the offer if they didn't accept within a certain period of time."

Jillian nods as her brain chews on the phrase Jordana just used—*ineffective assistance of counsel.*

"Personally," Jordana continues, "I would have subpoenaed and waited for the autopsy report from the medical examiner before advising my client to consider a plea. Sounds to me like Sketcher was being pushy. He wanted to look like a hero in the press by quickly slamming the cell on a defendant in a high-profile case. I would have played hardball if I were defense counsel. I would have pushed to see that autopsy report. It may have taken months, especially if the victim had a medical history and records were requested by the ME and they had to speak with his doctors—all that stuff takes time. The waiting can be grueling. You feel your life is on permanent pause, but ultimately, that's time *not* spent in prison— time that could help strengthen your case to *avoid* prison."

"Right. So you said something interesting and now I'm curious . . ." Jillian clicks the cartridge of her ballpoint pen up and down as she considers how to phrase her next queries. "What would qualify as ineffective assistance of counsel in this case? Did Cossofski have a responsibility to check in with the medical examiner or the prosecutor to get an update on an autopsy if his client already took a plea?"

"A defense lawyer isn't obligated to get that information. Should he? I think that's a no brainer. But is it a duty? No. Also, you should know that the medical examiner is obliged to send the medical records *only* to the DA—government agent to government agent— not to defense counsel unless defense requests it. If it were my client, I'd want my hands on anything and everything that could potentially help avoid jail time."

"And how about the district attorney? Did Sketcher have a duty to turn over an autopsy report that surfaced *after* Rudy pled guilty but before he was sentenced? The report showed the cause of death was a brain bleed, not bleeding from the arm. It could have helped Rudy."

"Did Sketcher have a *duty* to share potentially exculpatory information? Yes. Absolutely yes. Under the Brady-Giglio doctrine, prosecutors are required to disclose evidence that's favorable to the defendant and relevant to their guilt or punishment."

Jillian scribbles furiously in her notepad, trying to record every word verbatim.

"And remember," Jordana continues, "the prosecution has the obligation to prove guilt beyond a reasonable doubt. If it was a brain bleed that killed Bailey, you need to think about what the ME said. Bailey could have hit his head during the fight or before he ever laid eyes on Rudy. If it wasn't clear when that intracranial bleed started, then there's your doubt. That's all Cossofski had to say, and maybe Sketcher knew that and didn't want to share it."

Jillian shakes her head. She can't believe what a shit storm she's uncovered.

"Turn around," Jordana says and points to a framed gray and white print on the wall above where Jillian is sitting. "My friend, Becca, gave that to me when I passed the bar exam. The Hebrew words say '*Tzedek, Tzedek, Tirdof.*' In English that means 'Justice, Justice, Shall You Pursue.' When I became a lawyer I took an oath to do justice, not to win at any cost. Believe me, I know how imperfect and broken our justice system is—how bad things can happen to such good people. It's very disheartening. It would be a lot easier if the world were black and white—a clear right or wrong—but that's not life. We exist in the gray, and that's why this piece centers me. It's a reminder that even though the world may be broken, I'm getting up every day and doing my small part to repair it."

Jillian takes in the details—how the print's deep, dark charcoal hues and crisp, clean whites are blended with such precision it is impossible to delineate where one ends and the other begins.

"It's stunning," Jillian marvels as she reaches for her cell phone. "Mind if I take a picture?"

"Please." Jordana smiles.

When she returns home, Jillian turns the photograph into the screensaver on both her laptop and cell phone. *How funny*, she thinks. *I used to want to be a fly on the wall and observe the way others navigated life. Now I'm staring at a wall, finding direction for my own.*

21

Rudy

NOW

I t's Sunday afternoon and Rudy is standing in the cereal aisle of his local grocery store wholly transfixed by the variety of brightly colored boxes. There are at least twenty-five options on the shelves. Choosing a brand is hard enough, but needing to select flavors within those brands (honey nut, apple cinnamon, chocolate) and then doing the math to determine the most cost-effective package size for your household is simply overwhelming. *With only two cereals available at the prison commissary—offered only in tiny individual servings—breakfast was much easier*, he thinks. *Fewer choices, fewer decisions.*

As he weaves his cart through the aisles, Rudy makes several discoveries. First, there are intriguing six-packs of silver cans in the beverage department that resemble soda but are actually labeled "energy drinks." He makes a mental note to ask Tommy if he's tried them. Next, the produce section has a separate subsection for "organic" fruits and vegetables. He places a conventional granny smith apple in one hand and an organic version in the other to compare, and after inspection he shrugs in befuddlement. The conventional looks shinier and more appealing. He drops a few into a plastic bag and chucks them into the cart.

Of all the products Rudy sees that afternoon, however, there is only one that triggers a visceral reaction. While ambling down a row of facial tissues and disposable plates, he encounters three fully stocked shelves of paper towels that leave him breathless. *This*, he thinks, marveling at the multi-ply, quilted patterns, *now this is something!* Like sneakers, high-quality paper towels are a hot commodity among inmates. They are difficult to come by and valued at a premium. He'd gotten so used to the coarse brown version in prison that seeing so many rolls with layers of absorbency right there for the taking feels like Christmas. *Now this is where I'll invest in the family size*, he thinks, grabbing a twelve-pack bundle.

As Rudy makes his way to the checkout counter, he notices how so many customers are in a hurry. Even on this lazy Sunday afternoon, he senses he's traveling at a slower pace than the others. "Upstate," as he has come to refer to prison, is a place where he wanted to keep his gestures tight and compact because sudden movements could lead to punishment. Watching shoppers multi-task as they zip through the aisles and converse through earpieces linked to cell phones—a technological development that frightened him upon noticing several people talking to themselves on the street—makes him feel alien. This is the neighborhood to which he dreamed of returning, the one and only place he has ever called "home," and yet, Midwood has changed. The tweak is subtle but detectable, as if a small yet crucial tile in a mosaic is missing.

As he transfers the items from his shopping cart to the checkout counter, he hears his name.

"Rudy?" the cashier mumbles. "Rudy DeFranco?"

It's Dominic—a teammate from his varsity baseball days in high school.

"Dom?" he offers a half grin. In his former life, Rudy would have been ebullient and come around the counter to high-five or bro-hug. But now he has downshifted into first gear. *Stick to the mission and lay low*, he tells himself. *Get the groceries and get home.*

"I thought so . . ." Dominic studies Rudy. His head remains fixed as his hands glide items over the scanner.

This is awkward, Rudy thinks and busies himself by organizing items on the conveyor belt into groups—dairy, cleaning supplies, produce, etc.

"Didn't know you were out . . ." Dominic mutters coolly.

Yep, there it is. Rudy does a quick once-over of his surroundings. There's a woman in line behind him and a teenager helping bag at the end of the counter. Neither seem to be paying attention to his conversation.

"Long time away, huh?" Dominic asks flatly.

Rudy shrugs. There's nothing to say.

"Fifty. Three. Seventy. Five." Dominic draws out the cost of groceries as if he's addressing Rudy by his prison identification number. He crosses his arms over his brown supermarket-issued vest and leans his back against the register, blocking entry to the cash drawer.

Does he honestly think I'm going to rob him? When did the checkout line become a courtroom and the cashier a judge?

Rudy can feel Dominic's gaze as he counts out the cash Lorraine gave him for groceries. There's no way Dominic would know the money belonged to Lorraine, but he feels like a child running errands for his mommy. *This is mortifying*, he thinks as he digs a hand into his pants pocket for loose change. He can't retrieve the quarters fast enough.

It pains Rudy not to be able to cover living expenses for himself. He'd love to put the charges on a debit or credit card—it's the least he could do for his parents—but he has neither.

As he lugs the groceries home, Rudy notices how many of the retailers along Avenue J have changed hands. What was once a shoe repair shop is now a deli; a women's clothing boutique has transformed into an electronics store with gigantic advertisements for cell phone plans. *I feel like Michael J. Fox in* Back to the Future, *except in reverse.*

While crossing East 19th, he sees an elderly woman with an aide approaching from the other side of the street. With her bright pink lipstick and freshly coiffed hair, he knows instantly it is Bunny Fishbein—the bagel store customer whose generous tips he used to purchase the Swiss Army knife.

"Mrs. Fishbein," Rudy says gently, careful not to startle her.

"Yes?" she smiles upon hearing her name. She turns and when her clumpy mascaraed lashes settle on Rudy's face, she grabs her aide's forearm to steady her balance. "No!" she cries in disbelief. "It isn't you, is it?"

He places the grocery bags down on the sidewalk beside his feet. "It is. It's me, Mrs. Fishbein."

"Oh my! Come here." She reaches up and places her gnarled hands on his biceps. "You look good. Thank God. Now give me a hug."

Other than his immediate family and the Zagodas, few people made an effort to stay in touch while Rudy was away. He received a holiday card each December from Mr. Marino at the bagel store, a monthly note with an inspirational quote from his high school baseball coach, and every once in a while, a delivery of books from Bunny.

"Let's make a plan. You free tomorrow? It's Mediterranean lunch day in the dining hall."

Rudy knows that to visit Bunny at her assisted living facility, he'll have to submit a formal application to his parole officer, wait for approval, and lock it into the calendar at least a week in advance. Last-minute requests are reserved for emergencies, not Greek salads at local retirement homes. Plus, who knows what kind of security screening the facility has—they might ask for ID at the front desk, and he has none other than an expired driver's license. But this isn't worth explaining to Bunny. *Yes, I'm finally free*, he thinks, *but it's freedom with an instruction manual.*

"Unfortunately, I don't think tomorrow will work, but we'll make a plan soon. I promise."

"So glad you're back where you belong, doll," she says with a wink.

The following day, Rudy takes a bus to meet with Gene, his parole officer, who, after checking to ensure Rudy's ankle monitor is working properly, offers him a seat in the folding chair beside his metal desk.

"So, how's it going?" Gene asks as he begins to flip through Rudy's file.

Rudy pauses, unsure if this is a trick question. If it isn't, he's confident it's the stupidest query ever posed. "Um, great!"

"Great, huh?" He closes the folder, pulls off his readers, and gets right to the point. "Rudy, you were away for quite some time. Remember when you were first locked up?"

He nods. *Why does this feel like an interrogation?*

"You may not have realized it, but you went through an adjustment period. We call it prisonization. You slowly separated from free society and became part of that society. There are different rules on the inside, and you just spent a good chunk of time living by those rules." He clears his throat. "You know, they say the day you get in is the day you start thinking about getting out. Well, here you are. You're out now. It's 'great' as you say to be back, but there are challenges. Many challenges that you may not expect. And my job is to help make reentry successful."

"Yes, sir."

"Remember, we're all capable of positive change, son. We can't judge ourselves by the worst things we've done."

This stings. He knows this is meant to be encouraging, but he can feel an uptick in his blood pressure. *Yet another reminder of the consequence of choosing to plead guilty to a homicide I never committed—the world will forever think I did it. I'm out of prison, I've paid my dues, and still, the stain is right there. Right fucking there.*

Gene pulls a pamphlet out of his desk drawer and hands it to Rudy. "I want you to attend some of these classes. It's at an organization called The Prentice League. They have programs that help with reentry."

Rudy does a quick scan of the pamphlet with *Reclaim Your Life!* written across the top in bolded italics. In addition to helping people obtain their GED, they offer workshops on housing and employment, anger management, a writing class described as "a redemptive space to hear stories and dissolve stigmas," and a three-part series titled "Exploring Post-Incarceration Syndrome/Post-Traumatic Prison Disorder."

"Housing and employment are the top priorities for most people," Gene says. "The obstacles go hand in hand. Right? Can be tough to get a job if you've got a serious rap sheet and been locked up. Not many employers or landlords are willing to take a risk. Think about it. If you've been out of work for a long time and can't get a job, how are you going to get a bank loan or rent an apartment? And you know everything is electronic now. Gotta learn how to upload your résumé, download information, navigate job sites, email employers. The computers aren't like the ancient things you probably got used to upstate. Gotta learn the technology. Running into all those barriers is a major stress and can lead to recidivism. One tiny parole violation—smoke a little weed, be late for curfew, miss a check-in—and you'll go right back. Odds of getting arrested are a lot slimmer if you have a job. So that's our goal. Got it?"

"Got it." Rudy shifts uncomfortably in his folding chair. *This meeting is a buzzkill.*

Gene puts his reading glasses on and returns to Rudy's file. "I see you earned your bachelor's degree in engineering while you were away. Impressive. What do you hope to do?"

"Thank you, sir. I like mechanical, electrical, pretty much any kind of engineering. I'm good with my hands. Fixing stuff. But I also like being with people. My dad's a building super and I can work with him, and I'm sure I can get a job at the bagel store where I worked all through high school. I can do that in the mornings when it's busiest and then help my dad in the afternoons. That's sort of what I was thinking until I get a full-time position somewhere."

"Have you spoken with the bagel store about potential employment? Do you know if the building management will allow you to enter and service the apartments of the residents?"

"Uh, no. I haven't asked yet."

"I recommend you do."

The slight condescension Rudy detects in Gene's tone feels like a sock in the gut.

"Also says here you're living back home with your family. How's that?"

"Great!" Rudy says, trying to sound upbeat. He desperately wants to swing this conversation in a more positive direction.

"Just so you know," Gene peers at Rudy over his readers, "it's not unusual to experience tension with relatives or have some trouble reestablishing connections after being away for so long."

"Yes. I'll keep that in mind, sir."

"Family reunification can be tough. They may not be the same people you left behind years ago. Relationships change. But let it evolve naturally. Don't force the bond."

Rudy suddenly feels parched. "May I, um, have some water?"

Gene pulls a bottle out from the mini fridge near his desk and hands it to Rudy.

Though the passage of time is evident, Rudy knows that some changes—Barbara's wheelchair, new stores, Tommy moving out—are not wholly unexpected. Fortunately, for the most part, his core support system has remained intact. He sees his parents and brother constantly. The Zagodas are as present as they've always been; Lorraine and Barbara speak daily, and Steven brought Rudy an ice cream sundae from Carvel because there was a two-for-one Wednesday special. The most glaring difference between Rudy's life in Midwood pre- versus post-incarceration is the absence of April—both physically and, more surprisingly, emotionally. He was ecstatic to see her at the apartment the day of his release, and even though he detected something amiss, he wrote it off as stress. After all, he reasoned, three kids, a job, and being an only child living far away from her aging parents will do that to anyone. But since she returned to Chicago, Rudy and April have not spoken. She hasn't called and he hasn't wanted to nudge. And it's this surprising lack of connection with April, more than anything else, that Rudy knows will be his greatest hurdle to a successful reentry.

As Rudy gets off the bus and heads home, Gene's words stick in his head: "Reunification is tough . . . Relationships change . . . Don't force the bond."

Fuck it, I'm just gonna call her. Why the hell not?

When he returns to the apartment, Rudy makes a beeline for his bedroom and dials April's cell. It rings four times and just before he expects it will go to voicemail, she answers.

"Hello?" she says, a bit panicked and breathless.

"Hey, it's me! What's shaking? I miss you!"

"Hey, R—" She stops herself. "Everything okay?"

Rudy hears several voices in the background. "We gotta go," a man says sternly.

"Listen," she says to Rudy. "Can I call you later? I'm sorry, it's a little nuts right now."

"Uh, sure. No problem at all. Not like I'm going anywhere!"

His attempt at levity falls flat.

"Great. I lo—" She catches herself again. "Speak soon," she says before hanging up.

If he had the money and permission from the Department of Parole to hop on a flight to Chicago that evening, he would.

So this is it, this is the next chapter, he thinks and pulls The Prentice League pamphlet out of his backpack to peruse the list of classes. Just as he's about to circle the ones that look most intriguing, the phone rings and he can hear Lorraine pick up across the hall in the kitchen. He didn't even realize his mother was home.

I wonder if it's April. His heart swells. *I bet she's calling back.*

"Rud?" Lorraine taps on his bedroom door and then pokes her head inside. "There's a call for you."

"Ape?"

"No." Lorraine's brow furrows. "Some woman named Jillian Jones."

22

April

NOW

April stands with her spine pressed against the locked metal door of a middle school bathroom stall as she summarizes the contents of an hour-long meeting into a brief text. It's only 9 a.m., but she doesn't want to wait another second to report back to Peter. His scathing admonishment—*You did this, go fix it!*—coupled with her own heartbreak upon listening to Attie and Rosie recount hurtful snubs from friends was enough to compel April to schedule a meeting with school administrators and devise a plan to manage the headlines' collateral damage.

The fact that Peter was too overloaded "playing whack-a-mole" to join her was neither a surprise nor a disappointment. It was just as well, as April didn't need the frustration of watching Peter pout in a middle school principal's office, or anxiously cross and recross his lanky legs while the cell phone buzzed in his shirt pocket every few seconds. But, keeping him in the loop is important, and nothing says *I'm trying* or *I take responsibility for my part in this debacle* quite like bullet points delivered in a timely manner.

- Principal, school psychologist, and two guidance counselors in attendance
- They'll take turns keeping an eye out during lunch and recess for any stupid comments or ostracism
- Teachers will do same in classrooms
- School psychologist offered to be on call 24/7 for calls/ texts

After April presses send and unlocks the stall door, her phone rings. It's the DeFrancos' landline, which means it's Rudy calling. Again. He'd called late the night before, but she was asleep and given the 8 a.m. school meeting, she hasn't had a second to even listen to his message. She sends this call directly to voicemail—an act wholly incongruous with anything she could have predicted after yearning to hear the sound of his strong yet sweet timbre for over a decade. This simple tap sends her heart skyrocketing to her throat. If only she possessed the bandwidth for the marathon conversations of their youth, but that's no longer feasible. His frequent, borderline incessant phone calls are living proof of their divergent paths. The last three times he's called she has been either carpooling, in the midst of an argument with Peter, or wrapping up a call with her parents' lawyer about making April their health care proxy. Inevitably, by the time she has a moment to speak, assuming she isn't falling on her face, it's nearly 11 p.m.

Minutes later, as she shakes hands with the principal on the middle school steps and expresses her gratitude for his having her daughters' backs, Rudy calls again. Once more, she directs it to voicemail. By the time she walks past the school soccer field, there is another call, this time from a number with a 718 area code. As always, the sight of an unfamiliar number from New York City incites a wave of panic. *My parents! It's an emergency!* She picks up immediately.

"Hello?" she drops her tote onto a patch of grass and braces herself for the hit.

"Is this April?" says a woman on the other end.

"Yes?"

"April, this is Jillian Jones. I used to be Jill Colburn. Not sure if you remember me. We attended Rivington together."

Jill? Now that's a blast from the past. "Wow. Yes. Jill." April closes her eyes and exhales in relief that this has nothing to do with her parents. She plops down atop her tote, careful to avoid grass stains on her pants. "Sure, I remember you. It's been years. How . . . how are you?"

"Well, thanks. You?"

April's not in the mood for the pleasantry dance. *Cut to the chase. I have a to-do list longer than my leg and people I'd rather spend my time chatting with right now. It's not like we were close during the five seconds I lasted at Rivington.* "Okay. What's going on?"

"Well," Jillian clears her throat, "this may be out of left field, but I'd like to speak with you about Rudy DeFranco."

Oh my God. She's still obsessed with him after all these years? Is that what this is about? Does she want me to fix her up? I wonder if she stalked him in prison. Move on, woman!

"What about Rudy?" April knows she sounds curt but doesn't care. Jillian was psycho then and probably hasn't changed.

"I'd prefer to speak in person." Her tone is more serious. "It's actually regarding both you and Rudy. I have some new information about what happened years ago that you should know."

"I'm sorry, I'm not following you at all. What kind of information? And by the way, how did you get my number?"

"Your father gave it to me."

"My father?!"

Barbara and Steven recently mentioned that someone named Jillian stopped by the house, but neither one could recall Jillian's last name. They noted it was a peculiar visit, but neglected to share that Steven took the liberty of passing along April's number without her permission.

"Yes. April, the information I have pertains to Rudy's criminal case and your expulsion from Rivington. Although this investigation is a freelance project and has no connection to the newspaper, I'm a reporter at the *New York Times*."

"The *Times*?" April can hear the exasperation explode from her mouth. "I'm sorry, I can't speak with you . . ."

"Please, April. Trust me. You'll want to speak with me. I'll be on a plane to Chicago tonight. Meet me tomorrow. Any time. Any place. I'll be there."

How am I going to explain this to Peter? Speaking with a reporter? He'll divorce me on the spot.

"Can you give me a five-second preview of whatever this is about?"

"It's a lengthy conversation. There's a lot to take in."

April checks her wristwatch—a stainless timepiece Peter presented on their tenth anniversary. She needs to leave soon to get Simon to a midday orthodontist appointment, drive him back to school, do a quick Whole Foods run, pick up the girls, drop Rosie at physical therapy and Attie at ballet, and then throw dinner together before attending a cocktail event for Peter. She has no time for a long chat.

"I'd prefer to talk in person," Jillian continues. "I land tonight. Just tell me where and when tomorrow. I'll be there."

April releases a long, frustrated exhale. *Jill's as persistent and grating as I remember.* "Fine. Text me in the morning."

❧

The following day, while Peter is in yet another meeting with his team and the kids are at school, April drives thirty-five minutes up the Kennedy Expressway to Bucktown. When they first married and were exploring the city, she and Peter fell in love with the neighborhood's Brooklyn-esque vibe—its charming brick homes, hole-in-the wall shops, and cozy eateries like Club Lucky, an old-school Italian restaurant/cocktail lounge. She hasn't been back in quite some time, but given how removed the venue is from her home in the South Loop, it's the ideal location for a clandestine lunch with a reporter. And perhaps, she hopes, its moniker will bestow a bit of good fortune.

When April walks in at 11:30 a.m., she immediately spots Jillian nestled in at a red vinyl booth in the back. The place is nearly empty, but that doesn't stop Jillian from waving both hands above her head. April wouldn't be shocked if Jillian started hollering "Yoo-hoo! Over here!"

"It's nice to see you, April," Jillian says as she stands to greet her.

After an awkward embrace, April takes Jillian in. Her look still trends mousy but has a little more zhuzh than before—a bit of jewelry, sheer polish on her stubby nails, trendy eyeglasses. "Good to see you, too." April forces a smile before sliding into her side of the booth.

"So I'll get right to it," Jillian says, interlacing her fingers and leaning forward over the table. "I've thought about you and Rudy for years. I feel terrible about what happened. None of it—your expulsion, his sentence—ever made sense to me. But I was too pre-occupied with my own life to do anything about it. When I learned he was getting released, I started sniffing around a little, if you will. One thing led to another and here I am."

What's her real MO here? April wonders as she takes a sip from the glass of ice water in front of her. "Did you fly to Chicago just to meet with me? Just to tell me this?"

"I came to Chicago to let you know that I have some answers. First, I think I have an explanation for why you were expelled from Rivington. And second, what happened to Rudy was a tsunami of unnecessary bullshit. What I've learned won't change the past, but it could help smooth out his future. Significantly. And just so you know, I've told him the same."

April's eyebrows arch. "You've spoken with Rudy." She says this as a statement, not a question.

"Yes, I called him shortly before I reached out to you."

Oh my God, that's why he was calling nonstop. He wasn't being pushy, he was trying to tell me about his conversation with Jill! Damn it! I should have called back!

For the next hour, as they poke at their Caprese salads, April's head swirls with the facts and terminology flowing out of Jillian's mouth: ineffective assistance of counsel, medical examiner, autopsy report, the Jameson family's connection to Rivington University, Keith Jameson's mea culpa.

April pulls her hair into a messy bun atop her head and waves her hand too cool off the back of her neck.

"You okay? I know this is a lot to take in." Jillian's nose crinkles sympathetically.

"So basically you're telling me it was one screw up after another."

"Yes."

April stares at the table's salt and pepper shakers as she digests this information. The devastated part of her wants to roll around on Club Lucky's vintage red and black tile floor and scream like a toddler in a full-blown tantrum. The infuriated part of her wants immediate retribution and wonders who, among all the players, deserves the top spot in the blame game. The logical part of her knows she can't change the past and should accept the calamity for what it is—a prime example of "shit happens." But her gut knows better. *There's only one path forward, but I want to hear what Jill has to say.*

"What's your suggested next step?"

Jillian gently rests her fork on the edge of the plate. "I do believe setting the record straight is the best way to ensure justice is served. Going wide with this story is not going to make up for lost years of Rudy's life. It won't erase the trauma you experienced. And it won't bring back Bailey Jameson to his family. But if we do this correctly, I think we can try to right a whole lot of wrongs."

"What do you mean, *we*?"

"I've done the work. I've got the ingredients for a powerhouse story. The cherry on top would be getting you and Rudy on the record. He's already spoken to me about his side and I'm going back to New York tonight so I can chat with his family tomorrow. But I'm curious about you. He did the time, but his sentence impacted the people around him, and clearly, you're one of those people. It's sort of like an illness, right? It's not just the patient who gets affected by the disease, the loved ones suffer too, in their own way. There's a ripple effect."

Something about this analogy breaks April. She plucks two napkins from a dispenser on the corner of the table and dabs at her lash line.

No one has ever been this blunt or intuitive. The goal has always been some sort of clichéd physical aphorism—putting one foot in front of the other, staying afloat, moving on—as opposed to stopping to wallow in the pain. Healing has always been about forward motion, but perhaps, April thinks, she could have used some of Jillian's insight long ago. *Injustice is a disease*, she realizes. *If you don't catch that rogue cell early on, it can metastasize and annihilate everything, just like a cancer.*

"I think the sooner we run a story, the sooner Rudy gets his life back," Jillian says. "He's already lost enough time. I don't want him to have to waste another minute being restricted. We have a chance, right now, to make his life infinitely better. How many opportunities do any of us get to make a real difference and drastically change someone's world like this?"

"I couldn't agree more, but . . ." April says, her voice breaking. She chews on her lower lip as an attempt to thwart the emotion creeping up from her chest.

"But what?" Jillian pushes.

If she's this much of a sleuth, she must know about Peter's campaign, April thinks. "I'm not sure if you are aware, but my husband—"

"I know all about your husband," Jillian interjects. "Running this story now might actually help squash those headlines he's been dealing with. You think he'd speak with me?"

April shakes her head. "No way. In fact, I worry if I tell him *I'm* speaking with you, he'll go berserk."

"Really? Seems to me this story would be right up his alley—it's about criminal justice, it would clear the only obstacle in his path with this election, and it would help a dear friend of his wife."

These are logical arguments, but Jill doesn't know Peter. Hell, I'm not sure I even know Peter anymore. At this point, April can no longer contain the torrent of emotion inside. Tears cascade down her cheeks and she covers her face with her hands.

"I can't do this anymore!" she whimpers. "How does anyone do this?"

"Do what?" Jillian asks as she slides out of her bench and moves over to the other side of the table to put her arm around April. "I'm so sorry, I didn't mean to upset you."

"It's not you," April snivels and reaches for more napkins from the dispenser. "You're doing something incredible. But I can't. I can't do anything without disappointing or neglecting someone else. I can't give 100 percent to anything I care about, ever. I *want* to, but my hands are constantly tied . . . I'm constantly torn. I'd do anything to devote this time to Rudy and getting him settled back at home in New York, but then I'd be neglecting my kids, and my husband would likely kick me to the curb. But if I do what Peter wants, then I'm abandoning my best friend at a critical point in his life when he only has a handful of people in his corner. My kids are my priority, yes, but Peter and Rudy? I'm at a breaking point! I can't do right by either one! People always say, 'oh, just do the best you can,' but how? How do you give your best physically and emotionally when your loyalties are divided and top priorities conflict?"

"Honestly," Jillian says softly, "I don't have an answer for you. I was married very briefly. Never had kids. Never wanted them. My job has been my everything, until now."

"Until now?"

"I know it's not the same, but just like you're worried about Peter's reaction to this story, I know my boss is going to be royally pissed when he learns about this investigation. Years ago, I never would have jeopardized my career for anything. But I've gotta say, I've never had so much clarity in my life. For me, pursuing this story is the right thing to do. I know it's not totally analogous to your predicament. I can't imagine being pulled in multiple directions the way you are. I guess I'm just saying, I feel for you."

"Thanks." *Jill's definitely growing on me*, April thinks.

"Forgive me if this comes across as prying, but what do *you* want? Forget the reactions you might get from others. Imagine a judgment-free zone. I understand the kids come first. They are safe and well. Now what? Think about it. If you could do anything, what's the first thing you'd tackle?"

April can't remember the last time anyone asked what *she* wanted. She also can't believe she's getting a life coach session from the girl who annoyed the crap out of Rudy freshman year, but Jillian's calm demeanor is surprisingly comforting.

What do I want? I want to feel light. I want to feel weightless. I want the guy who won the gold medal for shot put at the summer Olympics to pick up the crater that has been compressing my chest for over a decade and hurl it into oblivion because even with all the joy I've been blessed with, it's still there. It has never gone away. This is my chance not only to help Rudy but to feel pure again. But at what cost? Peter? Will I just be swapping one heartbreak for another?

"I just want to do the right thing." April's voice quivers.

"And what's that?" Jillian asks.

He'll have to understand. If he doesn't, we have bigger issues. This is too important, April thinks.

"Run the story," April says with certainty. "I'll tell you everything, but I'm off the record. You can't quote me."

"Deal."

April takes a sip of water and for the first time in a very long time, she feels a sense of jurisdiction over her own life. "Okay. Where should we begin?"

23

Jillian

NOW

Last year, when Jillian's colleague, Meredith, resigned from the *Times* to launch an online news magazine, she thought her friend had lost her mind. Voluntarily relinquishing a stable paycheck, health insurance, and byline at a preeminent publication seemed absolutely batty, but Jillian also knew that Meredith felt shackled by the bias of top brass and frustrated that deserving stories never made it beyond pitch meetings. Meredith ventured out and founded *The Reporter's Notebook (TRN),* and over the course of twelve months has amassed nearly a million followers, a bevy of awards, and created thought-provoking content. So, when Jillian was placed on administrative leave for flaking on the overseas medical conference *and* lying to her boss about investigating Rudy's story, she knew exactly where to turn. *The Reporter's Notebook* was the perfect spot to run her exposé.

It has been only forty-eight hours since the article went live and the piece has already received a record-setting number of hits. To Jillian's utter shock, the hashtag #justiceforrudy has gone viral. She has been invited as a guest on five national morning shows, as well as PBS News Hour and NPR. She has garnered interview requests by more podcasts than she can count and received a bottle of champagne as a token of gratitude from Meredith for catapulting *TRN*'s reputation as a trusted news source. But Jillian will speak with no one—the hoopla shouldn't be about her. She's gotten Rudy's story into the zeitgeist and it's enough satisfaction to know she's shifting tectonic plates in the justice system.

As she sips her Monday morning coffee on the couch and scrolls through the latest comments on *TRN*'s Instagram page, Jillian's phone vibrates. "Private Caller" flashes across the screen.

She slides into her desk chair and flips on the lamp. "Hello?"

"Is Jillian Jones available?" a woman asks.

"This is Jillian."

"Hello, Jillian, my name is Cecily Barash . . ."

Jillian's mind races as she tries to place the name.

"I'm a dean at Rivington University."

Ahhh, so it's the other contingent that's been ignoring me.

Like the Jamesons, Rivington administrators have rebuffed all attempts at conversation.

"I'm here with our head of school and chair of the board of trustees. We'd like a minute of your time."

Are they calling to say they're going to revoke my diploma the way they expelled April years ago?

"Well, Jillian," Cecily begins, "it may not come as a surprise that we have read your article and are deeply saddened."

Oh, here it comes . . . they're pissed at me for exposing my alma mater.

"As I'm sure you are aware, there's a new administration now, and while we can't speak for the actions of past leaders, we can say with certitude that we are committed to being on the right side of history."

"Jillian," one of the men interjects, "I'll have you know you are among our most distinguished alumni. We are extremely impressed by your career achievements and though, frankly, your article isn't the best look for us, we respect and appreciate your work and are prepared to glean lessons from our past. We were wondering, Jillian, perhaps you would consider returning to the university as, say, a lecturer or adjunct. The greatest source of pride for an academic institution is when former students become our colleagues."

They want me to teach?!

"The students could use someone like you," Cecily says. "We think it would send a powerful message to budding journalists about the importance of truth in reporting and how it's never too late to right wrongs."

And the optics of such a grand, public mea culpa wouldn't hurt the school's image either, she thinks. *I see your angle, Rivington.*

"Thank you, I appreciate the kind words." *But you can't hire me to clear your conscience,* she wants to say.

"We would be extremely flexible," Cecily says enthusiastically. "Large lecture, intimate seminar, any topic, we'll work around your schedule. I could see an investigative reporting class being quite popular and filling quickly. We'd leave it to your discretion, of course."

Oh, how my twenty-year-old self would adore this ass-kissing, she thinks. "I appreciate your thinking of me, but I'm afraid now is not the ideal time." *What about April,* Jillian wonders. *Are they going to reach out to her, too? Maybe offer an honorary diploma? Ugh. I don't want to drag her name into this conversation.*

"Let it marinate," Cecily urges. "We'll circle back."

Later Monday evening, as she is taking Farley on a post-dinner walk along Madison Avenue, Jillian bumps into Jordana, who is exiting Butterfield Market with a cup of swirly soft-serve frozen yogurt in one hand and a spoon to her lips with the other.

Jordana's eyes grow wide and electric when they land on Jillian. "This is so weird! I was going to call you tonight. What are the odds I'd run into you?" she asks and points to the sidewalk benches outside the grocery. "Got a minute?"

Jillian glances at Farley and wonders if he'll be patient enough to sit through a conversation. "I don't think this little guy will last. Can we walk and talk?"

"Absolutely," Jordana says and scoops another spoonful into her mouth.

The dusk air is crisp and the illuminated storefronts along Madison Avenue make the city feel magically cozy, as if all of Manhattan is tucked in for the night. Taxis and buses roll by, but the space between them is generous, far from the congestion of midday traffic. In all her years of living in New York, Jillian has yet to grow disenchanted by urban rhythms—she loves the quiet early mornings with fellow coffee-toting dog walkers, the frenetic buzz of midtown at lunchtime, and the winddown, just before bed, when the tranquil side streets of her uptown neighborhood could pass for suburbia.

"So I learned something today that I thought you should know." Jordana licks a stray drop of vanilla from her finger. "I heard from a friend involved with the New York Bar Association that because of your story, they may initiate an ethics investigation into Don Sketcher."

"What does that mean?" Jillian asks. She knows this isn't great news for Sketcher but is unsure if this would be a simple note on his record or have actual implications for his career.

"It means Sketcher could be suspended or even disbarred if there is a pattern of misconduct."

"Wow."

"At least in New York. He passed both the New York and New Jersey bar exams, so he has the ability to practice in both states. I have no insight on his standing in New Jersey, but I can tell you it's not looking great for him in terms of keeping his license in New York."

Jillian takes this in. It's one thing to imagine your work inciting change, but it's quite another when there's a chance it could actually blow shit up. "That's big news."

"Yeah, well, you did the heavy lifting with your research. When a prosecutor conceals evidence the way he did by not sharing information with defense counsel, that conduct is considered bad faith. It was poor judgment. Depending on the circumstances, bad faith could be dishonesty, fraudulent intent, neglecting to meet fair dealing standards, untrustworthy performance of duties—I could easily make an argument for any of those with Sketcher. As you say in your article, he had the swagger. He desperately wanted this ADA job that had repeatedly rejected him. This was his shot. He was going to do anything in his power for a high-profile win. And when you combine that with a lackluster defense attorney, well . . ." Jordana stops walking and turns to face Jillian. "I think there's a chance we can get Rudy's conviction set aside."

"Set aside?"

"Yeah. The DA's office has a Conviction Integrity Unit, or we could go to the Innocence Project at Cardozo School of Law—I happen to be a lecturer there and know a bunch of people. There's a good chance Rudy could bring a civil lawsuit and seek significant damages. People have received millions of dollars for similar claims."

Now Jillian's eyes are wide. "Really?"

"In the right hands, yes," Jordana continues. "I'd be happy to help, and I have several friends, all excellent lawyers, who would jump on board too. Pro bono. No cost."

"That's incredible."

"Feel free to give him my number or I can call him directly, if he prefers. Just let him know he's got people ready to fight for him."

"Will do. Thank you."

The following evening, Jillian drives to Brooklyn to have dinner with the DeFrancos. Though she's had a longstanding rule of not socializing with sources, this story has broken rules from the get-go, so she decides to make an exception.

The night Jillian called to tell Rudy about her investigation, he was so overjoyed by her discoveries that he began dancing around the apartment while she was still on the line. In fact, Jillian could hear Lorraine in the background asking Rudy why he was sliding across the foyer in his underwear and socks like Tom Cruise in *Risky Business*. Jillian's news was met with joyous squeals from Lorraine and at least fifty exclamations of "God bless!" from Eddie. They were so grateful for her efforts that at the end of the conversation, they insisted Jillian come over for a homecooked meal. Lorraine pushed for her particulars—preferred dishes, allergies, aversions—and for some reason, her favorite color. They settled on six o'clock the following Tuesday.

As Jillian walks from her parking spot to the DeFrancos' building a few blocks away, she is accosted by campaign volunteers handing out flyers for local races. She accepts the pamphlets so as not to disrespect those who have devoted personal time to the democratic process, but when they turn away, she discards the leaflets in the trash. It's an ethical conundrum she has considered before—insolence toward humanity versus insolence toward the environment. Although she deems herself a responsible recycler and supporter of all things green, she prefers to err on the side of not being rude to someone's face.

When she rounds the corner, Jillian passes a public school with a queue of people outside the main doors. *Ah, voters on their way home from the office*, she smiles and immediately thinks of April. Though Jillian would not consider April a friend, their meeting in Chicago certainly fostered a kinship. She pulls out her phone as she waits for the crosswalk light to change on the corner of Avenue J and shoots off a text to April:

Thinking of you.

Rudy and his parents are standing at the doorframe of their apartment when Jillian exits the elevator.

"Hello! Thank you so much for having me. Here, this is for you." Jillian smiles and hands Eddie the bottle of vintage Dom Perignon she received from Meredith. She isn't too proud to regift. *They deserve champagne more than I do*, she concludes, but wonders whether presenting this to a source violates the Society of Professional Journalists code of ethics. She supposes it does not, but even if she's wrong, she doesn't care.

"Welcome!" Lorraine pulls Jillian in for a hearty embrace.

Her hair smells like coconuts, Jillian thinks while leaning in and awkwardly patting Lorraine's shoulder blades as if she's burping a baby.

"Thanks again for everything," Rudy says, coming in for a hug of his own. "Can I take your coat?"

When she turns around, Jillian is greeted by a sea of orange, her favorite color. The dining table is set with orange napkins, a large bowl of tangerines, miniature faux pumpkins, and a bouquet of orange lilies. Her name is even written in cursive on an orange place card at the head of the table. A lump forms in her throat; never has she received a more thoughtful or gracious welcome.

Are dinner parties always like this? Jillian wonders. She typically eats alone at her desk or in front of the television. Occasionally she'll meet a friend for sushi, but dinner parties are never on her calendar.

"Look who's here!" Lorraine beams, her hands covered in oven mitts as she places warm casserole dishes onto table trivets.

"Sorry I'm late." A man in a gray suit with a loose blue tie dangling from his neck enters and makes a round of kisses before extending a hand to Jillian. "Nice to meet you. I'm Tommy, Rudy's better lookin' older brother."

Jillian knows all about Tommy from her conversations with April and Rudy. *He's right*, she thinks, admiring Tommy's dark skin, high cheekbones, and long lashes. *He's even better looking than Rudy!*

Sitting across from the siblings, Jillian is mesmerized by their similarities—the way their smiles angle slightly to the left, showing the teeth on only one side of their mouth; the way they each watch to ensure Lorraine has taken food before making their own plates; the way they grip utensils with full fists instead of separated fingers; and how they both rise in their seats to fill Eddie's cup of water as soon as it nears the midway mark. It's as if neither son ever wants their father's glass to be half empty.

"So, I actually have something exciting to tell you all," Jillian states during the main course. She's uncertain if it is a guest's place to direct dinner conversation but dives right in with the news of Jordana's offer.

"Where on God's green Earth did you come from?" Lorraine gazes at her.

"I might just dance across the floor in my boxers again," Rudy laughs. "Really, Jillian, that's, well, that's just incredible. Thank you."

Jillian nods in acknowledgment. "We'll make it happen." She's prepared for queries about how Jordana can help or the potential consequences of an ethics investigation into Sketcher, but they drop it and she doesn't raise the subject again.

The remainder of the evening is filled with laughter and no mention of the events that brought them together. Jillian gets the sense they're talked out. Instead, they have boisterous, lengthy conversations about sports and reality television. After so many years of darkness, they seem eager to bathe in the light—to focus on anything other than what they have been immersed in for far too long. Jillian can't remember the last time she had this much fun—or found kindred spirits regarding *The Bachelor* franchise. Apparently, Lorraine is just as addicted as Jillian, and though he is reluctant to admit it, Tommy is too.

At the end of the night, as Rudy helps Jillian with her coat, Lorraine emerges from the kitchen toting a shopping bag of leftovers. "Everything freezes well," she says and places the bag on a small bench beside the front door.

Jillian thanks her profusely and then turns to Rudy.

"This is for you" she says, handing him a slip of paper with Jordana's number. "Call her."

"It's the first thing I'll do tomorrow."

"Good. And if you want me to be a part of the conversation or need anything, I'm here."

"Thank you."

Walking down Avenue J toward her car, Jillian hears her name. She spins and sees Tommy jogging in her direction, the bag of leftovers bouncing in his hand.

"You forgot this upstairs," he pants.

"Oh, I'm so sorry you had to hunt me down."

"No problem. I was on my way home anyhow. This gave me an excuse to slip out early and skip dish duty." He winks.

"Are you parked this way?" She points down the street.

"Nah, I'm like a fifteen-minute walk."

"Can I give you a lift?"

He considers her offer. "Alright. Thanks."

There's a fair amount of traffic on Flatbush Avenue for a Tuesday at 9 p.m., and it takes longer than expected to get to Tommy's building, but it's the best nightcap Jillian's ever had. There isn't a single lull in conversation. They begin where they left off with reality TV, and by the time she pulls up to the curb to drop him off, they've covered current events, books, dream vacations, and careers. It's this last topic that shifts the gears.

"You know," Tommy says somberly, far from his buoyancy minutes earlier when describing the ideal trip to Acapulco, "I thought I'd be further up the ladder at this point in my life."

Jillian nods. She learned from Rudy how Tommy's life, both professionally and personally, had been stunted. Rudy went into detail during their phone conversation about how Tommy stepped up to help their father during the day and spent years in night school to get his master's degree in accounting. He had no time to date and rarely saw friends.

"It's just frustrating when you have a clear vision for your future and suddenly everything gets put on hiatus," he says.

Tommy's grief incites a pang of guilt inside her. *I set this disaster in motion when I gave the cop Rudy's name, and Tommy's still picking up the pieces.*

"If you ask me," she says, "success isn't about scoring a big paycheck or impressive title by the time you're twenty-six. The real question is: Are you proud of the choices you've made?"

Jillian recognizes that while her own answer is a resounding *no*, Tommy's should be an unequivocal *yes*.

"Sometimes there's no choice." He shrugs.

"Oh, there's always a choice, Tommy. You can choose to be selfish or selfless. You can choose to tear someone down or lift them up. You can choose loyalty or abandonment," she pauses, "and in your case, you can choose to be your brother's keeper . . . or not."

Tommy gazes contemplatively out the windshield. "Did Rudy tell you he bought the knife to be like me? How's that for being my brother's keeper?"

The remorse oozing out of him is practically visible.

"How could you have known, Tommy? How could you have anticipated this happening to his life—to any of your lives? None of this was your fault. You're not responsible. I hope you know that."

As Tommy quietly absorbs her words, she wonders if anyone has ever expressed this sentiment to him before.

"He told me you've been a rock. Actually, I think the exact quote was 'friggin' rock.'" She smiles.

Tommy smiles back and looks Jillian directly in the eyes. The intimacy sends an electric current throughout her body.

"Would you like to go out some time? Get dinner or whatever?"

Jillian can feel her face flush. She's flattered yet nervous as she has not dated anyone since her divorce five years ago. "Yes. I'd love to."

At 10 p.m., Jillian slides into bed and opens her laptop to check email. Given the excitement of her evening, she has forgotten all about the election in Chicago but is reminded as soon as her inbox appears on the screen. Just as a Google alert kept her appraised of developments in Rudy's life, the same computer algorithm is keeping her abreast of April's world.

The first subject line reads: "Peter Nelson Wins State's Attorney."

The second declares: "Nelson Prevails Despite Controversy."

The third is a link to a photo of their family on a stage, hands raised high in victory. Peter is on one side, April on the other, the kids sandwiched between them.

Though April did not respond to Jillian's text earlier in the evening, she decides to send another. Jillian takes a moment to ponder and find the right sentiment. She thinks of all April shared when they met in Chicago—how much she has on her plate, how torn she feels by conflicting priorities, the stress of the election coinciding with Rudy's release—and then settles on three simple words:

Rooting for you.

24

Rudy

NOW

Rudy's palms are sweaty and his throat is parched. He stoops over the water fountain, angling so that the stream doesn't splash his suit.

"Shit," he mutters under his breath when droplets trickle down from his chin onto his collar. He pulls a tissue from his pocket to dab at the spots.

This is his third visit to Manhattan since his release and he wouldn't mind if it were his last.

On his first post-incarceration excursion, he broke out in hives while traversing the Williamsburg Bridge and needed to stop at the Duane Reade Pharmacy on Delancey Street for Benadryl. He was en route to meet the defense team Jordana assembled to discuss how to get his case dismissed and was horrified by his own tardiness, especially because they were taking time out of their schedules and not asking for a cent in return.

On his second trip to the city, he opted for an alternative route in the event the bridge was somehow to blame for his random case of hives. He crossed the East River underground through Brooklyn Battery Tunnel and unfortunately, while sitting in the back of the BM1 bus, experienced his first panic attack. His heart raced, his head pounded, his face tingled, and his vision narrowed. Luckily, an off-duty nurse was sitting nearby and recognized his symptoms. She talked him through some basic relaxation techniques, but he was in no position to meet with lawyers, so he rescheduled. As soon as Rudy returned to Brooklyn, the symptoms disappeared. All subsequent discussions were held via conference call.

Post Traumatic Stress Disorder (PTSD), agoraphobia, and even something coined "Post-Incarceration Syndrome" were terms he had seen written in pamphlets about the reentry process and heard mentioned in support group classes at The Prentice League. In fact, there was a corkboard in the second-floor lounge with a flyer listing potential symptoms along with a headline: "Have You Experienced Any of These? If So, You're Not Alone." It made sense, Rudy reasoned, that after so many years of being locked up he would feel anxious leaving his comfort zone and reluctant to return to the site of a trauma (upper Manhattan: the scene of the crime) or a place where escape could be difficult (lower Manhattan: the courthouse where he was arraigned and sentenced), but he never spoke with anyone about it. He wasn't depressed and if anything, he felt like he'd won the lottery compared to the men and women he knew struggling with family dynamics or forced to live at a halfway house because they had no home. He appreciated the blessings of his loving, stable environment and that was precisely his Achilles heal—he freaked out any time he had to leave it. Apparently, Midwood wasn't merely home, it was his homeostasis.

Though technically his attendance is not mandated, today really can't be phoned in. He *should* be there. He *wants* to be there. He *deserves* to be there. After all these years, he is finally having his day in court.

Unlike the arraignment and sentencing when he was escorted from the holding pen to the courtroom in handcuffs, Rudy is now sitting in the audience section dressed in his finest clothes, flanked by his attorneys and loved ones. The courtroom décor then and now is nearly identical—same wood paneling, matching light fixtures, similar burgundy rope separating the well from the visitors— yet somehow, what seemed ominous years ago feels propitious today.

When the court officer calls his case, Rudy and his attorneys stand at their spot in the pews and walk over to the defense table. Entering the courtroom's well triggers some of the sensations he had on the BM1 bus that morning. At first, he's not sure if the ringing in his ears is coming from a lightbulb or other source inside the room, but when he feels his vision narrow and pulse quicken, he knows. As soon as Rudy settles into his wooden chair, he loosens his tie and fills the empty glass in front of him with water from a pitcher on the table.

"Don't worry. Hard part's over," the lead attorney whispers in his ear. "Just some procedural stuff and we should be out of here soon." He gives Rudy a reassuring pat on the back.

Rudy doesn't hear exactly what is said during the hearing. He's too busy concentrating on not passing out. The prosecutor, standing, is doing most of the talking—something about evidence coming to light, the District Attorney's office doing an independent investigation that verified the validity of that new information, and moving in the interest of justice for this case to be dismissed.

The judge exchanges some unidentifiable legalese with the lawyers, stamps a few papers, and then looks directly at Rudy over the readers at the tip of his nose. "Mr. DeFranco," he says in a monotone, "by the people's motion, your case is dismissed."

That's it? Rudy wonders. He expects the judge to sermonize or deliver a dramatic soliloquy as one might expect at the conclusion of a movie, but there is no more. It is only when Rudy's attorneys lean in for a hug and flash broad smiles that he knows. He's a free man.

While the hearing may have felt anticlimactic, the scene outside afterward is the antithesis. Press swarm like vultures as soon as Rudy and his team exit the courtroom doors. Rudy holds Lorraine's hand tightly so they don't get separated, and Tommy extends his arms like a linebacker to block television cameras from getting too close to their faces. Rudy quickly whips his head to check on the Zagodas and sees April slowly maneuvering Barbara's wheelchair away from the crowd. *Good*, he thinks. *I don't want them getting jostled.*

"How does it feel to be a free man, Rudy?" one reporter shouts.

"What's going through your mind right now?" another calls out.

That I'd like to get out of this building and never return, he thinks. Instead, Rudy smiles politely. "I'm very grateful."

"Can we get a shot of the family, please?" asks a photographer with two cameras hanging from his neck.

The sea parts and Lorraine, Eddie, Tommy, and Rudy stand at the elevator bank, arms linked at the elbows, as if they are a human blockade against falling down an airshaft.

As camera flashes fire, Rudy notices the Zagodas taking in the scene from a safe distance. April's hands are wrapped around the handlebars of Barbara's chair, and Steven's blazer is far too large for his now delicate frame.

They look frail, he thinks, recalling how they were so robust and strong, his rocks, at the start of this process in this very building. The effect of time on Barbara and Steven is the clearest proof of the years Rudy has lost.

Rudy lifts his chin a bit and catches April's eye. He winks. She blows an air kiss. And at the exact same moment, they both reach for their earlobes and smile.

It's time to go home.

꙲

Though it has been heartbreaking to witness Barbara and Steven age with challenges, April's now frequent visits to Brooklyn to assist with her parents' care have created a window of in-person quality time Rudy and April would not have otherwise been gifted. When he first returned home, Rudy learned that substantive phone conversations with April were impossible given her demanding life in Chicago. With three kids, a husband in the public eye, and a life of her own, she rarely picked up his calls, and if they did connect, they were quickly interrupted. She certainly tried though. For a while, they exchanged lengthy voicemail messages providing updates and questions for the other to answer in their subsequent dispatch. That didn't last long. Once Rudy got a smartphone, texting proved to be a decent alternative, though it wasn't the same as hearing her voice. But now that she is back in Brooklyn every few weeks, Rudy can feel his equilibrium reset. And fortunately, the day of his exoneration happened to be scheduled right smack in the middle of a week she was in town.

Numerous post-courthouse celebratory options had been proposed—a fancy lunch at Peter Luger's (the Zagodas' time-honored milestone marker), a favorite homecooked dinner (Lorraine's suggestion), cigars on the terrace (Eddie's idea), darts at a local bar (Tommy's preference)—but all Rudy wants is a typical day in the neighborhood. It was all he dreamed of while he was away. Nothing extravagant. Nothing out of the ordinary. Just normalcy, or whatever he deemed normalcy given its shifting definition over time. His only special request is an ice cream sundae from Carvel before the day is over. It is Wednesday two-for-one, after all.

Later that afternoon, once the media circus has calmed and Rudy has changed out of his suit and into a hoodie and joggers, he walks up the block to thank the Zagodas for their support. He

knows it was not easy for them to rise early, shower, make breakfast, take their pills, get dressed, and leave the house in time to contend with morning traffic all while maneuvering a wheelchair in
and out of a car, past security, and into the pews of a courtroom.
People don't often think about logistics, but Rudy does. Just as he
appreciates every step required to fix a refrigerator compressor
pump or install a new faucet, he recognizes the minutia of what it
takes to get things done. He's a details guy. Always has been.

Though it's four o'clock when Rudy rings the Zagodas' bell,
April answers the door with an index finger pressed against her
lips. "Shh, they're sleeping," she says as if he's nearly awakened
twin infants.

"Is this a nap or a really early bedtime?"

"They're a little off schedule," she says. "Busy day."

"I'm sorry." *Damn it. It's my fault. I'm glad they were there, but if
I had known it would be so taxing, I would have insisted they not come.*

Rudy follows her into the kitchen. There are pill bottles lined
up along the counter and doctors' business cards with appointment
reminders taped to the cabinets. A folder with a picture on the
cover of silver-haired couples laughing sits in the middle of the table.

"What's this about?" Rudy asks, pointing to the packet.

April sighs.

Man, she looks exhausted, he thinks.

"I made an appointment to see that assisted living place in the
neighborhood. I'm just exploring options for my parents. Sort of a
reconnaissance mission, really. I was poking around their site and
ended up registering for promotional information. I have a tour
scheduled tomorrow morning before I fly home."

Rudy feels himself wince. He's still not used to hearing April
refer to Chicago as *home*.

"I don't know Rud, it would definitely give me peace of mind
knowing they've got someone making their meals, monitoring their

medicines, helping them run errands. I've tackled the food delivery—I order groceries for them online—but it's the little stuff like unpacking the food, doing laundry, cleaning the bathrooms—it's a lot. I got them an aide a few days a week and a cleaning lady every Wednesday, but I think they need more. I can't keep doing this. The travel back and forth to Chicago is catching up with me. I never see my kids."

"You know," Rudy says, "I've never *actually* seen your kids."

"That's absolutely insane. It's like the left and right ventricles of my heart are not connected. We need to make that a priority."

"I've never met your husband either."

Rudy can feel April tense. "Mmm. True. Want some tea?"

He can tell she is avoiding something but doesn't want to overstep so he attempts a joke. "Where are we, London? Having high tea at four o'clock?"

Her eyes widen with wonder. "Oh, Rud, you'd absolutely *love* London! You *must* go. Gosh, think of all the places you can travel to now! Chicago, London, LA is so cool. What else is on your list? Oh, we should make you an appointment at the post office to get a passport! This is so exciting! It really is like a whole new life!"

Rudy chuckles. "With what money, Ape? I ain't got a job! I mean, I've been pitching in on the morning shift every day at the bagel store and I get tips for helping my dad around the building, but I'm not exactly rolling in the duckets. There's no jet-set life happening here. Hell, I've never even been on an airplane!"

"Right. Sorry. Let's talk about that. Not the airplane part, I mean the job situation. I may have a lead for you. It's at an engineering firm."

"And they'd hire an ex-con?" He raises one eyebrow.

"Never know. It's worth a shot. My friend Georgia in Chicago, her brother Bob lives here and is the head of the company. I can put in a good word."

"Where's the office?"

"Midtown."

"Midtown Manhattan?"

"No, Rud, midtown New Jersey . . ." She rolls her eyes. "Yes! Of course midtown Manhattan!"

"Nope. No way." He holds up his hands. "Sorry, but don't bother."

"Whoa." April laughs. "What's your beef with midtown?"

"I just don't want to be in the city. Like ever."

April is quiet. He can feel her scrutinizing him.

"I just . . ." he starts but is suddenly antsy. He jumps out of his chair and over to the pantry to search for a snack.

"Rud?" She cocks her head. "You were saying?"

"I just don't want to be in Manhattan. I can't."

She grabs the cookie from his hand. "No Oreos until you talk to me. Tell me what's going on."

He sinks into his chair and goes into detail about what he believes are panic attacks. He tells her about the pamphlets he's read and the poster at The Prentice League and how the symptoms started only recently, but now whenever he sees an image of the skyline or even the word "Manhattan," he can feel his pulse quicken.

"I think there might be something wrong with me, Ape. You know, I'm a pretty chill guy. I've never felt anything like this before."

She reaches across the table for his hand. "You have no idea how common this is. When I worked at The Prentice League, people dealt with this all the time. Not exactly an aversion to the island of Manhattan, but something related to their incarceration or arrest where some aspect of their experience became a trigger."

"I'm scared I'm messed up in the head."

"Rud, you experienced an astronomical trauma. Honestly, I'd be concerned if you didn't have some sort of reaction and just whistled and skipped through the rest of your life as if nothing happened."

"How do I fix it?"

She hands him back the cookie. "Remember when you broke your ankle in seventh grade and needed to have those pins put in?"

"Yeah."

"So you know how you were convinced you'd never play baseball again because you thought you wouldn't be able to run quickly or slide to steal a base, but then you did physical therapy, healed perfectly, went on to play varsity in high school, and now all you have is that faded scar?"

He nods.

"Well, it's kinda like that. With the right support, the scars will fade."

"Not sure I'll be playing varsity sports again, though."

"Metaphorically speaking you will, and I know just the person to help."

The following week, Rudy walks half a mile to Bedford Avenue for his first appointment with Dr. Fiona Emmett—a former colleague of April's from The Prentice League. Fiona spent years directing The League's outpatient mental health clinic and has since opened a private practice in addition to her post as a professor of psychology at Brooklyn College. Her office is located just steps from Midwood High School, his old stomping grounds, in an unremarkable brick apartment building he must have passed a thousand times.

When Rudy arrives, he notices that the office's interior is only slightly less bland than the exterior. There are potted plants along the windowsill, a glass jar of individually wrapped mints, and a large, framed poster of Coney Island on the wall over a brown leather couch. Fiona's young receptionist, Isla, checks him in and hands him a clipboard of forms. He takes a seat on the chair opposite the couch so he can enjoy the art.

"Forgot to give you this." Isla walks over and offers him a pen for the forms. "I read that story about you in the paper. Just want to say I'm really sorry you had to go through all of that. How are you doing?"

The genuine concern in her voice is both heartening and unnerving. For so long he'd been treated like a killer. Now, thanks to Jillian's article, he's a victim. He pauses before responding to her question. *How* am *I doing?* he wonders.

"I'm sorry," she blushes, "that was probably a loaded question and none of my business." With her dark hair, wide eyes, and the way her cheeks redden against her porcelain skin, he can't help but think she bears a striking resemblance to Snow White.

"Don't apologize." Rudy chuckles. "That's why I'm here, you know, to figure out how I'm doing." He looks down at the clipboard and sees several questions asking him to describe his symptoms and what he hopes to gain from therapy. The mere thought of trying to articulate his recent experiences in Manhattan cause his upper lip to perspire. "Do I have to answer all of these?"

"It's okay, don't worry," she says gently. "Fiona will gather the same information by speaking with you. It's all good." She holds her hand out to take back the clipboard and he notices a tiny sun tattooed on her wrist.

"Thanks," he smiles and wipes the sweat from his philtrum.

Over the following months, Rudy finds his sessions with Fiona to be very helpful. The cognitive behavioral therapy techniques are useful and while he dreads their exposure therapy "field trips" to Manhattan, his symptoms improve with each visit. He can now look at an image of the skyline without an uptick in his pulse.

Ironically, bridges and tunnels are the conduits to Fiona, and they have in turn become pathways to other forms of healing. As well-intentioned and loving as his family is, they lack the training and experience to guide him through the emotional aspects of reentry or help him thoroughly process so many years of trauma. Mr. Marino, his boss at the bagel store where he has taken on daily shifts, always asks how he's doing, but Rudy plasters on a smile and employs his standard line, "Never better!" April is the person with whom he feels most at ease, but she is often unavailable. Either she's in Chicago, or, if she is in town, she's typically too busy checking off a to-do list with her parents to delve deep with Rudy. He has never spoken about their relationship with anyone or even labeled his complex emotions for her. But Fiona has provided a safe space for him to begin.

"When I got home from prison, I expected everything with April to be the same," Rudy shares during one of their sessions. "Like life had just been frozen in place for a really long time."

She nods thoughtfully. "Mmm, as if being released were the equivalent of releasing the pause button on your relationship."

"Exactly. I mean, we wrote letters the whole time I was away, I got updates . . ."

"Yes, and how wonderful that years of correspondence successfully maintained your bond. But do you feel it sufficed as a placeholder?" She pushes her retro cat eyeglasses onto the top of her spiky silver hair. "In other words, did receiving those occasional letters prepare you for your current relationship as adults?"

No, he thinks, but can't bring himself to form the word.

Who knows what could have been? was a familiar trope in his mind for years as he lay in his cell. Occasionally, he wondered if, had that fateful night never happened, their connection could have turned into more. He also questioned whether something between them would ignite upon his return, irrespective of the fact that she was married with three children. He never met her husband or kids or visited their home in Chicago. *Did any of it even exist?* The distance of it all just added to the mystique. Her grown-up world was hard to accept when none of his senses could experience it. He never shook Peter's hand or heard her children's voices. April did not send photographs to him in prison, so her written descriptions were all he had to go on. The first time Rudy glimpsed any of their faces was after he was released and visited the Zagodas' house where the walls had become a shrine.

"She's built a beautiful life for herself," Rudy finally answers Fiona.

"And how does that make you feel?"

That things have changed, are the words that come to his mind but he doesn't say. Instead, he focuses on the whirr of the white noise machine in the background while summoning the courage to speak without getting emotional. "I'm happy for her," Rudy finally replies. He clears his throat, pushing down the lump that has formed. "Very happy for her."

"That's lovely. Now tell me, what does being happy for April mean for you?"

"That I'll always love her no matter what, and I know she'll always love me."

"Yes, *and . . .*" Fiona touches the chunky craft-fair necklace resting on her collarbone.

Rudy takes a breath and lets out a long exhale. "And, it's time I build a life for myself, too."

Fiona smiles satisfactorily. "All of these things are true."

25

April

NOW

t's 7 p.m. on a Thursday when a text comes in.

Rudy: Hey, what's up?

> April: Well, in no particular order . . .post-dinner clean up, helping girls with homework, and trying to get my son to take a shower, but I fear that last one's a losing battle. 🤐

Rudy: FYI, IMHO IDK how u do it.

April bursts out laughing. For someone who has only recently learned how to navigate a smartphone and text, Rudy has caught up and embraced the multitude of acronyms at lightning speed.

Rudy: U around tonight for a call? LMK

April: 👍 Gimme an hour . . . 😶

With the kids in their rooms and Peter still out at one of his many weeknight rubber chicken dinners, the timing is perfect for a catchup with Rudy. She shuts the bedroom door and curls up on the upholstered chaise lounge by the window overlooking the L tracks. April has always enjoyed watching the Chicago trains zoom past her condo; the reminder of New York subway cars is comforting. She's just grateful to live in a building with soundproof windows.

"Okay," Rudy says, picking up on the first ring. "You wanna go first?"

April loves that they have returned to a point where they can skip greetings and pleasantries at the beginning of a phone call. Their rhythm is back. It's not the allegro pace of their youth with daily conversations, but it's a solid 4/4 common time beat.

"No, you," she insists. She knows her news will be a bombshell and they'll spend the rest of the call picking up the shrapnel. *Better he should start*, she thinks.

"Okay," he begins. "First, did you hear? I'm sure my mom told your mom."

"What?!"

"Tommy and Jillian are going out."

"My mom mentioned he had a girlfriend, but I didn't realize it was Jillian. Wow! That's, um . . ." she searches for the appropriate word to capture worlds colliding, "absolutely bizarre."

"Yeah, I know. But hey, if they're happy, I'm happy."

"Same."

"Okay so my other news . . ."

"Hit me."

"Mr. Marino pulls me aside the other morning and says his friend up the street who owns the hardware store is looking for a manager. Someone to deal with customers, man the floor, oversee appliance repairs, that kinda thing. Apparently Marino's buddy is planning to retire in a year and wants to groom someone now to take over. Marino wants to recommend me. What do you think?"

"Yes!" April exclaims and then lowers her voice so as not to disturb her kids down the hall. "A bazillion times yes!" she whispers emphatically.

"Yeah, I thought so too. I'd get salary, benefits, all that stuff. Don't want to get ahead of myself, but I'm pretty psyched."

"You should be! What does everyone else say?"

"Everyone's supportive. Isla too."

"Ooh, Isla," she sings as if they are kids again. April loves getting updates on Rudy's budding relationship. Every time they speak, a new detail trickles in. First, it was that Isla lives with her parents in Brooklyn, just like Rudy. Then, it was that Isla has a daughter named Sunny, the product of a high school pregnancy she didn't want to give up. Becoming a single mom so young derailed her life, but she got her GED and worked part-time as Fiona's assistant while completing her associate's degree at community college. All these nuggets were gleaned over small talk before and after his weekly sessions with Fiona. Rudy didn't want to ask Isla out while she was still employed by his therapist, but as soon as she graduated and got a full-time job elsewhere, he got her number. April even helped him plan their first date—a walk through the Brooklyn Botanical Gardens. The contentment she hears in his voice each time is a tremendous relief. For years she worried how he would fare in the dating world when he got out of prison. How would he navigate a dating app? How would he explain his past? Would he be transparent from the start or wait until a relationship felt solid, but then risk getting heartbroken if the woman couldn't handle dating a felon? *Thank goodness he's met someone so promising and accepting.*

"Alright, that's my news," Rudy says. "What's up with you?"

April takes a deep breath. "My parents are moving."

"Oh, to that assisted living place?"

"Well, they *are* going to assisted living . . . just not the one in Brooklyn. I found a place near me. In Chicago."

There is no sound on the other end of the line.

"It's just easier, Rud. I can't keep up this pace flying back and forth all the time."

"Yeah, makes sense." She can hear the disappointment in his voice.

"Every minute they're home alone is like Russian roulette. I'm losing sleep over whether they remember to take their pills, if they're taking the *correct* pills, if they left an appliance on, if they slipped in the shower, if they tripped on the stairs, if they're getting scammed when answering the phone. It's time."

"Talk about pills. This is a hard one to swallow."

"I know. It's not easy for me either. I can't imagine my life without a base in Midwood, but I need and want to be close to help and I can't uproot my family. Which, actually, leads me to the other thing . . ."

"There's another thing? I don't know if I can handle more news right now."

He sounds like he's kidding, but I'm not sure.

"My parents have an insanely good long-term care insurance policy. I met with their financial advisor and between the long-term care coverage and what they've got saved in the bank, they don't need to sell the house right away in order to afford assisted living. I can move them in tomorrow if needed."

"So that's good, right?"

"My point, Rud, is the house is going to be sitting there empty because I don't have the bandwidth right now to clean it out, list it with a real estate broker, and get them situated in Chicago. But I don't want to leave the property unattended. The last thing I need is for a pipe to burst and the basement to flood and not know about it because there's no one home. And I don't want to give a key to some random caretaker to check in, especially when all their stuff is still in the house."

"I can check on it for you. That's easy."

"I know. Thanks. I thought about asking you, but then I had an idea. Would you want to move in? Kind of be a live-in super like your dad, but at our house?"

He laughs. "That's funny."

"I know but think about it—it's a win-win. It gives me peace of mind that the house is in good hands, and it gives you a little space and independence, which you've been wanting. I know there are a lot of memories for you in the house—good and bad—but it has always been your home, too. It doesn't have to be forever, or it can be, we can figure that out later."

"Ooof," he lets out a loud sigh. "That's a lot to take in over one conversation. Possibly a new job, maybe a new home, a Zagoda-less Brooklyn . . . Geez."

"I know," she laments as she watches the L roll past her window. "I know."

"Thanks, Ape. It's a very nice offer. I'll check in with Isla, we'll talk about it, and I'll get back to you."

I'll check in with Isla?! April feels like she just got whiplash. *This conversation really is jam-packed with change. Would Isla move in with him? In my house? That's weird . . .*

"Are things getting serious?"

"I know what you're thinking, Ape, but I have no big plans on the horizon. There's no rushing here. Slow and steady. Isla's got a kid. That's a big deal. I'm nowhere near ready for a major commitment. I've got to get my own life together, especially the job situation. It's not like either one of us is baggage free. But yes, we're in a good place. I like her a lot."

"Rud!" April gasps and sits up in her chaise. "I've never heard you say that about a girl. Ever! I'm so happy for you!" *It's not love, but "like a lot" is a major step.*

"Maybe you guys can meet next time you're in town."

"I'll be home soon to move my parents. We'll do it then. I love you, Rud."

"Love you, too."

"I'll check in with Isla." April replays Rudy's words in her mind as she washes up before bed. *Now that's a partnership*, she thinks and vigorously spits foamy toothpaste into the sink.

She remembers the early days with Peter that were chock-full of promise, security, and indissoluble unity—a time when they discussed everything and were each other's first call for the good, the bad, and all points in between. There wasn't yet an embedded layer of ick tainting the purity as there is now, but perhaps, she thinks, that's an element of true partnership, too.

The intercom in the condo chirps twice, alerting her that there is motion at the front door. April checks the clock radio on her nightstand—9:48 p.m.—and knows it's Peter returning home. *He's early*, she thinks and shuffles down the hall in pajamas and slippers where she finds him holding open the refrigerator door and staring indecisively at its contents.

"On the left under the tin foil," she says. She doesn't need to ask to know he's craving something sweet.

"Oh, perfect!" He sighs as he unveils the mini Boston cream pie she set aside for him. "You know the way to a guy's heart."

She hands him a fork and kisses the back of his head before going to check on the kids.

April has no regrets about telling Jillian everything that day at Club Lucky. It was undoubtedly risky as she wasn't sure how Jillian would ultimately skew the article, but April knew in her gut that she needed and wanted above all to do right by Rudy, and fortunately, Peter came away unscathed. In fact, the wider than expected margin of his win was likely the result of the clarity Jillian provided. April knew that there was a chance the piece could benefit Peter, but there was no guarantee. It could have gone either way and had Peter lost the election because of his peripheral link to the scandal, April isn't sure what would have become of their marriage. Club Lucky turned out to be an auspicious pick.

In the end, election night went smoothly. Aside from a manicure and new bouclé tweed blazer, she prepared for the victory celebration by having both Georgia and Nina within arm's reach— Georgia to help out if needed with the kids and Nina to be April's public relations buffer in the event she was hounded by reporters for a comment about Jillian's story or Rudy's case. Both friends have been steadfast in their support. Like Rudy, April has had her share of circumspect side-eyed glances around town, but for the most part, she has found that people either avoid the topic or express heartfelt sympathy. On a few occasions, acquaintances used April's adversity as a gateway to sharing their own, and it was during these moments that April did more listening and consoling than speaking. Once, a woman pulled her aside in the produce isle at Trader Joe's to share how she was devastated and ashamed by her husband's gambling addiction that nearly bankrupt their family. Another woman revealed in the pickup line at Starbucks that she had done a brief stint in jail herself for shoplifting. April felt flattered by their trust but also uncomfortable that she had come to be viewed as an icon of misfortune, a poster child for *shit happens.*

The confessionals by these women reminded her of Bunny Fishbein's visits to the bagel store and how whenever Rudy asked how she was doing, she'd reply, "Eh, we all have *tsuris* darling, but I'm here and still standing, aren't I?" Bunny literally wore the Yiddish sentiment on her sleeve with a zip-up sweatshirt that had *Goodbye Tsuris, Hello Pension* written on the back.

For April, the best part of election night was the ride home. With the kids electrified in the back seat thanks to a combination of adrenaline and sugar, she and Peter had the middle row of the SUV to themselves. She feared the trip back to their condo might mimic the one following the press conference when Peter publicly praised April but was then privately apoplectic and cold. This time, however, when the car doors closed, Peter turned off his cell phone and reached for her hand.

"Thank you," he said, pulling her fingers to his lips and planting several kisses on her knuckles. "I'm so sorry. I'm so so sorry. I just couldn't imagine life without you by my side. I thought I was losing you. I just . . . I just couldn't handle it." A tear trickled down his cheek and landed on her thumb. "Highs and lows, Ape," he whispered as they drove down Lake Shore Drive and passed the Navy Pier Ferris Wheel. "What did I tell ya? Highs and lows and we're still side by side."

April grinned. She knew the emotional night was likely catching up with Peter and contributing to his sentimentality, but it was still good to hear. She didn't doubt his words were heartfelt, but she also never second-guessed her own decisions. She stood by her men as best she could all the while remaining authentic, honest, and true. So much of April's life had been dictated or defined by others' circumstances. Being forced to choose between Rudy and Peter elucidated who needed championing the most: herself.

"So what's the plan for your parents? When's this move happening?" Peter asks between forkfuls of Boston cream pie at the kitchen island.

"I'm thinking I'll fly out and get them packed up next weekend."

"Are you kidding? You're not moving them alone. We're doing it as a family. The kids, you, me, we're all going to New York."

Now this is the man I fell in love with, she thinks.

"That would be amazing—really meaningful for my parents and me. But I have to let you know, it won't just be us there. The DeFrancos are going to be around all weekend, I can guarantee it. I don't know how you feel . . ."

Peter takes a swig of milk and places the empty glass in the sink.

"Well, I'd say it's about time we meet."

26

April

NOW

The maroon carpeting in the Zagodas' living room is barely visible as every inch is covered by a box or crate. Rudy arrives early to help pack for their move to Chicago, just as he did when April left for college, but this time he's toting enough bagels and black and white cookies for her entire family.

The introduction is years in the making and April knows that if she thinks too much or overanalyzes the magnitude of this moment, she may pass out. It's only nine o'clock on Saturday morning and already she has had two cups of chamomile tea to calm her stomach. So, when she looks out the front window and sees Rudy walking up the stoop, she does the only thing she can think to do: grab her offspring and line them up like pageant contestants.

"Rud! These are my kids!" she squeals when he enters. It takes a few seconds before realizing she's standing on her tiptoes.

Though April has prepared Attie, Rosie, and Simon in advance, she can feel all three pairs of eyes scan him up and down and she knows exactly what her children are thinking: *This is the guy who went to prison—the source of our stress at school.* She prays they heed her warnings not to ask any questions or make references to his past.

"So Rud, this is Simon." She taps her son's shoulders. "He's a sportsman just like you."

Sportsman?! she hears herself. *When have I ever used that word? Athlete, yes, but sportsman?! My God, woman, get a grip!*

Rudy raises his hand for a high five, but Simon leaves him hanging and glances at April, seemingly for permission before vigorously slapping Rudy's palm.

"And these are my girls, Attie and Rosie." April twirls her fingers around their silky ponytails just as she did with her own at their age.

"Hi." Attie waves.

"Nice to meet you." Rosie flashes a polite grin.

"Gosh you two look *so* much like your mom," he says, clearly gobsmacked. "They're like clones of you, Ape!"

Attie turns and curls her arm around April's waist. She is certainly the most affectionate of the three, but when she nuzzles her head in the space between April's arm and chest, she can tell it's something more. *Maybe it was unsettling to hear my nickname uttered by someone she's never met?* April thinks as she rubs her daughter's back.

"By the way, I just passed your parents down the street," Rudy says. "Did you know they're going out to breakfast with my parents?"

"Yes, they wanted a farewell meal just the four of them. Isn't that sweet?"

Just then April hears Peter's footsteps slowly lumbering up from the basement. When he appears at the top of the narrow staircase, she notices he's lugging Barbara's beloved antique apothecary table and squinting to prevent beads of sweat from dripping into his eyes.

"Need a hand with that?" Rudy asks, instantly running over to help. He grabs one side so Peter can shift to the other.

Seeing them just feet apart is surreal. April takes a mental snapshot.

Suddenly, Peter's eyebrows morph from furrowed confusion to arched astonishment—proof he's aware that the stranger with whom he shares responsibility for the Zagodas' prized possession is none other than Rudy DeFranco.

"Thanks," Peter says as they lower the table onto the kitchen floor. He wipes his brow and extends a hand. "Peter Nelson. So great to meet you. I'm assuming you're Rudy, right?" He laughs.

April can tell by his awkward chuckle that her husband is uncomfortable, but she's grateful for his taking the lead. *Thank God he spared me.* Had he left the formalities to her, she knows her voice would have jumped at least an octave while making an awkward sing-song Rudy-this-is-Peter, Peter-this-is-Rudy introduction.

"So you're the lucky guy." Rudy shakes Peter's hand. "It's nice to meet you. You've got a beautiful family."

April's mind does calisthenics when Peter's only response is to fold his arms across his chest. He says nothing as he shifts his weight back and forth. 'I, um, I, I," he stutters. "I just want to thank you."

"Oh, it's no problem. Happy to help. That's why I'm here."

"No, no, that's not what I mean." Peter chuckles. "How do I say this?"

April has never seen her litigator husband struggle to find words. She moves within his line of sight for moral support, but not too close to cramp the space between Peter and Rudy.

"Every person who has played a major role in my life, in shaping who I am, I have known, like actually known," Peter says, now looking directly at Rudy. "My family, my friends, teachers, mentors, you name it. I've seen them all in person countless times. But you?" Peter shakes his head. "You're probably the most valuable, influential, behind-the-scenes player in my life, and yet we've never met. So I just wanted to say thanks. Thanks for being such an important part of April's life and consequently, a part of mine. I really do hope we'll now have a chance to make up for lost time."

Never would she have expected these words to emerge from Peter's mouth. She had no idea he was experiencing any of these emotions or thoughts, and while she wishes he had shared them with her sooner, she is grateful nonetheless. In fact, there is something quite beautiful about him articulating it all for the very first time directly with Rudy.

"Wow. Thanks, man. That's really nice. I'd like that too."

April is about to run over and throw her arms around both of them but refrains. *I want them to form their own bond and have a connection independent of me.*

For the remainder of the day, while she and the kids box up lighter items, Rudy and Peter lug the furniture her parents designated for the move into a U-Haul parked in the driveway.

Originally, April had planned to hire a moving company to transport Barbara and Steven's belongings, but then decided to ask Rudy if he'd be interested in the job. She would cover all expenses and compensate him as she would any professional mover. Plus, it would be a great way for him to see her life in Chicago and travel outside of New York State for the first time since his arrest. April knew he was working with Fiona to overcome his aversion to Manhattan, but she wasn't aware of any other locations that triggered his anxiety. Just in case, though, she suggested he invite someone to accompany him, perhaps Tommy or Isla. As soon as Rudy got clearance from his boss at the bagel store, he invited Isla and she jumped at the opportunity. This will be their first "vacation" together as a couple and April is pleased to have the peace of mind that he won't be traveling alone.

By 4 p.m., everyone is ready for a break, especially Simon, who has been begging to do something fun since he broke the label maker at 11 a.m.

"Is there a park or somewhere we can take them?" Peter asks. "I think the kids need to let off some steam."

"Avenue L playground," April and Rudy say in unison.

"It's actually around the corner from Isla's house," he adds. "She was going to come over here to say hi, but I'll ask her to meet us there."

April and Rudy sit side-by-side on a park bench watching her children run, swing, and climb just as their mothers did when they were young. The equipment has been upgraded—less metal, more safety surfacing—but otherwise, it looks the same as the day they first met.

"So is American Airlines gonna give you some kind of gift for all the miles you've racked up between LaGuardia and O'Hare? Maybe a free vacation or something?"

April laughs. "Actually, I don't want to go anywhere. I'm traveled out. I just want a normal routine again. Stability. Go to work, go home, make dinner, that kind of thing."

"Sounds good to me. I bet you'll be happy to get back into the classroom."

"Actually, I didn't renew my contract to teach next year."

"What? Why not?"

"I think I'm just ready for a change."

Initially when the scandal broke and Dr. Herman asked her to take some time off, she'd resisted. After Jillian's story cleared the air, he asked her to return, but given her frequent trips to Brooklyn and desire to be fully present for her kids, she opted to extend the leave. Dr. Herman agreed to hold her spot but said he'd need an answer when it came time to renew teacher contracts for the following school year.

Though she doesn't tell Rudy, the truth is that he is the impetus for the career shift. Having a front-row seat to his reentry experience has brought her back to her days at The Prentice League, and she can see the stark difference having an education and supportive family can make in determining a successful transition to life after prison. Rudy was lucky; most people aren't.

"So what's the plan?"

"Actually, when I initially reached out to Fiona about her working with you, she mentioned that one of her close friends is the head of an organization in Chicago similar to The Prentice League. I wanted to learn more so she connected me. I met with their team, and my plan once I get my parents settled is to work in some capacity with them. Maybe teaching, counseling, a combination of the two, administration. Not sure yet."

Rudy purses his lips together and shakes his head. "You really are something, Ape."

"Nah, it just feels right. I'm excited."

Just then Rudy points to the wrought iron gates at the entrance to the playground. "There she is!" He jogs over and greets a smiley, skinny-jeaned brunette with a hug.

April waves Peter over from the jungle gym where he has been keeping an eye on Simon. She wants him to share in this moment that suddenly feels less like the end of an era and more of a new beginning.

"You must be Isla." April smiles.

"And you must be April," she says warmly, reaching out and gently stroking the side of April's arm. "I feel as if I already know you."

The four of them chat for a while until the kids run over to the ice cream truck on the street. Rudy and April share a look. "Some things never change," she sighs.

While standing on line for cones, Rudy's phone rings and he

steps away to take the call. The image of him pacing back and forth on the sidewalk with a cell phone pressed to his ear strikes April as both unnatural and uplifting. *He's part of society again.*

"Isla!" he beckons. When she nears, he whispers something and she immediately beams.

"Everything okay?" April inquires when they return to the Mister Softee queue. If Rudy were alone, she would have sprinted over and pressed for details, but she knows there are boundaries now and wants to respect them.

"That was Mr. Marino," Rudy says, Isla's arm around his waist. "He called to tell me his buddy at the hardware store is interested. He wants to meet me."

"Oh Rud!" April cries. "You're gonna get it. I just know it."

"They'd be lucky to have you," Peter says.

Back at the playground, April and Rudy return to their spots on the green slatted benches and watch the kids frolic in chocolate-streaked clothing, just as the two of them had decades earlier. When Attie, Rosie, and Simon take turns ascending the slide, April can't help but reach for Rudy's hand and give a little squeeze. When he winks back, she knows he has the same thought.

"Thanks for waiting," he whispers.

She smiles and leans her head onto his shoulder. "You know I always will."

AUTHOR'S NOTE

I was raised in a home where a painting of the scales of justice and the words "Justice, Justice, Shall You Pursue" were prominently framed on our living room wall. My father began his career as a public defender and when I was young his colleagues would come over to our house and I'd listen as they prepped their cases around our dining table. Later, when he became a judge, I'd sit beside my dad on the bench and observe arraignments from his vantage point. I learned to appreciate nuance, the complexity of situations, and understood that behind every docket number was a human being. Most of the time, that human being had relatives and friends sitting on hard pews in the audience section awaiting their loved one's case. It didn't matter if they were on the side of the defense or the prosecution. Their angst-riddled faces were directly in my line of sight, and I couldn't help but wonder about *their* lives. *Their* backstories. How being on the periphery of a criminal case impacted *them*.

My mother's profession was equally formative. As an inner-city public school English teacher, she imparted her love of literature and creative writing to her students as well as to her own children. She saw beauty and potential in everyone, and like my father, encouraged critical independent thinking. She instilled in us the importance of doing our homework, of trusting but verifying, maintaining positivity and strength in the face of hardship, and always, always having compassion for others. Everyone, she said, has a story.

And so, this book is for my parents, Vicki and Joel Blumenfeld.

Thank you for being the ultimate role models and the best good people I know. You have inspired this book in countless ways, and I am so appreciative of your cheerleading, honest critiques, and endless devotion. I am blessed and honored to be your daughter.

ACKNOWLEDGMENTS

I conceived of the idea for *Such Good People* in 2019. The characters and plot have twisted, turned and marinated in my mind for several years and I am deeply indebted to many people for helping me see this book to fruition.

First, I am enormously grateful to those who have been on speed dial from day one helping me to fine tune the medical and legal aspects of this story: Dr. Michelle Bloom, Dr. David Goldstein, and Dr. John Shallat—thank you for your infinite patience explaining cardiology and emergency medicine in layman's terms. To Rachel and Lenore—thank you for every text, email, phone call, and photocopy of the New York Penal Code to bring me up to speed on criminal law. To R.J. for graciously offering to chat about very personal experiences. And to Michael S. Ross, Esq. for sharing his expertise and valuable insights.

To the team at SparkPress and BookSparks: Brooke Warner, Crystal Patriarche, Lauren Wise, Shannon Green, Krissa Lagos, Julie Metz, Cait Levin, Grace Fell, and Rylee Warner—thank you for believing in this book and for your steadfast commitment to uplifting authors and enthusiastically promoting their work. Also, special thanks to Jennie Nash, Nicola Kraus, Nicole Meier, and Anne Durette. Your wisdom, guidance, and editorial finesse at various stages of this book were tremendously helpful. I feel lucky to work with each and every one of you.

Thank you to my friends, family, and beta readers who have supported this book in various ways and continue to adopt my imaginary friends as their own: Lisa Barr, Dr. Kira Bartlett, Beth

Erdos, Jackie Friedland, Mark Fromowitz, Dr. Amy Sacher Goldstein, Stephanie Goldstein, Adam Hofstetter, Debbie Kamensky, Judy Kamensky, Rachel Levy Lesser, Lisa Lavitt, Leslie Levin, Andrea Lieberman, Kelly Mamaysky, Ann-Marie Nieves, Zibby Owens, Rebecca Raphael, Molly Rothstein, Ericka Schnitzer-Reese, Dr. Rebecca Schwartz, Michelle Shallat, Yvette Sharret, Rochelle Weinstein, Michelle Witman, and Samantha Woodruff.

As always, thank you to Dan for your endless editorial and emotional support, eternal optimism, kindness, dedication, and love.

And finally, to Mia Natalie. You are my prize. My heart. I am blessed and honored to be your mom.

ABOUT THE AUTHOR

AMY BLUMENFELD is the author of the award-winning novel *The Cast*. She is a graduate of Barnard College of Columbia University and received a master's degree from the Columbia University School of Journalism. Her articles and essays have appeared in various publications including *The New York Times, The Huffington Post, O, The Oprah Magazine*, as well as on the cover of *People*. Amy lives in New York with her husband and daughter.

Looking for your next great read?

We can help!

Visit www.gosparkpress.com/next-read or
scan the QR code below for a list
of our recommended titles.

SparkPress is an independent boutique publisher
delivering high-quality, entertaining, and engaging
content that enhances readers' lives, with a special
focus on commercial and genre fiction.